I0550589

The Malef Chronicles

Volume One:
The Sword Bearer

BOB HORBACZEWSKI

Copyright © 2008 Bob Horbaczewski

All rights reserved.

ISBN: 0615483607
ISBN-13: 978-0615483603

DEDICATION

To my wife Monique, my children Elise and Nikolai and my mother Ruth. Thank you for your belief and support in seeing this dream become a reality. You all are my inspiration.

CONTENTS

CHAPTER ONE

Endless darkness stretched to the horizon, disturbed only by the pinpricks of stars that lay billions of miles away. The deck of the Ares, one of the flagships for the U.T.A. or Unified Terran Armada, glistened against of the red sun of the Kodos system. She was a brilliant ship to behold, whether docked or hurtling through space. From bow to stern, the Ares measured in at seventy-five hundred feet. Numerous fighter squadrons lay dormant inside her belly, ready in a moment's notice to snap into action. Only the best pilots served onboard the Ares and they were her greatest weapon. Massive combat scarring lay hidden under a fresh coat of paint, a scattered history of battles past. The polished finish allowed even the faintest glimmer of light to radiate into a spectral glow around the ship.

Usually Terran ships were required to stay within the boundaries of known space; however, the spatial anomalies appearing in the Kodos sector were urgent enough to break that protocol. Just days into a much-needed leave, Admiral Nikolai Glovalkov had received orders to take the Ares out to the edge of known space to investigate.

As a member of the Galactic Council, the UTA was bound to the borders set forth by the Ter'Ok'Zhu, a race as old as time itself. An infinitely powerful race, the Ter'Ok'Zhu formed the Council years prior to put an end to the Great War. Traveling so far out pushed one of their sacred rules to the limit, which in and of itself told Glovalkov of the danger that waited them.

The crew of the Ares had become restless. Years of combat had honed them into a fiercely efficient crew and monotony was a foreign concept to them. No colonies nearby meant no communication beacons and thus no direct contact with anyone back home. Messages from loved ones, local sports news and even updates on the dealings of the Council were sent via data pods through the jump gate at Kodos One. The jump gates were built by the Ter'Ok'Zhu, technology so grand and complex that it seemed more magical than scientific. The gates were spread across the galaxy creating a super-highway of wormholes. Those wormholes allowed interstellar traffic to move in a hundredth of the time it would normally take. This grand gift also served as a assurance measure for the Ter'Ok'Zhu as no race wished to lose access to the jump gates.

Malaise had taken its hold on the crew. Caught up in routine they existed rather than lived; save for one individual. Colin Kinison was the son of Arthur Kinison, famed Senator of the Terran Alliance. Arthur was a hero to the Bellat people and yet a tragedy to his own, both revered and vilified for one momentous decision. Years prior Arthur chose banishment from the Galactic Council, taking the unjust punishment in place of his friend Fa'Sham, King of the Bellat. He sacrificed his career, just as it had begun to blossom, to right a horrible wrong. Many humans considered him a fool, but the Bellat adopted him as one of their own. Colin was Arthur's first and only child as his mother had died giving birth to him.

Following Arthur's banishment from the Council, he was appointed as an ambassador to the Bellat. The role was unique because few outsiders were allowed on the Bellat home world, yet alone ever permitted to live there. Colin in due course was raised on Bella Prime. For Arthur the duties of an ambassador usually outweighed those of a father, which allowed for a considerable amount of mischief to be had by the younger Kinison. Colin was in no way an average youth; the trouble he sought out always involved the most extreme of circumstances. A handsome young man by any races standards. Short, thick wavy brown hair framed his sharp face. High cheekbones, a strong chin and an angular nose were his most prominent features, though his eyes; as if his entire soul was compressed and forged into those two blue gems, were what seemed to get him in the most trouble. They shone as bright a blue as found at the base of a flame, yet their true spark came from Colin's penchant for mischief.

Days earlier, those eyes entranced a young female mechanic one long day during lunch. Charm radiated off him like the sun would a mirror and within seconds of sitting next to the girl she spilled forth the information he needed for his next bout of tomfoolery. Flight through space meant countless insignificant collisions with space debris and so the hull of the Ares was in constant need of minor repair. That job fell to the C-60 bots. The C-60's, or Seasicks as the crew called them, were equipped with a powerful magnet that allowed them shoot around the hull of the ship with no risk of being lost to the depths of space. The Seasicks were able to internally increase and decrease the strength of their magnets, which coupled with their high-powered external boosters allowed them to skip from one end of the ship to the other in mere seconds.

Colin now stood on the edge at the observation deck strapped into his flight suit, a hybrid design that allowed for freer mobility than a full space suit. It still protected its wearer from the harsh vacuum of deep space, though it could not sustain life for an extended period. He looked back at his squadron, fear and admiration covered their faces. His ice blue eyes caught the disapproving glare of Lieutenant Commander Sasha Rogers. The Yin to his Yang, Sasha was just as striking as he was with her flowing red hair and piercing green eyes. Hers was the only look of disgust amongst the squad. Her every thought packed into one angered look. He could feel her thoughts cut into his consciousness having heard them vocalized countless times before. *Always showing off. Arrogant. Prideful. Pointless.*

Colin simply gave her a nod, wink, and then placed his helmet on. The faceplate was in the shape of a black ebony skull, with bright red eyes. Many men, all leaders of the Reaper Squadron, the most elite squadron in the U.T.A. had worn this helmet, but none with such a blatant disregard for the rules of conduct placed before them. Arthur enlisted Colin in the U.T.A. in an attempt to create some sense of stability in the boy's life. Always a rebel, it only pushed Colin further in the intensity of his exploits. Colin always pushed his limits, both to test himself and in a vain attempt to draw attention from his father, even if it was negative. That desire allowed him literally to soar past his peers. His bravado, though at times regarded as fool hearty, had become the stuff of legend amongst the younger enlisted. Colin's daring was both his greatest strength and weakness. In respect to his father, regardless of the result, he would accomplish both of his goals today.

Colin walked through the shield that was protecting the interior of the ship from the vacuum of space out onto the flight deck. The view was divine, as if something beyond mortal had found a way to express itself tangibly. Even a few days in the brig could not erase the vision set before him. The red sun of the Kodos system was gargantuan and its reflection cast a ghastly red glow around the entire ship, as though a red ocean had flowed up and consumed the ship. The spectacle hypnotized him with its splendor.

Days prior when Colin first presented his idea of riding one of the Seasicks, cheers from nearly the entire squadron had greeted him. Sasha warned him of the consequences of such a stunt, as logic and a sense of duty ruled her motivations. "This is stupid. Overriding its control board could cause it to demagnetize and go flying off into deep space with you on its back. Knowing the Admiral he'd probably just leave you out there to teach you a lesson," she had said.

"What lesson, how to die a cold and painful death? He loves me too much to let that happen, but even if it did, my boots are magnetized. I'll be fine," Colin replied.

ZOOM! A seasick breezed by Colin, shocking him back to reality. Now the decisive moment had come. To turn back, Colin would face not only embarrassment and shame from his squad, but he would never hear the end of it from Sasha. He could not bear that fate, so out across the deck he walked to the seasick that had so recently buzzed by him. It chirped in response to his presence. "Hey there little buddy," Colin quipped at the robot, not that it could understand or respond to his comment, but the simple routine helped calm his nerves.

Colin removed a magnetic strip from his suit. A crude creation put together in his spare time, this small black strip of silicon and steel was Colin's ticket to glory. In theory the strip would interfere with the Seasick's primary functions just enough for him to directly interface and take control of the bot. Sasha had helped him design it, as countless failed attempts to dissuade him from his prior stunts had taught her that it was better to help keep him as safe as possible, than see what damage he would cause if left to his own devices. As with most schemes thought up in the middle of the night, this one sounded worse and worse with each passing moment. Colin reached the seasick. There was no predicting how it would react to him jumping on board, yet alone how its system would react to the interference from the magnetic strip. There was only one-way to find out; Colin leapt.

The most agile of leaps it was not, but it was beautiful nonetheless. Colin landed square on the back of the Seasick and made a grotesque thud. The air from his lungs rushed out of his mouth, leaving him mere seconds to regain his composure. The

Seasick would be alerting for help at any moment. This was his shining moment and suddenly ego overtook him. Colin's mind trailed off to the future, of the stories that would be told with such brevity. He looked back at his squad and waved in triumph. Not thinking Colin lost his grip and fumbled the magnetic strip, dropping it to the empty depths of space. All of his glory lost in a heartbeat, in a single act of foolish bravado. In desperation, Colin lunged for the strip. His legs barely hung onto the side of the Seasick as the strip floated further and further away, gone forever. The Seasick's alarm wailed. His failure was now complete.

CHAPTER TWO

Colin closed his eyes and hung his head in shame. His squad went quiet. Colin had faced adversity while showing off before, but never had he given up so easily. His confidence was infectious and yet so was his disappointment. Sasha smiled. Then Colin leapt up off the Seasick. The force of his jump sent him flying into space, accelerating toward the strip. "Idiot," Sasha snapped as she ran off back into the ship.

Colin's momentum accelerated him much faster than the strip, inches more and he would have it. In the distance, the Ares sped away. *GOT IT!* Colin grabbed onto the strip and looked down. The ship was moving dangerously farther away. Then he felt a growing rumble reverberate through the whole of his body. Colin turned and saw its source. The Ares' engines were getting frighteningly close and Colin could tell that he would be caught in their wake if he did not think of something fast. His squad clambered to see his status. Some gasped in horror at the thought of losing their leader. Colin smiled and pressed a button on his suit. His boots magnetized. For a second he hovered above the hull of the ship, frozen. Colin wondered if his boots were strong enough to pull him back down to the Ares or if he would indeed be burnt to a crisp and lost to the depths of space. Suddenly, his body jerked and he accelerated back toward the ship. Colin angled himself and landed forcefully onto the wailing Seasick.

He slapped the strip down across its head. Silence. Colin dared not to breathe and then the strip lit up with a very basic digital control pad. He keyed in some directions and pressed enter on the pad. Sasha walked up, fully dressed in her own flight suit, mouth agape. The Seasick's magnetic pad decreased its hold on the deck below. Colin pressed forward on the pad and the robot followed the command, boosters sent it screaming forward toward the bow. His squadron screamed in approval. All of them that is, except Sasha Rogers. A hint of smile threatened to sneak its way past her lips, but the disapproval in her eyes frightened it back down.

Colin sped along the deck, engaged the Seasick's magnets at the last possible moment and teetered on the edge of the ship. There was no point in playing it safe anymore. The Admiral and command crew were sure to be watching his every move by now. Colin looked up across the deck. The bridge was visible, though the blast doors were closed to protect the command crew from the harsh rays of the Kodos Sun; still Colin could feel the steely glare of the Admiral piercing down at him.

Admiral Nikolai R. Glovalkov sat in the middle of the bridge; embers of tobacco glowed a bright red inside the bowl of his dark brown briar wood pipe gently lighting his face. Smoke rose up like a ghost and kissed the Admiral's weathered face. His beard, once a rich tuft of black was now all but grey. Leathered skin and masses of wrinkles covered his face, a tribute to a life spent amongst the stars. His eyes, a deep chocolate brown, were the windows to his genius. Never had the UTA seen a tactician that could remotely approach his skill. Smoke billowed around his royal blue overcoat, a filthy habit all but given up on in this day and age, but for Glovalkov history was given life anew with each puff. It took him back to a time when men would brave the dangers of the oceans of Earth, in a vain attempt at conquering the unknown. His own ocean lay outside the ship, the endless black abyss of space. He knew that at his core he was no different from all those great men who were now but mere shadows of history. Therefore, Glovalkov indulged himself in the joys of the pipe, much to the chagrin of the rest of his command staff.

The bridge of the Ares was a large oval with two entryways at its rear. Standing between them at the weapons station was Crevall Litchen, the chief security officer on board the Ares. Carved from stone, everything about him was clean cut and by the book. He held himself with a strength that radiated in his posture. Crevall took his job with the utmost seriousness and was always ready for the worst. The Admiral's chair was located in the center of the bridge, raised enough that he could address his crew with authority, but not as high as to separate him from them. Glovalkov relied on each station to control the ship. After years of service together, the crew was able to anticipate his orders as he thought them. Glovalkov was proud of his crew, though he rarely allowed that emotion to ever be seen.

To the starboard side of the Admiral was the Communications station. Jalliet Perdu, a wispy French girl with long blonde hair and a child like face, sat and twirled her hair between two thin fingers. She seemed lost in a daydream, but her ears were trained on countless streams of audio. On the portside was the Tactical station, which housed Layla Frandis and Sumaya Hilloy. If ever there were two opposites in life it was Layla and Sumaya.

Sumaya wore glasses and had her hair tightly pulled back. She did not believe in having fun while she worked, even going so far as to chastise the rest of the crew. Layla was an explosion of cute as curls spilled out in a multitude of colors off her head. More so, the limit of how far she could push her uniform to accentuate the curves of her body was always stretched thin. Though, when called to action they worked as a single entity, monitoring the fighter squadrons as well as all external data of the ship.

Toward the bow of the ship, tucked below the floor was the Navigation station. Racken Donelly and Tanessa Vaughn sat in this area. Both were perfect examples of a soldier, Racken and Tanessa could easily have been images on a recruiting poster. Glovalkov relied on both of them as much as he did his own hands in his daily life. Theirs was a trust uniquely earned, as if they were his own flesh and blood. In the event that the Ares needed to separate, the Navigation station could detach itself from the bridge and travel down below to the lower section to function as a makeshift command center.

Two steel blast doors sealed the gigantic view port at the bow of the bridge. When opened the view was breathtaking, a living canvas painted against the backdrop of space. On most days Glovalkov found solace in that view, but the Kodos system's sun was too bright to allow a direct view, so instead he glared at the dull steel of the blast doors. The floor in front of the Admiral's chair appeared to be a large empty space. However, it was equipped with a massive Holovid system, which could display anything that the Admiral wanted, from a full tactical version of an ongoing battle, to a simple holographic projection of an incoming communication. At present it lay dormant, a morose pool of dark grey in front of Glovalkov. "Sir, one of the C-60's proximity alarms just went dead," Ensign Perdu said as she turned back to face the Admiral.

Glovalkov sat stoically in his chair, his eyes darted over to the tactical station and he barked in a gruff Russian tone, "Ms. Hilloy, bring up it for me please."

The Holovid sprang to life. Glovalkov leaned forward in his chair for a better view. Two streams of crystal blue light streamed out from the base of his chair, in an instant, tendrils broke off and spread out creating a glowing web on the floor. A faint ghostly image of the Ares appeared in front of him. Bits of the galaxy around the ship were also visible, fading out to nothingness as they reached the edge of the circle. A red light flashed along the deck of the Ares.

Glovalkov snapped out another order, "Magnification, five hundred percent."

He took a puff from his pipe as the flashing light zoomed in as if a camera was flying down to investigate the Seasick. When the viewer reached the desired magnification, the crew let out a collective gasp. "What the frag is that?" questioned Racken.

Glovalkov slammed a fist down onto the armrest of his chair. His eyes wrinkled even tighter as he glared at the image in front of him. The words hissed out of his mouth like venom, "KINISON!"

He spun his chair around so violently that he nearly spilled out of it. He stood up and bellowed to Crevall, "Send out security to take him to the brig."

"Already on their way sir."

"He'll destroy the whole damn ship with this stunt." The Admiral turned back and glared at Colin riding the Seasick. A part of him enjoyed Kinison's adventures, but his responsibility to the ship carried a far greater weight at the moment.

Back on the deck, Colin flew around with reckless abandon; he tipped the Seasick on its edge and then slammed it back to the deck. His squad ate up every moment. The cheers echoed in his helmet and fueled him with even more brazen foolishness. "One more lap boys. Just to set the record in case any of you get daring enough to try this," he spoke into the Comm in his helmet.

"Dammit Colin, haven't you had enough fun already? Security is on their way and you know what that means," Sasha barked.

"That there's no reason to turn back now. Hell, if I'm already being tossed in the brig, I might as well get my money's worth. Your complaint has been duly noted though Lieutenant." Colin gave her an obligatory salute and sped off. "Johnson, start the clock when I reach the bow."

A squad of security officers marched up to the observation deck, pushing their way through the Reapers. "Out of the way," the head officer ordered. "All of you back to your quarters now, or you can join the Captain for a night in the Brig."

Dejected the Reapers obeyed. Out on the flight deck Colin reached the edge of the bow and pushed the Seasick to full throttle. Johnson pressed a button on a small digital watch and tossed it to Sasha. "Let us know what his time was."

"I'm sure HE will," she responded.

As Colin sped toward the observation deck, his hands gripped onto the Seasick with every ounce of strength he had left. Adrenaline surged through his veins, helping ease the ache his body felt. He had not anticipated it would be so taxing to hold onto the Seasick, but then again how could he have known anything about the experience, as he was the first to have it.

Suddenly something in the back of his mind itched. It was as if someone was grabbing him by the shoulder. He looked up into depths of space and in that sea of black, a small burst of blinding red light erupted like a geyser, as if someone had drilled into the very fabric of space itself. The light spilled out and pooled into a circle. Then, in the blink of an eye, it was gone. Colin looked back at Sasha, saw her focus was drawn to the horizon as well and asked, "Did you see that Sash?"

"I think so," she responded.

"What was it?"

"I don't know, maybe some local phenomena."

That same itch grabbed Colin again but this time it would not be brushed aside and so he slowed the Seasick.

"COLIN, LOOK OUT!" Sasha screamed, but it was too late.

A large meteorite slammed into the deck of the Ares mere feet away from Colin and erupted in a hail of debris and electricity. Colin steered the Seasick as best as he could, his focus on maintaining his grip first, avoiding crashing second. If he let go, the flight suit's life support systems could keep him alive for an hour at most in the deep cold of space. Would that be enough time for them to find me, he thought grimly. As the Seasick steadied itself and found a grip on the hull, Colin breathed a heavy sigh of relief. Just then, a surge of power spat out from the top of the Seasick. Damage from the meteor had shorted out the override strip and caused a serious malfunction in the Seasick. The controls froze and its boosters fired at maximum capacity. Colin nearly lost his grip, but as he saw the Seasick's trajectory, a greater haste took hold of his actions. "Get out of there Sash!" Colin screamed. "I can't stop it."

She hesitated; her desire to protect him nearly overrode her sense of logic. Reluctantly Sasha turned and hustled the security officers out of the observation deck. Her eyes fought back tears as she closed the blast doors behind them. On the flight deck, Colin's hands danced around feverishly on the override strip; nothing. The strip was damaged beyond repair and would not yield control back to him. Colin knew that if he did not come up with a solution quickly, countless lives would be lost and he would be amongst their numbers. He had only seconds to think when suddenly the solution hit him. It was a gamble, but he was not in a position to take a safe route.

Colin swung his legs to one side of the C-60 and pressed the button on his suit to magnetize his boots. He slapped the strip onto the control pad on his belt. It snapped on and a bit of electricity surged along its edge. With what remaining strength he had left, Colin forced his boots down against the base of the Seasick. He hoped the strip would have the same effect on them as it did on the Seasick's boosters. It swayed but did not move. Colin thought to himself, *come on just give me enough room to maneuver.*

Again, he pressed down against the base of the Seasick, this time he disrupted the field just enough to nudge the Seasick an inch off the deck. That was all he needed. Colin leaned with all of his body weight in the opposite direction and pulled. The Seasick tipped a bit more off the deck, changed its trajectory and skimmed along the side of the observation deck, rather than into it. Colin let go and tumbled across the deck. The Seasick grated into the ship, tearing through the hull as it rode the wall and then flew off into the navigation tower. Both erupted into a giant ball of flame as they collided.

Colin watched in horror as the light from the flames in the distance illuminated his face. Then the realization of what had just happened finally hit him. He thought to himself that it might have been better to be consumed in that explosion rather than have to face the wrath of the Admiral. The navigation tower was gone, a mere melted mass of metal now, which meant the Ares would be flying blind, in a nearly uncharted sector of space and the only one to blame for that was him.

BOOM! A second meteor struck the deck of the Ares. It sent Colin flying into the side of the observation deck. His helmet smashed into the metal wall hard enough to crack his faceplate. In a breath, his world faded to black.

CHAPTER THREE

Zhu stood at the edge of the Ka'Dre'Kall, or Cliff of Kings. A thousand foot sheer drop stood between her and the ocean below. Cut by centuries of erosion, the black obsidian rock that formed the cliff face was a veritable myriad of protruding blades. Caves dotted the shoreline below, constantly beaten by the raging waters of the Dan'Gal Ocean.

Ter'Nag'La, the home world to the Ter'Ok'Zhu was home to an innumerable amount of breathtaking natural wonders. The planet itself seemed more sculpted than formed, none of the Ter'Ok'Zhu's own structures invading the environments in which they were set, so much so as they seemed a mere extension of them instead. However even among the Ter'Ok'Zhu, this particular spot that Zhu now stood in was favored best, for it was on this spot that their first king was chosen.

As passive and peaceful as the Ter'Ok'Zhu people were, such times did not always occupy their history. They were one of the first races born to the galaxy and they were adept with their control of the uR. From the dawn of their history, the Ter'Ok'Zhu wielded this power on a subconscious level, though over time they became aware and able to consciously control it. As with all great power, it soon corrupted their people. They became increasingly obsessed with control, status and wealth. Wars spread like plagues over time, poisoning not only their own people, but also the very planet itself. Through those destructive times, the Ter'Ok'Zhu made wondrous leaps technologically. War demanded an almost hyperactive production curve, though most of the inventions bore a destructive purpose. During their bloodiest war their people who were split into two separate tribes were dwindling in number, their planet was poisoned and on the verge of death. Ar'Tor, chief of the northern tribe, saw the fate of his people if the war continued unhindered and thus he issued an invitation of peace to the chief of the southern tribe, Mor'Dair.

Mor'Dair, like all of the Southern Tribe, was tall and stout. His face was painted black in tribal designs. He wore a heavy armor, ordained with golden symbols that displayed his status. On his head laid a skeletal crown. His hair was thick, long, black and tied into numerous braids that hung down to his chest. He entered the meeting with an agenda that did not include peace. Ar'Tor sought an end to the war. His hair was much lighter, a mixture of brown and white and worn pulled back. Ar'Tor wore minimal armor outside of his white robes. He wore no crown on his head and his face had a single adornment, one dangling earring that pierced three times through his lobe. He pleaded with Mor'Dair for a truce that would end the war and allow each tribe to live in peace. Mor'Dair saw his concern as a sign of weakness. He believed that the planet was his tribe's birthright and thus he was entitled to rule. Instead of offering peace, Mor'Dair offered a challenge to Ar'Tor. To end the bloodshed they would fight, one on one. The victor would have absolute power and rule both tribes. Ar'Tor paused and then accepted the challenge on the single condition that it took place on the Black Cliffs, the very cliffs on which Zhu now stood.

The sun splashed across the sky in a myriad of colors. Reds wrestled with oranges and were overseen by factions of yellow; the third moon glowed a pale silver blue, a perfect companion to the sunset. A hundred poets writing over the course of a century could still not do justice to the sight before her. The energy of the sun enveloped Zhu's very soul. More than just its warmth, she could feel the very tendrils of life in the falling rays. Zhu's elegant hands, a perfect contrast of ivory skin, strong and yet spindly, rested along the dark black edge of the cliff. She would never know of the exact events that had taken place so many years prior, yet their mark on history still resonated power in the rocks under her flesh.

Ar'Tor and Mor'Dair fought, hand to hand, blade to blade for hours. Sweat, mixed with blood, poured off their bodies. Possessed by their own means, neither could find an end through the combat. Their blades, infused with their own life force, sent sparks of energy into the air with each collision. Neither would yield and yet neither could find an edge. Mor'Dair, betrayed by his lust for power, ignored the honorable code to which was agreed. Concealed within the hilt of his sword Mor'Dair had placed a single poisoned needle. With a twist of the hilt, it sprang forth and he thrust it into Ar'Tor's side. The poison was strong. Brewed from the blood of a scrib, death was usually instantaneous for its victims, though, Ar'Tor was anything but usual. His constitution allowed him to take advantage of the blow, to get in close, as Mor'Dair was left vulnerable. Ar'Tor raised his sword and aimed it for a killing blow. Before he could strike, time began to slow and the world around him faded away to the vision of a possible future. One in which he had used his opportunity to slay

Mor'Dair. He saw his own death as well as that of his people. With both Kings dead, the Ter'Ok'Zhu once again stumbled into anarchy in a lust for power. They fought with an even greater passion, perverting their fallen chiefs into martyrs. They killed in their name, until there were no Ter'Ok'Zhu left.

Ar'Tor lowered his sword. Mor'Dair struck a killing blow to the heart. Ar'Tor fell back to the edge of the cliff. His blood flowed quickly from the wound. It was at this moment that the direction of the Ter'Ok'Zhu people changed. For it was at this moment that the great Fahl'ak, In'an, came flying up from the edge of the cliff.

The Fahl'ak were a sacred animal to the Ter'Ok'Zhu. Comparable to the human falcon, the Fahl'ak could fly just as fast, though they were nearly twice as large. They had the body of a lizard with feathered wings and a round, sharp golden beak. Their feathers were an assortment of red and gold that erupted in the daylight and glowed in the darkness. These creatures possessed a natural connection to the uR unseen in even the greatest adepts amongst the Ter'Ok'Zhu people. Their very essence exuded power and they seemed to shape the world around them.

In'an landed next to Ar'Tor. The ancient bird walked around his body, examining the wound with shimmering blue eyes. In'an nuzzled up to Ar'Tor and rubbed its forehead against his cheek. The gathered Ter'Ok'Zhu stood in silence. It was rare ever to see a Fahl'ak. Sightings spanned centuries and never had anyone made physical contact. Ar'Tor reached up and petted In'an behind the head, the bird purred in response. Ar'Tor spoke in barely a whisper, "Thank you friend. Thank you for the vision and thank you for fulfilling a foolish child's dream."

With that, Ar'Tor fell dead. Mor'Dair approached the fallen king, In'an snapped his head back toward Mor'Dair and let out a blood-curdling screech. Mor'Dair stopped and knelt down. He could feel In'an's disdain flowing through the uR. Mor'Dair hung his head in shame. The bird reached down with a clawed hand and pulled the sword from Ar'Tor's side. It threw the blade over the edge of the cliff. Then In'an raised his claw to his mouth and bit from his own flesh. The bird's blood fell down onto Ar'Tor's wound.

Ar'Tor gasped for life. The great bird flew into the air above him, spread his wings and screeched again. In'an hovered above as Ar'Tor rose to his feet. All the surrounding Ter'Ok'Zhu fell to their knees, staggered by the divine miracle which had just occurred.

Mor'Dair could not find the strength to raise his eyes. He wept out in shock, "Forgiveness. I beg of you. MERCY!"

Ar'Tor walked over and grabbed him by the chin. He looked in Mor'Dair's eyes, pulled him up and embraced him. "You have nothing to be forgiven for brother," Ar'Tor replied.

"I poisoned the hilt. I broke our pact. Yet you stand here and call me brother. Why?"

"You opened my eyes to the futility of our battle. The endless path of destruction set out by both our people. Let us start anew brother, emblazoned as protectors of life. TOGETHER!"

The Ter'Ok'Zhu rose up in a roar of approval. In'an screeched out again, voicing his own approval. Mor'Dair stood back and bowed down before Ar'Tor. Mor'Dair spoke, "Forever from this day forth shall I obey your rule Ar'Tor, for you have proven yourself the more worthy to lead our people. I pledge myself to you."

All of the Ter'Ok'Zhu began to chant his name, "Ar'Tor, Ar'Tor, Ar'Tor." In'an flew to the edge of the cliff and perched.

Zhu walked up to the bird, his feathers faded and worn from the sands of time. *Hello again In'an,* she spoke in her mind. *What news do you bring me today?*

In'an responded in kind, *O'Tel has returned. The Slai'Nor descends from the heavens as we speak.*

She reached out and scratched the back of the birds head; her love for him flowed from the tips of her fingers. *Father has returned! Thank you In'an. It seems as though the time between his trips increases with each that he takes.*

Zhu pulled a scrib out and tossed it to him. He snatched it out of the air and swallowed the bug in one gulp. Small, fist sized and hard shelled bugs; scribs were poisonous to every creature, save the Fahl'aks. For In'an, they were his most favorite treat. She ran off back toward the city of Tair Dal, anxious to see her father O'Tel.

The doors to the brig opened and in walked Admiral Glovalkov. The ancient officer breathed an air of respect. Everything from his posture, to his very stride reflected the years of experience that he had collected. Rarely was he seen off the bridge, preferring to leave the socializing to the rest of his crew, yet in moments like this that reclusive nature served a second purpose as well. He was able to strike awe into all of those who saw him, a veritable god walking amongst men.

There was always one way to know the mood of the Admiral, a precursor to what should be expected upon his arrival. The crew knew that if ever the Admiral was seen with his pipe dead and cold, his demeanor was sure to follow suit. As he walked into the brig, the crews' heads snapped up. Their eyes darted to his pipe; unlit. Glovalkov tucked it into the breast pocket of his overcoat. He placed his arms behind his back and stalked over to the cell. Without looking at anyone, he spoke, "That will be all gentlemen. This is a private conversation, understood?"

The cells in the brig were little more than metal boxes. A cot and a toilet were the only luxuries afforded to their occupants. In the last cell, Colin laid on a stiff cot, separated from the Admiral by a transparent wall of energy. He crossed his arms above his head and kept his eyes closed. The Admiral simply stared at him, motionless.

"How long this time?" Colin asked.

The Admiral removed his pipe and tapped the energy wall. It sparked in response. "I suppose you think of this as trivial Captain. Still haven't had enough of these walls, eh?"

"I'm getting kind of used to them. It's a bit simple, but it's home."

The Admiral turned away from the cell and hung his head saddened. He walked back to the control desk. "Arthur would be so disappointed."

Colin snapped up at the mention of his father's name. Years of anger flowed free as quickly as the nerve had been struck. "He never cared about anything except his career. It's always been about establishing his legacy. He's not the hero everyone makes him out to be."

The Admiral took out a pinch of tobacco and placed it in his pipe. "How little you know of your father Colin. He was, is, a great man. You may never know all that he sacrificed in his life. He never asked for that legacy, yet he carried it with dignity nonetheless. However, the disappointment I was referring to was my own."

"I'm not a child. I know what he sacrificed," Colin spat back kicking his cell. He walked to the back corner and sat down.

"Do you now?" The Admiral responded. He lit a matched and took a puff of his pipe. "So this is how you choose to repay that debt?"

"How long?"

"This is how your show your gratitude to your father? By feeding your own ego through all these idiotic stunts?"

"How LONG?"

"Putting countless lives at risk? This is what your father deserves from you?"

"HOW LONG ADMIRAL?" Colin slammed a fist against the wall.

The Admiral walked over and took another puff from his pipe. He stood and looked at Colin. Four years he had served with him. Four years since he paid back an old favor and took this brash young man under his watch. He had tried so diligently to shape and mold him. He had seen the potential that Colin possessed. He was the greatest pilot that Glovalkov had ever seen in all his years. Colin had a natural gift that gave him an edge over all of his peers. Yet he was undisciplined and lazy. Glovalkov had hoped the opportunity of command would help guide the troubled soul resting inside of Colin. However, with every opportunity for greatness came such disappointment. Glovalkov could not help but feel a failure. He had promised Arthur, that he would turn Colin around and help the boy become a man. Here he stood, seconds away from having to face his ultimate failure. Glovalkov's voice nearly cracked as he spoke the words. "Indefinitely Captain Kinison."

Colin was shocked and it was reflected in his voice, "WHAT?" The only words his brain could pull together. He stood up and stomped over to the energy wall.

The Admiral took a puff again. "You've left me no choice this time. Your latest stunt not only put yourself in danger, but the entire crew as well. Do you realize the damage you caused today? I have no choice but to court martial you."

"It wasn't my fault. There was a spatial anomaly. Those meteors came out of nowhere. Check the scanner logs; they'll back up what I'm saying. You know I wouldn't jeopardize anyone's safety."

The Admiral tapped the energy wall again, nearly touching Colin's chest. "Except your own."

"That's beside the point. You can't do this."

"It is still MY ship Captain," replied the Admiral.

At that moment, Sasha walked into the brig. Both men turned their attention to her. "Don't do this Admiral. Colin is too valuable to the fleet to just throw his career away."

"Get out of here Sash," Colin said.

Admiral Glovalkov turned, "Lieutenant, I appreciate your concern in this matter as I'd expect nothing less. However, as I told the crew before, THIS is a private conversation."

Sasha pleaded, "Admiral please."

"Unless you would like to join Captain Kinison in the brig, I suggest you retire with the rest of YOUR squadron."

She paused, weighing the cost of her next words, "Aye, Admiral." Sasha turned and left the brig, pausing for a second at the door to steal one last glance of Colin before the door shut.

BOOM! The ship shook under their feet. BOOM! The Admiral turned his attention to the control desk and hurried over to it. Colin snapped, "We're under attack?"

"Glovalkov to the command deck, Ensign what is our situation?"

The Ensign stuttered, "Admiral, I think it would be best if you came to the bridge to see this yourself."

"Admiral you need me."

"Lieutenant Rogers is quite capable of leading the Reaper squadron. She has their trust and respect based on the example she sets, not on the grounds of some outlandish stunt she has accomplished," the Admiral responded. "I'm sorry Captain."

With that, the Admiral strode out of the brig. Colin slammed a fist into the energy wall and screamed out, "Dammit!"

The Slai'Nor descended through the atmosphere of Ter'Nag'La, heat engulfed its hull in a bright blue ball of flame. The personal transport for the King of the Ter'Ok'Zhu, O'Tel, the Slai'Nor was as beautiful as it was legendary. Like all Ter'Ok'Zhu technology, the Slai'Nor was alive. The Ter'Ok'Zhu shaped machines, using the uR they merged technology and organic life; it was a rite of passage amongst their kind. Throughout the millennia, there had never been a greater savant of shaping than O'Tel. Not since the Maker himself, had there been one so accomplished. It was as if O'Tel was able to bring form to his very thoughts. Even among his own people, his creations were looked upon with a sense of wonderment.

Perhaps O'Tel's greatest accomplishment was his creation of the Slai'Nor. Its hull resembled the skin of an elephant, textured, wrinkled and yet undoubtedly stout. The coloring of the hull was at its base a golden yellow, tempered with shades of blue and grey that swam throughout. The Slai'Nor was long and narrow, expanding ever so slightly from the neck of the ship to its rear. The cockpit bubbled off the front of the ship, giving the profile of a greyhound without legs. Two wings spread out from the rear of the ship. When docked, they could fold up upon the hull like a bird's wings, meeting at the middle. The rear of the ship contained one engine, a wide cone with numerous exhaust ports slatted into its sides. The Slai'Nor itself was perhaps the fastest ship in existence; however in the hands of O'Tel it was also unmatched in its maneuverability.

As the Slai'Nor neared the ground, landing gear extended from the front and rear of the ship. It touched down gently on the earth and a rush of wind shot up around the ship as its engine wound down. The landing ramp opened and lowered to the ground. Light from inside seeped out and down the ramp walked O'Tel. Dressed in a cream color robe, O'Tel more resembled a monk than a king. His white mane of hair was pulled back in a tightly wound ponytail. His sparse facial hair punctuated rather than covered his long wrinkled face. O'Tel had already lived for nearly ten millennia, yet by human standards he looked a mere sixty years old. O'Tel wore no shoes, nor did he have any adornment on his body, save a simple black cloth belt wrapped around his waist. To meet the gaze of a Ter'Ok'Zhu was to stare into the depths of the universe itself. Their eyes bore only two colors, a small island of white that rested in the center of a blue pool of electricity. O'Tel smiled as he saw the small girl approaching him in a sprint. He had developed such a deep closeness to her over the years he had watched over her. Some part of him connected to her in a way he had never experienced with any other being. Pride, joy, concern and warmth melded together in one single emotion that overtook him at the sight of her.

Zhu ran up and hugged him around the neck. Quite a feat as O'Tel stood nearly a foot and a half taller than the five and a half foot girl. The greeting was still unusual for O'Tel, though he had grown fond of it over the years. She released him. "Father. It is so good to have you back. How long will your stay be this time?" Zhu asked in the Ter'Ok'Zhu tongue.

"Calm Zhu. You must learn to control your emotions, and though I adore the title of Father; I think you have grown enough to now realize that it is not a title that I could possibly bear."

O'Tel patted the ship and the ramp rose up. He walked with Zhu at his side, a slight smile on his lips.

"It is not one's blood relationship to another that designates their role in life Father. You have raised me and you are the only parent I know. In every way you have proven yourself worthy of such a title," she responded.

"Then it pleases me to carry it. Tell me Zhu, how does your training go?"

"Excellent father. Master Paow says that he has only had only one pupil who excelled better than I at the blade."

"I would expect nothing less from you Zhu, yet I sense there is more that presses at your mind."

"I have a present for you father." She smiled and dug in her tunic.

O'Tel stopped. Like all Ter'Ok'Zhu O'Tel did not cling to material possessions, an extreme taken by their people during their reform. His mind raced with curiosity and anticipation. Zhu pulled out a small metallic figure, only three inches tall. O'Tel's eyes grew wide; he nearly took a step back in shock. The younger races had shown that they were capable of producing uR sensitive individuals. In very rare cases, these individuals were able to gain a conscious control over their ability. Never had any race produced a Maven who could shape. Shaping was a difficult skill for even the most skilled of the Ter'Ok'Zhu to master. To do so was to take the raw force of the uR a mold it into a living creation of thought. Zhu's gift was beyond rare. O'Tel took the small man in his large hand. He bowed to O'Tel. "You've learned to shape? But how? Do your teachers know of this?"

"No. It came to me in a dream. He isn't capable of much, but I had hoped it would allow you to think of me when you are away," she replied.

The little man in O'Tel's hand began to dance. "Zhu. You are always in my thoughts. Thank you for such a magnificent present. Never in my life have I seen something so wondrous. Though, how do I make him stop?"

Zhu laughed and touched the little man's head. He stopped his dance and went still. O'Tel tucked the man into the inner pocket of his robes. O'Tel had known Zhu was a child of fate, but it seemed even he had underestimated what that meant. He walked again, Zhu followed. "Come Zhu; tell me of your days."

CHAPTER FOUR

Admiral Glovalkov walked onto the bridge in total silence. With a glance out of the view port, it was apparent why. Outside the Ares, a blinding red-hot sphere of energy just as Colin had seen before appeared, but ten times in scale. Glovalkov spoke orders as he marched to his chair, "Ms. Frandis, close the blast doors and bring the anomaly up on the Holo. I want to know exactly what we're looking at here." Frustration boiling inside as his crew stood frozen. "NOW Ms. Frandis!"

The snap of his voice jolted the crew back to reality. Ms. Frandis punched a number of buttons at her console. The Holovid sprung to life and the anomaly appeared in front of the Admiral, along with numerous amounts of extraneous data. Her counterpart turned to face the Admiral and spoke. "Scanners are reading massive amounts of tachyon emissions from the anomaly. It would seem it's some kind of jump gate sir."

Glovalkov was astonished. "Impossible Lieutenant. No ship can create its own jump point in space. Reanalyze the data."

Jalliet turned and said, "What about the Ter'Ok'Zhu sir?"

Glovalkov nodded. "True Ensign, but that is not the jump point of a Ter'Ok'Zhu ship; so unless another race has leapt ahead thousands of years from the rest of us, I would say that there must be another explanation."

Sumaya spoke up. "Sir, something is coming through."

All eyes focused on the Holovid. Through the red energy, an obsidian black ship began to slide into space. Shaped like a blade, white tendrils of electricity snapped off its hull as it entered regular space. Glovalkov slammed his hand down on his chair. He pressed a large red button on the armrest. Alarms sprang on all throughout the ship and the lighting changed to red. Glovalkov roared, "All hands to battle stations. All fighters launch immediately. This is not a drill. I repeat this is NOT a drill."

The Admiral released the button and spun his chair to face Crevall.

"Sir, I have multiple radar hits coming from the ship,"

"Shields at full, get the guns hot Lieutenant," Glovalkov spun back around to face the Holovid. He snapped a finger at Jalliet. "Send out a message on all frequencies, all languages. Let them know we are not hostile and to stand down."

"Sir, we have a transmission coming in."

Everyone went silent. Glovalkov rubbed his beard then calmly answered, "Put it through."

The Holovid snapped from the three dimensional picture of space to a two dimensional picture of a creature that no human eyes had ever seen before. Its skin, jagged, harsh and metallic, was a blue so dark it sucked the very light from the room. The creature seemed more mechanical than alive. Fire red eyes glowed as a mist of energy swirled up around them. Everything about the creature oozed violence and hatred, like the demons written about in myths and legend. It spoke, a guttural hiss of a language, completely unintelligible, but sharp cutting and wrathful. When it was finished, the Holovid snapped back to the exterior view of the alien ship.

Though the ships computer had not been able to translate the creature's language, its message was clear.

"Translation as soon as it's available," Glovalkov ordered out of habit.

Tanessa looked back at the Admiral and asked, "What was that Admiral? It's like nothing in the ships logs."

"Its origin does not matter Commander, only its intent, which I pray I am mistaken about."

"The computer was only able to translate the end of the message sir. Playing it now," Jalliet interrupted.

Over the loud speaker the translated Alien language spoke, "SURRENDER OR DIE!"

Sasha Rogers ran to her fighter. The Hammer class fighter was an amazing piece of machinery. It was the premiere star fighter of the human fleet and more than an equal to any other races best. The Hammer was unmatched in the destructive force of its weaponry, yet it still remained maneuverable. The cockpit rested at the end of a medium length neck. Two plasma guns were implanted in the nose cone. The rear of the fighter, counting the wings, was three times the width of the neck and cockpit and equally as deep. Two torpedo tubes rested on the end of each wing. On the back of the plane, side by side were the Hammer's engine turbines.

Sasha's fighter, Reaper two, was painted black with red trim. A picture of a silver skull with a crimson number two on its forehead smiled from each wing. Sasha hustled up the ladder to her open cockpit. Thoughts of Colin still raced through her head. She had never flown a mission without him. A piece of her was missing. Her squad needed a leader. When this was over she would unleash all of her tension in a rant that Colin would soon not forget. She hated him for being so selfish, so arrogant and so egotistical, but she also loved him for all those same qualities. Perhaps the Admiral would reconsider his punishment. She looked over at the rest of her squad and the rush of duty took over.

The top of the cockpit closed and an engineer smacked it to make sure it was sealed. Sasha's hands flew across the control panel without thought. She had spent so much of her life in the seat of some sort of a spacecraft that it had become as familiar as walking was to most. The Ares was manned by the most elite of the UTA. Countless tours served together allowed the crew to move without thought, but even as efficient as they were, it would still take several minutes to get every fighter launched. This time however, the situation was serious enough that the Admiral had ordered every available fighter to launch. Sasha knew that if in those few minutes that the orders to stand down were not issued, the situation would go from serious to critical. The Admiral obviously assumed an attack. She only hoped that for once his instincts were wrong.

Sasha looked out the side of her cockpit. The engineer stood, spun one arm and gave her a thumbs up with the other. She flicked the switch and her engine came to life. The entire fighter purred soothing her nerves. She eased the throttle forward and pulled back on the control stick. Her Hammer rose slightly from the deck and accelerated forward. Within seconds, Sasha exited the Ares into space. Hundreds of other fighters also exited the Ares, both from the flight deck and from the open ports at the bow of the ship.

"Form up on my wing Reapers," Sasha commanded.

Reaper squadron obeyed and in a heartbeat formed a perfect V behind her. Black, Gold, Alpha, Beta and the rest of the squadrons followed suit. Soon all the Ares compliments of fighters were on course to intercept the oncoming horde of Alien fighters. Sasha tapped her HUD. No information was displayed.

"Admiral, scanners are unable to penetrate target's shields. Any luck up there?" Sasha questioned.

Glovalkov's face popped up on her HUD, "No commander. It seems as though we will be going into this fight blind. We do know their intents are anything but friendly, so precede as such Lieutenant Rogers."

"Understood Admiral." She flipped a switch on her com. "Hear that boys. We have no recon on the hostiles, but this ain't a meet and greet."

"So we're flying blind and hot? Sounds like a good Saturday night," James Johnson, Reaper Three quipped.

"Engage when you're in range," Sasha responded.

"And hope their guns don't have a better range then ours."

"Cut the chatter three. Fifty clicks until they're in range." Sasha was already targeting an oncoming alien fighter.

The alien fighter's hull was a dark blood red with bright yellow and orange trim. Triangular in nature, they resembled extremely elongated pyramids. There was no visible cockpit or anything other than a smooth hull. They darted back and forth like a swarm of bees. It was an amazingly orchestrated chaos that spoke of the level of training they possessed.

BEEEEEEEEEEP. Sasha's targeting system locked onto one of the Alien fighters. She fired a plasma torpedo. It screeched out toward the alien fighter cutting through space so fast it left a trail of blue energy behind. "Reality time boys."

As it sped closer and closer, everyone's heart stopped anticipating the impact.

BOOM! The alien fighter erupted in a large explosion. "Light em up," Sasha ordered.

Both sides opened fire as they screamed pass each other. Around Sasha fighters exploded in some horrific fireworks show, lighting up the sides of her cockpit with flashes of death.

On the bridge of the Ares, the command crew scrambled around at their stations. The battlefield in front of Glovalkov was reduced to numerous blips, red for the enemy, blue for their own squads. Bits of data flashed around the action revealing crucial tactical information. In the distance, the alien mother ship maneuvered to face the Ares. Glovalkov tapped a few buttons on his chair and the mother ship became the central focus of the Holovid. "Ms. Hilloy, are our scanners able to identify anything about the mother ship?" Glovalkov questioned.

"Not anything directly about the ship itself Admiral. However, scanners are detecting a large energy build up at its bow," Hilloy responded.

"Madness," Glovalkov whispered in amazement.

"Sir?"

"Pull back the display to show the entire battlefield Ms. Frandis. Include the Ares and give me an infinite trajectory projected out from the center of that energy build up on the mother ship."

"Aye, Admiral," Frandis responded.

The display on the Holovid zoomed out. The Alien fighters were still engaged with the Ares's squads directly in between the two capital ships. Suddenly a beam of light extended out from the tip of the mother ship. It cut right through all of the fighters directly through the Ares.

"Ms. Perdu. Broadcast to all fighters. Retreat. Get them out of there now. Anywhere away from the trajectory of that blast."

"What blast sir?" The Admiral pointed to the Holovid and she understood. Jalliet shuddered, "They wouldn't. The losses to their own fighters."

"NOW Ms. Perdu." The Admiral stood up. "Commander Donelly. Turn the ship. Thirty-five mark one zero eight. Full engines."

"Aye Admiral," Donelly responded.

Sasha had another one of the alien fighters in her sights. She fired her guns, her forward lasers connecting and exploding the fighter as she flew through the flame.

"All fighters evacuate to these coordinates. Ten mark eighty-five mark thirteen. Repeat. EVACUATE IMMEDIATELY," Jalliet urged over the com.

"Admiral? What's going on?" Sasha asked.

"Not now Commander Rogers. Evacuate your squad. IMMEDIATELY!" He responded.

Sasha had never heard such desperation in Glovalkov's voice before and that frightened her more than anything. "Understood. All fighters form up and evacuate to those coordinates and don't drag your feet or you'll personally deal with me when we get on deck."

Sasha banked her fighter away from the battle. An alien fighter fired at her, lasers flashing across her hull, barely missing. After a few seconds, it gave up the pursuit and arched back toward the main battle. A majority of the other human fighters followed suit, banking away from the main action. On the bow of the mother ship, a large white ball of energy formed. Sasha looked over; nearly all of the alien fighters were still in the combat zone. A majority of them had shifted their focus to the Ares after the retreat of the Terran fighters.

"What are we doing Sash?" Johnson questioned.

"Following orders THREE."

"There's no way the Ares can withstand that large of an assault."

Just then, the mother ship fired a large beam of energy that cut through the battlefield and slammed into the side of the Ares. A huge ball of flame belched up from the impact, leaving a large charred gaping hole in the middle of the port side of the ship.

Colin flew to one side of his cell as the explosion tore into the Brig. The main door flew across the room. Flames engulfed everything beyond his shielded barrier. The ships extinguishers turned on and within seconds, the room was left a smoking charred mess. Colin got up from the floor and looked out. The energy wall had saved his life, but now it left him trapped; his only hope was that it did not fail before the exterior hull shields came online to seal the breach.

The crew on the bridge were tossed around from the impact. Glovalkov fell to the floor out of his chair. He caught himself as he landed, however in the process his pipe snapped in two. Glovalkov stared at his most prized possession, mourning it for the few seconds he could, then pulling himself to his feet he dropped it to the floor. Glovalkov dusted off his over coat and sat back down in his chair. The Holovid still displayed the battle scene in front of him. Tactical numbers on the damage done to the Ares flashed up next to the ship. "Damage assessment?"

"Shields are down to forty percent sir. We've lost a quarter of decks twelve through twenty-eight. I don't have casualties yet, but I'm sure it's high."

"Is the main cannon still functional?" Glovalkov questioned.

"Yes sir, but. . ."

"I want the main cannon ready. NOW!"

"Sir, I must remind you that firing the main cannon will leave the ship dead in the water for at least five minutes. If it fails. . ." Hilloy said.

"We are dead either way. I'm afraid the main canon is our only hope," Glovalkov responded.

Jalliet spoke up, "Sir, Captain Kinison is requesting to speak with you."

Glovalkov paused. He wondered if he should dignify Colin's request with such urgent matters on his plate. "Put him through."

"Admiral I'm begging you. Please let me help. I don't know what the hell we're up against, but for it to cause this much damage. . .please."

"No Captain. Your timing as always is inopportune. Steps are being taken that will either rectify our situation or ensure that releasing you from your cell would be a futile gesture."

"You can't fire the main cannon."

Glovalkov motioned to Jalliet to cut the transmission. "Status?" He questioned.

"One minute sir," Crevall answered.

Glovalkov watched the Holovid. The Ares slowly shifted in space, this time to face the mother ship head on. The smaller Alien fighters continued to attack the ship. A beam of energy streamed out from the Ares to the Mother ship, a small countdown beside it. Glovalkov tapped a switch on his chair, "All squadrons, prepare for firing of the main cannon. T minus ten, nine, eight, seven, six, five, four, three, two, one. FIRE!"

The Ares lit up a bright blue as energy surged over the entire hull. As the engines went cold and black, all of the energy crawled up along the hull and concentrated at the bow of the ship. Then the Ares fired a bright blue beam of energy at the mother ship. The explosion consumed the whole of the invader as it made impact.

CHAPTER FIVE

Cheers erupted amongst the fighter pilots and the entire crew of the Ares. Only Glovalkov stared at the explosion emotionless and silent. The bridge was dark, lit only by the emergency lights and the Holovid. The remaining alien fighters paused in their attack on the Ares as the explosion subsided.

The mother ship still stood, electricity snapping along the damage on its hull. Still functioning, its engines roared to life and the alien vessel pushed toward the Ares.

The crew's cheers turned deathly silent. The remaining alien fighters hastened back to the mother ship. Then as it neared a thick white beam snapped out and took hold of the dead hull of the Ares. "They've locked a tractor beam onto us sir," Hilloy informed the Admiral.

"DAMMIT ALL," Glovalkov spat out.

"Orders sir?" Sasha's voice chirped over the comm., breaking the mood.

Before the Admiral could answer, a hailstorm of lasers fired from the mother ship toward the Ares' fighters. Sasha screamed.

Fighters exploded as space became a wash of lasers raining down from the dark cloud of the mother ship. The surviving fighters retreated back to the Ares. Its massive engines struggling to come back to life.

Glovalkov slammed a fist onto his chair. "How long until power is restored?"

"Four minutes sir," Layla responded. Before Glovalkov could even ask his next question, the lieutenant spoke, "Ten minutes until the Mother ship reaches us."

"DAMMIT," was Glovalkov's only response. "Can we separate the ship?"

"Not while we are locked in that tractor beam sir," Sumaya responded.

"If we could disable it sir," Layla said.

Jalliet spoke up, "It's too risky. You saw the amount of firepower that ship possesses. It's a suicide run and beyond that, the fighters have sustained too much damage to even stand a remote chance."

Glovalkov took a second. He looked at the broken pipe on the floor then pressed a button, "Ready Captain Kinison's fighter."

Reaper One, Colin's personal fighter shot through space toward the mother ship. Trimmed in red and blue, it was overly adorned in order to stand out as the lead fighter. Suddenly, behind him sped Sasha in Reaper Two. "Don't think you can do this alone Colin. It's a suicide mission."

Colin's finger hesitated at the switch to turn off the comm. He knew what lay before him. He had seen firsthand what destruction the mother ship could do to the Ares, yet alone the number of his fellow pilots that had lost their lives on the receiving end of its firepower. Colin wanted so desperately to simply turn off the Comm and not have to address her. He knew more likely than not he was facing his death, but if he did not respond to her, she would follow alongside of him to her own just to spite him. He buckled, "Go back Sash."

"No, damn you. You can't do everything alone."

"You're right, but this is one thing I do have to."

"Let me. . ."

"NO! Go back to the squadron. Protect the Ares. We've only got one shot at this and I'm the only pilot that has a chance of pulling it off. You're throwing your life away if you follow."

Tears welled up in her eyes. She could not believe this would be the last time she might hear from Colin. Sasha thought to herself, *why of all the times you pick to grow up, you pick now?* Sasha banked her Hammer back toward the Ares; the tears now flowed freely. Her words choked in her throat as she spoke, "Don't do anything stupid."

"You know me Sash."

"Exactly."

Colin pushed his Hammer to full throttle. The engines glowed a bright blue and he burst forth in response. The stars streamlined as Colin accelerated toward the mother ship. Behind him, the Ares drew ever closer, still being sucked in by the tractor beam. A bit of light glinted off the hull of the mother ship and caught Colin's eye. A flood of laser fire poured down. Colin pulled on his controls and the Hammer slipped in and out of the assault as it closed in on his target. In a dance as precise as a surgeon operating Colin emerged unscathed.

His sensors were unable to penetrate the mother ship's shields. Luckily for him the giant white tractor beam was a sufficient visual marker. The mother ship was another matter, its dark hull allowed it to nearly blend into space, and were it not for the red traces of energy that lay interconnected within its hull, Colin might have crashed head first into the mother ship itself.

As Colin neared, the mother ship spat forth a flurry of fighters to intercept him. The Alien fighters swarmed out of every portion of the hull then made a direct path to Colin. He opened up his forward lasers and launched his plasma torpedoes. A sea of fire and death rushed out in front of him. Nearly by instinct Colin pushed his Hammer through the chaos, feeling his way through. The alien fighters descended in behind him as he continued on toward the tractor beam.

He maneuvered through the hailstorm of incoming laser fire from the fighters behind him, allowing it to tear into the hull of the mother ship. One shot glanced against his wing. He pulled back and launched his fighter back out toward the black emptiness of space. Fighters in his way exploded at the flick of his finger as his foreword lasers carved a path through the cloud of foreign steel.

Colin banked hard to the left then angled his fighter back toward the Mother ship, this time on a direct line for the tractor beam. Colin again pushed his throttle to the maximum and the alien fighters fell back, unable to keep up. As he approached the tractor beam, their lasers stopped, just as he had hoped. Colin flicked a red switch on his weapons panel. His targeting system flipped over to manual and the front lip of his wings popped open to fire his remaining payload. Each wing housed a full load of smaller missiles, like a honeycomb of death. Colin steadied the fighter, only seconds more and he would hit the point of no return. Though the Alien fighters no longer fired at him, they still pursued, lost in a bloodlust to kill this arrogant human. He had to be exact in his timing or everything would be lost and he would smash into the beam.

His mind screamed, *NOW!* He slapped a button and his entire payload fired. Colin pulled back on his control stick to reverse his trajectory and at the same time reversed his throttle. The move slingshot his fighter in a one hundred and eighty degree turn and the force of the maneuver nearly caused him to blackout. He shook his head and threw the throttle back to full as the alien fighters screamed past him. The plasma missiles connected with the tractor beam, obliterating it in a giant ball of flame. The alien fighters, unable to stop their own momentum crashed into the explosion as it expanded out toward space and threatened to grab hold of Colin's fighter.

On the bridge of the Ares, everyone cheered. Layla said, "He did it. The tractor beam is down."

Glovalkov got up and spoke, "Mr. Donelly, Ms. Vaughn, I will need you on the bridge. Begin separation."

"But sir, we're free. Captain Kinison disabled the tractor beam," Donelly replied.

"Have the crew evacuate to the command section immediately."

"Admiral?" Racken pleaded.

"Captain Kinison disabled the enemies tractor beam, not the enemy. In our current state, we are still vulnerable. Separation is our only option for survival."

"Then allow us to man the hull Admiral," Racken said.

Glovalkov stared proudly at Racken, but in his eyes were an unwavering message of authority. He knew the fate that waited for the hull section and as it was his ship, he would see it to that end. "Take the logs back to the council Mr. Donelly. They will need to see what has transpired" Racken began to speak, but the Admiral cut him off. "That is an ORDER Commander."

With that, the Admiral stepped down into the Navigation pod. He flipped a few switches and the floor to the bridge closed up over him. Gears in the Navigation pod began to whir and then in an instant it shot down through the bridge to the hull of the ship. The pod stopped suddenly and jarred the Admiral. In front of him, the view screen lit up and showed the space outside.

Sasha tapped her tactical screen. "Is anyone getting a reading on him? ANYONE? Colin do you copy?"

"Nothing Ma'am. That explosion is disrupting all our scans," Johnson replied.

"I'm going after him," Sasha replied.

Behind the squadron, the Ares groaned as it separated. Johnson spoke up, "We have our orders Sasha. Don't let your personal feelings get in the way. You more than anyone should know that."

Sasha sighed, looking on as the explosion faded along the mother ship. Her gaze shifted back to the Ares. "I don't care. I'm going after him."

Sasha pushed her throttle to maximum and sped out toward the mother ship.

"Good to see some of my bad habits found a way into that thick skull." Colin's familiar voice came over her comm.

She throttled down and yelled jubilantly, "COLIN!"

His fighter screamed past and she banked back to follow him. "We're not out of the water just yet," Colin said. "Reapers form up on the Ares, Zeta Thor formation. Reapers Two and Three on my wing. We'll provide cover for the Hull section."

"That will not be necessary Captain," Glovalkov chimed in over the comm.

"Admiral. What are you doing?" Colin responded.

"My duty. Protect the command section Colin. It is vital that the ships log reaches the council. They must be made aware of this new threat."

"This is suicide." Colin slammed a fist into his HUD.

The Admiral's voice rang in his ears. "Captain Kinison."

"Sir?"

"Tell your father that he was right."

"Yes sir."

"Good-bye Colin."

"Good-bye Admiral." Colin took a brief second to collect himself. He wanted to scream, cry or react a hundred different ways, but he had a duty as well. Colin flicked off the comm.

The Ares completed its separation and the engines of the command section as well as the hull roared to life. Each half took a separate direction, the hull towards the mother ship and the command section toward the jump gate. "Form up between them boys, we've got to give Donelly enough time to activate the gate," Colin ordered.

The Reapers darted past the hull section of the Ares, each of them looking one last time at the ship and commander whom they had spent so many years with. It seemed unthinkable that Glovalkov could be so soundly defeated, but then they had never encountered a threat such as the one that stood before them. Blips of energy lit up along the hull section as its cannons fired blasts out toward the enemy fighters.

As the Reapers neared the command section they came to a halt and flipped their heading back around to face the incoming threat. Colin tapped his tactical display on his HUD and saw the swarm of incoming fighters. A mass of them were destroyed, lost among the sea of fire being unleashed from the hull section. Enough of them made it though the barrage and they were headed straight for the command section.

Behind them Colin could see the mother ship advancing as well. It seemed on a collision course with the hull section and whether that was by their design or Glovalkov's Colin could not tell. Regardless the end result would be the same. "Let's go live up to our name Reapers," Colin barked.

"Two minutes to jump," Donnely stoic voice boomed over the Comms.

The Reapers and what was left of the Ares fighters engaged the alien fighters. It was a light show once again, the Terran fighters fighting with a fiery efficiency, where as the alien fighters only focus was on inflicting damage upon the two sections of the split Ares.

Suddenly space erupted with giant laser bolts, which were fired from the mother ship. They impacted the side of the command section, tearing a hole through one of its wings. "Jump gate active," Donnelly screamed out.

The mother ship stopped moving and intensified its assault. On board the command section the crew rocked back and forth with each blast that connected. Sumaya yelled across the chaos, "We can't make it through with all that incoming fire."

"Shields are down to fifteen percent efficiency," Layla added.

"Proceed through Commander. I will provide you cover." Glovalkov said over the comm.

Donnelly paused, then remembered his duty and answered, "Aye sir." He looked to his crew, "Engines to full. All fighters full retreat to the gate."

The command section along with the fighters pressed toward the jump game. As they found a distance, the enemy fighters simply abandoned their pursuit, as if hitting an invisible wall. Within seconds those fighters reversed their course and laid an assault on the hull section.

Glovalkov turned the ship, putting it in a direct path of the oncoming fire, providing a shield for the command section and also creating a blockade for the now advancing mother ship. Glovalkov laughed as his hands effortlessly danced along the instrument panels. Laser fire shook him in his seat and explosions consumed his surroundings. Blood stained his knuckles and lips, but he pressed forward. "So this shall be our end then?" he coughed as he pressed his velocity to full.

The engines of the hull section erupted in an explosion of force and accelerated the vessel at an unnatural speed. Laser fire tore into its steel, peppering the exterior with fire that peeled away its hide. In the cockpit, Glovalkov screamed a war cry. The hull section crashed into the mother ship and both exploded.

The other Terran ships reached the Jump Gate and warped into its stream of energy, free from the carnage.

The fireball faded away, metal debris floating through the Kodos system, creating a shroud which the mother ship floated through. Suddenly it snapped back to life. In the distance the same tear in space opened up and two white beams launched out. One attached itself to the mother ship, while the other took hold of what was left of the hull section. The beams retracted back, pulling both vessels toward the anomaly.

CHAPTER SIX

Fifteen Years Earlier

Alone in the darkness, surrounded by the dank smell of death, knelt Lord Xyrus, his body was frail and withered away from days of starvation. His arms lay bound together in front of his body by two interconnected steel bracers. Dark ancient steel, the Na'Dral were the most severe punishment given to a Belgae. A gift from their god A'Zag, the Na'Dral were unbreakable and once locked would only open upon their bearer's end.

Death's sweet touch caressed Xyrus's throat, gently squeezing the last breaths of life from his lungs. What small bit of light that remained in the utter darkness of the cave was now slowly fading. The month down in the Jahan had used all of his body's reserves. Were he not Dershaz, the most elite of all the Belgae warriors, he would have surely died weeks prior, but torture and pain were as natural to Xyrus as breathing was to others. As his death neared, Xyrus's mind began to fade back through his years of life. Xyrus saw himself as a child, a mere six years of age.

He was lost amongst a sea of other boys who were clearly years older than he was. Together they all stood in the center of a grand empty arena, gathered there for one single purpose, to fight. It was tradition amongst the Belgae that when their children reached the age of ten, they would be brought together to compete, to search out the strongest. The Belgae were a race founded on war and it was that core philosophy that allowed them to thrive through the galaxy. That day on the floor of the arena the children would be separated into one of two castes, soldier or slave.

He was far too young to have rightfully been included in this ceremony, but his father was a crooked man with no love for the burden that raising Xyrus brought. So it was that a large bribe gained the meager boy his place there. His father prayed for his son's failure, to see him taken away as a slave and to be rid of the burden of parenthood.

A large horn sounded in the distance and five heavily armored men, the Dershaz, walked to the edge of a platform high above the group of children. The man in the middle stepped past his peers and raised his hands out toward the children. His armor was fierce, black and stained red; whether from blood or paint was indecipherable. All along his arms sprang forth countless blades and spikes, along his shoulders a rim of coarse black fur. Zheresy, the Supreme Commander of the Belgae Military, was a legend.

Under his command, the Belgae had expanded their territory and inspired a level of fear usually reserved for myth. Only his genius matched his mercilessness in the field of strategy. Deep green skin, wrinkled and dark from his age, hung off his face like tar dripping from a branch. Large bits of bone cropping covered his face and the pieces of his body that were exposed. His eyes were still predominately red, but a light tinge of black clouding crept over them. Zheresy's voice was low and it boomed as it was amplified over the arena, "Young warriors, today you stand here on sacred ground. Here, today on Shadaz, you stand where generations of Belgae have before you. Today your path lies in your own hands, your destiny strongly in your grip. Today you chosen have this opportunity to walk amongst the stars as Shahd, today we find the exceptional amongst you, today we find who amongst you are truly Belgae."

A second horn sounded and the children erupted unto war, their bodies becoming a sea of carnage. Xyrus saw his younger-self surrounded by a group of significantly larger boys. Though his father was a horrible man, his neglect bestowed two unintentional gifts upon Xyrus, the will to survive and an uncontrollable anger. His father handed out beatings more frequently than meals and thus Xyrus had only two choices, survival or death. The older boys struck first, the impact of their blows awakening something terrible within his soul, it was carnal and chaotic, a rage that consumed Xyrus, fueling his attack. He exploded in a fury, using strength that was beyond what his meager frame was capable. Xyrus offered no mercy to those that would challenge him.

As the fighting died down and only a portion of the children remained standing, a third and final horn sounded. Again Zheresy spoke, "Enough. Those of you who still stand are welcome as my brothers. You have proven that the heart of a warrior beats in your chest as true Belgae. Join us now as equals."

Shahd soldiers entered the arena, ushering the survivors toward open gates at the end of the arena. As the last of the children passed through, something caught the general's eye. Standing in the middle of the arena, fists still dripping with fresh blood and panting was Xyrus. The other Dershaz stopped and turned back to see what he was looking at. "Boy," the old general billowed, "why do you not follow the others?" Two soldiers ushered

Xyrus closer to Zheresy. He refused to make eye contact, instead staring at the ground in silence. Zheresy yelled angrily, "WELL?"

Xyrus looked up, "If I am to be a slave, than I will not pretend to be something more."

The Dershaz protested at the insult, threats of death spat out and someone kicked Xyrus. Zheresy found a moment for reflection, as the truth of the words resonated in his mind. The old general laughed, deep and loud so that the four other men halted their abuse. "You are wise, even for one so small. What is your name boy?" Zheresy asked.

"Xyrus."

"You are right Xyrus. We are all little more than slaves, regardless of what caste we serve in. So for your insight I offer you this choice instead, serve at my side as my page and I shall teach you all that I know. In that, you will have the chance for true freedom. Otherwise you may rot with the rest of the scum left here. What say you, do you accept?"

The young Xyrus looked up at the general and knelt.

Suddenly, his life flashed forward, years becoming mere seconds as images of his life played out before him, countless battles, days spent at Zheresy's side, his life reduced to a slide show. Then everything stopped again and this time Xyrus saw himself standing in the hall of the Royal Palace. His presence there was anything but voluntary, the thick black chains that bound his hands and feet evidence as such. Seated in her golden throne across from him was Orphiannon. She was chillingly beautiful. Were she not born of royal blood, she would have still found a way into the royal palace through other means. Her face was powerful, wide and full. She had only small bits of bone outcroppings around her brow, under which rested red almond eyes, both unusual for any Belgae. High cheekbones framed soft full lips that completed her face. Her body, unusually slender for a female Belgae, still commanded strength about its form. Her skin as pale a green as one could get without being white. She was a warrior Queen, of that there was a certainty. However, unlike the Kings and Queens who ruled before her, Orphiannon preferred to wage her wars away from the battlefield. Orphiannon was as cruel and merciless a ruler as had ever seen. She was the Queen he had sworn to protect, the Queen he had sworn to obey.

She stared down at Xyrus with such contempt and disgust that it was palatable. Orphiannon wanted to spit in his face for his crimes, to humiliate him, but the moment called for the poise and control expected of her royal lineage. The hall was abuzz with the hum of whispered conversations. All of the Belgae Nation's eyes turned to the proceedings. Xyrus had become a hero through his treachery, succeeding if not surpassing Zheresy's own legacy. He was the leader of the Dershaz, a member of the Galactic Council and the Supreme General of the Belgae Military. He had won countless battles and even his few defeats carried tales of legend with them. Yet all of that was quickly disregarded at his trial. He was stripped of his armor, bound in chains and two guards at his side forced him to kneel like a common slave. Even through all his master's teachings he could not escape that fate.

Orphiannon knew that her task was one that needed a surgeon's touch, not only having to destroy Xyrus's standing amongst her people, but also to reinforce her own. Here was the time for judgment; here was her last chance to cut her people's sympathy for this fallen hero whom she now despised. Xyrus did not offer much during his trial, proud in his actions he refused to rebuke them. Orphiannon knew that any slip in her method could result in the loss of more than just face amongst her people. Though Xyrus was a legend in war, she was his equal with her political skills.

She slammed her scepter on the armrest of her throne and the crowd silenced. Methodically she rose up and stepped forward. Her eyes locked onto his and then she spoke. "Lord Xyrus, you have betrayed me and more so you have betrayed my people. You stand here shamed, a disgrace to the titles that have been afforded you, Supreme General of the Belgae Military, Leader of the Dershaz, Hero. You were appointed a seat on the Galactic Council, to represent our people, yet you have betrayed us all to serve your own prideful needs."

"No," he interrupted.

Orphiannon paused and cocked her head in shock. "You dare such lies?"

Xyrus stood up, shrugged off the guards at his side and stepped toward her. "I have never betrayed MY people."

"Liar!" she screamed as she rushed from her throne. Orphiannon snapped her scepter up and planted it under his chin. Its cold golden metal pressed hard against his flesh, but he would not yield. "Your petty grudge against the Bellat King has cost our race a seat on the Council."

"A worthless position my Queen. I simply released our people from the binds that such an obligation held us to."

She smiled slightly, enough that only he could witness it. Orphiannon lowered the scepter and strode out toward those gathered. "Such arrogance. Such pride. He presumes a lack of worth in our people's access to the jump gates. He presumes our people's ability to trade devoid of value, that our right to bring disputes to the council floor is but a fruitless obligation." She pointed the scepter at him once again, "For what right do you have to make such a decision? PRIDE? You let your petty hatred for the Bellat king blind you from your duty to me and to the Belgae people. Do you deny this?"

Xyrus could feel the trap but he would not fall into it. "No my Queen, I have sworn to obey and to serve. My life is for the glory of my people."

"No Xyrus, your arrogance and your pride have blinded you from that purpose. Your choice in the council shows that the only glory that concerns you is your own. You mistakenly sought to remove the binds holding our people, but instead you have utterly crippled us. There is only one punishment for such hubris."

Orphiannon pointed and two ornately dressed palace guards walked out carrying a large golden box. They stopped and knelt before her. She reached down, opening a metallic flap on the top center of the box and inserted her scepter into a medium sized hole. Mechanisms all around the box whirred and turned in a cacophony of motion. The masses gasped at the sight of it, their collective understanding of what she had decided. The box sprung open and Orphiannon removed a pair of interconnected bracers. The Na'Dral, black metal binds that were older then the Belgae people themselves. Legend told that A'Zag had come to Belgae to shape their people in his image. He had brought three great articles, forged by the Ancients.

The first was a golden scepter, given to the first Belgae King as a symbol of his nobility. The second was the Na'Dral, a pair of binds to be used in the most extreme need for punishment. Once locked nothing could open them save for the wearers death. The last article was a treasure that A'Zag did not share. All that was known about it was that its power dwarfed anything else known to the galaxy. It was said to be the source of A'Zag's power, but also the cause of his death.

Orphiannon moved close to Xyrus, the open Na'Dral resting in her hands. She smiled as their eyes met. "The Na'Dral! For the rest of your days now you shall bear these binds as a reminder of your arrogance, lest you would stand here in defiance of my judgment."

Without reluctance, Xyrus laid his arms into their cold purple steel. Orphiannon inserted her scepter into the top of each of the bracers respectively and as she turned it, the metal of the Na'Dral constricted and locked tightly around Xyrus's arms. The chain between them was only three inches wide and did not afford him much mobility.

She nodded and the guards at Xyrus's side forced him back to his knees. She turned and spoke as she walked back to her throne. "Take him to the Jahan."

The crowd erupted in shock and horror, for they all realized that no one escaped the Jahan.

His memories returned to the present. The guards at his side disappeared and the mass of people faded back to the shadowy red rock walls of the Jahan. Behind him a deep laughter crept along the shadows. Xyrus looked out into the darkness but could see nothing. He questioned whether his days in the belly of the cave had caused his mind to fracture, then something moved.

Xyrus stood up as fast as his body would allow him. The sudden change in position disoriented him, but he shook away the haze and searched the room for the source of the noise and movement. Then the laughter was suddenly behind him. Xyrus turned to see a large shadow of a figure, with piercing red eyes that glowed. "My lord," Xyrus muttered as he fell to his knees. "I have failed you."

The figure spoke in a deep bass of a voice. "Fool, do not think yourself as wise as to know the end game of this task we have set for you. You are exactly where we desire you to be."

"Forgive me master, but how can I serve you, how can I serve my people from this pit. The Na'Dral binds me till my death. How is this the fate you would have for me?"

The figure's eyes erupted in a fountain of energy that sent Xyrus crashing to the ground. The figure stood over him. "Patience Xyrus, you amongst all were chosen for a reason. You were brought to this place for a reason. Though your people have long clouded this cave's history with myth and legend, the truth still lies within these walls. Open your eyes, but more importantly open your mind and the answer will find you."

The shadowed figure disappeared and in his place, a ray of sunlight leaked in from high above at the caves opening. A hundred foot vertical ascent separated him from that opening. Complicating things further was the fact that the cave was pure Trillium. Known for both its scarcity and its durability, Trillium was the hardest and sleekest known material on Belgae. Thus, Xyrus was condemned to die.

Freedom. The words whispered in the back of Xyrus's mind, but the voice was not his own. He stood up and looked around in a circle, still alone. *Freedom.* The voice called out again. Xyrus searched for the source but could not find anyone around him. Then something caught his attention. A small stalagmite in the far corner of the cave seemed to be glowing. Xyrus walked toward it and a wash of energy flowed over him. It was warm, inviting and drew him even closer. The voice called out louder, almost deafening him, *FREEDOM!*

Xyrus fell to his knees before the glowing rock, focusing on the top and noticing something out of place; metal. He leaned in closer and saw what looked like the base of a handle. Again, the voice erupted in his ears, this time causing him significant pain, *FREEDOM!*

It would not stop and so Xyrus thrust the Na'Dral down at the rock formation in frustration. A large chunk of the rock broke off, revealing the hilt of a sword. Everything went silent. Xyrus understood. Feverishly he slammed the Na'Dral against the rock formation chipping it apart. When the last bit of rock had fallen, a near exhausted Xyrus looked up to see his prize. A sword sat plunged into the ground of the cave.

The hilt of the sword was thick and made of an ivory white material. Strips of gold rested around the hilt, as well as dark black jewels. At the base of the hilt, the pommel was shaped in the form of two serpent heads looking away from each other. Above the hilt, the cross-guard was four inches wide and an inch high. The edges of the cross-guard rose up toward the blade and were curved like an S. The visible portion of the blade was wide and made of steel that was so dark it seemed to suck in the light around it. Along each edge of the blade, three ancient symbols shone a bright violet.

Xyrus stared at the blade in awe. *Is this real or has my mind finally snapped?* His mind snapped back to reality as the voice screamed in his mind. *FREEDOM!* Xyrus nearly stumbled backward in shock. The weight of the Na'Dral on his arms awoke the memory of his master's words. He turned, knelt beside the sword and straddled his arms along the edge of the blade.

Xyrus pulled his binds hard and fast against the blade. After so many failed attempts at freedom, his mind had erased any possibilities of hope. He fell to the ground, the cold, hard bite of gravel rushed into his mouth, accompanied by the taste of his own blood. He wondered if in his exhaustion he had missed the blade.

Xyrus reached to his mouth and wiped the blood from his lips. Then, dumbfound he paused as his mind raced to process that simple action. Clarity began to fill his consciousness and he looked down at his freed hands. The Na'Dral was broken, chains sliced as easily as if they were paper. Xyrus stood up and walked back to the sword. Without thinking, his hand grabbed its hilt. He pulled it out of the ground and violet electricity shot through his arm. It flowed around his body, yet caused him no pain.

Free from the ground, it was clear to see that the sword's blade was broken. Xyrus wondered how long it had laid dormant in the cave. How long had his people overlooked such a magnificent weapon? Then he looked up and saw against the far wall of the outline of what seemed to be a throne, but its size was far greater than any that would seat one of his own race. Xyrus walked over and touched the rock outcropping and it fell apart before him, revealing an armor clad skeleton seated on the throne. "A'Zag," Xyrus whispered in respect. He stepped away and looked up to the entrance of the Jahan.

The sword was now free from its prison and Xyrus was ready to be free from his own. He walked to the wall below the entrance. His body was gaining an unnatural strength, as if his days in the cave never existed. His fatigue now replaced by a power that he could not explain. It was as if the sword had connected and enhanced him. Without thinking, Xyrus thrust the sword into the wall. It cut into the Trillium without effort. He pulled the blade out and cut into the wall again. It was a time-consuming process, but Xyrus's only focus was reaching the top and returning to the palace to speak once more with his Queen.

CHAPTER SEVEN

Colossal and magnificent in its architecture, the Great Hall that housed the Galactic Council seemed more fitting as a chapel than a political house. Grand pillars stretched up to a ceiling that seemed as distant as the sky. As with all Ter'Ok'Zhu structures, the Great Hall had been built synchronously with the surrounding environment into it rather than onto it. Yashin vines, had settled themselves along the smooth white stone of the ceiling. Pale pink tendrils stretched out like a gigantic spider web and bright blue bulbs grew in random places. Their scent was soft, calming and sweet rather than floral. Along the lip of the ceiling dome ran wide thin windows. Light from outside poured in and lit the pale ageless yellow rock that rested behind those vines. Peace and quiet reigned over the ceiling of the council chambers; a perfect contrast to the roar that echoes up from its floor.

Fifteen representatives made up the galactic council, three from each of the major races, the Sophos, the Bellat, the Voro, the Humans and now the Navia. The Galactic Council resided on Ter'Ar'Tor, one of the Ter'Ok'Zhu's own planets, near center of the known universe. Ter'Ar'Tor was a central home world for the Ter'Ok'Zhu in the ancient times. However, in more recent times, with their numbers dwindling the Ter'Ok'Zhu had relinquished the planet and allowed it to serve as neutral space for the younger races. In its early years, peace rarely existed and interaction amongst the races seemed only to accelerate their hostilities. Inevitably, war erupted, consuming the stars and threatening to annihilate a great number of souls. O'Tel interceded to end the bloodshed. Through his will the leaders of each race found bowed to the concept of peace. Their reward was the use of the Jump Gates. Battles once waged with steel and fire, now turned to a war of words.

In its infancy, O'Tel offered his council to the Senators, in hope of teaching them some sense of tolerance and compromise. His most trusted Ter'Ok'Zhu brothers served as guardians for the senators, protecting them and helping to enforce their rule throughout the systems. Though O'Tel allowed the council opportunity to settle their disputes, he alone reserved the right to make a final binding decision. However, as time progressed and the peace sustained, O'Tel involved himself less and less in the proceedings. The Ter'Ok'Zhu in suit withdrew their guardianship as well. The responsibility of planetary security fell to the Council Guards and each race provided protection for their own Senators.

None wielded the power of being a Senator with such delicate force as that of Draken Vulcanon. A tongue as biting as the sharpest blade, Vulcanon wielded his weapon as skillfully as a master sword smith. A master linguist and acclaimed historian, Vulcanon was able to speak and understand each race in their native tongue without help from any piece of machinery. He was unmatched in his ability to maneuver and manipulate situations.

Vulcanon's charm was not limited only to his silver tongue, but also his guise. Even at the ripe old age of sixty, Vulcanon was still strikingly handsome. He wore a trim beard, with short styled hair parted to the right. Both were black peppered with streaks of gray, very thick and full. Steel grey eyes sat back on his weathered face. Time had been kind to Vulcanon; however, a life of pampering had helped paint a bit of youth on his frame as well. Vulcanon stood six feet tall, his broad shoulders and muscular body defied his many years.

From a powerful family on Earth, Vulcanon's breeding predestined him to his seat on the council. He had attended the best schools, made countless partnerships and positioned himself for an easy election. However, his opportunity had almost eluded him, for his seat had once belonged to Arthur Kinison. In Vulcanon's eyes, Arthur Kinison had stolen his moment, his birthright. An upstart amongst the political scene, Arthur was a war hero and man of the people. He possessed as quick a wit as Vulcanon, but without the malevolent heart to use it for anything less than virtuous endeavors, Arthur did not seem a threat. In that, Vulcanon utterly underestimated his foe and for that folly he nearly paid dearly. Arthur won his seat on the council, one that was guaranteed until his resignation or death. Were it not for the dark stroke of fate in which Arthur chose to resign his position as a Senator, Vulcanon may have had to live life as a failure, if he had even lived at all. Smug, he sat and observed the two men debating on the Council floor.

Senator Mita Delosham, representative of the Voro people and of the fifth sector of the Known Universe stood in the middle of the senate floor. At seventy-five years of age, Mita was old even by his own people's standards; however, his substantial girth helped to hide the years from his brow. Greed and opulence consumed The Voro. Much as the Belgae who would wear intricately designed armor to show their rank, the Voro chose lavish jewelry to display the level of status that an individual possessed. As such, Mita was a profoundly covered in an innumerable amount of trinkets and baubles. His substantial girth, yet another status symbol amongst his own people, lent to whispered ridicule amongst the others on the Council. Some would jest that he should represent two votes for his people as he took up enough space to occupy two chairs.

Mita's skin was pasty and wet, with sweat that poured forth from every orifice of his body. His black tongue darted out of his mouth, wetting his thick and cracked red stained lips. Like all Voro, dirty yellow nails tipped his small plump fingers, closely resembling the claws of a bird. Repulsive in all manners of existence, the galaxy had rarely seen such a vile presence as Mita Delosham. Yet there he stood in the middle of the council floor, light glistening off all the jewelry dangling from his giant body. Dahaumn Tar'Sham, son and heir apparent of Fa'Sham, King of the Bellat, patrolled around the Voro senator. As considerable as Mita was in his opulence, Tar'Sham was in his humility.

The Bellat people were a warrior race similar in many ways to the Belgae, however brutality did not shape their culture but rather a strict code of honor. They saw no need to lavish their body in elaborate costumes. Their clothes were simple and efficient. Tar'Sham wore an elegant robe, black cloth adorned with random splashes of orange. His formal white jacket sat as a direct contrast to his brown fur. A feline-like race, the Bellat's fur covered their bodies in varied degrees. Tar'Sham wore his hair long and tied it back in a single braid. Sideburns stretched down past his chin to the midpoint of his neck. Even at only twenty-five years of age, Tar'Sham had earned a great deal of respect from his father and thus he was granted a position on the council. He carried his sword in the belt along his waist, though Tar'Sham knew better than to ever draw it while in the Great Hall. A lesson his father had learned so many years prior. Even through the formal robes, Tar'Sham's considerable build was obvious, yet it meant little to the tiny fat man that he now encircled.

Mita knew the rules of the council, knew that no physical harm could befall him no matter how vile his speech was, no matter what insult he spoke towards Tar'Sham or the Bellat people, no one would risk banishment from the council. He chose his words wisely, too wicked, he would lose support, too passive, and he would not provoke the proper response from his foe. "Fellow council members, how many hours must we waste listening to these preposterous arguments? We all know that the Bellat people are a violent and cruel race, their only goal in life, to engage in war so that they may die in battle. You know this to be true."

Tar'Sham stopped pacing and growled in disapproval. He swiped away at the air, as if he could wipe the lie from the room. "We do not begin conflicts Senator Delosham. You are a liar and you will not manipulate this council with false accusations."

"False accusations? Then would you stand here and tell this council that your people do not believe that death on the field of battle is the highest honor?"

"Of course not."

"So you agree that you seek out war."

Frustrated Tar'Sham turned to his father. Fa'Sham, the long standing King of the Bellat people, had faced numerous opponents on the battlefield, he was a proud warrior, but he was also a wise king. Fa'Sham understood, better than most that some battles laid not on land or in space; that some of the most important wars did not see even a blade drawn and yet those required the most skill. It took all of his willpower not to burst forth and rescue Tar'Sham, but he knew his son needed to find his own way so he simply folded his arms across his chest.

Tar'Sham hated the game of politics played within the halls. His people waged their battles on the fields. The young prince could find no honor in this exchanged, but they had little other choice in order to resolve the conflict. As Tar'Sham turned back, Mita smiled obnoxiously waiting.

"My people never seek war. Yes, we are warriors and death in battle is our passageway to Yaggrahal. We are a people that live by a code."

Mita saw an opportunity and pounced. He lunged toward the young Bellat, finger outstretched. "Yet you police the Jump Gate in the Tokar sector. You deliberately prevent my people access to our trade routes. You fire upon peaceful ships, sent only to open a dialogue between our races over this problem."

Tar'Sham laughed at the last comment. "Peaceful? Sending a warship does not seem to be a gesture of peace."

"Our diplomats require safety."

"Diplomats that have no place trying to negotiate in that sector. Have you not forgotten that such matters require the attention of this very council and MUST be negotiated here first."

Mita paused to gather his thoughts. "Yes, I concede that point to you, but you must understand the severe effect that your embargo has had on our economy. Innocents die under the crushing hand of poverty daily, as the Bellat continue to grow fat with greed. Waiting for the council to convene did not seem practical."

Again Tar'Sham laughed. Mita responded angrily, "You find humor in our plight, how typical."

"Perhaps you've forgotten why my people were compelled to enforce the embargo in the first place Senator. Perhaps your mind has overlooked what your people were doing in the Tokar sector."

Draken Vulcanon stood up and both went silent. He spoke with such biting force that the words seemed to carry a chill on them. "Enough. I believe this council has heard quite enough arguments for this day. Have either of you any evidence to punctuate your point, or are we to simply infer who is telling the truth by your quips and posturing?"

Neither of them could answer for neither had any substantial evidence. Senators brought cases to the council concerning disputes, which usually involved little more than a difference of opinion. Evidence rarely found its way into such matters unless it was assured that it would sway the vote. However, this time that was not the case. Tar'Sham growled under his breath in utter frustration at Vulcanon's statement. "Does the Bellat Senator have something to say?" Vulcanon sniped.

"Our evidence was destroyed during the last Voro raid."

"A diplomatic envoy! Unceremoniously attacked without provocation might I add."

"ENOUGH!" Vulcanon roared. "My ears ache from all this noise. I propose to the council a mutually beneficial solution. The Bellat people reopen the Tokar Jump Gate immediately." Mita smiled broadly at his victory. "However, all traffic coming through said Jump Gate must be reported to this council and must be escorted by a Bellat vessel to its destination. Agreed?"

The smiled melted from Mita's fat lips as those last words passed from Vulcanon's mouth. Voting was a simple process at the council. Each senator had a simple panel placed in front of their chair. On that panel rested three buttons, one to agree, one to differ and one to abstain. Six voted for the Vulcanon's resolution. Thomas Adams, a human senator, the entire Bellat delegation and Odesea Ephimira, a Sophos senator voted against it. The Navia delegation, as always, chose to abstain.

"Then the issue is settled, the proposal shall be put into effect immediately. Now, concerning the next matter on our agenda…" The door to the council chambers swung open, Draken Vulcanon's personal assistant rushed in and the entire council went silent. *The bloody Belgae army had better be on the brink of the Jump Gate*, was the only thought that raced through Vulcanon's head. Such an embarrassment was intolerable, but it struck even deeper with Vulcanon who based his entirety on maintaining a pretense of regality. His eyes let the boy know he would indeed kill the messenger. The young man trembled as he laid a data pad down in front of Vulcanon. Vulcanon looked down at the pad, his every mannerism controlled. He had learned early in his life that there was as much value in showing certain emotions as there was in hiding them and this was certainly a time for the latter. With a wave of his hand, his assistant disappeared and Vulcanon readdressed the council. "Fellow members I move that we adjourn for the day and move any remaining issues to tomorrow's docket, all in favor?"

Every light, even the Navia, shone in agreement. "Until tomorrow then."

Vulcanon stepped down from his seat and headed out of the council chambers. Only Fa'Sham could see the hurried pace at which he moved. "Where do you think the good senator is heading to in such a hurry?" Fa'Sham asked.

Puzzled Tar'Sham glanced over in time to see Vulcanon exiting the council chambers. "A hurry father? His pace does not seem hurried?"

A mighty paw slapped Tar'Sham's back lovingly and then gripped his shoulder. "You must look at more than just the surface of someone's actions cub. When have you ever seen Draken Vulcanon be the first to exit this hall?"

Tar'Sham tipped his head in acknowledgement, a slight bit of shame at not noticing it himself. "And has he ever held such a pleasant manner when being interrupted during a council meeting? No something is amiss, I'm certain of it."

"Shall I go after him father?"

Fa'Sham patted his son's shoulder with pride. "No, no, now is not the time to give chase."

"Then what shall we do?" Tar'Sham asked.

"We wait, observe, time will be our ally in this. For right now however, we drink. You've done our people proud today, though debate is not as noble an art as the blade, you were equally skilled on the floor as you are on the field."

"How I wish for the directness of a blade for that Scrib."

Fa'Sham let out a large laugh and walked toward the main doors of the council chamber. "Come Tar'Sham, perhaps we can substitute your taste for blood with the taste for some Krell."

Draken Vulcanon's office was a palace of decadence. Artifacts and trinkets from Earth's past adorned the walls, a tribute to his opulence. They served both to awe and to intimidate all who entered. Vulcanon's chair was more a throne then just a piece of furniture. Behind it, stretching from the floor to the ceiling, was a grand portrait of him. The room itself was an altar to Vulcanon's narcissism.

The exterior room was quite plain in comparison. Set aside for his personal assistant, Vulcanon did not afford the man any taste of the luxury that he himself indulged in. Sasha and Colin sat anxiously outside the door, ragged would be too kind of a description for their appearance. The trip back from the Kodos system left no time for rest or any other convenience. The recent attack clearly threw Sasha and her foot tapping rapidly on the floor made sure that Colin was aware of her discomfort.

The doors to the office slid open and a man entered. Without looking, both Colin and Sasha could feel his arrogance behemoth. Vulcanon strode past both of them, entered his office without even a glance and sat down in his chair. He laid a data pad on the desk in front of him and looked up as Sasha and Colin entered and took a seat. His fingers rapping on the desk, his eyes tightening and without looking up Vulcanon spoke, "Do you realize the burden you've put on me with this disturbance?"

"DISTURBANCE?" Sasha screamed. She tried to rise up from her seat, but the grip of Colin's hand on her wrist felled her ascent.

Vulcanon looked at her. "Yes, disturbance. I understand the depth of your concern over the loss of the Ares Commander Rogers, but in the grander scheme of things, it is a minor casualty to our forces and easily replaceable. However my time with the Council is not and simple military casualties are not something that should be brought to me as an emergent matter."

Sasha brushed Colin's hand away, stood up and pointed a finger at the Senator; though a better gesture could represent her feelings. "You arrogant bastard, don't you dare dismiss the loss of the Ares or of the Admiral as just simple."

Vulcanon sat cold and still, years of practice stalled his reaction. "Admiral Glovalkov; yes, his brilliance will most definitely be missed."

"He sacrificed himself so the rest of us could escape; so that we could bring that information to you and you blow it off as some inconvenience."

Vulcanon was a master at this game, playing Sasha with his every action, pushing her past her breaking point. His many years in the Council had taught him to recognize the subtlest of signals in a person's behavior. He had learned that all he needed was a simple turn of a phrase or a mere gesture to enrage someone. Here now Sasha was quickly becoming nothing more than a piece on his board. "Sit down Commander, unless you'd like to find other accommodations to vent your complaints."

Colin could see the game unfolding as well. Vulcanon turned his attention to Colin. His fingers tapped the data pad as the corners of his lips turned in a smirk. He could almost taste the sweet nectar of the words he was about to speak. "There is however the matter involving your court martial Captain Kinison. It was sent out prior to your attack, an incident involving some hot-dogging along the flight deck I believe."

Colin hid his anger at the mention of it, allowing only his eyes to squint in response. Nothing was more of a reminder of his father than this place and only one person in life left a greater distaste in his mouth; Draken Vulcanon. The old senator hated Colin's father with a furor and that hate naturally transmitted itself to Colin as well. Colin knew what Vulcanon wanted, a response. He could see the bait and refused to grab at it. Sasha however, was not versed in such games.

"The Admiral revoked that order while we were under attack," she snapped.

If he could not goad Colin, she would suffice. Methodically Vulcanon turned his attention back toward her. Enraptured by her passion, much as a shark is to blood in the water Vulcanon hissed, "Yet there is no record of any such order."

"Are you mad? Have you even taken the time to view what is on that data pad. Colin helped save us from whatever it was the

Ares encountered. How dare you accuse him of anything, you should be giving him a medal."

"Oh, I have viewed its contents quite thoroughly. Odd though isn't Commander that Captain Kinison destroys your navigation tower shortly after encountering the first anomaly and then conveniently is able to rescue your crew from the resulting attack just in the nick of time. So favorable for him to be in just the right place at just the right time. Perhaps too perfect a situation in my humble opinion."

Sasha stood out of her seat again. This time she kicked Vulcanon's desk in frustration. Colin reached out and grabbed her by the wrist. Sasha was usually so calm and controlled; he could not believe that she did not see the path that Vulcanon was leading her on. At any other time, she would have welcomed the concern, a concern that she had always dreamt of Colin having for her, but not here and with great certainty not now. Sasha ripped her hand from his with such force that it flew across the desk and sent a porcelain bust of the Senator crashing down to the floor.

Vulcanon rose from his chair, slowly and calculated, biding his time to quell the anger that was raging within. He adjusted his jacket, walked over to Sasha and picked up the porcelain head that remained. When he spoke, his words carried venom. "Not even in your entire lifetime would you be able to afford to replace this."

"Enough!" Colin yelled as he rose up.

"Sit down boy," Vulcanon ordered.

Sasha placed a hand on Colin's chest, but he moved past her and into Vulcanon's face. The senator cowered back and subtly pressed a button on his desk. "You're a damn fool Vulcanon and regardless of your history with my father, what is on that data pad is important. Important enough that Admiral Glovalkov sacrificed himself to see it here. I'm not going to let you manipulate this situation to bury it," Colin said.

Vulcanon sat down in his chair and picked up the data pad. He spoke with ice on his tongue, "This is mine now, and I shall do with it what I please."

The door to his office opened and two large guards entered. Vulcanon pointed at Colin. "Escort MISTER Kinison to the brig and if he struggles please feel free to use deadly force to subdue him."

The guards walked over to either side of Colin and grabbed his arms. Colin looked over at Sasha, stared into her eyes and saw something in them that had never existed before, mischief. "Sash, NO!" he begged.

She was deaf to his plea and in a breath she moved. Jumping up onto the desk and then leaping out toward him, Sasha kicked Vulcanon square in the chest. He dropped the data pad as he fell back out of his chair. One of the guards let go of Colin and went toward her. Colin shifted his weight as his arm became free, moving in one motion, spinning on his heel and thrusting his free hand into the throat of the guard still holding onto him. The guard crumbled down into a heap of unconscious flesh, the breath leaving his body. Colin rushed to the open window.

"Colin," Sasha screamed behind him.

It took a second for Colin to realize that she was not at his side. He looked back and his hand rose up instinctively, seeing the glimmer of metal a fraction of second before it would have smacked him in the face. He caught the data pad. Even in this moment Sasha still had had a plan, a foolish one, but a plan none the less. Their eyes locked across the room, exchanging an understanding look.

"Nooooooo!!!!!" Vulcanon screamed from the floor.

Colin turned, jumping out of the window and free falling through the traffic outside it. Vulcanon's office was nearly two thousand feet high and in the middle of the city. Vehicles flew by and Colin maneuvered himself to avoid being killed. He passed by a few of them until finally he landed into the back of a garbage transport. Though soft enough to cushion his landing, the smell of the contents were enough to turn his stomach.

Vulcanon stared from his window as Colin sped away. He returned to his office and walked over to Sasha. The guards placed her arms behind her back and locked them in place with a pair of energy cuffs. As the white bands snapped to life, consuming her wrists, she ceased her struggling, choosing instead to spit in Vulcanon's face as he came near. He laughed, grabbing her by the cheeks and squeezing as he moved his face inches away from hers. "I admire your spirit Commander, but you've simply delayed the inevitable." Vulcanon hissed.

"Frag yourself Vulcanon," she spat back.

Anger flashed across his eyes and he grabbed a stun stick from one of the guards. Vulcanon thrust it into the nook of her neck and Sasha screamed, falling limply into the guards grasp. "We'll see how long your spirit lasts in the mines fool girl. Take her away." he said.

CHAPTER EIGHT

Princess Zhu stood rooted in the center of the training dome, blade firmly grasped in her hands. O'Tel had retired to meditate and recover from his journey and so Master Paow seized the opportunity for training. His tone was merciless, spitting words as if they were the end of a cracking whip, but Zhu knew that Master Paow's true feelings were only of care and concern. He had seen her potential early on and he understood the potential for her to become a threat to herself if firm discipline did not temper that power. Paow drew his sword and took up a position across from her. If she did not give her all, he would leave her a very nasty scar to remember the experience.

The training dome was colossal, domed ceilings stretching several hundred feet into the air and alive with colors. Varying artistic expressions morphed into each other to create a kaleidoscope of light that covered the ceiling. The walls were plain white marbled rock and four grand pillars dotted each distant corner of the room.

Master Paow lowered his blade to the black stone floor and the tip sent yellow sparks into the air as he paced around his student. He voiced reverberated through the dome with authority. "You have showed much skill Zha'Toh. However, the blunt of the training sticks cannot inspire the same fear such as that of the blade."

Zhu responded, "I have no fear Master."

Master Paow stopped walking and silence filled the dome. *Such strength in one so small,* he thought. In all his years Master Paow had trained countless Ter'Ok'Zhu. He had run them to exhaustion much as he had done with her, yet only one had any had as much valor as the child before him. He cracked half a smile on his lips, "You should!"

With that he struck at her with his blade, its edge lunged forth towards her face. With barely an effort, her blade rose up to block it. Following the momentum he spun and flashed his blade back toward her. She arched back, like a willowy bird, and allowed Master Paow's momentum to carry his blade over her body. He followed its course, jumping into the air in an acrobatic flip and turning to land on his feet. As he landed, he swung his blade back behind his head and brought it down towards Zhu's arched body. She placed a hand to the floor, while continuing her bend, and pushed up sending her feet spiraling into the air. Master Paow's sword slashed into the floor, sending sparks and debris into the air.

He pulled it out and then heaved it at Zhu. His sword cut through the air in a barely visible blur, but she deflected it away as she landed. With but a breath he dashed over to her, reached out with a hand and using the uR pulled the sword from midair back into his grasp. As he reached her he struck furiously, she parried every blow, a beautiful dance of structured chaos. Zhu wielded her sword as a true master and even though Master Paow was failing to break her defense, he felt a great deal of pride in her performance. Her blade pushed past his and came within an inch of his flesh as the thought passed through his mind.

He reached out with his free hand and struck a blow in her midsection, reinforced by the uR it sent her flying across the room and separated her from her sword. Her momentum stopped as she smashed into the wall. Zhu's body slipped down to the floor and she caught herself in a sprawl, legs stretched out like a cat. Master Paow charged in. She glanced over at her sword and with but a thought it flew back to her hand. Then mere feet from her grasp it suddenly stopped. Master Paow slashed at her as soon as he was within range. *Does he truly mean me harm,* she pondered. Never had he fought against her with such resolve, the line between rigidity and aggression was dreadfully close to being crossed. She dodged around the blade, blocked the strikes and kicks that he threw, all the time using the uR around her to give her strength her body could not possibly possess on its own.

Zhu's dance of avoidance, a carefully orchestrated series of moves, allowed her to advance toward her still hanging sword. She lunged for it. The blade turned on her, obeying its new master and swung at her face. Zhu collected her feet under her body and her hand rose up, more by instinct then by conscious thought. The blade struck her flesh and stopped, held back only by the force of her will. Blood trickled out of the small gash on her palm. Her resolve doubled and in one grand movement, she released her hold against the blade and spun out of its trajectory. Her hand grabbed it at the hilt and carried it through its swing toward her master.

He raised his sword just in time to block the blow, but the force both chipped his blade and sent him flying back behind a volley of white sparks of energy. He collected himself and roared out, "Enough."

Zhu stopped and lowered her sword. She relaxed and bowed her head in respect. Master Paow walked over to her. "Do you fear now Zha'Toh?"

"No Zhi'Fah, I do not," she responded.

"Why? Do you wish for death?"

"No Zhi'Fah, I cherish life; but I do not fear death. It is only a transition."

He leaned in close to her face. "Where have you learned such things Zha'Toh?"

A booming voice responded, "From an old fool or have you forgotten our ways in your old age?"

O'Tel entered the training dome and Master Paow stepped back from Zhu, his hard exterior instantly melting away to one of reverence. "My King, I have not forgotten."

"I see only one wall damaged, far better than even my own trial."

"Yes, she is much more determined to prove herself than you were at her age." Master Paow smiled.

O'Tel walked over to Zhu, placed a finger under her chin and raised her face to examine her cheeks. His other hand touched a thin line along his own. "I see he did not find a need to leave a reminder of the cost of humility," O'Tel said.

Zhu smiled. Master Paow stepped over to them. "She keeps that lesson within and did not need a reminder."

O'Tel let go of her chin and focused his attention on Master Paow. Paow was shorter than O'Tel and far older. His skin wrinkled to the point that his eyes were but small slits hidden beneath a tuft of white furry eyebrows, but he still maintained an incredibly fit body. His facial hair was wispy at best, a long white goatee stretched down to his chest. He was bald and wore robes similar to O'Tel's, but royal blue rather than cream. "I require the Jahn'Do'Tor my old friend," said O'Tel.

Master Paow went dreadfully pale, he could only stand and stare at the mention of the *Sword of Kings*. Never was there a greater artifact in all of the Ter'Ok'Zhu's history. Legends and songs written about its exploits throughout the ages covered his races history. Master Paow had been in awe when presented with the task of safeguarding the weapon, but he had also hoped never to live to see its use. Only the darkest times in history had called for it and he dare not ask O'Tel for his need now. His fright was broke by O'Tel's words, "You do still have it in your possession?"

"Of course my king." With that, he bowed and hurried off. When Paow returned, he carried a sword wrapped in a deep brown cloth. He knelt and presented it to O'Tel.

The cloth wrapped around the blade puzzled Zhu. Never had she seen an animal that could produce such a smooth skin, it was like solidified oil. Something else seemed to grab at her mind though. Around the sword a strange emptiness seemed to hang, as if the object in Master Paow's hand was merely a ghost. O'Tel opened the cloth and a bright light poured out. Contained within was as brilliant a sword as one could ever dream. Its construction was simple and yet beyond elegant. The hilt was made of a deep brown wood, one so uniform that it seemed impossible to be organic. The pommel was even darker and capped by a smooth piece of gold, sturdy enough to bludgeon an opponent. At the top of the grip was an ornate cross-guard, yellow stone shaped in the form of a half circle housed a relief of a skeletal wings behind a Fahl'ak's head. O'Tel grabbed the hilt and removed the sword, its energy leapt out, engulfed his arm and then slowly absorbed into his skin until only the shimmering steel of the blade remained.

Paow and Zhu stood mouths agape. O'Tel lowered the sword and turned his focus back to his old teacher. He reached out and lightly placed a hand on Master Paow's shoulder. "I am afraid the words I have for Zhu are to be heard by her ears alone old friend. The tides run dark and it is time she saw what lies ahead for herself."

Master Paow looked over at Zhu. His concern over O'Tel's last statement echoed in his mind, but the steady grip on his shoulder brought calm to his soul. His turned back to O'Tel and knew there would be no argument, so he bowed his head, "With great respect then my King," and left the room.

"Come child, we have important matters to discuss and little time to do so," O'Tel said.

Zhu nodded in respect, following alongside her adopted father as curiosity filled her head. They walked along the edge of the cliffs, mist from the crashing waves hundreds of feet below wafted up to cool the air around them. They stopped next to a large yellow tree. Its trunk was ten feet in diameter and its bark fell off like sun burnt skin. Shades of brown lay smeared throughout parts of the tree, a desperate attempt to hold onto its youth. Hundreds of thin branches stretched out in random directions and a huge knot, the size of an adult's head, stared out toward the ocean.

O'Tel walked up and laid his hand on the tree. He seemed connected to it, as if he was having a conversation that no one else could hear. Zhu dismissed the thought as fancy; *surely, a tree could not talk*. O'Tel opened his eyes and looked at her. "Do you know this tree?"

Zhu paused and searched her memory. She was educated in numerous pieces of Ter'Ok'Zhu history, yet could not remember a single mention of this particular tree. "No father. I do not know its history. What is its significance?"

"It carries none that would be found in books or lore, but it is significant child."

"How?"

"It is where I brought you when first you came to this planet."

"Surely this is not the reason that you dismissed Master Paow, is it father?"

"No child there is more. Do you know this sword? Do you know its history?"

Zhu's eyes went wide, like a child about to receive a present. She knew a few scattered myths about the Jahn'Do'Tor, but very few knew the sword's true history. "Only what is whispered in legend," she replied.

O'Tel stared out at the sea in the distance and spoke, "The Jahn'Do'Tor predates even the Ter'Ok'Zhu, it was not forged by any of our hands. It was a gift bestowed upon our first true King. No weapon made since has been its equal."

Zhu seemed puzzled. "Father. Who possessed such skill as to craft such a blade?"

"Even as old as my people are, we were not the first to walk amongst the stars. At the dawn of time, it is said that there were a select few who existed as part of the uR. They could shape as easily as we can dream, their thoughts given instantaneous form. Of those first ones one was a master forge. It is written that when he shaped, he gave life, true life, to his creations. The Master Forge lived on a sentient planet, one formed by his own hand. There he created and shaped things that defied imagination. However, rarely did the Master Forge bestow his creations to anyone. The Jahn'Do'Tor was one exception."

"So the sword is alive? Can it use the uR?" Zhu asked.

"Yes child. There is no pure explanation of how the sword lives, it has an energy that is its own, a sentience, yet it needs an owner to connect to in order to thrive. That, however, is not what is

57

important for you to hear Zhu. You see the sword holds a terrible legacy. I must tell that legacy to you now, for I fear a great darkness threatens to consume the world once again. The sword has a twin, for in all that the Forge created he insured a balance. You see Zhu only in balance can one find harmony. Such that where this sword brings hope and life, its twin wields despair and death.

This sword was first given to Ar'Tor, our first true King and has been passed down to each successive ruler. The sword chooses who is worthy enough to bear it. Others may hold it, but in their hand the sword is nothing more than dead steel. Only in the grip of the Sword Bearer does it truly come to life. To bear the sword is to give up a part of yourself, such is but one of the burden's of the bearer. In that burden lies one of the greatest gifts given to the bearer as well, for the compounded knowledge of the past bearers is transferred onto he who bears the sword."

"I am confused father, surely Master Paow knows of the sword's history."

"Yes child and it is the next bit that I wished only for you to hear."

O'Tel plunged the sword into the ground and turned to face Zhu. "The Ter'Ok'Zhu are dying. Our numbers dwindle and I fear that my generation is our last. It shall be up to you Zhu to carry on our legacy when we are gone."

Zhu looked down at the sword, then up into his eyes. They gave her a sense of comfort, even though her heart felt such a great bit of sadness.

O'Tel raised her chin in his hand. "Though that still is not why I have dismissed Master Paow. You are beyond skilled with the uR; your connection is utterly natural. Yet there is still one gift that has been kept from you, the sight."

Throughout her teaching, Zhu had learned of the wonderful force that existed around her and within her. The uR connected all things, an energy that transcended time and existence, yet encompassed both. It had no conventional definition of how it existed, there was no portion of biology that produced it, it simply was; a universal idea of essence, translated by every race into their own culture's definition. She had become skilled in controlling that energy, but the way O'Tel had spoke about it, seemed as though the uR was something tangible, like a stream of water beneath their feet.

It was as if O'Tel could hear her thoughts, or else her confusion was so prominent on her face. "You cannot see the uR child. That is the other reason that I brought you to this spot."

"How could I see the uR father? You speak as though it were something physical, like the water out in the sea."

O'Tel looked at the old tree behind them, felt one of its roots at his side on the ground. Years had passed since last they both stood beneath it. He looked at her and shame filled his eyes. This horrified her. Never had there been anything but warmth and compassion in those two gems. O'Tel spoke in a somber tone, "When last we stood here, I took the sight from you. Master Paow and I argued whether it was right to do, or if it was even possible. In the end, we agreed that it would be best to keep this one gift from you, until you had gained a greater control over your ability. You are a Maven Zhu, the first of your race. You were feared for that and other reasons as well, but those are not to be told by my lips. However, that is why you were brought here, for your safety," He said.

"What of the sight?" she pleaded.

"You know of the uR. All creatures possess some level of control over it, through meditation, prayer or whatever means they employ. It is our connection to each other, to everything here and beyond. However, some are born Mavens, naturally skilled and able to control the uR on an unconscious level. Those few born with this gift are able to see the very uR itself. Very few outside our own race have ever been blessed with this gift, and as such, we were unsure how you would handle such a burden. That day that I brought you here, under this very tree, I suppressed your sight and allowed your mind to ease from processing so much information. However, Master Paow has told me how far you have come in the training and I have seen now that you are ready for this gift. It may seem overwhelming at first child, but remain focused and that will quickly pass. I wish I could better have prepared you for this, but time is already short. Are you ready? Hold onto my voice and I will guide your mind."

She nodded and O'Tel placed his hands on either side of her temples. He closed his eyes and a white energy rose from the Jahn'Do'Tor and consumed his hands. It flowed along Zhu's face and then in an instant absorbed into her body. She screamed out in pain and fell to her knees.

Zhu opened her eyes and looked up at O'Tel. The world had not changed. Every single detail was the same as before. *Was O'Tel mistaken? Perhaps I am not a Maven.* Then it began, slowly at first, a flicker of light along his head, then sparks from the tree and a river of color appeared around her feet. Everything around her erupted with a new exciting stream of life, it sang to her and mesmerized her, so much color, so much beauty. *Why did they think she would not be ready for such a gift?* Then a bright white light began to emanate from the Jahn'Do'Tor. It expanded exponentially, consuming everything.

Blinding power, growing larger and larger, as if the sun itself were no more than a few feet away, it threatened to consume her very being. She tried to step away, but she could not move fast enough. "Zhu, focus on my voice," O'Tel call out.

She tried to listen to him, but the world became overpowering. She placed her hands over her eyes. It did not stop. "Relax Zhu, focus your mind on my voice and anchor yourself. Zhu? ZHU?!?"

It overtook her and she was lost to its power. With a sharp scream, she feinted to the ground and the world of color disappeared to darkness.

CHAPTER NINE

Footsteps plodded along the black rock of Mount Arras in search of some bit of life to quench the hunger growing in the pit of its belly. The Crocena's black fur thrashed back and forth with every icy blast of wind that blew by but its blazing red mane remained matted down against the beast's body. The rising sun cast an unnatural sheen along the silhouette of its body. Its three clawed paws dug into the slick rock in a vain attempt to stabilize its massive frame. Measuring ten feet from snout to rear, this Crocena was large even by its own species standards. Its mouth opened and a purple-pitch forked tongue snapped out past rows of razor sharp teeth, examining its surroundings. No life flourished around the peak of the Mount; however, at times stray animals would find themselves lost to this desert of death. It could taste the nothingness, the terrible ache of hunger begging it to abandon this task and move on, then something overpowered its natural instincts.

Though every part of the beast's core screamed to leave, its body could not obey. Instead the Crocena stood frozen, the occasional flick of its tongue showed that the beast was still alive. Its eyes darted toward what looked like movement.

LIFE! FOOD! The smell of the meal became overwhelming and the Crocena let out a hungered roar. It turned and sprinted toward the source of the smell, bits of rock flew up as each paw slammed down along the mountainside. Warm saliva flew from its jaw down to the rock below, splattering as the beast rushed to its meal. The Crocena came to a skidding stop mere yards away from a small cave opening. Death and despair poured forth from the hole in the mountain like rotting flesh, yet something kept the beast frozen with anticipation. The bit of life that the Crocena had smelled was getting increasingly intense. The drool poured forth from its mouth like a broken spigot.

A hand reached forth from the cave and then a broken sword thrust into the ground beside it. Lord Xyrus pulled himself up from the bowels of the Jahan and breathed in the fresh, bitter air around him. The beast growled a guttural roar that echoed along the mountainside, as ferocious and violent as the Crocena itself. Ready to satiate its hunger the beast reared back on its hind legs, gathered its bearings and charged Xyrus. Spit flew wildly as the beast screamed another horrific roar. Xyrus stood and looked up at the charging predator. He watched as it neared closer, though he held firm and statuesque. It was nearly on top of him when finally he raised a hand and focused his thoughts.

The Crocena came to a halt mere inches from his hand. The hunger washed away from its mind as it stared at Lord Xyrus. Though the beast did not know him, it now felt a deep connection to the Dark Lord. Xyrus ran his hand along the beasts jaw, further strengthening the bond he was forcing upon it. He examined the Crocena closer. The beast was magnificent. Originally, he had simply intended to use it as mode of transportation, but now seeing what a spectacular specimen this Crocena was, he contemplated a longer attachment. "I shall call you Mardral," he said.

Mardral purred and nuzzled against his new master's hand. Xyrus patted the beast on his giant brow and then hoisted himself upon its back. He grabbed onto the beasts mane and smacked its flank. Mardral reared up and strode off along the mountain. In the distance, Xyrus could see the Royal Palace, even hundreds of miles away there was no mistaking its splendor.

At the base of Mount Arras stood the Belgae Royal Palace. Its outer walls were chiseled from Herak, a white stone that stood as a stark contrast to the black mountain before it. The walls were a solid mass, no windows or outcroppings graced their exterior. At nearly one hundred feet in height, the walls were virtually impenetrable. Guards patrolled at the top of the wall, but the majority of their forces sat stationed at its base in front of a giant gorge.

The only port of entry to the palace was through the main gate, two giant doors of steel which stood at nearly half the height of the wall itself. A colossal golden seal of the ruling house acted as not only a gigantic lock, but also as an entry ramp when lowered. A giant mechanical system that attached the door to the walls also pulled and slid them back behind it as well.

The Palace Guard were one of the Belgae's most elite group of warriors. Only the Dershaz stood as their superior. Clad in armor so dark a shade of green that it could be mistaken for black, the Palace Guard oozed intimidation and professionalism. Every movement was calculated and echoed their discipline. Faceless solid black masks rested on bright red helmets; the smooth glass reflected the world outside of each soldier's existence and prevented any ounce of individuality to exist amongst their ranks.

Twelve guards patrolled the entrance outside of the great wall carrying Viper class rifles, far superior a weapon than that issued to common soldiers. A double-barreled blaster, with a grip at the front of the gun. A small band of steel allowed it to rest on the forearm of its owner, when viewed from below the barrels held a shape similar to that of a cobra's head. As they patrolled the wall a call came in over their Comm unit, "We have an unidentified hit on long range scanners. Approach vector thirty-five mark sixteen. Fray, darag and nak move to intercept."

The three guards moved in unison in response to the orders. They formed up a slight distance away from the wall and raised their weapons. "Permission to fire?" asked one guard.

"Negative. Wait until we have a visual," the Commander responded over the comm.

The blip in the distance was moving toward them at an accelerated pace. The HUD inside their helmets enhanced their vision and crosshairs lit up with a display of distance of the target. They stood motionless, obedient, fingers at the ready and the muzzles of their guns tracking the movement of the ever-approaching threat.

Xyrus pressed his body as firmly to the back of Mardral as he could bear. Even though the uR now gave him unnatural strength and sustained his health, his time in the Jahan left him far from his best. The icy cold bite of the wind stung deep into his flesh as Mardral strode at breakneck speed. The great wall was growing closer with each step the beast took and soon he would have his revenge. He knew that the guard could see the beast's approach and assumed their weapons were locked onto its every movement. A bit further and he would know definitively what his next move would be.

As the former leader of the Dershaz, Lord Xyrus had trained the Palace Guard himself. Naturally curious, the wildlife had a tendency to wander around the palace's perimeter and during his regime, Xyrus had trained his soldiers to ignore such disturbances. The Crocena were easily irritable and especially difficult to detain or kill, so firing at them was more trouble than it was worth.

The beast was now within visual range of the guards. "Stand down. Target is a non-hostile. Just another Croc looking for food. Return to patrol," the Commander barked over the comm.

The guards lowered their rifles and filed back to join their fellow soldiers at the wall.

Xyrus did not need the uR to tell him that his plan was working. The cold silence that filled the air was answer enough. He felt a wave of hesitation as the beast came closer to the main gate. Xyrus reached out through the uR and touched the beast's mind. Though Mardral could not fully understand him, Xyrus could fill the beast's mind with certain emotions. He pushed the fear and anxiety aside and replaced it with anger and hunger. As Mardral charged harder, Xyrus focused his own body. Soon the guards would realize that this situation was not as typical as it appeared. Soon they would see riding on Mardral's back and understand their failure. For as long as he remained focused, Xyrus would insure it would be their last.

Mardral charged within twenty feet of the palace. The commander took a step forward and shot a blast in the path of the Crocena. Hot dirt splattered across Mardral's face, but he was unphased pushed into an unnatural lust for food by his master. That is when the commander first saw Xyrus. He lowered his weapon for an instant in disbelief, but that moment of hesitation was all Xyrus needed.

"Defensive positions," the Commander screamed into his Comm, as if force would accelerate the words delivery, "Target is hostile, repeat target is. . ."

The Commander never got the chance to finish his sentence. Mardral was on top of him, razor sharp teeth engulfed the whole of the Commander's helmet, shredding through his armor and finally filling the beast's stomach with a morsel of sustenance. From Mardral's back Xyrus leapt into the air. He sent a thought to Mardral, *flee*. The Beast had done its job in delivering him, even better than Xyrus could have hoped. Xyrus could now call on Mardral through the uR, so there was no need to risk the animal's life any further. Mardral grabbed the Commander's lifeless body and fled.

Even without the uR, the Palace Guard stood little chance in a direct fight with Xyrus, his skill was so unmatched. However, now with the uR firmly at his side, the conclusion to this skirmish was all but determined the moment he set foot before them.

Xyrus drew the Jahan and its desire for carnage consumed him. Euphoria rushed through his veins, as if he were consumed by a drug. Red flashes of laser fire streaked through the air. He gripped the sword tighter and it smoldered a brilliant dark purple hue of energy. Xyrus used both the Jahan and the Na'Dral to deflect the incoming volley of laser fire as he pressed on toward the Palace Guards, forcing them to retreat to the main gate.

With a leap into the air, Xyrus was on top of them. His feet thundered down into the ground from his impact. As he swung the Jahan, flesh and steel melted away, leaving only hot red glowing remains in its stead. The sword granted him the ability to tap into the uR but it was also as if it had somehow amplified his own natural aggression as well. Two guards screamed out in pain and with a wave of his hand, Xyrus sent their bodies hurling away into the distance several hundred feet. The remaining guards formed up and continued firing at him.

Red blasts of laser fire screamed past his ears. The Sword also drastically enhanced his senses, almost to the point that he could sense the blasts before they were fired. One of the guards screamed into his Comm, "Perimeter breached. Intruder alert, repeat, the outer wall has been breached. . ."

Xyrus reached out with the uR and a purplish coil snapped out from his hand and wrapped around the guard's throat. He could feel its strength, stronger than anything his own grip could produce yet a part of him none the less. Xyrus squeezed. The guard let out a horrific gurgling sound as the life left his body and then he fell limp.

The palace alarm erupted, deafening the exterior with its thunderous bass thump. Within minutes, the whole of the Palace Guard would be upon him, but Xyrus no longer cared. It did not matter how many bodies he would have to lay at his feet this day, his only goal was to reach Orphiannon. Xyrus darted at the remaining nine, moving in and out of their ranks. The Jahan cut through some while others Xyrus simply tossed aside with the uR; hurtling their bodies through the air.

The giant seal rotated to the left and clicked open. The echo of its mechanisms were so loud they even overpowered the exterior alarm. The seal detached from the giant steel doors and headed down towards Xyrus. The large mechanisms pulled the giant door back and behind the walls.

Xyrus looked up, dropped the sword and as if out of instinct raised his hands to catch the twenty-foot wide seal crashing down toward him. His flesh did not touch it, instead two streams of energy reached out and gripped its edge. Even though he was not physically holding it, the sheer weight of the seal still pressed against his muscles. The rays of the sun shone brightly against its surface, reminding him it was Orphiannon's seal in his grip. Her visage flooded his mind and fueled his hatred. His days in the Jahan had given him ample time to become lost in his thoughts, to reflect not only on his past under her rule, but also on his people as well.

Orphiannon had sentenced him to death, attempted to strip him of his honor, but inadvertently her decision had brought him to his destiny, to the Jahan. However, even with his new-found direction, he knew that his people were still lost. Their race's lineage had become corrupted by the impure ideals of the Galactic Council. It was by her will that this infection of thought had been allowed to spread. Xyrus had sworn an oath to serve his people and in his time in the Jahan, he had understood what that now truly meant.

He pulled back on the seal and the joints that held it firmly against the base of the ancient wall groaned in protest. Xyrus dug his feet into the ground and pulled again. His muscles labored and his feet drove into the around from the strain. The joints of the seal creaked and then finally snapped. As it tore free, Xyrus flung it like a giant discus back toward the mountain.

Hundreds of soldiers and guards rushed forth from the opening in the wall. In an instant they stopped, awe struck by the incomprehensible sight just witnessed.

Xyrus turned his attention to them; sweat now covered his body and his lips curled in a devilish smile as his eyes filled with a bright purple fountain of energy. Xyrus raised a hand and the Jahan flew up into his grip. As it made contact with his flesh, the blade erupted in a violent purple flame. He pulled it back behind his head; then thrust it forward and a beam of dark energy shot forth into the soldiers before him.

Those caught in the beams path were smote to ash, their screams silenced before they could meet the air. Xyrus leapt across the gorge to the opening. Their collective fear became palpable, sweet nectar that flowed heavier with every step that he took. Soon he would find her, but for now, he would take pleasure in the death he would reap upon the unfortunate masses that stood before him.

O'Tel sat staring at Zhu. Though he did not consider himself worthy of the title of father, he cared a great deal for her. He was not surprised that the Sight had overwhelmed her. In time, she would learn to control her gift, learn how to filter out the unnecessary bits and to see the uR as a gentle stream rather than a crushing ocean.

He placed his large hand at the top of her head and brushed the hair out of her face.

Her eyes fluttered and then opened wide. At first, the world was as she had remembered it, plain and without color. She wondered if it had been a dream or hallucination. Zhu looked up at O'Tel's face and a smile gently rose from her lips. Then it began again sparks of color surged forth from the world around her, growing exponentially. She closed her eyes; tried to shut away the world. Fear tried to creep into her mind.

"You must not fight it, let go of your fear. Calm yourself Zhu, focus your mind and let go of all you have known. Now look at the flame that casts the shadow, it will not blind you. Let your mind relax and remember your training."

Zhu heard his words and trusted them. She breathed slow and focused her thoughts. Her fear was simply a reaction to that which she did not understand, her mind's natural reaction to something foreign. She knew that O'Tel would not have given her such a gift if he did not trust that she could control it. With an exhale, she opened her eyes to a sea of color. Energy surrounded the world around her, washing over everything. It threatened to consume her as the energy flowed out of control, chaotic and frenzied. She forced her body to relax, forced the fear out of her mind. The she allowed the energy to consume her. Nausea rose in her stomach as the sensation overwhelmed her. She wondered, *how shall I learn to control something so alive?*

"Focus!" snapped O'Tel. "The world has not changed child, only your perception of it. Focus your mind, control what it is processing, do not allow your emotions to control you. Bend your mind to what you see and all shall fall back in its regular place."

Zhu obeyed his instruction and as she calmed herself the sea of energy faded back. Splashes surged forth every so often and threatened to pierce her control. The uR shifted about O'Tel as he stood by her side, sending ripples throughout the uR. It was a wonder to Zhu how one would learn to read those currents and know the things as O'Tel seemed to.

The energy directly around O'Tel glowed warm and white, much like that of the Jahn'Do'Tor. It moved like fire, dancing in a wondrous rhythm that was controlled and yet somehow chaotic. Around the room, the sea of colors flowed into one another.

"This is the uR?"

O'Tel chuckled, "In a sense Zhu. The uR is not something that should be defined, for any simple construction would only serve to lessen your understanding of it. However the currents you see are a visual representation of the uR. It is our life, choices, decisions, possibilities and outcomes. In time perhaps you will learn how to read those currents."

O'Tel gathered himself and took a breath. Zhu could sense a change about him. "What is wrong father?"

"I fear I must impart something to you Zhu. A great darkness is upon us, the Malef sword, the Jahan, twin to the Jahn'Do'Tor has returned and bears a new master. I fear it is only a matter of time until he discovers this place. Your fate is upon you Zhu, a burden I wish you did not have to bear."

Suddenly a dark red tendril pierced through the door and the uR in the rest of the room stood still in response. As it cut through the air. The tendril left no trace of its existence, simply melding into the uR that it passed. At first, it moved slowly, then as if it recognized O'Tel, it turned and slithered toward him at a fearful pace. Zhu's eyes widened in terror and the uR around her swelled in response, her concentration faltered in keeping it at bay.

"It is not hostile child," O'Tel said in seeing her fright. He turned his attention from her to the tendril.

It stopped, rising up, assessing him and then shot into his forehead. O'Tel became entranced. Only his assurance kept her from calling out. She had no idea what was happening, but she could sense a calm radiating from O'Tel. Then in an instant, the tendril disappeared, as if it had never even existed. O'Tel returned his gaze to her. *Was this how he read the tides,* she wondered?

Before he could speak she asked, "What was that?"

"The calling child," he responded. O'Tel did not expect her to understand, nor did he have the words fully to describe the experience to her. "The Prophet calls. I wish I had more time Zhu, but you will understand in time why I do not."

Her hand tightened around his. Zhu did not want him to go again, yet she could see the importance of this matter. She let go of him and smiled, a vain attempt to mask her true feelings.

"In all my years, I have never seen a being, from my own race or any other, which as much ability as you Zhu. You bring me such pride when I think of the path you shall tread in the times ahead and the mark you shall leave on this life."

She looked into his great blue eyes and forced the tears that demanded release back into their cages. "Be well father and safe journey," she said.

"May the tides watch over you as well child."

O'Tel rose up and left the room. Zhu rolled over, closing her eyes and in that darkness she drifted.

Orphiannon stood at the edge of the pulpit. Her throne sat a few feet behind her, salvation amongst the madness that preceded her down below. Here Orphiannon had to wear her royal garb, black as her heart and trimmed with a brilliant green, material covered her from collar to heel. Bits of garish red armor, sharp and angular, covered her arms, thighs and midsection. An equally black and green cape laid on her back, billowing out in its regality. Her bust was prominently exposed and nearly drew attention away from the crown she wore on her head. It encircled only half of her head, from ear to ear, and came down along her jaw line to thin curved triangular points. Her hair was pulled back in a tightly wound and extravagantly styled bun. She held a golden scepter in one hand and her chin in the other.

Were she born male, Orphiannon would not have had to put up with the league of males now bickering over what would be her best course of action concerning her people. Were she male, her legacy as one of her people greatest rulers would be certain. Instead, her gender handicapped the way she could deal with those that came before her. As a male, the force that she wished she could dispense on those fools would find honor and respect, though she would never earn either and thus came her dependence on maintaining the facade before her.

She detested her formal attire even more so than she detested her advisers below. Orphiannon wished she could dress as the Shahd, devoid of the heavy uselessness of the armor she now bore. She wished she could replace her crown with a helm, such as her generals wore into battle. Her red eyes squeezed in hatred for her place in life. Her hand slid down from her chin and dug into the wood banister. "You assured me of his death, his dishonor Grimwurm."

Grimwurm was frail and meek by any races standard, but exceedingly so for a Belgae. He had a very feminine look about him, old, but not aged, Grimwurm wore only formal robes as he did not care for the weight of armor. His garments were notably expensive and he wore an excess of garish jewelry as well. He slithered up to the queen's side and responded, "Perhaps you should flee then my queen. It would appear as though our plans have been spoiled and I highly doubt Lord Xyrus has seen the error of his ways and now returns to simply ask for forgiveness."

She looked out once more at the sea of madness before her and did all she could to maintain her composure. She spoke, "A herd of cows."

Grimwurm tapped the banister and waved a hand, encompassing the mass of Belgae below. He replied, "They only care for our people Majesty."

"Their care has done nothing but tarnish me. Were I a man I would end them."

"But you are not my Queen. So perhaps prudence would be your best course of action."

Orphiannon's hand snapped to her side and grabbed the white Herak handle of her blade. In the time it took to breathe, she had its edge to Grimwurm's throat. Years of repression erupted, hate poured forth from her eyes and fear wrapped around the base of her spine, her hand did not tremble and her purpose was clear. With Xyrus's impossible return from the Jahan and her own life now at stake, she needed to know where Grimwurm's loyalties lay and the end of her blade carried the most efficient route to that answer.

"Choose your next words with great care Grimwurm, for they may prove to be your last. Where do your loyalties lay?"

A bead of sweat formed at the base of his brow. He had little time to formulate a response. What answer was she seeking? Should he try to guess? The blade pressed into his flesh and sent the most unnerving feeling through his body. Grimwurm detested the barbarism that was a standard for his race. He preferred the use of his wits to overcome and progress. Nearly sixty years he scraped through the muck of the political battleground, making move after move to reach his current status and not once had he met the edge of a blade. Ironic that now, when the battlefield would never have the chance to soil him, he felt the cold steel edge of death pressed to his throat. Were the situation not his own he might laugh at the irony. Instead, he pondered his next words with great care, for that was his only true skill.

"With our people my Queen, but by the subtly of your presentation, I assume the question you would rather have answered is the question of my honor," he responded.

"Yes Grimwurm, astute as always. Have you betrayed me then, your final play for the crown?"

He met her gaze straight on, with as much resolution as he could muster. "I have no hand in the Dark Lord's return my Queen; nor does the council to my knowledge, which is quite broad as you know. None in our history has ever survived the Jahan, yet alone the Na'Dral; it is incomprehensible that he now stands alive, yet alone that he assaults the palace. In that single realization I find more terror than even that of your blade at my throat."

"I cannot flee."

"Then we have no option my Queen."

The door chimed, breaking their conversation. She turned her attention toward it and lowered her knife. "Enter."

General Simura entered. A dark red streak lined the edges of his black armor, as if stained with blood; it denoted that he was an elite warrior. The arcane rune on his left breastplate signified his rank as one of their highest Generals. Simura wore a leather eye patch on his left eye; the old scar ran under it from his scalp to his jaw. He bowed then spoke, "He has broken through the perimeter my Queen. I gauge that the Palace Guards are little more than an impediment to his progress."

Grimwurm asked, "How long?"

"Ten minutes, perhaps less."

"We have no options then," she conceded.

Simura stepped forward and ventured, "There is the Shahd."

"But they are loyal to him Majesty. Do you think it wise to take such a risk?" Grimwurm asked.

The entire Palace shook in response. "Are you sure none have assisted him in this assault?" she asked Grimwurm.

"None. His sentence assured as much," he replied.

The queen looked at General Simura. "We have no other option. Call the Shahd. Kill him."

"Yes highness," said Simura and with a bow, he was gone.

CHAPTER TEN

Bodies lay scattered amongst the debris from the Palace wall, a field of death reaped by one man. Xyrus stood alone, sweat and gore covering his body. He hunched over, his shoulders anchored by the weight of the sword. His body rose and fell aggressively with each breath, hatred filled his lungs and fury coursed through his veins. The hue of energy that consumed the sword's blade shone a dark purple against his body. Xyrus reached out to a building in front of him with the uR, streams of energy snapped out like fingers and tore into the wall. He pulled back and the entire face of the structure ripped away. Stone crashed down on top of him, but Xyrus, protected by a sphere of energy, avoided harm. Debris that hovered on top of the sphere fell to the ground as he dropped the shield and a cloud of dust rose up from the destruction. Xyrus looked up as the remaining portion of the building gave out and collapsed in onto itself.

Xyrus scanned the rest of the Palace. He knew where Orphiannon would be in theory, but now he could feel her presence; taste her fear. *Soon I shall return to you my Queen, to reward you for your generous gift to me. I shall bring to you the glory of the Jahan and you shall fully reap its woe.*

He turned in time to catch an incoming blade. He was too focused on his revenge and the lapse of concentration nearly cost him dearly. The edges of the blade dug into the flesh of his palm and pain surged through his system. He allowed it to consume him, an affirmation of the fact that he was indeed alive. The uR flowed through his body, enhanced his strength and reinforced his skin as he crushed the steel in his grip. He tossed the crumpled blade aside, disgusted that it nearly reached him. He looked at the source of blade and smiled.

A virtual sea of death, the Shahd were the only family that Xyrus had truly known. He was a legend amongst their rank, but now they stood against him on her command. Though it pained him to have to kill so many of his brothers, Xyrus knew that their sacrifices were necessary, still even as his foe, he found pride in seeing them once more.

The Shahd wore limited body armor, red with smears of color randomly applied, spikes and blades accented each piece unique to its wearer. Their helms however were uniform varied only by the soldiers rank.

Xyrus drew back the Jahan poised and ready for the inevitable battle. Before he could strike, the Shahd parted and from their ranks stepped a single figure. Heavy footfalls, a result of the man's massive girth, echoed against the ground. The man stood a good half foot above the rest of the Shahd, his armor far more decorated and fearsome than the others; a spiked skull molded into each shoulder connected an immense flowing blood red cape. His helm was shaped like the head of a Crocena, but more artistically dramatized to emphasize its more violent features. General Lordakai, once second-in-command to Xyrus himself, now the leader of the Shahd, moved toward Xyrus.

He stepped out in front of his warriors and stood face to face with Xyrus. Lordakai unsheathed his sword, a gigantic blade nearly a foot in width and made of solid black steel. Its edge was jagged and worn from years of use, yet undeniably still sharp, it shone in the falling rays of the sun. Lordakai stopped, taking pause mere feet from Xyrus.

Xyrus spoke first, "Have you come to challenge me Lordakai? Do you so desire death's company?"

Lordakai slammed the blade of his sword into the ground. He reached up and removed his helmet, then placed it on the hilt of the sword at his side. His face was a portrait of war. Were it ever considered attractive in his youth, that description could serve it no justice anymore. His right eye was shrouded in a ghostly white tissue, the left of his lips spilt and scarred from top to bottom and his skin marred from an endless number of scattered scars.

Through all of his disfigurement there was still an aura of power, as though his years of war formed into something tangible, a badge of honor. Lordakai did not fear death, nor did her fear the man who stood before him, instead, he maintained a deep respect for both. He locked eyes with his former mentor and responded, "I welcome it my Lord, as do those behind me, but why waste so many lives on this glorious day? How would that serve our people?"

"I will not serve her will; I will not bow to her any longer. The only glory to be found on this day is when her flesh meets with my blade and her life spills forth as payment for her sins against our people. If you will not yield than I shall force my way past you," Xyrus spat.

"You are wrong m'Lord."

Puzzled Xyrus's stance softened. "What?" he puzzled.

"You assume that the Shahd serve the will of the Queen. Has it been so long since you have sat with us? Have you forgotten our pledge?"

He could kill Lordakai with but a thought, snap his neck for speaking with such disrespect, but the words were true. He had forgotten, but how could he have faith in anyone? How could he trust, even in those he held as close as family, when none had stepped up to defend him, none had stood at his side!

Lordakai continued, "We serve the Belgae people m'Lord. Orphiannon has become weak and blind. To allow her to infect our race with such poison would be the same as striking the blow ourselves."

"Then what purpose do you have here?"

Lordakai smiled, knelt down on one knee and bowed his head in respect. "We come to serve you in your aim, as it serves all our people it you succeed. Will you have us at your side on this glorious day Lord Xyrus?"

Xyrus walked to Lordakai's side and placed a hand on his shoulder. He looked out at his brothers, the elite of all the Belgae, their strongest and most capable warriors, worth more than thousand of any other soldier. Victory wet his mouth and a smile consumed his lips. "Rise up old friend."

Lordakai rose to his feet and turned to face the rest of the Shahd. They shifted slightly, more of a natural reaction than an emotional response. Xyrus planted the Jahan into the ground and took a step toward them. The uR poured forth connecting him to the Shahd. "The time has come for us all to rise up my brothers. The time has come for us to purify the plague of weakness and cowardice that has infected our once noble race. We are Belgae. We are the Chosen. We do not negotiate. We take what is ours in battle; we allow the truth found in that honor to be our only judge. Brothers, today we return our people to their rightful legacy. Today we stand together. Today we rise up together, FOR BELGAE!"

The Shahd roared their approval in response. "Cry havoc and let slip the hounds of war!" screamed Lordakai.

The Slai'Nor descended through the mist of clouds along the lower atmosphere of the planet; it broke through a mere mile above the surface. The planet was beyond abundant with life; flora overgrew along the surface creating an ocean of dark green. The

Slai'Nor accelerated forward, air screamed along its hull as it shot along the surface of the planet, continuing to descend closer and closer to the ground until the plant life below could virtually reach up and grab hold.

Suddenly, the vegetation receded and O'Tel knew he had arrived at his destination. The Nahk'Bet Pe Wahjet or Temple of the Mother stood alone on the landscape. Two black pillars stretched up to the clouds above, a third sat decayed and broken, as a cruel reminder of the First War. Hundreds of feet up on each pillar a white band, twenty feet tall, was carved into the whole of the pillar itself. Ancient runes were etched onto the bands in a language even O'Tel did not know.

When viewed from above, the pillars formed a triangle. The temple was simple in design but majestic in detail, resembling the ancient Ziggurats of earth. The layers of stone that in an ancient past would have created the beautiful square base segments, were withering away. A long extension of steps extended out past the front two pillars. Remnants of the fallen third pillar were still scattered about the ground. At the base of the steps, two giant stone guardians stood watch. Each holding a GahngNr, giant spears whose heads housed an ornate decorative base below a V-shaped blade. The Guardians held them crossed over the base of the steps. At the top of the temple four small columns dotted each corner, standing fifteen feet tall, seemingly carved that day, as if time had not weathered the beautifully sculpted scenes that covered their bodies. In the middle of those columns stood a giant sphere of white energy. A slight mist rose up, covering it in an ethereal haze.

The Slai'Nor landed at the base of the steps. O'Tel exited as rain began to fall all around him. He walked to the steps and stopped in front of the two giant statues. He looked up at them and they spoke in an ancient tongue, slow and powerful, "*Who seeks the truth?*"

"*I have been called,*" O'Tel responded in his own tongue.

"*O'Tel, King of the Ter'Ok'Zhu, you may pass.*"

Both statues pulled their GahngNrs back against their bodies; dust flied into the air covering the steps. O'Tel bowed his head and proceeded up to the top of the Temple. Beams of energy shot out from the ball of energy in the middle to the posts surrounding it. Then, a single tendril extended out from the sphere. It reached out toward O'Tel, until it stopped inches in front of his face. He closed his eyes and bowed his head. The tentacle lashed out into his forehead and his eyes filled with the same white energy as the sphere. It snapped back into the sphere and O'Tel's body collapsed.

He awoke in a room of white light. Torn from a dream, this place had no physical boundaries, no walls, no floors, just an endless sea of white. O'Tel stood in that infinite sea and waited. He had been here before and so the experience, though daunting, did not unsettle him. Before him in the distance another presence rapidly approached, the Prophet. In a breath, she was next to him. O'Tel bowed his head in reverence.

Ancient and barely of a physical form, her race was imperceptible, all that could be discerned was that she was undeniably feminine. In comparison to O'Tel, she was a frail creature, with as much substance as the wind. Her hair crept down along her body, stopping at her feet. She was nude; flawless supple skin covered by well placed pieces of her hair. Her face was long and angular, thick curved red lips rested below a sharp perfect nose, pink almond eyes glowed as if they held a secret gateway to heaven. Her voice reverberated, a soft light hum, "O'Tel, King of the Ter'Ok'Zhu, it is with a heavy heart that I call you again."

Her silenced prompted his response, "Whatever my path, through darkness or light, I am prepared to walk it."

Her body hovered in the air before him, as if she were floating in an invisible glass of water. She closed her eyes as she spoke again, "The tides of the uR have darkened. Surely, you have seen this for yourself. The great Malef sword of old has been released from its prison. It has chosen a new bearer. The balance is once again threatened; do you understand?"

Her hand waved to the right and an unseen hand painted a floating fresco of Xyrus wielding the Jahan standing on Ter'Nag'La. In the sky behind him giant black Malef ships dotted the horizon. O'Tel's brilliant blue eyes stared in disbelief, "Then I have failed?"

With another wave, the picture changed. Xyrus was replaced with a visage of Zhu standing along the cliffs. The prophet turned her attention to O'Tel. She opened her eyes and reached out to touch his face. "You are wise and powerful great king. You read the tides as no other that has come before you, but even you cannot change the path. Some things simply must come to pass."

"Then why have you called me yet again? I have done all that was asked of me."

"You have done more than simply what was asked." She waved away the picture. "Though, do not worry for I do not judge you O'Tel, it is not my place."

She waved a hand and images of the past began to spring up around them, a few at first, then more and more, a constant haze of images spewing out of each other creating a slideshow of O'Tel's life. "You have lived thousands of years O'Tel. You have seen much and done even more.

You question why you have been called and for good reason. Never before has someone been called to me twice, never. The future is always uncertain, yet certain moments bind the paths together. I fear that a great imbalance is set before us, one that threatens to consume the universe in darkness. You have served your role righteously. It is only now that I hope you are ready for the burden of this understanding."

From her eyes, a radiant ethereal pink light poured forth into a solid beam. It shot out into O'Tel's eyes and he screamed. The room channeled itself through her body and a black emptiness replaced that which was once white, until there was nothing but darkness.

Then O'Tel was standing at the top of the temple. He stood frozen, his eyes burned bright with pink energy and then they faded back to blue. After a brief pause, he turned and walked down the steps hurriedly. With a thought, the Slai'Nor opened its bay door and he entered the ship. Once inside, he spoke, "We must return to the council old friend, as quickly as you can manage."

Its engines roared to life and sent dust flying into the air. The Slai'Nor rose from the ground and rushed up toward the sky. The two giant statues again crossed their GahngNrs, returning to their original position.

Grimwurm trembled in the corner of the room as explosions echoed throughout the Palace. His voice cracked as he spoke, "I told you majesty, I told you! Now he comes, death on his heels. He will show us no mercy for what we have done."

"Silence!"

"Prey that it is quick. Let him end it fast and not torture us endlessly."

The crack of the Kah'gashi startled him to silence. Orphiannon now stood tall and proud, in her hand was the ancient weapon, passed to her upon her ascension. The Kah'gashi was roughly two feet in length when not engaged. Its docile form was that of a golden scepter. As regal of a symbol as there was amongst the Belgae people, its adornment functioned to mask the lethal weapon hidden within. With a subtle change of grip, the rod unleashed a five-foot long black braided metal whip. Few knew the Kah'gashi's most deadly secret, housed within the scepter was a most deadly necrotic venom.

The crack of the whip was enough to silence Grimwurm. She looked out to the men assembled below; their fear fouled the air and disgust lay written across her face. "Let him come for me," she said, "Let him stand before me and take my life if he so dares. Though I assure you if he is to succeed, I will at the very least, leave him with a permanent reminder of this day to carry with him through the rest of his pathetic life."

She gripped the scepter and the whip retracted. A burst of purple energy tore through the room below. Screams silenced as quickly as the bodies that housed them disintegrated. Lord Xyrus and his Shahd army entered the hall. Those that had survived the initial assault met their end courtesy of the Shahd's swords. Xyrus looked up to Orphiannon's chamber and saw her walk away. As casual as some would take a step, he leapt up to the opening and landed softly barely making a sound.

"Mercy my lord, I beg of you," Grimwurm cried out.

A wave of his hand was Xyrus's only response. Grimwurm's head turned in an awkward angle, bones cracked and he crumbled to the floor, silent.

CRACK! The whip snapped out and wrapped around Xyrus's neck. He merely smiled. With a thought he could tear the whip from her hand, he could tear that very hand from her arm. *Oh, the ways I shall make you suffer.* The skin along his throat burned with seething intensity. All his thoughts focused on the pain. He grabbed at the whip and the fire took hold of his hand as well. *What madness is this?* He buckled to his knees and dropped the Jahan. Now it was Orphiannon's turn to smile.

"Does the taste of the Kah'gashi not suit your palate?" she asked.

"It is a shame that poor Grimwurm could not see the shock in your eyes, the sudden realization that all of your effort was for not.

That even though you survived the Jahan, you shall still die on your knees, disgraced, dishonored and a failure. Our people shall write of this day Xyrus. It shall be echoed for generations to hear. The day a soldier stood up to his queen and was crushed."

He closed his eyes, closed his mind to the world and focused on the pain. He would not let his life end like this.

"The venom has no cure. Soon it will reach your heart, killing every cell it touches along the way."

He focused on his hate, used it to pull the uR in around him. The Jahan called out, too soft to hear. He opened his eyes, but only darkness greeted him, life was nearing an end.

He reached out again, every ounce stretched toward the sword, his last bastion of hope. It refused to respond to his cries for help. The Jahan would not serve weakness. She spat at him, "Your death shall see the end of the Shahd as well. Their failed Coup has sealed their fate."

Come to me NOW, so I may strike the life from her with my last dying breath, he screamed at the sword. The Jahan tasted his hate and sprang to life in response. Xyrus felt the uR flood into his body. His neck cooled and his sight slowly returned. He pulled the sword to his hand with his mind and slashed up at the whip as it reached his grip. The Kah'gashi snapped in two and Orphiannon stumbled back.

"Impossible!" she screamed.

His mind focused on repelling the venom coursing through his system and it poured out of his wounds.

"You should be dead!" she screamed.

"No my Queen," he said through gritted teeth, "it is you that dies tonight."

Xyrus limped toward her, the dark sword firmly in his grasp. He swung it and she raised the Kah'gashi up to block the blow. He struck repeatedly, but each time she parried. They danced about the room locked in that violent dance, for as skilled a warrior as Xyrus was Orphiannon was nearly his equal.

The room took the brunt of the damage from the fight. The Jahan, though focused on keeping Xyrus alive, was still strong enough to cut through all it encountered, save for the Kah'gashi. Xyrus pressed Orphiannon, trembling and covered in sweat, into a corner. She screamed at him between his blows, "You betray your oath coward. You would strike down that which you swore to protect?"

"I would not."

"LIAR!"

The blade glowed as the rage within him gave it life. Her doubt and accusations sickened him. "It is you who is the liar!" He yelled. The scepter chipped. "You who is the poison to our people. It is for their glory that I strike you down," he roared.

With that, all of his hate, all of his rage and all of his fury found a home within the sword in his hand. It erupted in a brilliant purple blaze as he slashed it down toward her. This time the scepter did not protect Orphiannon from the blow. Her scream echoed through the room; then went silent as her body fell lifeless to the floor. Exhaustion overcame Xyrus as he fell down to his knees and dropped the sword.

Lordakai burst through the door, Shahd warriors at his side. They stopped and took in the scene before them. Lordakai hurried over to his master and placed a hand on Xyrus's shoulder. Instinctively he snatched Lordakai by the forearm and gripped a hand around his throat.

"M'Lord, it is over," Lordakai offered.

Xyrus released him and then stood up. He looked down at his former Queen. "She is to be honored Lordakai, as no other ruler has been before her."

Lordakai bowed. "Of course m'Lord. What is our next course of action?"

Xyrus stared out to the carnage below them, "For now we rest old friend. Today has yielded enough honor in death."

With that, Lordakai and the Shahd exited the room. Xyrus walked over to the throne, sat down in it and closed his eyes.

CHAPTER ELEVEN

The Ventured Spirit rested in the heart of Ter'Ar'Tor. More than just a simple cantina, it was a haven to the more disreputable clients that visited the planet. The interior of the Ventured Spirit featured high vaulted ceilings, a large bar that stretched from wall to wall and enough darkness to allow even the most illegal of transactions to take place. Dregs of all sorts piled inside the room leaving just enough space to get around. Barmaids wore enough to remain decent, but not much was left to customers' imagination. The character of the characters that close this particular locale was never in question, for discretion was severely enforced.

Never was there more of a perfect place to disappear and that was exactly Colin's plan. He felt it better to lose himself at the bottom of a glass then risk life dealing him any other blows. His mind wandered, questioning everything that had just happened. How many people had he failed? What was he to do with his life now? His career was over. He pulled the U.T.A. emblem from his chest and dropped it on the table next to his empty glass.

A waitress stepped up to his table, a buxom young Andromedean, whose pale white skin was contrasted sharply by her flowing orange locks of hair and black lips. She snatched up the glass and scuttled away, a certain sway to her walk that was meant to draw the wrong kind of attention. Colin played with the U.T.A. emblem, flipping it up and down along his fingers. What little light that existed in the bar caught its edge every so often. Colin was lost in the motion, desperately waiting for his drink to return so that he could further lose himself in it.

The Waitress returned to the table and placed a full glass in front of him. Colin looked up at her, smiled out of the corner of his mouth and winked. "Thanks."

His charm washed over the young Waitress, but before she had time to get properly flustered, a large Baan warrior pushed her aside. The Baan were a gruesome race. They had no hair; save for a wispy collection of black strands that draped along their jaw. Sharp, fractured features detailed their pale, leathery, yellowish skin. Two dark brown horns that pointed toward their rear rose up along the top of their head. Long, brown claws tipped their fingers. Their mouth leaked a putrid black drool that stained the skin around their chin and was as morbid to look at, as it was to smell. The Baan wore primitive armor covered in spikes and animal fur.

Never was their more primal of an example of their race as Kale. The Baan warrior stood before Colin. He hated humans much like his entire race, however after spending countless years in the confines of the U.T.A. mining prisons, his hatred drove even deeper to his core. Kale took personal offense in seeing a human officer sullying his personal. He felt that the human's language was foul and disgusting, but years of imprisonment forced a crude education upon him. "You NO allow here HOO-MAN," he snarled.

Colin smiled in response and stood up, the opportunity for trouble enticed him. Even if he had not been so influenced by the drinks in his system, Colin still would have answered the Baan the same. "I guess it's true what they say, Baan ARE more stupid than ugly."

Kale roared in response, slammed both fists on the edge of the table and nearly sent Colin's drink into the air. The entire bar shifted their attention to the altercation, hopeful for bloodshed.

"Hey," Colin uttered, "be careful of my drink."

Kale reached across the table, grabbed Colin by the breast of his shirt and pulled him across the table as his other hand swung up to meet Colin's face.

Colin blocked the blow, used the momentum and hurled himself up over Kale's head. A quick sweep back toward the large Baan's feet caused him to crash forward into the table face first. The table shattered under his weight, tipped over with his momentum and sent the drink sliding down toward the floor. Colin caught it as it met the air and then with his other hand offered a hand to the fallen Waitress.

He slammed down the drink and tossed the glass aside. Colin raised his eyebrow cockily and smiled at her. "My apologies miss; I think you were what we like to call collateral damage. Nasty brute though, even for a Baan."

Her eyes widened with terror. He could almost see the reflection of the beast behind him in her pupils. Colin never fought a Baan and was only familiar with them through stories, which he assumed were greatly over exaggerated. The crack of a blaster overshadowed the crude screech of the steel table ripping from the floor.

"Kale, if you have to fight do it outside or down in the Arena, but I'll be damned if I'll have you tear up my bar. You both can rest in a grave first," yelled Dale Cobb, the owner and bartender of the Ventured Spirit.

Dale commanded an unspoken authority. A human, he was a good six and a half feet tall and had a long beard peppered with grey and black to compliment his wrinkled, tan, old skin. A glutton on the simpler pleasures of life, Dale's body was a reflection of such indulgence. The blaster in his hand was blocky and old, but what it lacked in beauty it more than made up for in efficiency. History had shown that his words were a statement of fact rather than just idle threat.

"HOO-MAN COWARD. No fight, RUN HOME TO OO-TAH!" Kale spat out mockingly. A roar of laughter filled the room.

"Where's the arena?" Colin responded.

Draken Vulcanon sat in his office, pitch black save for two candles that burned on opposite sides of his desk. His eyes closed, he listened to the hum of music that played from an antique record player. A symphony from one of the great masters of old poured forth and filled the chamber. Vulcanon was fascinated with all of Earth's glorious history, using his massive wealth to collect all kinds of artifacts, indulging in only the most prestigious of those here in his office. He listened and marveled at the utter brilliance of the ancient tune, so much purer than the offerings of current society. Human music was scattered, chaotic and influenced by the countless number of races now in contact with them. Vulcanon despised such pollution.

He had more than one motive for being in his office at such a late hour. As if in response to his state of calm, the Comm rang and a green button lit up on his desk. The senator placed all five fingers of his right hand on black touch pads surrounding the button. Needles pierced his flesh and scanned his DNA, a security measure to ensure only he could access these calls. The button turned red in confirmation and he pressed it down. Panels on each corner of his desk opened and small silver pillars rose in their place. When all four fully extended, a snap hiss of energy surrounded the desk, further preventing anyone from monitoring the conversation, a field dampener of sorts. The middle of Vulcanon's desk opened, panels receded to either side and the holographic image of a shrouded armored figure stood before him. He bowed his head in reverence.

"How may I serve you master?" Vulcanon asked.

The figure shifted briefly and then spoke in a dark hiss, "A task that must be completed. Your services are required to see it done."

"In what way?"

"Another of our agents must pierce the shield of the planet undetected. His task is of great importance."

Vulcanon did not know how to respond. He could not fathom how to accomplish such a task, but more so he did not understand the point of such a risk. So much had been done, so many plans set into motion. *Why would he jeopardize all that we have done?* Vulcanon let slip, "This was not part of our agreement."

"It is of no concern to you how I choose to serve our agreement. Do not mistake this as pleading or some negotiable request."

"Of course. How long do I have?"

"Four hours."

Vulcanon almost lost his composure. *Has he gone mad?* He had connections to many operations throughout the planet; however, what he was asking was as reasonable as stopping the sun. The planetary shield was impenetrable, and it was controlled by Senatorial Guard, the last great gift from the Ter'Ok'Zhu. "It will cost," was Vulcanon's only response.

"Currency holds no value to us. Your coffers will be filled beyond measure if you succeed at this task. However, fail us. . ."

A hand gripped at Vulcanon's throat, but he was alone. It squeezed tighter and tighter. Vulcanon choked as his body gasped for air. *How is this possible,* he thought?

The figure continued, "and it shall be your *coffin* instead that is full."

The figure released him. Vulcanon gasped for air and said, "Yes, I understand. It will be done."

"You shall get your war. That much we promise!"

The figure faded away and the energy field around Vulcanon disappeared. The record player stopped as he thought of how to accomplish the task set before him. He had so many avenues to exploit, yet in this occurrence, he could think of none that would succeed and not lead directly back to his own involvement. Then it came to him, the solution to this horrendous problem. He knew of one man who was so bereft of morality that he would operate purely on a capitalistic motivation. Vulcanon's fingers flew over his keypad. The Comm lit up and the man's image appeared before him.

Sleeping and quite haggard looking he answered, "What do you want waking me so late?" His eyes blinked until he saw Vulcanon and snapped to attention, "I'm so sorry Vulcanon. I didn't realize it was you. How can I be of service?" he croaked.

Vulcanon knew the man could be trusted, if not out of his passion for wealth, than at the very least out of his fear, for the consequences of failure. "Mita," said Vulcanon, "I have a task for you. It is quite dangerous, but it will make your pockets a great deal deeper than even you could want."

Mita's tongue flicked over his lips wetting them, "Ooh, tell me more."

Vulcanon flicked the switch and the energy field again covered his desk.

The arena was located below the bar itself, torn through time and deposited in the bowels of the establishment. Reminiscent of those from ancient Rome, the arena was oval in shape, its floor covered in red dirt that puffed with each footfall. Legend around the bar was that the dirt was originally brown, but countless washing in blood had stained it the current hue of red. Two metal rectangles sat on either end of the Arena, an entry point for each combatant. On the left side of those was a large weapons post, both of which could retract into the floor. The steel wall was ten feet high and thoroughly worn from countless impact. Six large energy spikes extended up toward the ceiling and provided an energy shield to protect the spectators from any errant attacks.

The crowd from the bar lined the seats a bloodlust consuming them. They did not expect the fight to last long as Kale had a fearsome reputation for his brutality in the arena. He was a champion and the only thing larger than his number of wins in the arena, was his hatred for humans. The floor opened and up he rose. He was stripped of his armor and only leather pants adorned his scared, muscular frame. Kale raised a hand into the air and screamed to the crowd. They roared in response and chanted his name. The Baan smiled and black drool oozed out between his sharp jagged teeth. The platform stopped and he stepped to the weapon post. Kale shook with anticipation hungry to maim his opponent.

The opposite platform opened and Colin rose into the arena. Kale licked his lips at the sight of the human. Colin looked out at the debauchery going on about him and sighed. He thought, *maybe this is where I belong. No one to fail but myself here.*

The top of the post to their left flashed red and a buzzer sounded concurrently. After three flashes, the light turned a solid green and the buzzer silenced. A series of weapons materialized from the post, dangling down like racks of beef, they ranged from non-lethal stun sticks to very lethal energy blades.

A veteran of the arena, Kale snatched his favorite weapon from the rack, a large scimitar with a spiked grip. He yanked it away, the entire post rushed down into the ground and he charged at Colin screaming.

Colin's own post flashed red again. Though he did not know the exact meaning of it, Colin knew it was bad. The roar of approval from the crowd snapped his attention to the oncoming Baan. Only a few more feet and he would be on him. The post went a solid red and slowly receded into the floor. The movement caught Colin's interest and he dove for a weapon. His hand latched onto something he could not see and he yanked it away just before the post dropped fully back into the floor.

Something tingled in the back of his mind and he dove forward in a roll. Kale's blade struck the ground, dust rose up and energy exploded where Colin had so recently been. The Baan roared his disgust. Colin looked at his hand to examine the weapon he had retrieved. A beautiful long sword, sleek and roughly three feet in length, its weight brought back memories of his youth on the Bellat Home world.

His father had insisted on him learning the art of swordplay, whether his goal was to have Colin fit in amongst the Bellat culture or just to preoccupy the boy's time and keep him out of trouble, it accomplished neither. At least now, it had found some purpose, but he knew better than to expose that fact, at least not until it played to his advantage.

Kale struck at him again, an untrained brutish blow. The blades exploded in a hail of white energy as they met each other. The blow pushed Colin back toward the hall. He had heard how strong the Baan were, but those stories did them no justice.

Three more blows followed, each blocked by Colin in sequence, until the arena wall pressed against him. Kale was noticeably frustrated. His human victims were usually the dregs of society, the only kind who frequented a place like the Ventured

Spirit, so he had come to expect humans as subpar warriors. This one however was well skilled in the art of combat.

Kale swung again, this time pressing his sword against Colin's as the human parried his blow. The energy of both swords spit off into the air like drops of water from a tiny fountain. Kale reached toward his back and pulled a small hidden shank from his pants. He thrust it toward Colin.

Perhaps it was the look in Kale's eyes, the subtle shift in his weight or something all together unexplainable, but Colin sensed the hidden blade coming. He shifted out of the way and the swords passed dangerously close to his face. For a split second, he was exposed and had Kale not been thrusting the shank forward toward where Colin had been, he could have taken that advantage.

Instead, Kale's sheer strength thrust the blade deep into the metal wall. He turned his head to stare at Colin, amazed the human was still alive, not realizing he was now exposed. Colin did not strike, instead he stepped back and bowed, more to mock than out of respect. Kale roared with hate. The crowd went silent, shocked at his tactics. He charged Colin, his sword flying recklessly through the air. Colin parried blow after blow, never making an offensive move. "How long do you want to embarrass yourself Kale?" Colin taunted.

Kale swung a heavy blow overhead. Colin spun out of the way and kicked him in the back as he flew by. Kale crashed to the ground in the dirt, a cloud of dust rose up around him. He picked himself up to his knees and yelled, "I KILL YOU HOO-MAN!"

Kale charged and threw his sword in one motion at Colin. Colin deflected the blade, but absorbed the full contact of Kale's shoulder as the Baan tackled him to the ground. Colin's sword flew out of his hand as did the air from his lungs.

Colin protected his head from the downpour of uncalculated blows raining down from Kale. Though Kale did not have a dominant position, his blows still carried a great deal of strength behind them. A stray that connected to a vital area would end this fight and quite possibly Colin's life as well. Colin braced his feet into the dirt as best he could, his timing would have to be perfect and his body would have to be precise. As Kale thrust a heavy blow toward his head, Colin pushed with his feet, thrust with his hips and pulled his upper body down in one fluid motion.

The momentum thrust the Baan forward past his head and slightly into the air. Kale's fist slammed into the dirt as Colin slipped out underneath him. Back on his feet, Colin felt confident he could end the fight. Kale laughed as he rose to his own feet. This puzzled Colin, as he was sure the Baan would answer his last move with another frustrated roar. Instead, he was greeted with a quiet jagged black smile.

The crowd roared with a bloodlust as Kale raised the scimitar into the air. He charged at Colin and swung madly, leaving his success to chance rather than skill. Masterfully Colin managed to avoid each blow. Perhaps by luck, Kale managed to press Colin to the arena wall yet again. Colin asked, "Is this what the Baan consider a fair fight?"

Kale laughed and swung his sword, "ALL FAIR IN FIGHT, WE LEARN FROM HOO-MANS!"

Colin looked back, gauging his distance to the wall when he noticed the shank still stuck in it. He smiled as an idea formed in his head. "Spoken like a true coward Kale."

"KALE NOT COWARD! CHAMPION!" His blade swung heavier with hate.

Inches from the wall Colin stopped, put his arms out and said, "Then kill me, if you can."

Kale raised his scimitar up and swung it at Colin recklessly. Colin stepped to the side, avoiding the blade by mere inches. He grabbed Kale's wrist and pulled him forward. The Baal slammed into the wall and froze. The scimitar sunk into the wall above him and he let go of it. Colin staggered away and tripped over something on the ground. He looked down, his sword. Colin kicked it up into the air and snatched it. Kale pulled himself from the wall, a large gash on his stomach. He staggered a few steps toward Colin and then fell to his knees. The wound should not have been so fatal. The crowd chanted, "KILL! KILL! KILL!"

Kale answered Colin's questioning look with a crooked grin, "Poisoned." Then he pleaded, "KILL ME!"

Colin looked out to the crowd disgusted. He was not a murderer and he would not satiate their lust. "No Kale."

Kale spat some black blood on the ground and grabbed the wound on his stomach. "NO HONOR, DIE LIKE THIS."

Colin walked up to his face, leaned in and said, "Then that is how you will die, but not by my hand and not here."

Again, Colin looked out to the crowd who still chanted for blood. He raised his sword, they screamed with glee; he looked down at Kale and then threw his sword aside. The cheers instantly turned to jeers. Colin yelled back, "I will not kill him!"

The posts powering the shield crackled with energy, the result of the crowd hurling debris at him. Colin feared the worst. Would this be his last decision? Killed by the mob or was there an even worse fate awaiting him? Beams of energy shot out from the post and hit both Colin and Kale. Everything went to black.

The sun set along the Alecean Coast. Waves from the raging sea caressed the black sand; white foam reflected what little light remained. Lush green vegetation lined the top of the twenty-foot cliffs, but none dared to climb down the rugged black rocks. The waves pushed further up the shore with each pass, threatening to engulf it. Leaving a path of deepening footsteps, a single lone figure walked the shoreline.

Draken Vulcanon walked as a stark contrast to the environment surrounding him. Dressed in an illustrious suit of white, countless medals he could not have possibly earned adorned his dress jacket, from his shoulder to hip clung a red sash and perfectly creased pants that tucked into tall black boots which finished the outfit.

His face told of his desire to be there, but still he had gone through much, both financially and politically to get his master's agent through the Planetary shield unnoticed, only such an isolated spot set a proper location for their meeting.

"I see subtlety is not your forte Vulcanon," a deep voice spoke from inside a nearby cave.

"This is not my only meeting and as it must maintain the burden of appearances, especially in as auspicious of circumstances as these," Vulcanon responded.

Out from the cave, clad in full body armor, Xyrus walked onto the shore. He no longer resembled the broken creature that had spent so much time in the Jahan years past. His armor was terrifying, a deep black that shone in the fading light and was stained with multiple splatters of red and orange. The chest plate was sculpted, a charging Crocena with a victim in its mar, stabbed by numerous blades and with fallen combatants that rained down along his sides. The forearms and shoulders added to Xyrus's already considerable frame, dotted with spikes and three blades on each piece. Skeletal finger guards were tipped with bright red claws. Hip leggings were formed in the mold of his actual musculature. The flow of each piece, so seamlessly designed that the armor became an extension of his flesh.

"Lord Xyrus. Interesting. Do you think your own attire any less conspicuous, or shall we simply announce your arrival to the Council?"

Xyrus stopped, raised a hand and through the uR a stream of energy lashed out to grip Vulcanon's throat. "Do not forget your place in this Vulcanon. I shall bring you your great war, but in no way am I your servant."

Vulcanon crumbled to his knees, the oxygen could not reach his lungs and the burning of asphyxiation coursed through his mind. He reached to his neck to remove the hand, yet there was nothing for him to touch, only a deadening pressure. "My apologies." he wheezed.

"I could kill you Vulcanon; your purpose here is finished. Though…" Xyrus released his grip and stepped closer. "You make a strong point. I cannot simply walk the streets."

"Whatever you need of me, I am at your disposal."

"I need nothing from something as lowly as you. My resources extended beyond that which can be bought with currency or coercion."

Vulcanon ran white with fear. Would this be the end of his life? He knew the cost of his actions and believed in their worth. He would accept his fate if it served that purpose. There were others in place that could finish the work he had begun.

Xyrus raised his hand up, as if gathering some unseen item from the air above. It burst into a bright hue of throbbing purple energy. Vulcanon's eyes threatened to pop out of his head at the sight. *What power is this?* He had only heard in myths and legend of the Ter'Ok'Zhu being able to do something so magical.

Xyrus pulled the energy down over his face and it spread out like a gel over his body, morphing every bit of mass that it touched. Xyrus's green skin changed to a pale white. His hard Belgae features transformed into that of a diminutive human male and his armor morphed into the plain black suit of an attaché. Vulcanon could not find the words to remark on the spectacle before him.

Xyrus smiled and spoke in a new voice, "Come now Senator, we must get to the council. It wouldn't befit the great Draken Vulcanon to be late to a Council meeting."

"How is this possible?"

Xyrus pulled the senator to his feet. He turned and traced the path of fading footprints in the sand. "There are things in life that require more than an educated mind to grasp Vulcanon. Simply understand your place in this and more so now understand the true wealth of my resources."

Vulcanon followed after Xyrus, his mind raced trying to wrap itself around the events that had just unfolded before him.

CHAPTER TWELVE

Colin awoke to the familiar feeling of his feet dragging along the ground. His eyes had a difficulty in focusing and he could not make out the two hulking men who carried him. What he could make out from their clothes and their stench was that they worked at the bar. *At least I'm alive,* he thought. Even without his vision fully enabled, the rest of his senses told him where he was. *Back in the bar.* The growing white blur hinted at where they were taking him. As they reached the front door, the two men stopped, gathered their strength and hurled Colin through it.

He came crashing onto the metallic street outside. His hands and chest took the brunt of the fall, but his face suffered some collateral damage as well. He looked up to see his reflection starring back at him in a pair of perfectly polished black boots. A deep, boisterous laugh echoed out from nearby. "I see your son has finally learned to pay you some respect Arthur. Though kissing your boots may be a bit much," Fa'Sham bellowed.

Colin picked himself up and dusted his clothes off. He hung his head, as if it was attached to a stack of weights, every bit of arrogance and pride washed away at the sight of his father. Colin feared meeting Arthur's cold disapproving eyes and even now he could feel their weight bearing down on him. They both stood frozen, neither willing to break the unbearable tension between them.

Arthur was far past middle age but physically he showed very few signs of it. He was quite fit and carried himself as such. It was years since his time on the council, however Arthur still bore the appearance of a man of importance. His hair, now fully white, served as a perfect frame to accentuate his ice blue eyes. Fortunately Fa'Sham had watched the scene countless times before and knew best how to defuse it. Arthur was his dearest friend, a brother of sorts. Fa'Sham walked up, embracing Colin in a gigantic bear hug and lifting him high off his feet he roared, "How I have missed you young Kinison."

Onlookers burst into laughter at the sight. Fa'Sham, still in his formal robes, a half-foot taller and several hundred pounds heavier than Colin, looked as though he was picking up a child, rather than the grown man that was in his arms. Even Arthur managed a slight chuckle at the sight.

Colin pushed him away. "Save your affection for your Queens Fa'Sham. I already feel like my ribs are broken."

His laugh, pure and hardy nearly shook the promenade. Fa'Sham placed Colin down and slapped him on the back. Colin looked to his right and made eye contact with Tar'Sham, his childhood friend and the son of Fa'Sham. "So have they relegated you to guard duty now Tar'Sham?"

"Colin!" snapped Arthur.

Tar'Sham rested a hand upon Arthur's shoulder. "Such a position would be an honor was it mine."

"Tar'Sham has been appointed to the Council. Old age has begun to bite at my heels, so he takes my seat there," Fa'Sham said.

"I see your time in the Alliance hasn't changed anything. How is Admiral Glovalkov?" Arthur asked.

Colin's heart sank; he could not believe his father did not know, it would seem Vulcanon's influence was far greater than he could have imagined. Then the icy grip of guilt took hold of his heart and his eyes returned to the ground. He longed to tell his father of the battle and of his confrontation here with Vulcanon, but his shame drove his tongue to silence. Even the two Bellat could feel how serious the question had affected Colin. Fa'Sham's once boisterous demeanor went deathly serious and he grabbed Colin's shoulder, brown clawed fingers gently dug into his clothes. "What is it son?" Fa'Sham asked.

Colin responded in the only way his body would allow, he reached into his jacket and removed the data pad. A glint of the sun shone off its face. So much had been lost because of the events recorded on that pad. How he wished he could simply erase them from existence, something Vulcanon had literally tried to do himself. Colin handed it to his father.

"What is this Colin?" Arthur questioned.

Tears gathered behind his eyes and then without force poured forth. He had lost so much, Glovalkov, Sasha and even his career, how could he tell his father without admitting that shame? How could he open his mouth without opening up his heart to all that sorrow again. Vulcanon's sick cruel face appeared in his mind, that wicked smile mocked him, flashes of images of Sasha being subdued. Colin could not let him win, even if it meant admitting his failure to the only man whose approval mattered. Colin wiped his face off and spoke. "Glovalkov is dead. This is the log. We tried to bring it to the council, to Vulcanon, but he wouldn't see it. Sasha got herself," the words refused to come out, "Vulcanon tried to cover it up. He tried to have me arrested, but I ran."

Arthur put a hand on Colin's shoulder. "It's alright son, but we need to go to my quarters and view this. If Vulcanon was trying to cover it up, there must be something dreadfully important contained in the log."

"And inherently evil," Tar'Sham chimed in.

Fa'Sham gave a gentle tug on Colin's shoulder, "Come on now. My personal transport is waiting. We've no further time to waste on discussion; action is what's required."

All four men disappeared into the crowd, moving quickly toward the king's awaiting transport.

The Holovid snapped off as the Ares exploded. Arthur's face sunk at the sight of such horror. Glovalkov had always been a close friend, but more than that, he seemed immortal, legendary for his incredible military mind and battlefield tactics. To see him defeated so soundly spoke volumes as to the level of threat that the crew of the Ares had faced. Arthur stood up from his desk and removed the data pad. "Light."

The room snapped to life, bathed in the warm white light. Arthur's office was simple, adorned with scattered portraits of battles from centuries past. The furniture was modern, but minimal, almost to an extreme. All four men now stood at Arthur's desk, starring at the data pad in his hand.

Colin still could not look at his father, but he offered, "Vulcanon tried to bury it, why wouldn't he want the council to see this?"

Fa'Sham spoke gruffly, "Foul piece of trash. Vulk's never raised a finger unless it served him personally in some way. I swear it was a dark day on the council when he replaced you Arthur."

"It would have been far darker had we lost you instead," Arthur replied.

Fa'Sham nodded in agreement. Tar'Sham spoke, "There may be something he does not wish the council to find out about. What of the ship that attacked you Colin, the recording does not seem to offer any identification or details about its origin."

"We couldn't identify it. Scanners didn't work properly and the sheer power. . ." His voice trailed off remembering the horrific battle. "It wasn't anything that's been encountered before. I can be sure of that. Even Glovalkov knew that. He died so that we could get this recording into important hands."

Fa'Sham slammed a fist onto the desk. "That Vulcanon would not want this log brought to anyone's attention affirms his ill intentions. Let me present the pad to the council myself and watch the scrib squirm before me."

"We must be cautious with our next move old man. He will be on the lookout for this pad and we can be sure that he will stop at no end to prevent it from being shown to the council." Arthur said.

Tar'Sham spoke up, "He has already placed an alert on the streams for Colin's arrest."

"That fragging coward," Colin screamed.

"All the more reason to be prudent," Arthur calmly added.

Suddenly Arthur's desk chimed and a single light flashed. Arthur tapped it and O'Tel's face appeared. "M'Lord," Arthur said as he and the other bowed their heads.

"Arthur, I dare hope that I am not too late in this. Is Colin there with you? Is he safe?" O'Tel said.

Arthur nodded, "Yes M'Lord, but why?"

"I fear the tides have shifted and new plans have been set into motion. I shall arrive shortly, make sure the boy stays safe."

"Of course M'Lord," Arthur responded.

He pressed the button again and the image disappeared. Arthur raised the data pad to emphasize the words he spoke, "This must reach the council. It seems now that our hand is forced and so we'll just have to play it as best as we can."

"You two," Fa'Sham pointed at Tar'Sham and Colin, "Stay here and wait for Master O'Tel to arrive."

"I want to go with you," Colin pleaded.

Arthur stepped to him and placed a hand on his shoulder, "Of course you do, but you would only be playing into Vulcanon's hands and you know that. You have a far greater fate than working the mines. Patience Colin, please this once have patience."

Colin bowed his head in acceptance. Arthur patted his shoulder and left with Fa'Sham.

Fear and anxiety filled the Council chamber. Voices exchanged queries carried on whispers. This was not the first time the council had been convened for an emergency meeting, but what was unusual was the fact that Vulcanon had called for it.

In all his years of service on the council, Draken Vulcanon had established an aura of control. It seemed his every move, even one as small as wiping his nose, was thought-out and calculated. He was a master at his craft and as such, his need for an emergency meeting terrified those now gathered.

The doors to the chamber opened, startling the room to silence and Draken Vulcanon walked in. Vulcanon's confident stride and oblivious arrogance overshadowed the unfamiliar man trailing behind him so much that all eyes focused solely on Vulcanon. He motioned to his right and Xyrus, in human guise, walked over to an empty chair, dutifully playing his role. Vulcanon walked to the center of the room and stood. He looked around the room, silence and curiosity wrapped around him like a warm blanket. He knew he owned this moment, that the Council was at his command, pliable to his will and his words.

His eyes smiled in place of his mouth. Vulcanon thrived on this rush, the thrill that power could give a man. He allowed them a second more to stare, allowed their minds to dash furiously in random directions, an endless journey deciphering the riddle of his motivation. His deception needed to be perfect, his part crucially played to separate him from the events that were about to take place. As the tension rose to a crescendo and his fellow senators began to shift in their seats uncomfortably, Vulcanon, fingers interlaced at his chest, spoke. "My fellow Senators, I apologize for convening the council so hastily, but my reasons for doing so are both urgent and dire."

His feet moved slowly as he circled the room, his hands assisting his words to give them added emphasis. He continued, "As many of you know, some from direct experience, the Belgae still remain a major threat to us all. Some would contend since their banishment from this council that that threat has elevated. The attack on Zelda Four and consequently the loss of that entire system is an indisputable testament to such a fact.

I have pleaded before you in the past for a unilateral strike. I have sought the use of the Guard to quell their violent progression through our sectors. The Belgae race itself poses an immediate threat to not only our physical well being, but to the very values that make up the core of everyone seated here at this council. Sadly my calls to action have gone unanswered, tied to endless hours of debate and posturing. The urgency of this matter has gone unheard.

So I come to you today, my fellow senators, in this time of crisis and with evidence so compelling, so horrifying, that this council's only answer can be a pre-emptive strike against the Belgae war machine, lest we simply wait for them to gain enough strength and power to erase all that we together have worked so diligently to conserve."

The door to the council chamber thrust open. Fa'Sham stormed in, hatred in his eyes. "Have the old ways become tiresome and no longer any use to you Vulcanon?" he bellowed.

"Do not use your own tardiness to find blame in my manner of operation Fa'Sham. You were informed of the time of this meeting in the same timely manner as those seated about us."

"I was delayed," Fa'Sham answered.

Vulcanon rolled his eyes and turned his back to Fa'Sham. "Were the taps running slow today?" A small chuckle escaped his lips and jumped to a few of the other senators as well.

"No Draken, though they overflow if the truth be told," Arthur replied.

The chamber froze. Vulcanon's eyes went wide with confusion, but he dare not turn to face the man. Xyrus gritted his teeth, a meager attempt to hide his hatred. Arthur had interfered in his attempt to kill Fa'Sham so many years prior. More so than that, Arthur had sacrificed himself to spare Fa'Sham from banishment. Xyrus desperately wished to lunge out across the Hall and kill him, but greater things were a foot and so he buried his blood lust.

After a beat, Vulcanon spun on his heel and faced them as they approached. He raised a finger at Arthur and yelled, "You are banished from this council. I see the years have not diminished your blatant disregard for the rules of this Hall."

Arthur came to a halt a few feet from Vulcanon, his presence enough to disrupt the Councilor's demeanor. Two Senatorial Guards slithered up to his side. The Guards were the only ones allowed weapons in the Great Hall. They wielded a Desh'Kai, a three-foot golden lance. On one end rested a wide black steel curved blade, much the same shape as a scimitar, and on the other end was a bright red ball, no bigger than a fist, held by three talons. The ball could fire bolts of energy of varying levels, much like a blaster.

The Guards were a mysterious group. Left behind from the Ter'Ok'Zhu. Many questioned if they were even alive. None had ever seen under their black hoods, which obscured nearly all of their facial features. Across their eyes, they wore a tinted glass visor, which connected to metallic square housing hard wired over their ears directly into their skull. This allowed them to process data at a rate faster than any normal soldier could. Thousands of the Guard protected all of Ter'Ar'Tor and their skill as warriors was legendary. They answered to two masters, the Ter'Ok'Zhu and the Council.

"My banishment extends only to my service as a senator, as you are well aware Vulcanon. My attendance here today is simply as an urgent messenger. I would assume you would offer such a matter for vote rather than simply having the Guard usher me out unheard."

The council erupted in chaotic agreement and Vulcanon raised his arms to quiet them. "Unfortunately wants do not direct this council. There are traditions and rules of conduct that take precedence, or have you risen above such demands Arthur? You have been banished. . ."

Arthur stepped forward and waved off Vulcanon's comment. "From SITTING on the council Draken, nothing more, I still have a claim to enter this Great Hall and speak."

Vulcanon scowled and his eye twitched at the truth of his statement. "Only members may address the council, unless called forth."

"There have been exceptions," Arthur countered.

"This shall not be one of them Arthur. You chose your path long ago and though you may very well find a right once again to enter the sanctum of this Great Hall, you shall not undermine that punishment which you brought down upon yourself. It is your burden to bear. If you will not leave the Hall of your own accord than the Guard shall remove you, preferably with force."

Fa'Sham took a step forward, but Arthur raised a hand to stop him. He smiled confidently, much deadlier a weapon than any blade Arthur could have wielded. "I concede to you then Senator. You are right in that I have no right to address the council. I have been banished and I have honored that burden without qualm. Traditions serve to guide us past simple wants and needs, yet sometimes one must go beyond the comfort that following such traditions brings. One must risk if the need is great enough. Since it is your will that I leave without addressing the council, then I shall respect that request and allow their curiosity towards my purpose here to go unanswered."

Arthur bowed and turned to walk out of the large doors, the Guards shadowed his every step. The council interrupted his departure with a roar of disapproving voices and comments. Halfway from his departure, Arthur stopped. He raised his hand and the council went silent. Arthur reached into his breast pocket and removed the data pad. He strode back toward Fa'Sham and said, "However Draken, though I may not address the council over the contents of this data pad, Fa'Sham, as king to the Bellat people has every right to."

Vulcanon recognized it immediately. "That pad belongs to the Alliance."

Arthur stopped next to Fa'Sham; he did not anticipate that Vulcanon would be fazed so quickly. A voice from the Sophos Council spoke up, "How does the Senator know this, when Ambassador Kinison has yet to disclose any information regarding its contents."

"A valid point Draken," Arthur agreed.

Vulcanon scanned the room, it seemed to be growing in size with each passing second, or was he simply shrinking, such an unusual feeling, it reminded him why he hated Arthur so. His mind failed him, all of this was so unexpected, but none more so then the pad itself.

"It does not matter. It is property of the Terran Alliance and as such out of King Fa'Sham's jurisdiction to present to this or any council."

Fa'Sham grabbed the pad out of Arthur's hand and yelled, "Damn your fool rules Vulcanon. The council has a right to see this."

"I am the only one who can make such a judgment. Give it to me and I shall determine if its contents validate such a need."

"I would sooner surrender my own life," said Fa'Sham.

"Regardless, the pad does not belong to you and if you refuse to relinquish it, then I am sure the circumstances in which I shall have it procured will not be as pleasant as what I offer you now," Vulcanon spat.

"You dare threaten me?" asked Fa'Sham.

"Royal privilege does not exclude you from the equity of the law, or do you hold yourself above such simple things?" queried Vulcanon.

"Enough," screamed Xyrus. Still in his human guise, the outburst seemed even that much more awkward. Xyrus reached out with the uR and pulled the pad from Fa'Sham's grip. It flew across the room past stunned eyes. He crushed it as it reached his actual grip.

"What witchery is this?" Fa'Sham asked.

As if in response, Xyrus allowed his guise to fade away. Electricity crackled down his body as his human flesh melted away to reveal his true appearance. Most of the senate screamed in terror. Fa'Sham let out a colossal roar that shook the room. "Have you come to face defeat once again Xyrus?"

"Guards stop him," ordered Vulcanon.

Xyrus reached out with the uR and threw Vulcanon across the room into a mass of the Senators. Like a snake ready to strike, the Senate Guards slithered forth to confront the Dark Lord. They raised their Desh'Kai in tandem and struck. Xyrus met each blade with the Na'Dral on his wrists. Energy exploded and the Guard used the recoil from their attacks to enhance each successive strike. Again, Xyrus blocked their blows. The Senate Guards were fast, they pushed his limits as a warrior, but he had an advantage they could not match.

He blocked a blow and with the uR pushed one of the Guards across the room, slamming him into the wall. The Guard fell to the floor unconscious, an imprint of his impact left behind. The second Guard swung at Xyrus's head. The blade stopped an inch from making contact. Xyrus turned his head and his eyes erupted with power. He reached up, grabbing the Guard under the jaw, hoisting the man up into the air, and energy flowed from Xyrus's forearm to the base of the guard's head. He let out a bloodcurdling scream as his body quivered and trembled. Then the life left it and he hung limp and motionless.

Xyrus tossed the Guard's body aside, a mere afterthought of action as he strode toward Fa'Sham. Xyrus raised a hand and the fallen Guard's Desh'Kai flew to his hand as he spoke, "Now, finally I shall revel in the feel of your blood flowing along my skin and stare into your eyes as death claims you."

"As I've always known, the only way you could ever face me down is as a coward. You have no honor. Come fool, I assure you I will not die with as much ease as you think."

Xyrus allowed the blade of the Desh'Kai to slide along the floor, creating a trail of sparks as he neared Fa'Sham. He did not care if he would be looked at as a coward, striking down the Bellat King unarmed, history was written by the victors, honor had no place for him on the field of battle, only glory. Xyrus raised the blade up as he came within feet of Fa'Sham; the King stood proud and unmoving.

CRACK! Xyrus was not sure if he heard or felt the blast hit him first. His armor took the brunt of it, scorched and burned. He looked up to see Arthur across the hall, in possession of a Desh'Kai. The remaining Senators rushed out of the giant doors to freedom. Xyrus frustrated, thought to himself, *not again!*

Tar'Sham and Colin sat in Arthur's office. The two had grown up together on Bella Prime, but Colin's time away had created a gap between them that the few hours now spent together would not cross. Once inseparable brothers, the two were now polar opposites.

Tar'Sham sat with perfect posture; everything about him was in its place, where as Colin leaned to the side, legs spread and his chin arrogantly resting in his hand. They had nothing but time to burn and rather than spending it in an uncomfortable silence, they chose to play Darbash.

Darbash was a game of strategy and skill, but luck also factored into it. A Bellat game, it had since found a strong following in other sectors of space as well. Colin was a much better player than Tar'Sham, but the Bellat's skill had vastly improved over the years.

"I see you have not forgotten how to roll the Bash," said Tar'Sham.

"A few boys onboard the Ares liked to play, easy marks, but they kept it fresh."

Colin spun his roller and it flashed the number twenty. "Darka!"

Suddenly the door opened and they both shot up to their feet. The sight of O'Tel eased their nerves. He hurried up next to them, moving Colin's pieces and then nodded to them both. "Darbash, a most excellent way to pass the time, but I'm afraid you are defeated in twelve moves my young prince," O'Tel said peacefully.

Tar'Sham studied the board for a second and then slammed a fist against the table in angered acceptance. O'Tel looked over to him and asked, "Has he been told yet?"

"No. A more urgent matter drew father away before he had the opportunity to," Tar'Sham replied.

Colin interrupted them, "Tell me what? You act as if I'm not even here."

O'Tel slowly turned his attention to Colin and drew in a breath for strength. He spoke with a heavy heart, "Colin you must come with me. You have a fate, a path in which only you can walk. There are matters at hand that threaten to reshape everything, things which even now are unfolding."

"What are you talking about?" Colin questioned, visibly shaken from his words.

Before O'Tel could respond, a call rang through on the Holovid on the desk. Colin eagerly pressed the buttons on the keypad to answer it. The game disappeared and was replaced by a female Bellat who was quite distraught. "My Prince, I am sorry to disturb you."

She bowed her head toward Tar'Sham and he returned the gesture. "You have not, what news have you?"

"My Prince, King Fa'Sham has been attacked."

Colin blurted, "Impossible."

"How?" Tar'Sham asked.

"I don't know m'Lord, but those who escaped are reporting its...."

"Who, who is this assailant?" Tar'Sham demanded.

She paused, pressing a finger to her ear. The color drained from her face as she listened. Trembling she looked up to Tar'Sham. "Xyrus."

They both spoke in unison, "XYRUS?"

Without haste, they rushed out of the room, but O'Tel stopped them. "NO! Colin you must not face Xyrus," O'Tel demanded.

"My father is in danger. I'm not going to just stay in here and let him die," Colin responded.

"It is written, if you face him, you will die."

Colin was taken aback by the words, but after the shock of it passed he moved back to exit the room. O'Tel raised a hand, holding him in place with the uR. "LET ME GO!" Colin screamed.

"No! I have sworn to protect you. It is your fate to die if ever you face him, it cannot be changed, trust me in this. I will not allow you to see it fulfilled so rashly."

Colin fought desperately to get free. He stared straight into the ancient man's eyes and said, "You've no right to do this. You're not supposed to interfere, is this truly the Ter'Ok'Zhu way?"

O'Tel paused and then released his grip on Colin. "It is your fate Colin, I have seen it."

"I make my own fate," Colin spat back, rushing out of the room.

"Colin wait," O'Tel yelled to no avail. Tar'Sham hurried after Colin. O'Tel paused as something far away, a terrible danger, suddenly crept into his mind. He forced himself to follow after them, dismissing the warning.

The Great Hall was all but empty, only Arthur, Fa'Sham and Xyrus now stood within. Xyrus reached out a hand and with the uR slammed the doors shut. His eyes locked with Arthur's as he stepped away from Fa'Sham. "You only delay the inevitable Kinison." He spat the last name from his mouth as if it were some foul tasting brew.

"I don't know what sorcery you've learned Xyrus, but even that won't ensure your victory here," said Arthur.

"Perhaps," Xyrus said with a crude sneer.

Xyrus reached out, flung Arthur into the giant doors and using the uR held him suspended in the air. Xyrus squeezed his hand shut and the stream of uR constricted around Arthur's body.

Arthur could feel his bones conceding to the pressure, as if some mechanical vice was bearing down on him, and he screamed out in pain. His mind searched for options, but the darkness had already begun to consume him. Then, the glint of the Desh'Kai in his grip sparkled at the edge of his vision. Arthur tried to raise the blade, but his arm firmly locked against the steel door behind him refused. The pressure on his chest intensified and one of his ribs cracked.

Time was running out. Xyrus walked closer. "You see now Kinison, my powers are far beyond anything you could comprehend. Your feeble attempt to play hero shall only serve to extend the amount of pain I shall reap upon your friend."

Arthur wrestled the Desh'Kai up enough to fire a blast. Xyrus waved a hand and swatted the bolt away, as one would a charging insect. The brief change in his focus loosened his grip on Arthur, his body crumbled down on the floor. Arthur gasped for air.

"You continue to fight a battle you simply cannot win. WHY?" Xyrus asked.

Arthur clenched an arm around his midsection as he grudgingly pulled himself to his feet. "Because I must," he said.

"Concede! Concede to my pre-eminence and I promise you both a quick death."

"NEVER!"

Arthur fired another volley of shots and charged at Xyrus. The Dark Lord deflected each blast, using the uR to protect himself from harm. Arthur neared within feet as the last deflected bolts flew to the sidewall. He raised the Desh'Kai and swung at Xyrus's neck.

Xyrus reached a hand up, stopping Arthur mid motion. Xyrus clenched his hand and Arthur felt the pressure squeeze around his throat; the Desh'Kai was mere inches from Xyrus's flesh. "I shall find great pleasure in tearing the life from your body," Xyrus hissed.

CRACK! Xyrus's attention turned to see a large pillar swinging directly at him. He released Arthur and braced himself for the impact. Stone slammed into his body and sent him flying across the room. The Desh'Kai fell to the floor from Xyrus's grip. Fa'Sham came running over, picked up the weapon and knelt over Arthur. The smell of sweat and dirt were not much of a comfort, but they were familiar. Fa'Sham wrapped a furry arm around his fallen friend and hoisted him to his feet.

"Is there still breath left in you?" Fa'Sham asked.

Arthur coughed and a bit of blood rose to the edge of his lips. "Not much old friend, but enough."

"Gather what you can, I fear there is still more fight left in the Dark Lord."

The pile of debris where Xyrus had landed trembled and then exploded.

"It seems as though he still wants to dance," Arthur said.

"At least he is no longer armed."

Xyrus clapped his hands together; they erupted in a purple haze of energy, and as he separated them a solid beam expanded in kind, connected to each palm. After reaching a four-foot length, he stopped and grabbed it with his right hand. Electricity crackled up and down the beam as it took a more defined shape, that of a sword.

Arthur and Fa'Sham looked on in amazement. It was as if a horrible nightmare had suddenly taken form. Arthur patted Fa'Sham on the shoulder. "No better way to die old friend."

"Aye!"

Arthur and Fa'Sham struck first, though aged; the two warriors were still fiercely skilled. They moved in a seamless dance, countless years of experience together gave them an intuition about each other's next move.

If ever there was a match to their skill, it was Xyrus and now infused with a greater skill from the uR he was able to meet each strike with a parry. His own blows nearly connected with each swing of his blade. Arthur and Fa'Sham struck with an unending pace, aware that if the Dark Lord was given an opportunity to focus on more than their oncoming strikes, he might be able to tap into the force he had displayed earlier.

Beleaguered with the stalemate, Xyrus risked. He reached out with the uR and delivered a blow to Arthur's chest. The feel of his flesh striking the human's gave him intense pleasure, feeling bone break for a split second before Arthur's body propelled through the air across the room. Arthur's body crashed through one of the stone pillars across the room and he fell to the floor behind it. Fragments of stone crashed down around him, just barely missing his broken body.

The change in focus drew strength from the shaped weapon in Xyrus's hand and as Fa'Sham struck down with a blow that was blocked, it shattered. The top of the blade fell to the floor and Xyrus was exposed. Fa'Sham drew back for a killing blow, Xyrus's gamble had failed and now he would pay for it.

The giant doors to the Great Hall burst open and there stood Colin and Tar'Sham. Colin's eyes snapped to his father's broken body and he screamed, "Father!"

Fa'Sham's attention shifted to the voice as Colin ran towards Arthur's fallen body. Xyrus used the opportunity, waving a hand at Fa'Sham, the uR streaming out to send him flying across the room crashing through a council pod. "No!" Tar'Sham screamed and rushed after his father.

Arthur looked up to see Colin rushing toward him. His eyes darted over to the Dark Lord as he was standing up. The broken half of the uR blade rose into the air by Xyrus's side. Clarity filled Arthur's head with the realization of the blade's target. A surge of adrenaline rushed through his body as he tried in vain to scream at Colin to get down, his lungs collapsing as they filled with fluid under his fractured ribs.

Blindly Colin rushed forward to his father, nothing else mattered any more, and he had to save him. Colin saw his father rise up, visibly weakened, waving his arm in desperation. Colin glanced over to the Dark Lord just in time to see the light glint off the broken purple faux-steel of the uR blade as it came screaming directly for his chest.

CHAPTER THIRTEEN

It pierced his flesh, the blade slicing effortlessly through muscle and bone, straight through to his heart. Colin screamed out in pain, a deeper pain than he had ever felt at any moment in his life. He fell to the ground and blood oozed out of the wound over the faux-steel to the floor.

Colin fell to his knees and grabbed his father's body. "NO! WHY?" he screamed.

Arthur had used what life was left in his body to intercept the dark blade, taking the mortal blow himself. He lied in his son's arms and felt the life flow out of his chest. He reached up and held Colin's cheek in his hand. "I love you Colin," were the last words he uttered before the breath left his body permanently.

Colin grabbed his father's body firmly in his arms and wailed in denial. Arthur could not die. It was a foreign concept to him. "Now, now boy, at least do his memory some value and die with dignity, not blathering about like some fool woman," Xyrus spat out at him.

Colin looked up at the beast that stood over him. The broken sword raised, Xyrus readied himself to finish the job. Colin stared with unwavering hate at the man who had killed his father, the tears now only a scant memory along his cheeks. "Much better child," Xyrus said.

His blade flew down at Colin's neck, ready to taste his blood and end his life. Instead, it shattered as it met the steel of the Jahn'Do'Tor. White energy showered down on top of Colin and he looked back. Xyrus recoiled, nearly falling to the floor. His eyes filled with shock as he gazed upon O'Tel. The Ter'Ok'Zhu King stood, arms outstretched, a guardian angel over Colin and his dying father's body. Xyrus could feel the power radiating from O'Tel and the sword, it washed over him like a wave washing up against the shore.

"You shall not claim his life on this day Xyrus," O'Tel proclaimed.

Xyrus reached out with the uR and tried to thrust O'Tel aside. Disgust filled O'Tel's face and he furled his brow in response. "Such arrogance," he said.

Without motion, but rather only a thought, O'Tel focused the uR and sent Xyrus flying across the room. Only the opposite wall stopped his momentum. O'Tel leapt effortlessly toward the Dark Lord, landing soundlessly mere feet in front of him. Xyrus looked up, blood dripping down his chin as he smiled. "You may be able to save his life false King, but you can no longer hide her from me. Their will shall be done."

O'Tel stepped back in shock. *How does he know of Zhu,* he thought. His hesitation gave Xyrus his moment for escape. The Dark Lord turned and pressed a hand to the wall behind him. It exploded outward in a burst of energy and Xyrus launched himself outside with the remains.

O'Tel turned and saw Fa'Sham walking with help from his son Tar'Sham. He snapped a hand in Colin's direction and spoke to them, the force of his conviction wrapped in the uR allowed his voice to carry more meaning then the spoken words alone could, "Watch over the boy, his life is vital to all our future. He must be protected."

With that, O'Tel dove out of the break in the wall after him. Xyrus's body plummeted through the air alongside Mount Arrash. The Great Hall from which he had begun his flight quickly shrunk away into the distance with each passing second. He could only imagine the thoughts of those residing in the scattered buildings resting along the edge of the mountain as he screamed past their eyes. Xyrus concentrated on the uR; he could feel it gather about his body, as he drained the life out of the very world around him. Then something else tugged on his senses, something familiar and something that he hated with every fiber of his being, O'Tel.

Xyrus turned to face the ancient king. O'Tel plunged toward the Dark Lord at an unnaturally fast speed, as if some unseen force propelled him. Xyrus placed his hands in front of his chest, as if he were holding an invisible ball. Suddenly a pale red orb materialized and grew as he pulled apart his palms. As it snapped out bits of electricity he thrust it out toward O'Tel.

O'Tel screamed through the air, wind tore past his body and caused his robes to flap noisily. With the uR at his back, he closed in on Xyrus, hopeful that he could catch him in time. He felt the orb before his eyes could fully see it coming. His mind marveled at Xyrus's ability to manipulate the uR. His skill so strong and so soon. Few outside of the Ter'Ok'Zhu had ever produced beings capable of willfully manipulating the uR and never had he seen someone blossom so quickly. It was as if years of training were imprinted onto Xyrus's mind. O'Tel did not alter his descent. Even though Xyrus's ability had increased significantly, his control obviously had not grown equally in measure.

The orb missed the ancient king, but Xyrus assumed it would, O'Tel was not his target. Instead, the large outcropping of stone above them had been his aim the entire time. The orb crashed into it and a hail of rock exploded out of the side of the mountain. Xyrus smiled and turned back toward the ground. His mind drew up the uR for a much more difficult task.

O'Tel turned at the sound of the explosion, *not as reckless as I thought.* The fragments from the explosion rained down on the buildings along the mountain. O'Tel reached out with his mind and pushed the mid-sized pieces to paths that would cause minimal damage. However, one particular section was so large that there was no place to divert it to without causing a significant loss of life. O'Tel raised a hand and aimed it at the boulder. A white beam of energy laced with electricity shot out and tore into the stone. It exploded in a burst of force, leaving only bits of dust. O'Tel turned back toward Xyrus and continued his pursuit.

Xyrus's eyes turned a bright purple and a beam of energy shot forth from his forehead out in the air fifty feet in front of him. It formed into an oval, roughly the same size as him. His body plunged into it and he was gone, as was the oval of energy, without a trace.

To any other, the escape would have seemed flawless, as there was no tangible evidence of Xyrus's destination. O'Tel however was blessed with a sight that saw beyond the spectrum of the rest of the world. To him the uR was given a tangible form and his eyes could trace the subtle shifts in its tides, reflected in each action of every being that existed. Xyrus was careless, an obvious statement to his lack of understanding about the full nature of the uR. His path tore through the tides, as visible as if the Dark Lord had left a jet stream behind for O'Tel to follow.

O'Tel had surprise on his side and he would not waste it by rushing in to confront the Dark Lord. The ground was nearly upon him and even with all his strength and skill in the uR; such a collision would end only in his death. Fear did not take a hold on him.

The Slai'Nor came screaming through the air and flew up alongside its master. The cockpit opened and O'Tel used the uR to nudge himself inside. The ship pulled up hard and streaked toward the Dark Lord's location. The smell of the interior and feel of the seat brought a further sense of calm to O'Tel. He cleared his mind and prepared for his confrontation with Xyrus.

Peace. Quiet. Tranquility. Crisp air rolled in through the bay window, a fresh wind from the laden snow that sat along the hills outside, a chill still on its breath. It rolled off her cheek, gusting through her hair. Queen Helaya stared out at the fading sun, lost in her own meditation.

The leader of her people since the death of her beloved husband Menalae, Helaya had learned to capture each free moment as if they were bubbles of air amongst a giant ocean. The yellow sun lit the sky of Vysan in a display of flowing color. The upper atmosphere was filled with a mixture of gases and moisture, which always projected a sea of extravagant shades.

However, in the failing light the sky truly was poetic in all of its glory and it now filled her private quarters with an ethereal glow, transporting her away from her regal duties if only for the briefest of seconds. She was beloved by nearly all her people, whether by admiration for her success following her husband's demise or by pity in remembrance of the man he had been. Helaya had helped fortify her people's place amongst the stars in ways that no other leader had in the past. No other race owned as much territory or had made as great of strides in technological advances. However, as glorious and well received of a leader as she was, the Sophos Queen still had some amongst her own race that desired her fall.

Her door banged, a large thumping of the metal knocker slamming against its wood base. The Sophos were odd in their designs, relishing mixing opposites to create synergy. "Open," she responded and the doors swung inward of their own accord, mechanized.

Minas entered, he waved his own attachés aside, the message was clear for them to remain outside of the room. He bore brilliant blue robes trimmed in white. Black gloves covered bejeweled hands, one of which carried a tall golden staff, twice as adorned as the man himself.

His robes flowed like oil along the ground, allowing only brief glances at the perfectly polished boots underneath. His face was weathered and worn, even though he had only but reached middle age. Outward appearances taking a priority over any sense of practicality, every bit of his body was pampered and readied for presentation.

Minas had served the Imana all his life and thus he had risen quickly through its ranks to his current role as its leader, never in their history had one so young reached the position of Patriarch. He alone was in charge of the direction of their people's faith. The honor of such an appointment allowed Minas a candidness with the Queen that others would never be afforded.

"Hello Minas. You are early," she said.

The doors closed behind him. She stood up, turned to face him and the windows closed behind her. Helaya motioned toward an empty pair of chairs. "Of course majesty, thank you for seeing me none the less," he replied.

They walked to the chairs, fine leather pieces that dwarfed the occupants. An awkward pause passed between them then they sat. The Patriarch tapped his staff on the ground and it retracted into a smaller hand held version of itself. "Have you forgotten your faith?" he ventured asking.

The statement was meant to shock her, as no one spoke in such accusatory tones to the Queen, however, it did not. Helaya pressed a button on her chair and the doors to the chamber opened, allowing her handmaid, Jonella, to enter. She carried a large silver platter with a bevy of Ichar, similar to English Biscuits on Earth in texture, yet their taste was closer to a vegetable paste such as creamed spinach. "Far more important matters have required my attention Minas."

"Your duty to our people demands your presence at mass, as an example to the rest of us. To show the populace that your faith comes in second to other duties is simply unacceptable majesty."

She took an Ichar and bit a small corner. A nod of her head and look from her eye gave thanks to her handmaid, as well as an unspoken order to leave. A press of the button allowed Jonella to escape and gave the Queen the ability to speak to the Patriarch with more candor. She detested his fascist attitude toward religion. He believed with such passion that it often clouded his mind and prevented him from using any sense of reason. "My location in regards to the practice of prayer has no relation to my level of commitment to our faith."

He scoffed at the notion, "Your intensions in the matter are irrelevant. Your role supersedes standard operations of behavior, as perception should be your only concern in this."

She placed the cake down, upset at his tone. Her eyes squeezed tightly as her glare dared to cut through him. "So should I now cater to the whim of the masses? Is it no longer my place to lead them, but function as a simple figurehead?"

"I would make no such suggestion majesty, rather a simple request to show support and inspire those whom you so lead. In times such as these. . ."

Her eyes widened at the words, *how much did he know* she thought. His words were ambiguous enough to simply be an inquiry. "What times Minas? Our people stand in an age of great prosperity."

He hung his head low. "Empty whims of glory majesty, we expand our empire and gain in wealth, yet spiritually I see our people straying and I fear, I fear for the future of our people as a whole."

"I too have questioned the direction of our people, but I think for different reasons than your own."

"Perhaps they are closer than you think my Queen." He stood up, shook the golden rod in his hand and it extended into the staff once again. "Come with me," he said. She stared at him unmoving. He offered her a hand and said, "Please."

She accepted it and together they walked to the window. The sun had all but set in the distance and the sky threatened to go black in its absence. "What do you see Helaya?" he asked.

She stared out at the horizon, her mind dissecting his question for any hidden meaning. "The sun setting in the distance," she replied.

"It is indeed, in its simplest definition that majesty, yet I see so much more. I see a gift from our maker, celestial beauty encapsulated in tangible forms, a reminder of his glory. Have you ever in your travels seen such beauty as can be glanced on our own planet?"

"There are great wonders beyond the reach of our own planet, Minas."

"But none so glorious, none that strike an inner chord like those witnessed on Vysan. Yet more and more with our people's devotion to technology and our expansion throughout the depths of space are such reminders of our maker's glory, of our righteous place as his chosen people, lost," he said.

"You see all this in the failing light?" she questioned.

His eyes widened at the statement, "I see much more majesty. That is why I pray that you will change your perspective, come to mass as an example to your people, a reminder that even in such glorious times our faith must remain our first priority."

She turned away as the sky turned black, returning to her chambers. "Your faith is moving Minas, but there are things in life that test the limits of faith, things so terrible their stain can never be erased. So as much as I understand your point, I fear my own faith lacks in comparison and to do as you ask would only be an empty gesture."

"I assure you it would not," he interrupted.

She waved his comment off and continued, "For you I shall be sure to attend on this week's end, but do not hold a space for me permanently."

He nodded respectfully. "An honor my Queen, I shall prepare a sermon so moving as to fill your soul again with an unwavering faith, to blind what dark things you have seen with the light of the glory of our maker."

She nodded, pressing the button on her chair, the door opened on its own, understanding came over his face and with a smile he was off. Jonella returned to her side with a fresh cup in hand. She lifted the tray still full with Ichars. "Did he not care for the Ichars?" she asked.

Helaya cupped the drink in both hands and allowed the warmth to filter through her fingers. "I fear the Patriarch has deeper motivations for this visit than the joys of Ichars."

"Shall I see after him m'Lady?" she asked the Queen.

Helaya replied, "No, that will be all for now Jonella. I need to tend to my thoughts."

"As you wish," she said and with a slight curtsy, Jonella left the room.

Helaya's thumb rubbed the smooth surface of the cup. She missed her King's company so very much in times such as these and only the fragrance of the Ambrita seemed to bring him back to her.

The Slai'Nor came to a halt above the cave along the shore. Inside the cockpit, O'Tel sat confused. He removed his right hand from inside the control stick, tapped a group of silver buttons on the console in front of him and then waved his hand at the large view screen above it.

The world outside the ship appeared, bits of information scattered alongside points on the image, spewing forth countless bits of inconsequential information. On the console, next to the pad of silver buttons, a rectangular display showed the ships thoughts. Foreign words scrolled at a hurried pace along the screen. O'Tel glanced down at them then said, "It is odd old friend. The trail is gone, as though he suddenly ceased to exist, but even that would leave some taint on the currents. Something unnatural is at play."

PAIN! Violent severe pain flooded O'Tel's senses. The Slai'Nor, as it had no voice, screamed out to his mind. Something had attacked the ship and the blow was substantially more than a glancing one. With but a second to react, O'Tel opened the cockpit and jumped free of the ship. *FLEE*, he instructed the Slai'Nor as he flew through the air. Even wounded it did not want to leave its maker. *GO, NOW,* he pressed at the ship. Reluctantly it flew away over the sea, O'Tel saw the large gash along its belly as it departed.

He landed gently onto the sand and instantly felt the menace and hatred before any other sense could react to the incoming blow. O'Tel raised an arm covered in uR and caught the edge of the blade. It erupted in an explosion of purple and white energy. Shock spirited itself behind O'Tel's eyes at the sight of Xyrus. The Belgae's skill with the uR was unprecedented; his arrogance was its only equal.

Xyrus smiled and laughed as he paced around the Ter'Ok'Zhu King. The blade in his hand radiated power, sucking in the life around it. "Surely by now you understand, does its image not trigger a recall locked away in your consciousness."

O'Tel's eyes drew to the blade in Xyrus's hand, the Jahan, the blade given to the last Malef King and banished away at his defeat, now was mere feet from him, released from its prison. The Jahn'Do'Tor inundated O'Tel's mind with instant understanding, recognizing its twin. It was now clear how Xyrus had become so powerful. He struck again; O'Tel blocked each strike as they circled each other on the beach.

"I see the clarity pass before your eyes. You recognize the blade, but more importantly, *IT* does," said Xyrus.

He shot beams of energy toward O'Tel, which were dispelled with a casual wave. The Ter'Ok'Zhu King went on the offensive, never using the sword to strike, but rather as a shield for Xyrus's blows. O'Tel moved gracefully with each strike, as if he were water flowing down a twisting canal. The two engaged in what seemed a well choreographed dance along the beach, neither gaining a distinct advantage, but only O'Tel connecting with his attacks.

"You may now possess the Jahan and the will to bend the uR," O'Tel snapped between strikes, "but knowledge without the wisdom to use it is both dangerous and futile."

"What do I need of wisdom, when I have so much power?" Xyrus screamed. He thrust forth with a blow that connected to O'Tel's chest. Reinforced by the uR the jolt vaulted O'Tel through the air into the side of the tall cliff.

Xyrus willed a group of stones through the air toward O'Tel. As O'Tel blocked them Xyrus struck at O'Tel with a blast of energy from his palm. O'Tel was able to deflect the debris, but a bit of the energy blast connected. The rock behind O'Tel melted away from contact with the beam. A black char covered his clothes and smoke rose up into the air. "Fool. Your ideals of honor and wisdom have grown old and stale and your race is at an end. What do I need to learn of control with these powers? Would you like to feel their full scope?"

Xyrus drew the uR into a single orb, just as he had done before. Lightning flickered about him, radiating off the growing orb between his hands, he laughed a hideous cackle as a circle of black death grew about the ground around him.

O'Tel stepped forward. "Your arrogance makes you a fool." With a thought, O'Tel allowed his own soul to reach out to the life about him, interlacing his own energy with that of the environment itself. Xyrus would never grasp such a use of the uR, his way was of greed and pain, and he had little concern to the discipline needed to allow for such a connection.

Two tendrils of sand rose up from the earth and struck at Xyrus, as if they were extensions of O'Tel's own arms. The blows disrupted Xyrus's concentration and his ball of energy diffused. After a few more blows the tendrils engulfed Xyrus's body, his frantic blows unable to break them apart, and then they solidified, creating a cement like prison. The Malef Sword glowed and a new blast of earth struck it out of Xyrus's hand.

O'Tel stepped forward and lowered the Jahn'Do'Tor to his side. "Physical strength is no substitute for perception, for perception is the key which unlocks the intangible powers of the spirit. You, Xyrus, perceive nothing."

O'Tel stopped in front of him at arm's length, raising his sword to deliver a mortal blow and then he stopped. Under the mound of earth Xyrus laughed, slowly at first and then uncontrollably. O'Tel saw the shift in the currents and turned his attention to the giant shield generator located in the center of the city.

It rose out from the ground, a giant blue tower. Power surged throughout the entire structure and a beam of energy shot upward into space, creating the massive planetary shield that rendered the planet impenetrable.

The generator had no symmetry to its shape, yet it still was pleasing to the eye. It was as if a giant icicle had formed on the face of the planet, stretching out towards space. The generator was housed in a crater that had no visible bottom.

"Impossible," was the only thing that came to O'Tel's lips.

Small explosions detonated along the outer hull of the generator in the distance. Though miles away, its sheer mass kept it within O'Tel's normal visual range. That he could see the explosions with his naked eye told the most frightening truth about the extent of the damage that was occurring there. O'Tel released his hold on Xyrus; all of his attention was needed for the task ahead of him.

The earthly prison turned from its cement like state back to that of loose sand and fell to the ground. Xyrus raised a hand and the Jahan flew into his grip. He contemplated striking at O'Tel, but he knew his place was to escape. The Dark Lord's plans were unfolding just as he was foretold.

O'Tel turned in time to see Xyrus teleport himself away. The Niit'Horg flew out from the cavern and the trail from Xyrus's teleportation streamed directly into it.

BOOM! The sound of the generator called for O'Tel's attention. He closed his eyes, focused on his destination, the generator, and the uR flowed around him. It pierced into his flesh; in an instant, he was gone.

CHAPTER FOURTEEN

Alea ran along the hillside, the Sophos Royal Palace a distant backdrop behind her. A mere peasant or Helos of the Sophos tongue, she did not concern herself with the proceedings that went on within those far off walls. The only fancy the children took was viewing the splendor of the Isris, the Queen's personal transport, as it came and went.

In the summer months, Alea would work the land with her family, for it was their charge to do so. In the winter months such as this, free time was much suppler and the children made sure to use as much of it as possible amongst the fields.

An enormous black mountain range rose up at the border of the hills. The black giant split in two directions, forming a deep valley inside each face. Light rarely touched that corridor and in the minds of the children, it became a mystical place, home to all sorts of terrors and horribly imagined monsters.

It was here on the outskirts of such fright that the children could also find wilds Horgs. Docile creatures, though at a glance they seemed more of a fierce predator, the Horgs were herbivores. They had giant square block teeth which they used to chew the local brush. A single large rear toe complimented two front ones. Their bodies were anatomically similar to that of an Earthen lion, though their heads were longer and narrower like a horse. Solid black eyes rested on either side of their head and two ridged slots formed its nose. A large tuft of coarse brown hair ran down the beast's spine, reaching its tail, which was thick, equal in length to its torso and covered in extremely short hairs. The Horgs were very agile and fast. They usually grew to three feet in height and five in length.

During the warmer months, the Horgs roamed the village surrounding the palace looking for both food and potential playmates. Now though they stayed nearer to the entrance of the corridor at the base of the mountain. Warm winds rushed out from the valley to the nearby hill, providing the Horgs with a year round supply of food.

The day prior, Ta'Lor had challenged Alea to catch a Horg, a significant task even when not considering the time of year. Alea was never afraid of a challenge, she relished the opportunity instead. Through such obstacles and in conquering her own anxieties and doubts, she found strength and confidence. Helaya, the Sophos Queen, was her personal hero and she felt compelled to strive to be like her.

As the children reached the edge of the hill, the white sheet of frozen water evaporated into a sheet of green life. The kids dove into the snow, their warm layers of bundling preventing them from feeling its cold bite. "Do you see one?" Jabril asked.

"Quiet, you'll scare em off," Alea replied.

"If none show then you still lose the bet," Ta'Lor chided in.

"What?"

"The bet was that you couldn't catch a Horg, so unless you do, you lose," he said.

"That isn't fair," Jabril said as she hit Ta'Lor.

He rubbed his arm then retaliated in kind. "It is so."

They wrestled in the snow for a few seconds, then the wave of Alea's hand along with a shush brought their ruckus to a halt. She whispered, "I see one."

Alea rose to her feet and the two other children looked down to where she was pointing. "What are you waiting. . . " Ta'Lor tried to blurt out, but she was off before he could finish his thought.

Alea dashed down the hill, slipped on a patch of melted snow and went skidding down. Her butt thumped on the ground as she came to a stop at its base. The Horg's head snapped up, startled by the noise. Its small ears helped it to hear in the echoing chasm, but out in the open of the hills they became a hindrance.

Alea rose to her feet cautiously, the Horg's eyes firmly focused on her every motion. One wrong move and the Beast would flee into the recesses of the mountain and she would fail. "It's okay," she said in her most soothing voice.

She reached down, tearing a patch of grass from the ground and then held it out in an offering. Back on the top of the hill, Ta'Lor snickered, "That'll never work."

"Quiet," Jabril replied.

The Horg's nostrils sniffed at Alea, the smell of the fresh dew filled its senses. Cautiously the beast stepped toward her. She nearly squealed as the Horg approached. It would be so satisfying to see Ta'Lor's face when she proved him wrong, to show him she was just as strong as a boy. A few more steps and the Horg would be upon her. It came near enough to take the food from her hand. Its mouth opened and its tongue pulled in some grass. Her leg twitched, a small and subtle movement. It was noticeable enough that The Horg's instincts told it to run. Alea sprung forward and grabbed the Horg by the neck.

"She got him," yelled Jabril.

"Not quite. Look," Ta'Lor said.

The Horg ran and shook violently, trying to free itself from her grip. She would not oblige. That is until he pulled up sharply to a stop. The sudden change in momentum sent Alea flying off the Horg into the grass. She rolled and caught herself enough so that she was standing as she stopped. Her eyes locked with the Horg's, determined and ready to challenge its will.

She charged and the beast ran for the mountain pass. Alea knew she had one chance to succeed and took it. Altering her path, she sprinted with all her might. The Horg ran as fast as it could as well, but instinct pushed it to follow a straight path to the corridor.

They neared a collision point and the Horg seemed poised to win, moving too fast for Alea to keep up. Then the beast saw something from inside the darkness of the chasm, an unfamiliar gleam of light that caused it to slow down.

It was all the opportunity that Alea needed. She dove into the air and tackled the Horg with all her force, tumbling with it up to the base of the mountain. The beast whimpered under her weight. She kissed it and stood up. "It's okay. I'm not going to hurt you. It was only a game," she said.

She stood up and waved to her friends in the distance, triumphant. The Horg sprinted off as soon as it was free. "Alas, I am afraid I cannot afford you the same offer child," said Lordakai, an army of Shahd standing behind him as he exited the chasm.

He raised his sword high and the setting sun shone off its blade, bathing Alea in a shaft of warm light. Her eyes went wide as she stared up at the hulking man, but she did not cower from him. The blade moved quickly down toward her head, leaving just enough pause for her to wonder if the blow would hurt, closing her eyes, she accepted her fate.

KLANG! She opened them, unsure of what miracle had saved her. Before her, inches from her face was the end of a solid black metal lance. Its owner was clearly a Sophos male, his sleek body covered head to toe in black. His gloved hand pulled the lance away, silently and effortlessly as if it was an extension of his arm. Large heavy black robes, topped by a hood covered his body and kept his face hidden in silhouette. Still, she could see his eyes, a blue as brilliant as the cloudless sky; they pierced her to her soul, connecting them instantly. "Go home child, your place is at your parent's side for the night," he said.

She rose and scurried off toward her friends in the distance. Lordakai threatened to give chase, but the stranger's lance snapped up to his throat in response. "That is enough Lordakai. You've no quarrel with that child."

Lordakai swatted the lance away and challenged, "What authority do you have over my actions? It is not your place to issue commands."

The stranger rested the staff at his side. His eyes locked with Lordakai's, "Your mission here is singular Belgae. It is on my stead that you have gained access to such hallowed ground that now rests beneath your feet. It is through my will alone that you shall accomplish what goal your Dark Lord sets before you and it is only because it serves both our purposes. Stray from that path and our pact is broken. Spill one unnecessary drop of blood and I shall see each of you dead before me; your task a failure."

Lordakai contemplated the argument, every bit of his mind knew the words were true, yet he desperately yearned to find a flaw in the logic. Seeing none, he yielded, "Agreed then. We shall bring death to them another day, when the Belgae take this planet as our own."

"Perhaps, but there is only one who so needs that gift tonight."

Together they walked toward the Royal Palace, behind them, the sun fell below the horizon and the sky turned to darkness.

Explosions tore through the blue metal of the shield generator, blasting plumes of fire into the air. Workers hurried out across the main bridge, screams of terror heeding their charge. The generator required nearly enough people to fill a small city to maintain its operation and now it seemed they were all fleeing at once.

There was no precedent for what was happening. The shield generator was Ter'Ok'Zhu technology and ancient to even them, as such its destruction seemed impossible. The workers had had no plan for evacuation and now their more primal instincts were dictating their actions. At the base of the bridge, O'Tel's body slipped in through the fabric of space, as though he had stepped through an invisible curtain. His senses paid little attention to the chaos of flesh that stood before him, he was a rock amongst those raging waters. His only focus was the destruction of the generator that stood thousands of feet away. His mind absorbed and translated information from the uR. He tried to rationalize a scenario that could account for what was happening, but none came to mind.

Another explosion came billowing out from the bottom of the tower. It engulfed the bridge along its side and the workers fell under its concussive force. O'Tel rushed forward, his mind and body operating on separate paths.

CRACK! The sound stopped him in his tracks. A slight rumbling along the bridge sent the workers into an even greater frenzy. They rose to their feet and rushed toward the city. People's regard for each other's safety now secondary to their own sense of survival, they pushed past, over and through one another. O'Tel could not only see the fear rushing through the crowd, he could feel it as the wave of uR threatened to drown him. He focused, bracing himself for the next few moments.

SNAP! The bridge buckled and started to give way. All those now trapped in its belly would be doomed to death by the failure. The last explosion had caused more damage to the supports underneath the bridge than what could be seen. The supports along the tower side gave way and the bridge snapped away toward the gorge. The workers screamed in horror and fell down from the explosion. O'Tel stood tall and allowed his own uR to flood out over them, his calm became their calm.

He bowed his head, closing his eyes, focusing all his thoughts and then looked up. His eyes opened with a burst of power, pure white from the energy of the uR pouring out around them. O'Tel took a step forward, spinning on his foot in a half circle and raising a hand up as he completed the turn. The bridge stopped. O'Tel made an elaborate motion with his other hand, keeping the former still as though it held some giant invisible weight. O'Tel's free hand seemed to weave the air around him; occasionally he would thrust it forward and send waves of white uR toward the opposite end of the bridge. The energy ran out along the open chasm and latched onto the former entrance to the bridge. In moments the bridge was complete again. "Hurry your way off the bridge children. You are not safe," O'Tel said, his voice projected beyond its normal volume.

O'Tel knew that if the destruction within the shield generator was not stopped there would be no distance in which they could find safety. As the last person exited the bridge the white uR disappeared. O'Tel stared up as he fell down into the gorge. Then he rushed to its side and leapt. Wind sped by him, licking his cheeks and bringing the smell of ash to his nose.

O'Tel angled his body toward the base of the mighty tower; he flipped himself over so that he approached feet first. Energy shot out from his hand, struck the outer shell of the generator and disintegrated the metal, leaving a perfectly sized entry point for him. With the uR, he slowed his descent and neared the tower until his feet made contact with its surface. O'Tel ran down its base as explosions erupted around him like geysers. He reached the opening he had just so recently made and slid down into the tower as if swallowed whole by its unmoving mouth.

Inside the base of the generator was a maelstrom of random destruction. A day earlier an occupant would have found smooth floors, walls that blended with countless data ports and mechanisms used to regulate the shield itself. In operation, the light show produced by the number of processes was hypnotic.

Now though, the room was black and burnt. Mechanisms lay scattered, charred and in ruins from laser fire. O'Tel knew the reactor core was only two levels down and from the pattern of destruction, he assumed that whatever was reaping it knew that fact as well. He pushed forward.

A hail of blaster fire greeted him. His sword was out to deflect the bolts as swiftly as they flew through the air. Loud clanging metallic feet and the familiar hum of mechanics whirring told O'Tel what was coming for him. Giant spider mechs rushed forward, grotesque and twisted silver metal beasts, their red optics scanned the room, assessing the new target. Four blasters sat along the corners of their heads, and their legs were made of polycarbonate steel mined from the Noth sector, which sharpened as they were allowed the spiders both flexibility and enough strength to cut through almost any obstacle.

It had been well over a thousand years since O'Tel had last seen the Noth mechs, remnants from the First War. Pure killing machines, they were used by the Malef and their presence here greatly disturbed O'Tel. However, their advance on his position afforded him no time to focus on the feeling.

More laser fire rained down on his position. He blocked it with the sword. One of the Noths slashed down toward his head.

O'Tel grabbed the end of its leg at the point. His hand clenched around it and the metal crushed like paper. He flung the beast aside into a second approaching spider and they both exploded into the far wall. In the darkness beyond the corridor, hundreds of red lights flashed on and rapidly approached. O'Tel readied himself for the onslaught, his goal still two levels down. If the generator was breached all would be lost. The Noths spewed forth, an endless metal stream of death. Lethal jagged talons tore at O'Tel's body, while a sea of laser fire followed just behind. The Ter'Ok'Zhu King moved with a tranquility that contrasted the chaos of his foes. Every step carried a soft grace and brought with it the iron strike of his hand or the crisp edge of his blade.

As quickly as O'Tel was able to dispatch one of the Noth mechs, three more were ready to take its place. A blast of energy from O'Tel's hand melted a deep line in their numbers. With a thought and clasp of his fist, those nearest to him were crushed by a storm of white uR, their bodies left folded in upon themselves.

Those that remained attacked him all at once. He deflected their blows with the sword, slid in between strikes when necessary and struck back only when he knew his blow would be fatal. Soon all that remained was a sea of twisted, liquefied metal. O'Tel hurried down the dark corridor ahead, when suddenly he came to a stop. Behind him, through the very entry point he had created, hundreds of Noths began to enter into the generator. However, this time their eyes flashed and followed in tune by a shrill beep.

Distant memories of these foul creature's methods flashed into his mind, foreshadowing their destructive intent. He reached out to the uR around him and shaped it into an orb that surrounded his body. As the Noths filled the room, the front mech's eyes ceased flashing and went a solid red. It exploded and set off a chain reaction amongst the rest of its brethren. Within seconds, the entire room was engulfed in flames.

Inside his shield, O'Tel felt the concussive force of each blast. His mind pressed hard against the assault and his body seemed ready to break. Suddenly the floor beneath him fell apart. More Noths followed through on their death march, tearing through the structure inside the generator. O'Tel came to a moment of clarity. The loud hum of the reactor core was close, just one more level down. Then the floor gave way again.

O'Tel knew what must be done. He closed his eyes and focused. The orb that protected him unraveled and expanded. He opened his eyes and pressed forward with his hands. His shield exploded out and up tearing through the entire length of the generator. In its wake, the Noth mechs fell dead, as if hit by a giant electromagnetic pulse.

O'Tel plunged down as the floor collapsed. His body, burned and bruised, crashed hard against the floor of the lower level. BEEP! BEEP! Impossible, he thought. He knew that the Noths could not have survived his attack. O'Tel looked up; a terror took a grip on his heart. A large Null Bomb was attached to the shield reactor core staring back at him.

CHAPTER FIFTEEN

Sefas stood watch at the base of the outer wall of the Royal Palace. His eyes scanned the dark hills that rolled into a sea of green in the distance. Not one of glory, Sefas cherished his position for his duties held a grave importance. The palace had one vulnerability, a hidden escape passage at its rear, built in secrecy, its existence known to only a select few amongst the Sophos and Sefas was proud to be one of them.

SHINK! He did not hear the blade and barely felt its sharp embrace along his neck. Sefas fell to his knees and then limply to the ground, the life ran out of him like a falling waterfall. Lordakai stood in his place, wiping his blade clean and then sheathing it quietly. A few motions of his hand were the only commands needed to instruct the Shahd now formed up by his side. He looked over to the man in black, nodded and then followed his men into the Palace.

In the courtyard, common citizens, women and children meandered about. Lordakai's bloodlust compelled him to strike, to tear through the masses and rush directly toward his goal. He was a warrior and the only judge in his life was the skill of his blade. He detested sneaking around like some common thief, yet it was by Xyrus's order that he now moved, for there was a greater death to be had at the end of this mission.

The Shahd moved as a living shadow, quietly slipping through the darkness of the courtyard. As they reached the inner wall, they fired grappling hooks up on its side. After checking the security of the lines, they hurried up them. They moved as one fluid beast, even breathing in sync. Lordakai was the last to mount the rope and even his large frame provided no sound as he climbed.

At the top of the inner wall, they could finally see their objective, the Royal Tower. Its peak sat several hundred feet above them. The tower shone bright, reflecting the light of Vysan's two moons. Lordakai pulled a data pad off his armor and tapped it to life. Schematics of the palace appeared on the screen. He tapped a section that showed his position and the map zoomed in, the palace dissolved into simple framework. Lordakai chronicled the display into his memory and put it away.

A quick series of hand signals told the Shahd of their orders and they moved effortlessly into action. Six of them took position and aimed their blasters. The Shahd preferred close quarter combat to test themselves against their opponents. Such an honor would have to wait, for on this day success would only be found in the completion of the mission.

The Shahd blaster looked as if someone had waved a magnet over a pile of spare parts and then set them together. 'U' Shape, the blaster had two barrels, which rested on either side of the wielder's arm. A handgrip on the front of the blaster allowed it to blend into their armor. A small housing on the top of the blaster contained a miniature shield generator, which could produce a small circular shield two feet in diameter. Each of the Shahd gripped their weapon, anxiously anticipating the order to attack.

Lordakai shouted, "FIRE!" in Belgish and lasers tore into the sidewall of the Palace Tower in front of them. Within seconds alarms blared throughout the courtyard. Lordakai and the Shahd charged forward to take the tower.

Inside the tower, they entered a massive hall. Numerous white columns connected green marbled floors to the ceiling fifty feet above. Staircases rose up along different sections of the wall, some reached up to the ceiling while others only made it halfway. Instinctively the Shahd moved into a defensive position. Within moments Sophos lasers lit up the entrance.

The Sophos Palace Guards were excellent fighters in their own regard. They had trained for battle their entire life, yet this was their first real taste of it. They poured laser fire down at the Shahd, hopeful that it would slow down the invaders long enough for Captain Hayator to arrive. Their reaction was robotic and trained, unlike their enemy.

The Shahd returned cover fire as the rest of their members came into the room. They took careful regard to only distract, not kill the Palace Guards. Under cover of their shields, they pressed further into the room. Lordakai was the last of the Shahd to enter the room. He stopped and relished the taste of the battle around him. He knew there was no glory to be found at the end of a blaster and standing in the gaping hole, cold wind biting violently through his body, undoing his armor and letting it fall to the floor, he hungered for his flail. On his waist was a large skull that seemed to function much as a buckle would, though as he removed it, it was obvious the skull was not a fashion accessory, but rather Lordakai's weapon of choice.

It was attached to a thick black chain, which was wrapped around Lordakai's body. Methodically he unwove the flail from around his body until that last link pulled against its housing at the front of his waist. Lordakai inserted his fingers into the back of the skull and squeezed. It formed into a ball and spikes shot out all around its surface. Another twist of his hand and a brilliant red energy leapt out and snaked its way along the chain up to the skull itself.

He wrapped the base of the chain around his forearm and swung it around in a violent arc about his body. Lordakai ordered his men to stand down as he stepped out into the hailstorm of laser fire. Even swinging the flail, Lordakai was able to move without limitation. It almost seemed as though he moved with more grace, using the weight and balance of the flail to counter balance his own steps. Lordakai used the chain to deflect the oncoming blasts.

The laser fire deflected off of it back to the other parts of the room. A sound of Palace Guards rushed in from one of the side staircases. Lordakai caught the movement out of the corner of his eye. With a spin of his body he launched the flail at the staircase. The metal sliced through the rock like a hot blade through butter. The blow took out the supports and the entire case collapsed on itself. Those guards that survived the fall wearily rose to attack, only to suffer the same fate as the case itself. Lordakai flung the flail around, deflecting more blaster fire, than allowed it to wrap back around his body. He screamed out, "For the Honor!" and the Shahd rushed forward.

The timer, coded in an ancient language that only O'Tel understood, continued to count down. He refused to accept the information his eyes presented, *Impossible*. Everything about the bomb, its harsh angular shape, the black red stained metal, and the very numbers that continued to count down, all pointed to its Malef origins, but O'Tel could not accept that conclusion.

The Malef had used the Noths during the First War, but they had not built them. The bomb before him was an entirely different circumstance. A Null Bomb was technology that was unique to the Malef. O'Tel had witnessed firsthand in his youth the monumental destruction that the device could reap. He prayed it was simply a poor copy, fashioned by whoever had designed the attack on the generator. O'Tel knew there was only one way to truly know.

Up until this point, O'Tel had tempered his vision while at the generator. A machine forged directly from the uR, the shield generator was a virtual sun to those with the sight and thus O'Tel was forced to filter his vision rather than risk being blinded by the fountain of uR that surged forth from the generator.

He now had to stare into that star, only then could he tell if the bomb was truly of Malef origin, its mark on the uR unmistakably absent. O'Tel stood up, closed his eyes and meditated. He removed the blocks piece by piece, allowing his senses to absorb every facet of stimulus around them. He braced his system for the shock as he opened his eyes. The white light erupted from the generator, threatening to consume him and burn out his eyes. Then amongst all of that brilliance, a spot of darkness pulled the stream of energy back in towards it. O'Tel's gaze locked onto it and his heart dropped.

Where there should have been some trace of uR on the bomb's exterior there was only black metal. O'Tel turned his back to the abomination, his worst suspicions now confirmed. The Null Bomb created what amounted to a small black hole. Upon detonation the bomb would implode, using the very power from the generator it was attached to as a source for destruction, a horrible mechanical parasite that would suck the life out of the world around it.

As O'Tel suppressed his vision back down to normal, the timer on the bomb went solid, then black. It exploded into a sphere of light, the deep bass hum vibrating through the entire generator. As quickly as the orb manifested, it collapsed back in on itself until it all but disappeared, replaced by a small black sphere that pulled in the very fabric of the world around it.

O'Tel reached out and streams of energy poured forth from his hands toward the black hole. Like liquid steel, they took form into a larger sphere around it and then solidified. The force of controlling the uR against the pull of the hole was so great that O'Tel instantly was covered in sweat. His face was pale and drained as he finished. The room went deathly quiet and he fell to a knee. He lowered his head and panted, exhaustion had quickly taken hold of him. O'Tel reached out to the uR to help him recover his strength and it obliged. A warm white light hovered and penetrated his flesh.

CRACK! His eyes looked up in dread as the sphere he had created to contain the black hole began to fracture. Without notice it imploded and the black orb replaced it, larger now and more powerful.

The orb drew in the world around it and all the mass destabilized as it made contact. O'Tel drew the Jahn'Do'Tor and thrust it into the floor. The blade was the only thing in the room that did not concede to the pull of the black hole and thus it became O'Tel's anchor.

The generator acted as a catalyst to the orb's process, increasing its strength and size exponentially. Even tethered to the Jahn'Do'Tor O'Tel felt the pull of the black orb on his body. As his feet tried in vain to find footing on the sleek floor, his mind searched for a solution to his current dilemma.

More so than just its gravitational force, the orb seemed to pull the very life from his body. It grew almost to three feet in diameter. O'Tel tried to draw the uR to aide him, but any bit he could bring to his side was promptly pulled away into the black orb. Only a few feet away, O'Tel could feel each cell in his body being torn apart. It took every ounce of his concentration to pull away from its grip.

Being so close, O'Tel finally understood the anomaly. Now activated, there was no way to contain it, for any energy or mass that approached the orb was absorbed into it. His only hope was to find some way to siphon away all of that energy out of the orb.

O'Tel focused on his connection to the Jahn'Do'Tor, allowing it to consume him. He turned and stepped toward the orb. O'Tel imbued his hands with what little uR he could and thrust them forward. Two streams shot out and latched onto the orb. A sickening darkness crept over his body as he was connected to the orb. He could feel it snake its way up through that connection into his body, pulling on not only his cells, but on his very soul as well. O'Tel ripped at its core with all of his resolve. He felt the orb shift against his attack, ever so slightly but enough that it was noticeable. His feet sunk into the metal floor and his body trembled from the strain. The drops of sweat that poured from his forehead were instantly sucked into the orb.

O'Tel took a step backward and the orb shrunk, expelling its darkness into him. He tried to pull away further, but his body remained. Frozen in place O'Tel tried again, his muscles shaking from the strain. He felt his grip falter and his arm snapped forward toward the anomaly. He relinquished his grip and fell backwards. Failure. He had come so close, but even his strength and skill was not enough to pull the orb apart.

The generator snapped with a crackle of electricity and O'Tel's mind lit up with a sudden epiphany. *Of course*, he thought. The answer had been sitting in front of him the entire time, not quite in plain view, but with the proper perspective, it was there. The generator itself could serve his purpose beautifully. He knew that it was directly connected to the black hole, feeding it from its own limitless power source. All O'Tel had to do was reverse the flow of the generator so that it would draw in energy instead of spewing forth. He hoped that the connection to the orb would hold and thus it would be its undoing.

One complication in O'Tel's plan was finding a way to reverse the generator's flow. With the strength of the orb, the only way O'Tel could connect to the generator was through direct contact. That placed him dangerously close to the orb's pull. Beyond that there was the chance that the generator itself might kill him upon contact. However at this point, O'Tel had no choice; the orb's mass was approaching a critical point.

O'Tel reached out to the Jahn'Do'Tor and it flew into his hand in response. He braced himself, drawing uR from the sword to fortify his muscles and then charged at the orb. As O'Tel approached it, he leapt and thrust the sword down into the floor. The orb pulled at him like a thousand hands, threatening to separate O'Tel from the sword. His fingers squeezed against the metal of the hilt, his knuckles turning a bright white, he could not allow his grip to break. His mind blocked out the thousands of signals from each nerve ending, all crying out in such agonizing pain. The Jahn'Do'Tor ripped through the floor, stopping a few feet from the orb.

O'Tel looked up and smiled. Now was the true decisive moment, he reached a hand to the blue metal and made contact with its cold surface. Pain rushed through his body, a combination from the surge of energy of the generator and his cellular structure tearing apart from the gravitational pull of the orb. He wanted to pass out, but his concern for the millions of lives above him kept him sharp and aware.

He reached out into the generator, melded his being with it and intertwined his consciousness with the generator's mechanics. O'Tel searched throughout the machine for its core operation center. He needed only to reshape that small portion of the generator. O'Tel traveled along the generator's many parts, searching desperately.

PAIN! His mind shot out of the machine and back to his own body. The orb was now as large as O'Tel and his body began to be pulled into it. Its time was at an end. O'Tel blocked out the pain, if he was lost here, if fate had shifted and this was to be his end he would at the least see the planet saved, no matter the cost.

O'Tel plunged his mind back into the machine, searching deeper and faster. With every passing second, he could feel his body succumbing to the orb's grip. Then finally, he found it, buried at the base of the machine, at its heart. He focused on this one chance for success. He pressed his will on the ancient components, shaping was a natural gift for O'Tel, but reshaping the ancient machine was a monumental task.

As he finished, his mind was torn out of the machine and returned to his body, which now drifted toward the orb. Seconds more and his cells would be torn asunder, absorbed into the increasing mass of darkness, never to know the result of his gamble. The generator shifted, its color turned white and it reversed the flow of energy. Two streams of energy latched onto the orb. O'Tel smiled as he let go of his conscious self, allowing his body to succumb to the pull of the orb.

The moon full and glowing a deep red reflected in the aching eyes of Helaya. The threat, only hundreds of feet away, drew ever closer. The Queen held no fanciful thoughts concerning the possible outcome of the night. She tasted the betrayal on the air, foul and painful, it turned her stomach.

Rarely were outsiders even let onto the planet, but never had one set foot in the Royal Palace. Someone with power, and knowledge had planned this attack. They must have calculated its outcome many times prior to its execution tonight, so very few could see such a thing done.

Her handmaid did not share her bleak view on the situation. In her heart hope still beat, she was still so naïve to the cruelty of life. Jonella reached out and grabbed a hold of the Queen's arm. Her desperation rattled in her bones and shook Jonella's grip. "M'lady we must leave, they shall be through the rest of the guard in minutes."

Helaya took a deep labored breath and glanced into the sky once more. She did not fear death anymore, rather she welcomed it. The years of pain from the loss of her husband and daughter now laid their full weight on her shoulders. She turned to face Jonella, the only person she felt a true connection to. "My place is not in escape Jonella, it is here."

She pulled herself away from the Queen; a moment of emotion overcame her training. Jonella was born into servitude, trained since adolescence to serve, unconditionally programmed so that it was a part of her being. Years by the Queen's side had served to facilitate a relationship that pressed beyond professional. She cared for Helaya as if she were her own blood. Usually those emotions were easy to dismiss, but in the face of such a real threat, they now surfaced. "You will die if you stay," she blurted out.

Helaya nodded, "I know child."

"Then why do you so easily surrender to that fate?"

The Queen walked to her and lovingly placed a hand on Jonella's cheek. She admired the young woman's passion, but did not have the time to convince her that escape was impossible. So many years had she been in Helaya's service, but never had she so wonderfully shown her loyalty and care as she was now. "There are times when there is no escape from the path fate has set forth for you and to try to escape it would only serve to bring forth a greater degree of destruction, than simply facing those things that you must."

Jonella reached up and took the Queen's hand in her own. She released it and reached into the sleeve of her tunic. Jonella withdrew a small curved dagger, its metal a mixture of blue and white; its artisanship spoke of the blade's ancient age. The blade curved like a snake crawling along the sand. It snapped to life with a hum of energy as she squeezed the hilt. "If your decision cannot be changed, I shall stand by you in this," she said as the battle outside drew deafeningly close.

Helaya reached out and lowered Jonella's arm. "No," she said, "I have a different task to ask of you."

With those words, Helaya pulled off the amulet from around her neck. Jonella's eyes grew wide at the sight of the ancient artifact. "The Heart of Alea!" she gasped.

The Heart was a bright white blue circular stone, housed in a web of silver and gold metal. It hung on a braided necklace made of a similar mix of metals. Given to the first Queen of the Sophos people eons ago, the true nature of the Heart lay wrapped in myth. It was a mystical object and all their people knew any more of the amulet's legacy was that it had been entrusted to the Sophos Royalty to be passed down through out the ages.

"I have no heir to pass it directly to. You know its value better than any other does. Even if I fall, it must not fall along with me. Therefore, to you Jonella, I entrust it. Guard it as you have guarded my life, for it is no longer safe here."

Helaya placed the amulet around Jonella's neck. She hugged her closely, as a mother would hold her own daughter. Helaya released her and Jonella ran to the opposite side of the room. The Queen stood next to her chair and pressed a hidden button located at the top of the chair. A secret door at the back of the chamber opened. "Go, before it is too late!" Helaya screamed.

Jonella dared one last glance and then rushed off into the corridor, the door slammed closed behind her.

The Queen's chamber was a mere twenty feet in front of him. Only four Shahd had paid for this mission with their blood so far. The Sophos guard had not been as fortunate. The remaining guards were obviously the most skilled for they had drawn the Shahd to a stalemate and so it was fitting that his hand alone would tip the scale.

Lordakai's flail was housed on his pelvis once again. It was far too dangerous to the integrity of the room to use such a violent weapon. Instead, he chose to rely on the power of his hands alone, the ultimate test of his honor.

Lordakai tapped a button on his forearm and a shield snapped to life in response. He walked out into the battle as casually as most would approach the market. His body bent and moved to avoid both incoming blows and blasts of laser fire.

The first guard's fate was quick. His necked snapped as Lordakai passed by. The Belgae General deflected incoming laser fire and stalked over to the next guard. This one saw the threat, drew his sword and attempted to attack. Lordakai dodged each swing of the blade waiting for the opportunity to strike. His hand moved almost too fast for sight, belting the guard directly in the throat. The man buckled from the force of the blow. Lordakai grabbed him by the collar and flung him into two charging guards.

He picked up the guard's sword and continued forward. His was the dance of death, slow, deliberate and learned from years of practice. The guards fought with heart and valor, but they could not match his skill. Soon they were simply decoration for the floor.

Lordakai paused as he finished the last guard. The Shahd followed his lead, their silence tribute to those who had fallen so gloriously on both sides of the battle. Though they were their enemies, the Shahd still respected the guards who had fallen, for it was in the battle that they were afforded a chance for honor. Lordakai looked up at the large wooden door in front of him. His mission was nearly finished; only one more task lay before him.

He turned and faced his men. "None shall pass until this last task is finished my brothers. Lay down your lives, for glory lies in the death of those valiant enough to face it without fear."

With that, he turned back to the door and thrust his foot into its middle.

BAM! The great wooden door at the front of the chamber flew inward in a shatter of splinters, she did not move. In the opening stood Lordakai, a sickening blood lust splattered across his eyes as he stepped into the room. His mouth could not help but sneer at the sight of her, defenseless and alone. *Too easy*, he thought.

She spoke, her back still to him, "You come unannounced."

"Oh yes M'Lady," he snarled, "but with great purpose."

She heard the heavy metal footfalls of his boots with each step, the scraping of the sword against the marbled floor and the shifting of his armor as he approached. "How one could so low be granted a purpose?" she asked.

"Face me M'Lady and I shall show you," he replied.

"If you've come to deliver my death," she said as she turned, "I am afraid your task may face more difficulty than you planned."

He looked around and laughed, "You are alone M'Lady, unarmed. I see no such difficulty as you speak."

He was only a few feet away from her, coiled like a lion ready to pounce on its prey. When she touched her chair, a rapier shot up into the air out of the armrest. Helaya caught it and went into a defensive stance. Lordakai laughed at the sight and stopped moving forward. "You truly think that shall change the outcome of this?" he asked.

"Though I may feel Death's breath on my cheek, taste his kiss on my lips, I assure you it is a fate you shall share with me this day."

He paused then struck, his blade meeting hers. They repeated the dance a few times. "Death does frighten me M'Lady," he said, "only failure."

They continued around the room. Helaya's speed with her sword was as breath taking as his raw strength. Lordakai's missed blows struck destroyed the room. As skilled as Helaya was, she was no match for his blade, only able to defend rather than attack. "The rest of the Guard shall be here shortly and you will have to face your failure Belgae," she quipped.

Her pompous attitude fueled his rage. Lordakai struck down at her with heavier and heavier blows. PLING! Her blade snapped in half under the force of one of his blows. He raised his sword, ready to end her life. She stood proud, fearless and accepted her fate. "Finish it then," she ordered.

For a second Lordakai contemplated delivering the final blow, but his sense of duty overpowered that selfish desire. "No," he replied.

Lordakai threw the blade far away from them both. He leaned in close to her. "No, M'Lady," he laughed menacingly, "your death is not my goal here."

"Then what is your. . ." she began to ask.

However, before Helaya could complete her question, Lordakai's flail wrapped around her throat. He disconnected it from his waist and wound it around his forearm. "My purpose here M'Lady is to make you scream so that the very heavens themselves may hear you."

With a tug on the chain, red energy consumed its length, flowing through both Helaya and Lordakai. She recoiled from the pain. It felt as though her flesh was melting off her bones, but she would not allow herself to fulfill his request. "Louder M'Lady, surely you can do better than that."

He pulled again, tighter, with more force and yet still she would not scream. The pain of this torture showed on Lordakai's face as well. He whirled the chain and lashed it towards her, wrapping more of it around her body. Her flesh was blackened where it touched the metal.

Lordakai gripped the metal and the energy flowed between them once more. This time she did scream, as did he. Every nerve in her body burned with pain. It was too much and no bit of will could sustain her resistance to its bite any longer.

The Queen's faltering only fueled Lordakai's own resolve. He relished in the pain that the torture was causing him, a necessary means to his end. His arm was severely charred. The chain utilized his own life force to deliver its energy and thus he not only felt its bite, but offered his own life as sacrifice. This effect was transferred doubly over to Helaya. "Nearly there now highness. Perhaps just once more and we shall both embrace death," he said.

In the distance, Lordakai could hear the Shahd beginning to fall. The Sophos reinforcements had arrived and soon they would outman and overpower his warriors. He had to finish this task or all their deaths would be in vain. Lordakai wrapped what was left of the chain around her body. He leaned in close to her ear. She gasped for breath, her body still overrun from the pain.

"Scream! Scream so that you daughter will hear you with your last dying breath," he said.

The mention of her daughter broke Helaya's resolve. Tears streaked forth from her eyes, but then came puzzlement. How could he know of her lost daughter? It had been so many years now, and her fate was one of the Sophos's most closely guarded secrets. As if in response to her thoughts, Lordakai said, "Oh yes M'Lady, she lives. Did they keep that secret from you? Pity you find out now, with no chance to ever see her."

She's ALIVE, she thought. Lordakai activated the chain, energy tearing through the both of them once more. Together they screamed out in pain, their flesh burning beneath the metal. Tears streamed down the once proud Queen's face and her soul screamed out to the daughter she did not know.

Zhu shot up in bed, startled awake by the echo of a woman screaming across her mind. She tried to make sense of the strange dream. It was so violent and so foreign to her that she had no ability to relate to it. She had seen the woman in her dreams before, always seeming so sad and lost, but now she was in great pain.

Zhu's mind searched for an explanation, for something to make sense of her dreams origin. The woman looked exactly like her, but she dressed so strangely. Zhu had never met this woman, but she felt a bond to her. In all her time on the planet, Zhu had barely seen anyone, save the Ter'Ok'Zhu that trained her. Only in fantasy had she ever escaped the confines of the planet.

Master Paow entered her room and came to her side. "Are you alright child?" he asked.

"A bad dream Zhi'Fah. The same woman from my other dreams was crying out in pain. Such terrible pain."

Master Paow shot up; terror covered his face, a horribly unfamiliar expression for him. "Why was she in such pain Zha'Toh?"

"She was in danger and she was crying out, as if her heart was being torn from her chest. What does it all mean?" she asked.

Master Paow gathered himself and rubbed her head, hoping she had missed his concern. "It was just a dream Zha'Toh. Relax now, you need your rest."

Zhu nodded and lay back down to sleep. Master Paow crept out of her room, concern now returned in force.

Lordakai let go of the chain and fell to his knees badly disfigured. His task was nearly complete. A Comm chirped in his ear. He pressed a series of buttons along his forearm and a small hologram of Xyrus's face appeared. "Lord Xyrus! Is it done?" he asked.

Xyrus nodded, "Yes Lordakai. I have her location. You have served our people well."

"Then I shall see you in For'Dowas M'Lord," he replied.

The transmission ended and Lordakai tapped another button on his forearm. A blade popped out from the tip of his bracer by his wrist. He lifted the Queen up again so that he could speak to her. She cringed as the blade pierced her flesh. He spoke into her ear, "The poison works quick M'Lady. Have no worries though, you shall see your daughter soon enough."

With that, Helaya passed out, the poison finishing what the news of her daughter had already wrought onto her heart. Her body collapsed to the floor, lifeless. Lordakai limped up to his feet as the Sophos Guards entered the room. They were lead by Captain Hayator. He glanced at his Queen's lifeless body and then up to her murderer. All thought left Captain Hayator's mind and he charged forward, as did those following behind him. Lordakai stood poised, smiling and ready to be delivered in battle to For'Dowas.

CHAPTER SIXTEEN

O'Tel reoriented himself, as he stopped moving and floated in mid air, facing the orb. He reached out with both arms and focused his mind on the two wild streams of energy that connected it to the generator. He could feel the raw force of the uR flowing around him, but he calmed his mind, breathing deeply in and out.

The tendrils of energy slowed their dance. With O'Tel as a focusing point, they operated with an even greater efficiency. The black hole in front of him collapsed in on itself, shrinking exponentially as its mass was fed directly into the generator.

As it returned to half its size, the orb's pull on O'Tel waned and his feet touched down gently on the floor. Then the orb spasmed, bursts of thermal energy shot forth out into the room, giant plumes of plasma. Instinct told O'Tel that something bad was about to happen, but logic dictated that he must finish his task regardless of the hazard.

Suddenly, the orb imploded in on itself disappearing from the visual spectrum. Then a gigantic burst of energy tore through the room, followed by a solid deafening boom. The tendrils of energy streaming from the generator diffused. O'Tel was thrust across the room from the force of the explosion. The generator began to shut down as the burst of energy consumed it, like a giant wave rolling over a sand bank. All of its life disappeared and the metal faded to a deep black.

O'Tel pulled the Jahn'Do'Tor from the generator and gathered himself up. The room went deathly black. He waved his hand and a false light consumed it. The light gathered up and rose into a sphere in the air above him. It did not cast a great deal of luminance, just enough for O'Tel to see directly in front of himself.

He opened his vision, allowing the flow of the uR to appear, but no colors sprang forth. *Impossible*, he thought. O'Tel looked down at the Jahn'Do'Tor and saw streams of brilliant color flowing around it, fading into nothingness as they touched the generator. It was more than broken; it was dead and with that death went the great shield that protected the planet.

In the center of the great hall Colin sat frozen, his mind racing to calm itself, tears running of their own accord from closed eyes. His father's body lay under one of the torn tapestries unmoved from where he had sacrificed himself. Hundreds of thoughts tore through Colin's mind, a hungering for revenge, a mourning for his the loss of his father, an ache in his heart from his inaction. Never in his life had he felt so helpless.

BOOM! The sound of the explosion reached them before the full force of the shock wave hit. Colin snapped up to attention and popped to his feet. The whole world seemed to shake beneath them. All three men ran to the opening on the side of the room. In the distance, they saw the source of the explosion. The shield generator was dead, black lifeless metal consumed by the glow of fire that spat out randomly from its surface.

"Impossible," Fa'Sham uttered in disbelief.

Their eyes tracked to the sky, clear and devoid of the shield that so recently protected the planet. Suddenly, behind them O'Tel phased into the room. The wear of his ordeal at the generator hung on his body language

Fa'Sham rushed to his side. "Master O'Tel, has the generator fallen?" he asked.

"I am afraid it has Fa'Sham. Yet our problems extend far beyond its loss. Where is Arthur?"

The mention of his father's name sparked hope in Colin's heart. The Ter'Ok'Zhu had performed countless miracles over the course of their existence. They had control over a force that was so foreign and unknown to the other races, that some claimed it to be magic. At this point Colin did not care what the origin or source of O'Tel's power was, only that there was a chance the ancient king could save his father's life.

"He lies under the cloth," said Fa'Sham pointing.

O'Tel took a step towards Arthur's body, Colin's hand springing up to stop him. O'Tel looked at him, reading the uR surrounding him. The words Colin wished to say were etched there, emotion poured forth so strongly from him.

"Can you bring him back?" Colin begged.

O'Tel wept; tears were such a rare thing for his race, yet the only appropriate response to a plea so heartfelt and innocent.

"No child. Many years have I walked the stars and many miracles have I seen, but never have I bore witness to staying the cold grip of death."

He patted Colin's hand in a weak attempt at comfort. Colin let go of O'Tel's arm and defeated went back to the opening. "I am sorry Colin, but your survival ensures that his sacrifice had worth."

Colin did not respond. Instead, he locked his gaze to the horizon and lost himself to the distance. O'Tel walked over to Arthur's body and knelt down beside it. He placed a hand onto the tapestry and focused the uR. It flowed out from his hand and interlaced with the tapestry. In moments it became an extension of O'Tel's own essence. O'Tel pushed his will onto the tapestry and it transformed into a pool of energy around Arthur's body.

O'Tel raised it into the air, then reshaped the pool around Arthur. The mass of energy expanded, contracted, bubbled and gurgled as if it were being shaped in a forge. The others looked on in awe. Tales of the Ter'Ok'Zhu did not do justice to the wonder before them. Suddenly the liquid shell crystallized and hardened into a crimson pod. O'Tel lowered it to the floor. "In that vessel his body shall escape the trials of time, forever as a testament to his courage and honor," he said.

Fa'Sham bowed his head in respect. "Master O'Tel I ask that we may take his body to Bellat so that he may rest as a hero."

O'Tel looked over to Colin and said, "It is the son's decision."

Colin turned, walked to the two Bellat royals and replied, "Of course you can Fa'Sham. It's what he would have wanted. He truly loved your people, loved Bella Prime as if it were his own."

O'Tel walked over to the three and lowered his head. Then, Helaya's scream flooded his mind O'Tel's eyes opened in shock, the sheer agony causing him to cry out and collapse.

The Niit'Horg tore through the atmosphere, heat billowing around it from the friction, the black of space hidden behind the overwhelming hue of the planetary shield awaiting him. Mere miles and he would be free, the first stage of his design a success.

Suddenly laser fire tore into the rear of the Niit'Horg, erasing his moment of brilliance. *Not so easy then*, he thought. Four ships raced after him. His ship's shields had absorbed the first of their shots, a result of his focus being too centered on what was to come. Xyrus knew that Lordakai would be nearing his objective. He had little time to rid himself of those pests on all would be for not.

Xyrus pushed the accelerator as far as it would go and the Niit'Horg shuttered in response. He weaved back and forth through the barrage of laser fire behind him. Bolts of energy streamed ever so close to his ship yet none were able to make contact. The shield closed and in seconds he would meet its edge. His senses exploded as he passed through its curtain. The shield had been designed to allow safe passage from within its confines, while protecting the planet from any exterior threat, this Xyrus knew. However, what he could not have prepared for was the effects of passing through a blanket of pure uR. Every sensory receptor exploded with information whitening out the world in a brilliant flash. Xyrus screamed a silent burst of pain as his mind shut down.

Xyrus awoke on the floor of a great throne room. Giant steel bowls lined the walls, a small fire danced in their belly, casting the room in as close to shadow as one could get. The room was deathly silent, each move Xyrus made echoing through it as he rose to his feet.

The room carried the emotions of solace and death. Its furnishing, a deep dark brown wood, were elaborately carved and trimmed in gold. Paintings of battles hung on the walls and countless oversized statues stretched as high as the arched ceilings fifty feet above standing as guardians of the rooms belongings.

Centered along the rear wall, two gigantic pyres raged beside a magnificent golden throne. This seat was decorated in tribute to the man who sat in it, detailing his greatest victories. The throne belonged in a museum. Twice his size, it still oddly fit him and only further dwarfed those that stood before him. The light from the pits of fire at the throne's sides caressed the front edge of the chair, casting him in silhouette.

Black and red splashed armor covered the entirety of his body. The little bits of armor that peaked into the light were visibly scarred from countless battles. In one hand, steel covered fingers gripped the hilt of a massive long sword. Its red blade appeared as though it had recently tasted blood.

The crimson splashes of light reflecting from the blade caught Xyrus's eye and drew him in close. As he neared the shadowed warrior on the throne, two beasts leapt out from the darkness. Catlike, the beast bore coats of long bristled violet fur. Were it not for the shine of their teeth and white tipped paws Xyrus may not have seen them at all. The pile of skulls behind the throne told Xyrus that others had not been so observant.

They stopped a foot beyond his reach, a gigantic black chain stretching taught to its limit and pulling on their collars. "You have come Lord Xyrus. I am honored," the shadowed warrior said.

Xyrus paced hoping to catch a glance at the man's face. The warrior clapped his hands, muttering something in an ancient language, causing the two beasts to retreat to the shadows. "It is a useless task. I have worked the shadows so that I always linger in them. No angle shall give you access to my face."

"What manner of coward hides himself in the darkness?" Xyrus challenged.

The shadowed warrior laughed hard and loud, amplified by the size of the room.

"You are brash, as legend has told, but know this Xyrus, I hide my face not out of cowardice, but for reasons that your small mind would only fail to comprehend."

Xyrus stopped moving, puzzled he asked, "What *legend* is this you speak of? My time is now, yet you speak as if it has long past."

"So short sighted, focused on only yourself and the now that you are blinded to that which is yet to come," he replied.

Xyrus felt the power radiating off the shadowed man. It penetrated the air and sifted its way into his senses. He would not be talked to as such, "What is this place then? If you will not reveal yourself perhaps you may enlighten me with at least that bit of information."

After a pause he replied, "No. The who and where have no relevance to this moment."

"What right have you to say as much?" Xyrus yelled as his patience was now fully used up.

Xyrus gathered the uR into his hand, the energy glowed a deep purple along his flesh. He threw his hand forward at the man and the uR fired out in a beam.

Without any movement the shadowed man deflected the attack away, sending the beam fractured into smaller shafts back toward Xyrus. They lashed around the Dark Lord's arms and legs like glowing ropes, pulling him to the floor.

"Fool! Your arrogance blinds you to the gift you have been given in this. Dark Lord, Planet Killer, such undeserved titles, for in your madness you miss the details. You waste your life consumed by anger. It is your strength Xyrus, but without control it shall be your undoing."

The flames at the man's side rose higher, illuminating the wall behind him. Along the wall on the other side of the man, something caught the light, shimmering. The ropes forced Xyrus to look at it.

"Your time here is done Lord Xyrus. Take head this advice, for the path you walk shall leave your name burned into the stars."

The two items on the wall came into focus. Xyrus's eyes widened at the site of them. Two suits of honor hung with reverence. To the man's left was a strange red and black suit. It was jagged and very coarse in the flow of its design, as if it belonged on the edge of a cliff. Xyrus knew of no race that wore such armor.

Then his focus shifted to the opposite side of the chair and his eyes went wide with shock. The sight of the armor rocked his consciousness and his mind could find no way to rationalize what he was seeing. *HIS* armor, the same as the one he now wore, hung on the shadowed man's wall. It bore only one difference, a fracture over the chest plate nearly six inches in diameter, a killing blow.

Then a new pull on his body became overwhelming. It threatened to tear his flesh from his bones.

"Release me," he screamed.

"As you wish," the man responded and the energy bands disappeared from Xyrus's body.

Instantly he was pulled back out of the room. The man in the shadows sighed deeply and the flames retreated down, leaving the room in nearly total darkness.

Xyrus opened his eyes, he was still screaming in pain, but now he was back in the Niit'Horg. He had only seconds to gather his bearings as the metal tips of the Council Guard's ships exited the shield behind him. Xyrus grabbed the control stick flipped the ship and squeezed the trigger. His forward cannons fired. Bright bolts of red energy screamed through space and connected with the first ship.

It was only half way out of the shield when it exploded in a hail of fire, Xyrus continued to fire as the next ship tore through his comrade's debris. The other two followed suit, returning fire back at the Dark Lord.

Xyrus banked down and away. His ploy had worked, yet not as effectively as he had hoped. His experience passing through the shield still sat heavily at the back of his mind, but the seriousness of the situation pushed it aside.

The three guard's ships formed up and gave chase. He weaved his ship effortlessly, avoiding their laser fire as if it were passing him in slow motion. Xyrus spun his ship back toward the planet. He knew that there was no passing back through the shield now and that impact with it was certain death, yet the shield presented his only option out of his current predicament. He accelerated, his ship's purr amplifying to a roar that vibrated around him. Xyrus knew the guard ships would follow suit, blind only to their goal rather than their own safety.

Xyrus armed a torpedo and focused his mind. The HUD in his cockpit showed the distance of his ship from the shield and in red counted down the distance to the point of no return from his dive. The red counter went to Zero and alarmed, Xyrus ignored it and pressed the ship even harder. The uR filtered into his senses and he fired the torpedo, not at those following him, but rather at the shield itself. His hand gripped his control stick and pulled back. With his opposite hand, Xyrus manipulated the uR around the nose of his ship, assisting it in this impossible maneuver. Metal groaned and strained as the Niit'Horg yawed away from the planet.

His torpedo made contact with the shield and exploded along its surface sending a ball of flame outward back into space. The Niit'Horg completed its maneuver and thrust past the oncoming guard ships. They too were trying to pull away from the oncoming impact, but without the aid of the uR their maneuver was doomed to failure.

The first guard's ship was hopelessly lost, flying through the explosion, contacting the planetary shield and adding into the force of the explosion. Shrapnel flew out into space and tore through the second guard's ship, destroying it before it could meet the shield.

The third ship however, was able to pull away in time, using the concussive force of the other explosions to aide in its yaw away from the planet. Engines opening up full bore, the guard's ship tore back into space, the flames of the explosion licking behind it. The guard opened fire upon the Niit'Horg.

Xyrus spun his ship back around toward the oncoming guard and returned fire. The guard barely banked to the right and both ships screamed past each other, their bellies nearly kissing. Xyrus's time was running short. Lordakai would be nearing the end of his task and he knew he had no time to play with the annoyance of the guard any more. His eyes caught a glimpse of the guard's ship flying towards his own. Xyrus killed his engines and focused his mind. He stretched out a hand. With only a single target Xyrus was finally able to concentrate, sending forth a blast of uR that engulfed the guard's ship, and with a clasp of his fist the ship crumbled and exploded.

BEEP! BEEP! BEEP! A red light flashed on Xyrus's console, Lordakai had begun. He had no time to find a safer haven and would have to trust his safety to fate. Death would be a worthy price to pay for the chance to gain all that was before him. Xyrus tapped a series of buttons that put the ship on autopilot and began to meditate.

"I'JAI!" The old Malef word stung his mouth as it passed his lips. In front of him the uR took form, pooling together in a black mass of tar. Xyrus felt the power from the object in front of him, exuding power as a sun would warmth. He uttered the word again, *"I'JAI."*

This time the tar took action, striking out and attaching itself to Xyrus's face. It seeped into his eyes, until all that remained was two black holes in his head.

In seconds the world before him exploded in a cacophony of light and color. Xyrus tried to cover his eyes, to shield them in some way, but it was impossible. Finally, he accepted this new gift, calmed himself, and remembered the things that his masters had told him.

"Helaya," he muttered, *"I'JAI* Helaya."

Suddenly his sight was thrust forward, though his body remained in its place. His sight rode the currents through space and time until they rested on Vysan. Waves of energy rose up from the planet, likes strands of silk flowing in the wind. They crashed into each other, constantly shifting and changing.

Xyrus knew he must be patient, he must trust in Lordakai. Than as time seemed to stretch for an eternity, something fired out from the planet, a stream of pain and desperation, brighter and more powerful than the others. It was as if he could hear her scream on its tail. Unconsciously he willed his sight to chase it.

It streaked through the galaxy at a pace that reduced the stars to mere streaks of light, tearing past countless planets, moons and suns. Xyrus wondered if it would ever stop or if he would simply chase this beam of energy throughout space until someone discovered his prone body and destroyed it.

Finally, the beam struck down on a giant planet. A blue hue covered most of its surface, tempered by scattered greens of the continents along the surface. Three moons rotated at different depths in the space surrounding the giant planet. The smallest of which was a subtle shade of blue. In the distance a sun that was equal in size to the planet, roared and shot life out into space. This portion of space was pure, untouched by technology. It seemed unthinkable that the princess was here, but the beam of energy had struck down on the planet's surface and thus it must be her location.

"*LA'GA'KAI,*" Xyrus said.

Power erupted from his sight and then shot back to his body. His com chirped, obviously the Queen's was dead and Lordakai's task was complete. Xyrus tapped the console and a hologram of Lordakai appeared. "Lord Xyrus, is it done?" he asked.

Xyrus nodded, "Yes Lordakai, I have her location. You have served our people well."

"Then I shall see you in For'Dowas M'Lord," Lordakai said.

The image disappeared and Xyrus knew that his great general had served him for the last time. He punched the coordinates into his computer. The location of the planet he had seen did not appear on the star maps, only black empty space, but Xyrus knew that the princess was there. He forced the ship to accept the coordinates, overriding the safety warnings.

There was no jump gate to use that would bring him close enough to the planet, nor would he risk making such a jump even if there was one. He was relegated to using the ship's fold drive, a slower mode of travel and more risky, but it seemed his only option. With a push of a button engaged the drive, space and time folded in on the Niit'Horg as it propelled forward and in a instant it was gone.

O'Tel caught himself as he nearly fell to the floor, Fa'Sham rushed to his side to offer assistance, but with a quiet raise of his hand, O'Tel let him know he was fine.

"Master O'Tel, are you alright?" Fa'Sham asked.

"Yes child, though I fear Lord Xyrus has indeed found her," O'Tel said.

"Found who?" Fa'Sham asked.

O'Tel paused, then spoke with a measured tone, "Zhu, daughter of Lady Helaya and rightful heir to the Sophos Throne."

"That is impossible," Fa'Sham protested.

Colin now turned his attention to the conversation. "Why?" he asked.

"Because she is dead and has been for years," Fa'Sham replied.

"No, Fa'Sham, she lives," O'Tel said.

"How is that possible Master O'Tel? I have spoken with Helaya, seen the pain in her eyes. If her child lives, why would she not know?"

"She has known Fa'Sham, for not even my own ability can fully block the connection of parent and child. Her knowledge of Zhu is only in her heart, in her dreams and her hopes; for that dark endowment, I have carried the burden as well all these years."

"You've what?" Colin asked.

"We have little time, but the telling of this has value. You, I have no doubt, are aware of the story that has been told of that fateful night sixteen years prior. How shortly after Zhu was born, an assassin came to the Royal Palace and tried to kill both the Queen and her child," O'Tel said.

"Yes, news of such tragedy was impossible for them to contain," Fa'Sham replied.

O'Tel nodded and continued, "There are bits of truth to the lie that was told about that night. There was an intruder that night and his mission did involve the Queen, this much was true; but it was to save her life not end it."

"How do you know that is the truth?" Tar'Sham asked.

O'Tel hung his head in shame. "For I was the intruder at the Sophos Palace all those nights ago."

Fa'Sham stepped back, astonished by the revelation, "But that does not explain why she is lost to the knowledge of her daughter. She truly believes her dead."

"I hid the memory of that night for her own safety, allow me to explain," O'Tel responded.

He reached out to them, the uR shooting out from his hand and into each of their eyes.

In an instant, they were transported to another time, sixteen years in the past, on Vysan, outside of the Royal Palace. They now shared O'Tel's memory of that fateful night.

Before them, O'Tel walked along the courtyard unnoticed. It was night and rain poured down heavily. O'Tel walked past countless guards who seemed unable to see the man before them. The vision flashed forward and O'Tel was now inside the palace, only feet from the Queen's chamber, which was quiet, before him lay numerous Sophos either unconscious or devoid of life. Suddenly a woman's scream in the distance hurried his pace. He waved his hand at the door and it flung open.

Inside of the room Queen Helaya stood, restrained by two young priests. A third, much older, was standing before them holding in one arm a tiny babe wrapped in a blanket. The child wailed as the old man raised a blade in the air. Helaya fought violently against her captors flinging her body towards the elder man in a vain attempt to knock the blade from his grasp.

"It must be done highness," he screamed.

"Stop!" yelled O'Tel.

The man's vision snapped up to the intruder. "you know the prophecy better than any here my lord. The child is an abomination. She bears the mark, she is not pure and she will bring a great darkness to all."

The elder man thrust the knife down toward the child and Helaya let out blood curdling scream that shook the fiber of all those around. Inches away from the child's heart the blade hung in the air. Both man and steel enveloped by a stream of uR. The man pressed with his might to finish his blow, but O'Tel would have no more. With a flick of his wrist, he flung the blade harmlessly across the room.

"Your arrogance is superseded only by your foolishness. What right have you to think your interpretation of this matter is absolute? That you may find justification in taking a life, in particularly one as young, appalls me Regent. No, you are a traitor to not only your people, but also your faith."

O'Tel reached the elder man and grasped his arm holding the child. Energy erupted from his palm and pulsed up the elder man's arm. The two young men tossed the Queen aside and charged at O'Tel, weapons drawn.

O'Tel's head snapped up and with a thought he flung the men into the air. They each crashed into the far wall, unconscious. O'Tel returned his gaze to the elder man still in his grip.

"You must let me finish my lord, they both must die. Their deaths will spare millions of others immeasurable suffering. You know I am just in this. I have consulted the scripture," the elder man said.

"All creatures face death Regent. Yours is not the hand to decide when that time shall come for anyone."

"Then you must kill me my Lord, for my faith in my mission is unwavering."

"No," O'Tel said as the uR ran back up the man's arm. "There are other choices in this."

Suddenly the elder man gasped as a blade pierced through his chest. He fell to the ground, dropping the child.

"No!" O'Tel yelled, as he reached out and caught the child.

Helaya stood over the elder man and wept. She fell to her knees. "Is this to be my fate? How many shall have to fall for her to be protected. She is not pure, it is undeniable. Others will come just as the Regent did."

O'Tel looked at the fallen man. "His death was not needed."

The roar of footfalls echoed in the hall behind them. She looked up at him, "What shall I do my lord? How do I face this?"

O'Tel shifted his vision to the child now in his arms. Her face was angelic and soft. Bright red eyes looked up to his own and connected them in an instant. He looked back to the Queen. "There is a way for both of you to be safe M'Lady, though the hardship will be absolute," he offered.

"I will suffer any burden to see her safe my lord."

He paused; the footfalls were growing in volume. "I shall take her to be raised on my planet. I will be her personal guardian M'Lady and I promise that no harm will come to her while I live, but the cost is that you shall only know her in your dreams."

Puzzled she questioned, "How my lord?"

"Unquestionably I can shape your memory, erase this night. Though the cost of such a thing is that in its loss you shall believe your daughter to be dead."

"NO! There must be another way," she pleaded.

He looked to the door, then back to her and said, "It is the only way I see for both of you to be safe. You must hurry and decide, our time draws to an end."

Helaya took a second to contemplate the decision. She knew the power of the Ter'Ok'Zhu first hand. She had seen the wondrous things that they could do, yet knowing that she would never again know her daughter. Helaya gathered herself up and stepped over to hold her child once more. "You say I will know her in my dreams," she asked kissing her daughter's hand.

"Yes m'Lady, though she will seem a distant memory at first and then a mere stranger as time passes, there shall always remain a connection between you both."

"You swear your life to protect her?"

He nodded. "Hers is a special flame that burns bright and I shall ensure none snuff it out as long as I draw even a breath of life."

She hugged the child close and returned her to O'Tel. "Will I never know of her true fate?" she asked.

"O'Tel closed his eyes. "At the moment of passing, you shall know her as though you had walked every step by her side, but through your life, no."

Helaya rested a hand on Zhu's cheek, tears erupting from her eyes. "Then I accept that burden my lord. Her protection is all that matters."

O'Tel reached a hand out and touched it to her forehead. He tucked the child close to his body as energy flowed forth from his hand and consumed the Queen's head.

Just then, the Palace Guard stormed into the room. "Assassin," Captain Hayator screamed.

O'Tel broke the connection with the Queen and covered himself with his robes, shielding his identity from those in the room. Helaya collapsed to the floor. He looked to the window and leapt through it, deflecting laser fire with the uR as he ran.

Suddenly all four men were back in the Great Hall. It took a second for Colin, Tar'Sham and Fa'Sham to reorient themselves, but finally they gained their composure. "For sixteen years I have honored that vow, but I fear I can no longer fulfill it on my own. Ancient forces work against us now and I fear Xyrus is their tool. He goes to kill Zhu, Helaya's daughter".

"Whatever you need of us is yours Master O'Tel," Fa'Sham offered as he and Tar'Sham bowed.

"I shall need all of you in this task if we are to save her. Even you Colin," O'Tel said.

He shook his head in disbelief and stepped back. "No, no, no. This is all too much, lost princesses, magical power, and ancient races. You don't need me, don't need my help. I'll just screw it all up, failure is the only thing I do well."

Fa'Sham walked over and placed a hand on Colin's shoulder. "You must not let self doubt deafen you to your fate's call Colin. Honor your father."

Colin brushed the hand from his shoulder and said, "No. My father is dead. My crew is dead. It's all my fault. I'm cursed. You're better off without me."

With that, Colin stormed out of the Great Hall. O'Tel raised a hand to stop Fa'Sham from chasing after him. "The decision must be his to make Fa'Sham," O'Tel said, "Come we must tend to the Slai'Nor, she is badly hurt and our time grows short."

All three left the hall. From the rubble rose a single man, Draken Vulcanon. He was disoriented, but quickly gathered himself up. Draken cleaned off his attire and stepped down to the floor. He cleared his throat, then hoarsely said, "Convene the council."

"Affirmative Senator Vulcanon," the computer replied.

CHAPTER SEVENTEEN

The dew on the grass tickled the bottom of Zhu's feet. The horrifying image of the woman in such pain still haunted her, yet here in the grass she was able to find some sense of solace. Zhu opened up her senses to her true sight. The world awakened to something so much more brilliant. Streams of color washed over everything around her, from the stone of the buildings in the distance, to the very blades of grass underneath her feet, each piece of life became interconnected in a single flow of energy. The uR, individualized and yet united.

Zhu found that every movement, every choice, every pulse of life altered that flow. Her mind began to understand how O'Tel had been able to read its currents, but could not fathom how she would gain such knowledge for herself.

Zhu allowed her vision to all but fade away, leaving but a simple glow about the world.

Zhu reached out with her mind and connected to the environment, feeling the cool moisture of the dew at her feet, the warmth of the sun bringing new life to the world and even the insects and other smaller microscopic forms of life skittering about along the ground below her.

She reached out to the large tree and was able to see into its past. She saw life from the tree's perspective, time unwound as she pressed back through time. The surroundings changed as the layers of years peeled back.

Suddenly something ripped her out of the vision back to her own time. She allowed the tides to open up to assess where the disturbance had come from. The tides shifted, as if the world was trying to pull away from this new intruder. A deep black stream carved its way through the light. Zhu followed its path until her gaze stretched towards the sky. In the distance a great pool of energy hovered, as if a small piece of the morning sky had been plucked out and replaced with night. The black force moved closer toward the planet, searching for something.

She had never seen such a thing and instantly a morbid sense of curiosity drove her to investigate. Zhu extended her own perception beyond that of her corporal self, instantly traversing the distance to the black pool.

The planet reached out and tried to pull her back, but she was enthralled in her discovery and brushed its grip aside. She neared to the black mass, until she was but tens of feet away. Three tendrils snapped out of it and wrapped around her arms and her waist. The contact sent waves of sorrow and pain through her.

Zhu tried to scream out, but one of the tendrils covered up to her mouth. She thrashed against her new binds, but no amount of force seemed to gain her an advantage. The tendrils forced her to look into the center of the black mass. A face suddenly formed in its center. It smiled a sickly smile of overconfidence. Sharp jagged feature highlighted by scars, the face was one that had seen its share of battle, yet it was noticeably masked by the darkness.

A brilliant golden light shot up from the planet, consuming both Zhu and the black mass. The face in its center screamed out silently in pain. The tendrils that pulled Zhu's essence, disintegrated and she fell back down along the shaft of golden light to her corporal self, which was now held by Master Paow.

She opened her eyes and the tides subsided, leaving only the natural world. Paow spoke before she could herself, "Are you alright child? Did he harm you?"

Zhu looked up to the sky, puzzled. "Was that real then?" she asked.

"What did you see child? Be exact in your words and be swift."

Zhu could see the seriousness in his eyes as helped her to her feet. "I saw a black dot in the sky and as I approached it a face in its center, someone who had been tested through many battles."

Paow looked to the ground and closed his eyes. It was as if the words had hit him like a blow to the stomach. "Then he knows you are here. We have little time Zha'Toh; you must go to the Temple."

"Who Zhi'Fah? Who knows? What was the black mass in the sky?" Zhu asked.

"No! No questions Zhu. You must simply obey now. Our time dwindles too fast for debate. Hurry!"

He grabbed her by the wrist and pulled her toward the Temple. Zhu obeyed. The worry in his voice was all the convincing that she needed.

Xyrus screamed, grabbing at his eyes, an evil laughter filling his throat. The old man's move only delayed the inevitable. Xyrus knew where the girl was and now it was only a matter of time before she would be his.

He tapped a series of buttons on his control panel and the active display showed a three dimensional model of the Niit'Horg, the word *Jamming* flashed next to it. Xyrus pressed a large red button and several small satellite dishes rose out from the ship's hull.

He tapped a second series of commands and the display shifted to a map of the planet below. Coordinates scurried across the screen until they triangulated on a single point. *Target Locked.* Xyrus leaned back in his chair and pressed a circular orange button.

Two handles emerged on each side of his body, perpendicular to his shoulders. As he gripped them both, his chair rolled back into the ship and the floor beneath him sank slightly.

Xyrus now stood upright, arms outstretched in the handles. He turned each of them clockwise and then pulled. A sharp hiss followed and then metal shot up around his body, forming a black sphere. This sphere lowered down and the base of the ship opened to allow it access into space.

As it made its way out into space, hovering in place, it was held by the ship's tractor beam. Inside the sphere, Xyrus pressed both of the handles forward. Boosters in the rear of the sphere fired and the pod shot toward the planet. The black metal of the pod burned amber red as it tore through the atmosphere. As the pod shot into the troposphere, it tore through a giant grey cloud. Inside the pod, Xyrus stood patiently, his head down and eyes closed.

The interior of the pod functioned as one giant display, creating a view that made it seem as though he was in free fall. The pod offered a small bit of maneuverability, but none that would soften his landing. The moisture of the cloud cooled it off and created bits of steam along its hull. In an instant Xyrus was through its mass and the ground seemed to be approaching at an alarming rate. Xyrus embraced the speed. His hands ached from holding the current position, so he used the uR to fortify his strength. The computer alarmed as the pod neared impact.

Suddenly the ground exploded as the black metal slammed along the planet's surface. Top soil flew up into the air along with a sea of other debris. As the dust settled into the air it combined with the steam that now decanted forth from the cooling exterior of the pod.

In the distance hundreds of footfalls pounded against the earth. The dust settled around the pod and from its creases, streams of mist exuded into the air. The four sections burst apart and slammed into the ground. In their wake stood Xyrus, a dark heaving gargoyle, his arms curled and resting at his side, ready to unleash hell on any who would oppose him.

Along the opposite hill, the battalion of Guardians stormed up in unison. Shimmering gold appendages attached to brushed silver trunks, the Guardians were at a quick glace flesh born, limbs and contours mimicking the sleekest and most agile athlete that any race could offer. Even their faces carried a trace of humanity, though masked by a solid golden face plate that held a single blue visor, no wider than an inch to see through.

Hundreds of those soldiers marched across the field in perfect unison, a solid singular moving force, operating in a fashion that echoed how far from humanity they truly were. Every movement, even down to the slightest twitch of a finger was unitary.

The Guardians were robots, alive and shaped from the uR by Master Paow. They reflected his virtues and commitment to discipline. Though mechanical in nature, the Guardians were far more than simple machines.

As with all of the technology shaped by the Ter'Ok'Zhu, the Guardians were alive and thus able to manipulate the uR. Their unity echoed across the countryside, several hundred feet moving at once. The ground shook in response.

As they saw Xyrus they all stopped as one. Each Guardian wielded a lance with a blade housed in its end and together the front line slammed the base of their weapons into the ground at their side. Xyrus looked up, a snarl passing across his lips, disgusted that his time would be wasted, and that the Ter'Ok'Zhu would cower behind such pathetic trinkets. He spread his hands out to his side and allowed the uR to pool underneath them gathering up in a vile purple cloud. *A pity*, he thought, *that so many should fall with such ease.* "Pathetic," he spat with hate under his breath.

In a motion, Xyrus pulled the uR up and fired it out toward the Guardians. A shaft of purple energy discharged out from his hands, five times his own width.

Their oneness created an easy target for him. The beam screamed through the air between the two foes and the ground was reduced to black soot beneath it. Xyrus gloated as he awaited their destruction. The beam nearly upon them, the Guardians moved into action. Together those in the path of the beam thrust their lances out toward it. The instant the beam was upon them, they flung their lances overhead toward the warriors behind them. This task was repeated consecutively through their masses, effectively wrangling the beam and then splitting it. The Guardians then redirected the beam back toward Xyrus.

He stared half in amusement and half amazement. *This fight may indeed be worthy of me*, he thought. The beam shot back at Xyrus, directly along its original track, but before it was upon him, he merely raised a hand in the air. The beam slammed into an invisible wall mere feet in front of the Dark Lord. Energy splashed outward and dissolved into the air harmlessly.

When it was done, Xyrus reached back behind his head and grasped hold of the Jahan. Its power surged through his body the moment his flesh made contact with its cold steel. He pulled the ancient sword from its new hilt, a solid red shaft that rested firmly along his back, and brought it to rest at his feet. Sleek and jagged, the blade reeked of evil. Countless pools of blood had been spilled along its blade over the centuries, and yet not one had left a stain. The blade had now fully adapted itself to Xyrus, thicker and jagged, it still possessed a dark beauty, but that was equally tempered by the new hint of brutality reflected in its overall design.

In the distance, the Guardian army gathered themselves up. "Ha'Trag," one of the warriors shouted and the whole of the army surged forth, as though a dam had been suddenly removed from the base of a river.

Their collective charge shook the earth all the way to Xyrus's feet. The metal panels from his pod bounced about. The Guardians did not scream or roar along the path of their assault. They were incapable of such primitive feelings such as fear.

A silent rush of bodies flowed toward Xyrus up the hill, amplified by the echo of their footfalls. Still he did not move. Xyrus twirled the sword in his hand and stared at the crest of the hill as the thunder of his opponents neared.

Fear threatened to take over his mind. The enormity of his task became all too palatable as the situation invaded his senses. The roar from the Guardians approach, the mass of bodies charging up the countryside at such a violent pace, all became overwhelming. Then the first line came charging over the crest of the hill and he was returned to himself.

Xyrus raised a hand toward the horde of Guardians and the ground itself opened up like a giant mouth around them. He turned his hand over and slammed it to the ground. The earth collapsed on top of the Guardians, burying them beneath tons of dirt and rock.

Unphased by the assault the trailing lines of Guardians continued to push forward. With a wave of his hand, a giant wall of rock rose out of the ground in front of Xyrus. He pushed a hand at it and the stone shot forward at the Guardians.

Those in the path of the stone stopped their approach. Together they flung their lances about their bodies in a rhythmic yogic dance and then thrust them toward the oncoming mass. A golden beam of energy shot forth into the stone, detonating it on contact and leaving a plume of dust in its wake.

Xyrus used the uR and grabbed hold of the remnants of his pod. He raised his hands up to the sky and the four pieces rose in response. The pieces spun in a circle around him, reaching their top speed as the Guardians arrived. The first few were sent flying away through the air, unaware of how best to penetrate this new defense. The next waves of Guardians swung their lances at Xyrus's moving shield, but their fate was the same as that of their compatriots.

The Guardians flowed in around Xyrus, surrounding him like water around a lone stone in the field. Unable to get through his barrier of spinning steel, the Guardians altered their method of attack. Together they focused the uR and pressed it in on the pieces, pressing them in back onto Xyrus.

He pushed against them, trying in vain to stop their progress, but still they closed in. His focus shifted, the four pieces stopped spinning around him and now stagnant they continued their progress. Xyrus focused his entire mind and pushed against the oncoming pieces of steel, but even as strong as he had become, his power alone could not hold up against so many aligned against him. Like a coffin, the steel closed in on him, sealing off the light. The sea of Guardians pressed in further, each using the uR to help contain the Xyrus within the steel tomb.

Under the weight of the metal, Xyrus felt his body begin to give in. His nerves fired off signals to his brain, relaying the severe amounts of pain that were being applied to them from the crushing metal. The Malef sword glowed, blazoned with power that surged out of the steel of the blade.

The power coursed into Xyrus's body and his flesh took on the same purple hue as the energy that poured out from the blade. It was as if it had been dipped in some fluorescent liquid. Energy arced out from his eyes and poured into the darkness. He was no longer in control of his own movements, the sword had taken over his body out of instinct.

He crouched down into a ball, drawing the uR in and, then he thrust himself up and outward. His flesh contacted the steel and a concussive wave shot out across the field. It sent the pieces of metal flying away from him through the Guardians. Others were sent into the air from the force of the blow.

The nearest Guardians still on their feet attacked. With the aid of the uR they flew across the field with tremendous speed, jumping into the air to deliver their blows. Xyrus dodged the first two and caught the third by the heel, using the Guardian's momentum to fling him around in a circle. Xyrus released his leg and the Guardian's body hurled through the air, crashing into his comrades.

Xyrus continued this dance through the Guardians, evading their blows and delivering his own. He made very little progress, for though he dispatched numerous foes, the distance at which he gained toward his target did not decrease. His time table did not allow him such a luxury as seeing this fight to its conclusion.

His sword blazed with hunger and Xyrus swung it through his nearest enemy. The blade called for blood and so he cut through them with a chilling ease. The Guardians struck back with their lances in a series of blows, but Xyrus moved the Jahan through the oncoming attacks, bisecting weapons and appendages alike.

He swung the sword overhead and thrust it forward. A beam of energy shot through the Guardians, disintegrating all whose path it crossed. As he pulled the blade back a tail of energy remained attached to it, like the thong of a whip. Xyrus swung it over his head in a circle and then lashed the whip out through the horde of oncoming Guardians. It cut through its victims so effortlessly that it seemed as though it was a mere illusion. Only when the Guardian's bodies fell in two was the reality of its power visible.

With his other hand, Xyrus deflected oncoming attacks, the Na'Dral once again proving their worth. He shot out his free hand and manipulated the earth. It rose up, crushing and engulfing the Guardians down then.

They fired their own beams of golden energy at Xyrus, but the Dark Lord deflected them with both his sword and the Na'Dral. Even though their attacks were seemingly unsuccessful, their overall goal of detaining him from the child was working. Xyrus extended both arms and a circle of force pushed away and crushed his nearest attackers. The Dark Lord pulled the sword close to his chest and concentrated.

The Guardians swarmed in like water flowing down a drain. Electricity crackled around the Dark Lord and he rose up a foot into the air. A purple ball of energy took form around him. The Guardians fired bolts of energy, but they were deflected off the exterior of the sphere. Those closest assaulted the orb with their lances, but none of their attacks could penetrate it or stall its growth.

Suddenly the Dark Lord looked up and the orb began to crack with a surge of energy, electricity spit off its shell into the air. Inside the sphere, Xyrus shot his arms out and the orb expanded exponentially out through the countryside around him. It engulfed the masses of his enemies, shooting bolts of purple electricity along their bodies as the sphere passed over them. They fell to the ground lifeless as it dissolved.

Still hovering in the air, Xyrus looked across the hills to the city in front of him. It was far off in the distance. He alone would be the tool used in this assault on the ancient city. His gaze shifted to the sky, to the stars beyond, which were lost to sight by the sun. His purpose seemed so clear and direct to him. He looked back to the city and leaned forward. His body flew across the field, the grass parting as he passed.

Master Paow stood at the entrance to the temple, Zhu at his side. The building itself was daunting, an extension of the edge of the cliff, it rose up twenty stories into the air. The local flora crawled along its exterior, seemingly trying to pull the structure into the cliff. Elaborate carvings of figures and historic events lined both the base and top of the temple.

Its entrance was a simple arch, embraced by two giant columns. Along the steel door were arcane runes, symbols of power from a far away time, they still carried a great deal of power that echoed off their frame. *Find truth behind the veil of a closed eye, down the corridor of an open mind* was carved in the Ter'Ok'Zhu native tongue along the arch above the door.

Usually the Temple was a place for peace and tranquility where those who entered could escape the many distractions of the world and focus inward uninterrupted. The building was made so that it filtered out the flow of uR outside of its walls, allowing only a small amount of it to flow inside, that which resided in those in its sanctum.

Now the temple would serve a much different purpose, one of protection. Master Paow grabbed his pupil by the arms, stopped her in front of its entrance and spoke, "You must stay inside the temple Zhu, do you understand, do you hear me child? Stay in the temple no matter the circumstance."

She sputtered back, "What is happening? Why must I. . ."

He cut her off, "We have no time for explanation. I feel his presence nearing. You are not safe here. Pray this onetime Zha'Toh, heed your master's request without struggle."

Zhu stopped her tongue as a natural desire to question that which she did not understand or agree with rose up from her throat. His eyes told the majority of his argument, so she simply buried that desire and bowed her head in acceptance. He smiled and said, "Thank you child. If we live through this day I promise to yield to the no doubt endless stream of questions that your exuberant mind must have, but for now into the temple."

With that he hurried her inside the hulking steel doors. The last image he saw was her smiling gentle face staring back at him, darkness slowly engulfing it. The slam of the doors reverberated through his body, shaking his very bones. Master Paow raised his hands up in an elaborate series of movements. The uR streamed up from the earth and engulfed the edges of the archway, illuminating the door as it danced its way to the top. The Runes glowed white hot as the new taste of energy streamed over them. Paow finished his movements with a clasp of his hands and all traces of the energy disappeared into the temple. The great Ter'Ok'Zhu master turned around, feeling the dark presence before his eyes could bear witness to him.

"Xyrus, you have made a bold and grave error in coming here," Paow said.

Xyrus scoffed as he allowed his feet to gently touch the ground. He walked toward Paow unphased. "Do you think stone shall hide her from me old man?" Xyrus questioned.

Paow spoke, "She is safe from you now. Not even with the dark blade of the Jahan shall you see her harm."

"You underestimate my strength, a mistake your Lord O'Tel has so recently made as well."

"I do no such thing. Come forth if you are not afraid," Paow responded.

"I shall rip every stone from its base and use them to bury you old man."

Paow bowed. "Proceed."

Xyrus reached out with the uR, sought some grasp on the building, but there was none to be had. He focused and reached out harder, probing the building for some spot to grab hold, yet he could find nothing. It was as if the building did not exist. Instead there was a void in its place, an empty blot amongst the uR. "What madness is this?" Xyrus protested.

Paow walked out away from the temple, his hands clasped together, as if he were teaching a student. "Your power is great Xyrus, but your grasp of it is not grounded. You choose to assume rather than search for real truth."

Xyrus's anger boiled inside his stomach until it was so great he could no longer contain it. His eyes and body tracked Paow's movement, shifting to keep him in his vision. He gagged on his hate, his frustration having grown so severe. "Your race breathes its last breath, grasping on to an ancient glory. You think that trickery shall pull me from my path? You dare presume to hide her from me?"

"You think this all an illusion, are you truly so small minded? You are not the first to challenge me Xyrus. Your life is but a blink of an eye when placed against my own for comparison," Paow responded.

Xyrus pointed to the steel door on the temple. "Open them or I shall exact my frustration on you old man."

Paow laughed and stopped walking. "You think my life matters in this? Even now you look upon me and miss the veracity of this situation. You imagine the world as you would like it to be, rather than see it for what it is."

"The only thing I see before me is a coward and a corpse," Xyrus countered.

"Come then Xyrus, come and test the mettle of your words," Paow challenged.

With a visceral roar Xyrus charged toward Master Paow, his sword tearing into the ground behind him. Sparks flew up from its edge and a line of molten rock lay in its wake. As Xyrus reached his target, he swung the sword forward, its edge aimed for Paow's neck.

Paow arched his entire body back, drawing his own sword as he did and struck behind Xyrus's sword as he avoided the blow. The dark blade slammed into the ground and erupted in a sea of sparks.

Paow rocked his body back and rolled it forward, concentrating the uR behind the palm of his free hand. His flesh struck Xyrus's chest. Paow moved in such a flowing and effortless way that the blow appeared to have no force behind it, but coupled with the uR it was as if a hundred men had all struck Xyrus at once.

Unprepared, Xyrus took the brunt of the blow full on. His feet slid back as his body shot away from the Ter'Ok'Zhu master. He stopped himself and looked down at his chest plate. The armor bore a slight imprint from the attack, bent but not broken. "Is that your best?" he questioned with a sadistic laugh.

Xyrus reached down to the soil and with a push of his hands sent a giant shock wave of earth toward Master Paow. Paow pulled at the wave, separating it and sending it rolling behind him into the building where he had so recently trained Zhu. In its wake Xyrus charged, his sword at the ready. Paow shifted himself and brought his arms forward. The wave of earth responded and rushed up over his head, forming a giant shell.

The darkness of his cocoon was pierced almost instantaneously by the blade of the Jahan. Its purple energy coursed through the earth, casting a deathly light over Master Paow. Tendrils of light spider webbed their way through the structure, fracturing its integrity and then exploding the rock into a cloud of dust.

The Dark Lord came crashing down after Master Paow. Their swords clashed, sending sparks of energy into the air with each connection. Naturally gifted as a fighter and swordsman, Xyrus moved as if his weapon was a mere extension of his arm. His grace was parallel to that of a dancer and his ferocity was its only match. His blade moved as quickly as a thought, darting in and out and forcing Master Paow to defend rather than strike. Xyrus was not as rash as his first assault had seemingly painted him.

Not nearly as skilled at the art of the blade as the Dark Lord, Master Paow made up for the gap with his years of experience. A master of the craft in his own right, he seemed as close an equal as Xyrus had ever faced. Perhaps if the fight had taken place in his youth, Paow would have an outright advantage, but age had taken its toll on the Ter'Ok'Zhu master. The sands of time slowed Paow enough that it was evident that given enough time Xyrus would surely best him.

Yet time was the only thing that Paow could now cling to. Every second that he could delay Xyrus, was one more he could give O'Tel. The thought of his king was so strong in Paow's mind that it seeped into the very air about him. Xyrus could feel the thoughts as if they were his own. He glanced into Paow's eyes as their blades danced about each other. Xyrus laughed at the utter futility of his opponent. "Your thoughts betray you. Do you not see that your efforts here resound with futility?" Xyrus spat.

Paow continued to counter his strikes, replying in between blows, "There is no futility in my actions. My end lies not in success or failure, but in my faith."

"You truly think your king will come?"

Paow used the momentum from a parry and leapt away. He raised an arm and a giant wall of stone nearly fifteen feet high rose up between them. *How can he know?* He pondered.

Xyrus thrust his fists at it, sending a stream of uR that pushed the wall down upon Paow. He looked up as the wall buckled and snapped back from his thoughts. Paow sliced upward with his sword and a stream of golden energy flew through the air into the falling wall of rock. It exploded and the remaining two halves crashed harmlessly to his side. Behind them a ball of purple energy crackled through the air. Paow barely had enough time to raise his sword and deflect most of its impact.

The orb exploded, searing his robes as well as much of the earth around his feet. Before he could even take a breath, the metal of Xyrus's blade was at his throat again. Paow all but did not block the blow, but its force was so great that it shattered his blade in two and sent him to the ground in a plume of smoke.

Xyrus stood proud and arrogant, his figure silhouetted by the sun. Light reflected from the Jahan across Xyrus's face as his lust for blood gleamed down at Paow. The ancient master's own face was calm, as if he were easing himself for a slumber. It queered the Dark Lord. "Do you crave death?" Xyrus asked.

"I do not fear what awaits me in the next life. I have stared across that chasm many times and I have faith in where my end lies," Paow replied.

Paow's eyes stole a glance at the temple and Xyrus caught it. "You think she is safe? You still believe your King shall come to rescue her?"

Paow laughed, "The temple is more than just stone and steel. Its creation predates us all, and while in its belly, she shall indeed find safety from you. So kill me if you must, but do not expect to find success in your mission, for you have failed."

"Noooooo!" Zhu screamed out from inside the temple.

Both turned their attention to her. Paow reached out to her, primal instinct taking control of his body. "Stay in the temple Zhu!" he pleaded.

Xyrus flung his hand at Paow and energy shot out from the tips of his fingers. It pierced through Paow's skin and the sword crackled with energy as he screamed out in pain.

Xyrus pointed to the temple, "Do you see him child," he bellowed, "Do you see the pain you are causing your master? Come out so that we may play instead."

"Do not listen Zha'Toh," Paow managed to utter.

The streams of energy intensified and Paow's body arched up in pain. "His suffering ends when you come out to face me child."

Xyrus moved his hand and Paow buckled in on himself, he screamed out in agony, burnt flesh encircled the beams of energy and the very color drained from his skin as if sucked out of his body. Still his eyes gazed at the temple, "Do not listen!"

Xyrus pulled his hand into the air and Paow rose up, like a marionette on a string. The Dark Lord slammed the sword deep into Paow's chest, pressing the Ter'Ok'Zhu into the ground. His skin decayed instantly where it made contact with the steel of the Jahan. He let out an agonizing scream, as if his soul had been torn asunder from his very being. His eyes rolled back into his head and he simply squirmed in pain.

Xyrus bent over the ancient master and looked over to the temple, "Come now child, have you no heart? How much more shall he bleed before you come to his rescue? How long will it take for you to find the courage to face me?"

The skin around the beams of energy decayed even further, black rings expanding like ripples in a puddle. His screams went silent, a sickly gurgling the only sound no able to exit his throat.

Zhu could stand the scene no longer. She thrust out at the steel doors, drawing in the uR around her own body. They flew out, exploding off their hinges, directly at Xyrus.

The Dark Lord raised a hand and the doors stopped in the air, hovering in place mere inches from his face. He cocked his head, "Impressive. Perhaps this will not be as simple a task as I had thought old man."

Xyrus waved away the doors and they flew off in opposite directions. He grabbed his sword, still implanted in Master Paow's body, twisted it, and then drew it into the air. The old Ter'Ok'Zhu crumbled with a final scream. He looked up to see Zhu at the temple's entrance. With his last breath he whispered, "No!"

Xyrus flicked the blade, sending fresh blood to the ground. "Come child, come to your death."

NO!

The voice was both familiar and yet foreign. It screamed in Xyrus's head. *SHE MUST NOT YET DIE!*

In his hand, the sword began to burn, as if his flesh had been dipped in liquid magma. Still, even through such harsh pain, he could not free his grip from the blade. His body buckled over in response.

Zhu clasped her hands together as she charged forward. She knew there were no weapons available to her, lest she create one herself and so she did just that. As Zhu pulled her hands apart, a beam of light blue energy expanded between them. In the distance, she could see the assailant fold over in pain.

Zhu dared not allow the entirety of her vision to be seen, lest she be overwhelmed in this fight. She could feel the power dripping off this new threat, almost taste it along the wind.

With her hands slightly further than three feet apart, she broke the connection and then grasped the beam. The blue energy consumed her hand as she continued to stride toward Xyrus.

With a thought, she connected to the uR in her hand. A crackle of electricity ran up and down the beam, its hue grew brighter and brighter, then collapsed down as the energy transformed into a steel blade. Zhu was all but a few feet from Xyrus when she leapt, sword raised for a killing blow.

SHE MUST NOT DIE! DO YOU UNDERSTAND? The voice screamed in his head. Xyrus looked up and saw the girl create a blade from the air about her. His mind finally connected the voice's origin to the blade. It seemed as though it would sacrifice his life rather than allow him an ounce of disobedience.

"I understand," he conceded to the blade. The pain disappeared as if it had never existed.

As Xyrus looked up, he saw the girl's blade coming down at him. Instinctively his arm snapped the Jahan up to intercept the blow.

Zhu landed softly beside him, using the momentum from the impact to redirect her body. Immediately she was on the attack. Her sword moved swiftly, like an insect flying through the air. Yet every strike ended in failure, either deflected or altogether avoided.

With the uR, Xyrus pushed his free hand towards her and sent Zhu sliding tens of feet away. She dug her heels into the ground, buckling it under her force of stopping and charged back.

Xyrus waved his hand and a sea of earth rose up around her, forming into a solid sphere. "Far too easy," Xyrus scoffed as he walked towards his creation.

Suddenly the ball of earth exploded into a burst of blue light. Zhu stood posed in its center and as the dust settled, she returned to her charge.

Xyrus reared his blade back and gathered his strength for the upcoming blow. As Zhu reached him she swung her blade overhead, Xyrus matched the move bringing his sword up from his side to meet hers with a deadly kiss.

As the two collided, their impact caused an explosion of power. The Jahan did not buckle even slightly on its path. The sword was crafted in an ancient time and that quality was evident every time the blade was tested in the field of battle. The Dark sword tore through Zhu's fresh creation, sending the top of her blade flying into the distance.

The blow had been so clean however, that it allowed Zhu to follow her strike with a kick to Xyrus's side. Zhu enhanced the blow with the uR and the power behind it sent the Dark Lord flying. His sword fell from his hand.

Zhu charged forward, her sword broken she tossed the remains to the ground and they dissolved. Her fists and feet shot forth in a flurry of attack. Xyrus was able to counter most of her strikes and he brought himself to his feet while parrying her blows.

A stray kick allowed Xyrus the opportunity to grab and throw Zhu. Her body flew through the air and crashed through the wall of the building she had so recently used for training. Were her body not fortified by the uR, the impact could have been fatal. Instead, the rock crushed as she passed through it and she was only afforded a minor amount of pain.

The rubble piled on top of her body, her over confidence had cost her a bit of dignity. Revenge had consumed her mind, as she had nearly forgone all the lessons that she had been taught by her fallen master, even more so apparent by her current location. She pulled herself free from the rocks.

Xyrus leapt through the air and landed at her side. She tried to sweep at his legs, but the Dark Lord simply drove a foot into her knee, pinning her back to the ground. He reached down and grabbed Zhu by the neck. His grip was cold as ice. His flesh pulled the heat from hers, leaving a sensation of a thousand needles prickling underneath his grip. She grabbed his wrist with both of her hands, desperate to break his clasp on her. Xyrus bent down to her face and spoke, "How can one so small be worth so much? I should kill you here, now and be done with it all. Fate, however, has larger plans for you and your destiny lies elsewhere."

"As I breathe, I swear I shall see you dead," she spat at him.

He laughed, "Still so full of pride, I fear that no matter your binds you will find a way to test my patience and I have no time to deal with such meaningless annoyances. I see only one solution to this dilemma."

The muscles in his arm flexed as he swung all of Zhu's body through the air, his hand still squeezing her throat, and then slammed her into the ground.

The impact was so great that it sent shockwaves across the courtyard. The training building, now compromised from Zhu's earlier collision, began to buckle. The ancient stone that comprised its exterior cracked, buckled and then collapsed. The entire building collapsed inward sending a colossal cloud of dust into the air.

Xyrus waived his hands over Zhu's unconscious body and purple cocoon engulfed her. With a second motion, it rose into the air. Xyrus strode out past the temple, through the dust cloud, the cocoon at his side.

He raised his hand and a beam of light shot into the sky. Xyrus turned and looked at the destruction he had just partaken. The sun was setting in the distance, draping both him and the landscape in darkness. He smiled as the Niit'Horg descended from the sky above.

CHAPTER EIGHTEEN

The great hall still lay in chaos. The destruction that Xyrus had so recently reaped upon it was repaired as best as was possible, but echoes of the battle still rang across the air from the scarred landscape. The senatorial chairs had been either salvaged or assembled together to be presentable. In the center of the room, Vulcanon stood bruised, bloodied and nearly broken, though he still found some bit of strength, or perhaps vanity with which to carry him in an air of regality. In his healthy arm, Vulcanon grasped a far too ornate walking staff. It seemed more likely to snap in two, rather than support the whole of his weight, as it overcompensated in beauty for what it lacked in stature.

The last of the council members took their seats, the room did not stir, nor did anyone risk making a sound. The feeling of the room was one that was more familiar to the walls housing a funeral, then those that usually housed the senators.

Vulcanon relished in the somber atmosphere, feeding off the silence, allowing it to build to a maddening crescendo. Xyrus bathed in the focus of his peers, savoring the hook of everyone's vision focused on him. He craved the power that now rested in his hands, his own private addiction. A tragedy like Xyrus's attack created a sense of confusion and fright amongst the senators. Their once assured attitude had be replaced with confusion and a desire to simply follow.

In the next moments of his life, Vulcanon would be able to shape his world. His choice of words would echo throughout the channels of time.

There was no hesitation in his pause, he had decided long before this moment on what path he would choose. Rather, he simply soaked in the moment, playing on the uncertainty of his peers.

His lips nearly betrayed him with a smug smile, but he swallowed it down before any eyes could fall upon it. His face looked up to the ceiling and he closed his eyes. Vulcanon drew a long breath and walked around the chamber.

Arms tucked behind his back and crossed, Vulcanon spoke in a rough tone, "I dare risk the assumption that you, my fellow council members, know my reason for calling this meeting.

"This great hall," he stretched his arms out to emphasize the point, "has seen many days through the ages, both good and bad.

None, I fear, has carried with them as heavy of a darkness as today. Lives have been taken, ruin has been volleyed upon us and the very sanctity of this hall has been forever compromised.

I have called to you with concern in the past, fears that so many pressed as unfounded and futile. Never have I wished more to be wrong than at this very moment."

Again Vulcanon paused and stared up at one of the broken columns. The other senators sat quietly, absorbing each word from his mouth as if they contained some measure of salvation.

Vulcanon pointed to an empty chair. The seat was used by O'Tel in days past, when he still felt the need to oversee the council. It had now become a relic, a visual connection to the first days of the council. "They have abandoned us. The Ter'Ok'Zhu no longer care about this council or about this planet."

Vulcanon pointed to the gaping hole in the wall, "Their promises of protection have not held up. One, not an army, but one single man has brought down all of the securities that we held so dear. So in this, I ask you councilmen, where are the Ter'Ok'Zhu in this, our greatest time of need?"

The council simply sat in silence, none dared to venture a word against the ancient race. Vulcanon shook his head in disgust. "Absent. They have no need for us and so they have abandoned this council."

Vulcanon took a deep breath and sighed, allowing the others to share in his pain and exhaustion. "Perhaps the rationale is just. Dark times no longer are simply whispers along the wind, they are here upon us. The Belgae have in no small fashion declared war on us all. They call on us for action, for a response and yet all this council has been able to accomplish is a mandate of inaction, buried beneath the guise of debate.

It pains me to accept this fact, but the council has failed in its design. We have failed to take the measures to ensure that the peace is kept and in doing so we have lost our way. For those reasons alone and in the wake of this attack I see only one course of action that offers each of our people safety, I must move to permanently disband this council."

As soon as the words exited his mouth the council erupted from their malaise. Emotions overcame theirs sense of protocol and they erupted in response to Vulcanon's request. He gave them a minute, allowed their emotions to fester and boil. Such boisterousness as had rarely been seen inside the council walls now served to betray those from which it sprung forth. Vulcanon used it to affirm his position. He raised his hands to silence them, but his motion went unnoticed, their outrage was so strong.

"Enough," he roared, "we still have a protocol in this hall and it shall be followed."

"You cannot disband the council," Senator Adams said.

Vulcanon shot him an ice filled glare, "As Chancellor elect it is my right to bring the motion to the council."

"We must vote on this if the Chancellor wishes to bring it to the floor," Mita said.

Vulcanon nodded to him, "Of course, as I said we have procedures and they must be followed, even in matters as extreme as this. So my fellow senators, I ask you for your vote."

The Voro senators were first to vote, affirming Vulcanon's motion. Next, were the Navia, two of them voiced affirmation, while Toros Dampel voted against it. The Bellat unanimously voted against the motion. Two of the humans also voted in favor of the motion, whereas Thomas Adams did not.

Vulcanon smirked, feeling a sense of accomplishment, as though the last domino was now set in place and ready to start the chain. The votes had tallied up to a draw, six to six. Procedure in the Great Council was that in the event of a tie, the Chancellor Elect was given the deciding vote. The council had been set up to seat fifteen representatives for this very reason, as it was nearly impossible to an imbalance in such a setting. Vulcanon spoke, "As the Sophos delegation has decided to neglect this meeting. . ."

Bellat Senator Mor'Dral stood up and slammed his fist on the table in front of him. He roared dissent, "Their Queen has been attacked, there is rumor she may have been assassinated, this is outrageous to exclude them from such an important vote. There is no honor in this decision."

Vulcanon turned his head, the rest of his body statuesque. "Outrageous to expect them to still tend to their commitment to this council? Outrageous to think that they should still represent the hundreds of systems in their charge? Outrageous for them to HONOR their duty?"

The last words struck as sharp as a dagger to the Bellat's heart. The foundation of the Bellat civilization was a strict adherence to a code of honor. Vulcanon's words also stung for they carried a barb of truth in them. Defeated, Mor'Dral sat back down.

"Now back to the matter at hand. As the Sophos have chosen to abstain from this meeting, so to shall that be expressed in their vote in this matter. As such the final vote in such an instance as this where the council has reached a stalemate lies in my own hand and in that I have brought this matter to the council it is clear that my vote lies in seeing an end to the farce this council has become."

He smashed his walking stick into the ground for effect. The council members who had voted against him shouted their disdain as he walked out of the room, the smile on his face deflected any criticism from reaching him.

The shield generator, once so vibrant with life, now reached up to the sky like a barren giant. Its exterior, grey as stone, broken and burnt from the recent attack cast a stale taint in the air.

Seated on the broken bridge across from the generator was Colin, nearly as morose as the structure itself. Tears fell from their red swollen homes, uncontrolled and voluntary. One hand partially covered his lips, a faint attempt to contain his angst.

So much had been lost in short a brief amount of time. His life seemingly sound and direct one moment was now ripped away from him so violently. The things that had provided him with a sense of stability were now gone forever, at his time of most need. He had lost his purpose, but more than that his direction. That struck at him the deepest.

He no longer could trust his judgment, his faith in his decision making ability was beyond shaken. So much grief had stemmed from decisions that at the time had seemed so sound. Now he was left adrift in life and all he could see around him was an endless ocean on which to be lost, or worse sucked into too. So here he sat, the generator the company his misery so very much desired.

The quiet surrounded him in its absence and the cool lick of the wind caressed his skin. He looked down into the chasm below; his eyes became spellbound in its endless darkness. How simple it would be to simply join that endless silence, to succumb to its offering of an end.

A warm hand anchored onto his shoulder. Its touch radiated calm through his body, relieved the ache in his heart. He looked up, half expecting to see his father, but instead it was O'Tel, his white-blue eyes piercing into Colin's. Colin returned his gaze to the chasm and spoke, "How did you find me?"

O'Tel responded, "Your despair Colin, it radiates from you like a flowing beacon of light along the countryside."

"I'm allowed to feel aren't I? Or have you come to take that from me too?"

O'Tel released his hand and sat down beside Colin. "I would never try to deny you your feelings."

"Then why are you here? What do you want from me?"

"You still have a destiny Colin, whether you wish to deny it or not, it lies before you."

"I could leap and end it all. Then where would my destiny be?"

O'Tel shook his head in frustration, "You could take such measures to try to escape your fate, to rip yourself from this path, but then I fear your father's sacrifice will have been a fruitless one. That which has touched your heart so would be an utter betrayal to his memory."

Colin stood up, "What do you want?"

O'Tel rose to join him, "The man that killed your father."

"Xyrus?" Colin asked, a bit of hate left on his tongue from the name.

O'Tel replied, "Yes, Xyrus. He has taken a girl from my home world."

"And that requires my involvement?"

O'Tel paused, his own gaze turned to the fallen tower. "There is too much to give you every detail, but her life is intertwined with much more than any personal connection. You must come with me Colin, we have little time. If she is to be rescued it will take your help to see it done, of this I am certain."

Colin turned to walk away, his eyes focused on the ground beneath his feet. His confidence was visibly shaken, reflected in his sunken posture. The life was strained even in his voice. "Every choice I've made has ended in tragedy. How do you know you wouldn't be better off without my help? How do you know that I won't fail again?"

O'Tel paused, his eyes shifted from Colin to the lifeless generator. The silence caused Colin to stop, so unexpected that it sent chills down his spine. He wondered if his words had indeed struck a chord with the old man, that some bit of truth had caused him to question his choice in Colin.

"We all risk failure when the effort is put forth. I cannot guarantee success, but there is a certainty of ruin in inaction. To simply abandon a cause, to forgo the risk of failure in favor of what seems to be the safer alternative of pause in the face of malevolence, is to simply surrender ourselves to that very malevolence. It is the hope, the faith in our success which we must cling to, for the risk is what truly makes a man valiant."

Colin closed his eyes, damming the tears back. "My father bore that risk O'Tel," he opened his eyes and walked away, "and you see where it got him."

Perched on top of his balcony, Draken Vulcanon stared across the skyline, hundreds of ships were launching out into space. Though still neutral territory, the planet offered little else to those who remained. The Great Council was now fractured and each territory was left to fend for itself.

Inside Vulcanon's quarters his servants feverishly packed his belongings into hovering storage boxes. It was a difficult task to be both delicate and yet swift. Failure was nearly a literal death sentence.

Vulcanon reached down and grabbed a bottle of Macallan's whiskey. The glass was cold and smooth on his skin. He marveled at it, yearning for a glance into the history it had seen, a past when Earth still thought it was alone amongst the stars, such simpler times. Ages later now and yet here still was this trinket of attachment to that past.

Vulcanon had saved the bottle for a special day, a day when his name would be burned into the very fabric of time itself. He had flirted with breaking its seal when he first gained his seat on the council, but so many others had sat in those same seats throughout time and yet so few had left their mark through simple bureaucracy. He had hoped to taste its sweet nectar after being named Chancellor, yet even then it seemed to be but a passing moment. Now however, he knew that his name would forever be remembered, for he had done something no other had before him.

By his hand alone the council was broken, a moment that would be remembered by countless generations. He would let time be his judge whether his decisions were just or not. He believed in them and that was all the justification he needed.

Thus he opened the bottle, allowed it to exhale its century's old air. The aroma of the whiskey, the dark fruits, cloves and toffee filled his nose and invaded his spirit. He dared to taste a bit and was overwhelmed. His face cracked an orgasmic smile as he was transported in the moment. He felt at peace and then the green light on his desk flashed.

His eyes snapped to his chamber, announcement enough for his servants to take their leave. He walked over to the desk, sat and placed all five fingers of his right hand on black touch pads surrounding the button. He pressed the button down as the door closed.

Again he was engulfed in the sphere of energy and again in front of him appeared a holograph of Xyrus. The Dark Lord was clearly in a cockpit of some sort. He spoke, "Is it done Draken?"

"Yes Xyrus," he responded, "The Great Council has been disbanded, by my hand as promised."

"Then you have your war?"

"Not as of yet, but without the protection of the council to hide behind, it should be a simple matter to formalize upon my return to Earth."

Xyrus smiled broadly. "Then this is where our agreement reaches its end. When next we meet expect it to be at the proper end of my blade."

Vulcanon laughed at the comment. "Do not succumb to over confidence Lord Xyrus. I assure you these measures were not taken so that Earth would fall to Belgae rule."

"Time shall be our judge then?" Xyrus hissed.

The Dark Lord chuckled under his breath as Vulcanon became physically struck by the comment. Vulcanon slammed his fist down on the red button and shook his desk violently as he ended the transmission. The force of the blow caused the bottle of Macallan's to tumble off his desk. His eyes could only watch in disbelief as it sped to the floor and exploded. He stood there still, unable to process the last few seconds. He wondered if Xyrus could hear his thoughts, or if the turn of phrase was simply a lucky bit of words spoken by the Dark Lord. Vulcanon knew better than to assume such a thing, but then the alternative, which had so easily riled him, was that he was nothing more than a simple puppet to the Dark Lord. He pressed another button on his desk and the door opened. His servants followed suit shortly after it.

Vulcanon vented his frustration on them, "Why is this room not finished? Do I pay you to sit around or do I get this aggravation for free? I expect everything packed within the hour so we can get off of this God forsaken planet and return to the warmth of Earth." He walked past the broken bottle and his anger rose to his face again, "And clean this mess up." He stormed out of the room and slammed the door behind him.

In the vast space that now filled Docking Bay Nine sat one ship, the Harin'Horn, Fa'Sham's personal transport. Bay Nine was reserved for the high level diplomats that stayed on the planet. Its security systems were more complex and offered a level of safety for those who were able to afford the high cost for its use.

However, with the recent circumstances have so dramatically changed the complexion of the planet, those dignitaries that so recently house their vessels here had now taken them and returned to their own systems. The speed at which the news had spread was not surprising, but the reaction of the planet's inhabitants was. Whether it was a hidden fear of the now unrestrained Council Guards, a lack of reason for staying or a general irrational fear, people fled the planet as if there was the discovery of some incurable plague.

Much like the planet itself, once teaming over with the noise of the populous, Bay Nine now sat lifeless and silent.

At the base of the ship, straddled by four battle worn Bellat guards, sat the crimson tomb of Arthur Kinison. Guns shot up to the ready as the sound of footfalls approached. Even in such a secure area, the Bellat guards took no chances. Arthur had always been revered by their race for his actions at the council so many years ago, but now in his death he had become nearly sacred. The Bellat lived by a code of honor and thus few of even their own race exemplified that code as much as the man who now rested in that crimson tomb.

As the guard's eyes focused on the source of the footfalls they instantly lowered their weapons and their heads in respect.

Colin bowed his own head back to them, a token of respect, and then walked up to his father's tomb. It hovered in the air on its own accord, obviously the product of O'Tel's creation.

The tomb itself was cold to the touch. Hundreds of facets lined the crimson surface, reflecting pin pricks of light that seemed to cause the cocoon to glow with a warm red cloud of energy.

The crystal itself was solid, but as Colin stared down upon it he could see the faint outline of his father in its core, almost a specter of the actual man that so recently was alive. He traced a finger along its edge, all the pain of that moment in time rose into his throat. It threatened to overwhelm him and Colin closed his eyes for fear that if they were exposed he would not be able to hold back the flow of tears that searched so passionately for freedom.

The Dark Lord's face snapped into his mind. He replayed the moment. The shard again flying through the air across the Bay, every second becoming an eternity. It made him sick and disgusted at his own inaction which had cost him so much. His father's voice suddenly interjected into his mind, "I'm proud of you son."

Even through his failures, his father still loved him, still saw him for more than he could see himself as. How he longed to be able to seek his father's advice, to hear his voice just one more time, if only once more.

The Guards snapped their guns up again and then almost as fast, they were lowered. The first of the four spoke, "My lord," he said in a deeply respectful tone.

All four guards bowed deeply as Fa'Sham came up to them. In his wake were Tar'Sham and the entire of Reaper Squadron.

Colin opened his eyes, but did not turn to face the Bellat King. Fa'Sham waved away the Guards. The first guard attempted to speak up, but Fa'Sham's gaze cut him off before a sound could escape his throat.

"Save your arguments Captain Safir, you and your men shall serve a better purpose in emptying a challis of Krell right now, then deafening yourself to the conversation that is about to come forth."

The Guards bowed in acknowledgement of their King's request and were off. Fa'Sham stepped up beside Colin and rested a large hand on his shoulder. The Bellat King stared down at the crimson tomb in both grief and awe. "An amazement in what the Ter'Ok'Zhu are capable of."

"Ridicule is all this is. My father would never want to be display like some inglorious statue for the masses to stare at," Colin replied.

Fa'Sham patted his shoulder and then placed his hand on the tomb itself. He looked at the shadow of Arthur's face and smiled. "True that your father was beyond humble and would never have sought such recognition as this, but he also understood his place in the grand scheme of life Colin. He understood that there are times when universal needs must take precedence over our own personal wants."

Fa'Sham turned his gaze directly upon Colin, "Speaking of which, I have heard that you have refused Master O'Tel's offer."

Colin looked at those around him, the pressure of their stares only added to the already sick feeling in his stomach. "I would only fail him if I went along."

Fa'Sham scoffed, "Foolish youth, you think you have such omniscience? Yours is not to question or wonder why. Your life is but a heart in comparison to his. Do you not know how honored you are to be called on by a Ter'Ok'Zhu?"

Colin lowered his head and answered as if he were being scolded by his own father, "No."

"They have been walking amongst the stars when we were still but swimming in the seas. They know things about the world that we can only dream to comprehend and one of them, if not the greatest of them has called specifically to you for aid. Do you not see the importance of your answering that call? O'Tel would not ask if he did not have utter faith in you Colin. We all have faith in you; even your father knew that you possessed some great strength and that you were bound for a noble path in this life."

The mention of his father broke the dam holding back his emotions, they pounded out from him and he yelled back, "He died for that! He died trying to save me, because he thought I was so important. He was the important one, not me. He should be going with O'Tel."

Fa'Sham did not move, not even an inch, the words had frozen every part of his being. "Yes Colin, he died because he believed in you. So now you must decide if that sacrifice was worthy or not. Look around, look into the eyes of those here and you will see what our answer is."

Colin now looked past Fa'Sham, truly seeing the other men around him. Tar'Sham, like a brother, looked on with pride and love. Each member of Reaper Squadron too offered their support. Tar'Sham stepped up next to his father. He growled a bit, swallowing some of his own pride before speaking, "It is true Colin. All our lives I have watched you, looked on upon you with envy and awe. You blind yourself to what you could be out of fear of what you may not. Look at your shipmates, to every last one of them they believe that you could move the planet if it was called upon you to do so, and though it pains me to admit, I do as well."

Fa'Sham interrupted, "So in this hour of darkness reconsider your choice. Come with us, with O'Tel, so that we may still foil that foul beasts plans and find an ounce of vengeance for your father."

A new feeling crept into Colin's heart at that announcement, "You all are going?" he asked.

Fa'Sham laughed, "Of course! Did you think the glory would be yours alone?"

Colin paused and looked down at his father's tomb. The Dark Lord's face once again appeared, mocking him. His heart grew stronger with contempt. He looked up to Fa'Sham, the embers of a new flame lit in his soul burning behind his pupils, "I'm in."

CHAPTER NINETEEN

The once innocent silver eyes that had stared at the Royal Palace in such awe were now red and swollen from the steady flow of tears that poured forth. Alea had always admired their Queen, always dreamed of the woman that ruled her people from the palace in the distance. Her life was not filled with ignorance; her family worked the same land that she called her playground. She had seen the animals taken for slaughter, gotten her taste of the reality of life and death, but none of that could have prepared her for the news of the Queen's death.

It seemed so unreal, like a horrible nightmare that she could not wake herself from. In the deep distance she could see the palace doors open. The sound of the giant steel echoed across the hills to her ears. The guard, barely visible, exited in formation.

Alea knew their path would take them past her, she knew that she would be able to see the woman that she had only met in dreams before and that is why she now cried.

A black gloved hand gripped her shoulder, far too firm to be comforting. She looked up; her vision slightly blurred from the tears in her eyes and saw the man in black. He had been there when the off-worlders had caught her. He had saved her life, but not through force. His actions and the circumstances at hand spoke of a dark involvement by this clouded stranger that now stood behind her.

"Do not shed your tears for her child," he spoke.

She tried to pull away from his grip, wishing that she could run toward the funeral procession. Thousands of her people had gathered in the distance and more would be arriving at her location soon. All she had to do was scream to alert them to the man at her side, but she knew the futility in such an action.

"You don't scream for help? Good, perhaps there is a greater reason I spared you from the end of that sword."

"Let me go," she muttered under her breath.

He pulled her in close, the heat of his breath brushed her cheek through the shroud on his face. "In time, but first I must know something of you. You seem to have value, to have a spark that most have either extinguished or never possessed and for that I offer you this query. What shall you say of the other night if asked? What will your mind tell your tongue to say?"

He grabbed her by the throat and caressed her jaw, hinting at his desire to tighten his grip. Fear threatened to take over her body, to make her pull away or worse to scream. Alea killed her fright and used it to draw strength. She closed her eyes and muttered, "Nothing."

He released his grip and stood up. She knew his purpose and if she did not convince the man that she was not a threat, then her voice would be silenced forever. "In death she shall serve her people far more than she ever could in life."

Alea did not move, she only wished that he would leave, that he would not ruin her moment to see her fallen Queen.

"Do you know why they are taking her through this village? Why this march is so special?" he asked.

She focused on the guards in the distance. Alea could see they carried a huge metal coffin. He continued, "They carry her to the valley of the kings, out most sacred ground. Only one other woman rests there. Helaya's ideals shall carry on and her name shall echo throughout time. Perhaps one day you shall join her," he paused, "but not today child, not today."

With that he left. The guard neared and with them the horde of mourners followed. Alea stood still, her mind tried to erase the image of the shrouded man in black, she tried to focus on her Queen instead, to fill her heart with the admiration for that great woman.

A warm feeling fell over her, as though her mother was standing beside her and Alea embraced its tenderness. She looked up, but no one was there. She blinked her eyes and for an instant she saw the hints of a figure standing beside her, as if a shadow of light had risen from the ground. The woman's feature struck an all too familiar chord with the young girl.

Then as quickly as she had appeared, the woman was gone. The roar of the approaching masses snapped Alea back to the present. She turned her attention to see the guards walking down the path, her Queen in their tow. The young girl looked on and the tears resumed their flow down her cheeks. Within moments she was lost to the mass of bodies that walked along past her, consuming her as one of their own.

The sun was close to setting and the masses that had been following them had now subsided, leaving only the Royal Guards who were there to escort the Queen to her final resting place. Above all else, the Sophos people respected their traditions. Their adherence to their customs was what separated and elevated them from the other races.

Now the Guards, lead by Captain Hayator, stood at the entrance to the Valley of the Kings. Two red stone giants stood watch at the face of the valley. Fifty feet tall, the stone statues had become worn and their features were smooth, without detail. To and from along their bodies' bits of flora had taken over. Deep shadows ran over the guards as the sun retired behind the statues.

The men parted at the entrance to the valley. It was both frightening and yet majestic at the same time. The air was chilled, moist and caused the men's breath to become visible in the air. A slight mist covered the valley floor, as if the spirits that rested within were lying about.

Giant trees rose up hundreds of feet into the air, true keepers of the valleys past. The cliff walls of the mountains shot vertically into the air. Storms and time had cut deep grooves into the sides. The valley itself seemed endless, twisting off into the horizon until it simply became a blur to the eye.

This valley was home to the greatest sovereigns of the Sophos people, Kings whose names had been etched in time and now rode on the backs of myths and legend. There was never a visit paid to this sacred site that was one of joy, as it was only marked by the company of the living when they brought a member of the dead.

Captain Hayator waved to his men and the four that held the Queen's tomb followed him, the others stayed at the Valley's entrance. These five moved through the chasm, bathed in its history, specters of the past stared down at them as each King's likeness had been carved into the mountain on either side, spaced in a random fashion.

A chilling silence filled the valley, tempered only by the howling bursts of wind that froze their souls and tested their mettle. Finally, after trekking the chasm for miles, they reached their destination. Before them carved wondrously into the wall of the mountain stood King Menalae and beside him was the likeness of Queen Helaya. Fittingly they would now spend eternity together, immortalized for generations to come. Their love was as tragic a tale of star crossed love as ever existed.

The men stopped and it seemed as though time did as well. A pair of birds flew from the top of King Menalae's statue. Their caw echoed across the stretch of land. Captain Hayator walked ahead to the base of Queen Helaya's statue and removed his glove. His flesh chilled in the wind as the mist around him kissed it. He tucked his glove into his belt and removed a small blade from his hip.

The polished steel shone bright in the failing light. Captain Hayator kept the knife in pristine condition, a gift from the King countless years ago. He felt a special connection with the blade; felt it was charmed as it had saved his life countless times before. Now it had a far nobler task. Each tomb was designed with a DNA encoded lock, which once set would only open for immediate members of that person's clan. It was one of the greatest honors and responsibilities bestowed on one of the Sophos people.

Captain Hayator raced the edge of the blade against the meat of his naked palm. Like a surgical instrument, the knife ran cleanly through his flesh. It caused him no pain and within seconds his blood began to seep forth. Captain Hayator pressed his palm against the base of the Queen's statue.

Suddenly, a surge of blue electricity shot out along the rock against his hand. Like a fracture in the statue that towered above him, the electricity ran up its body, lighting the entire valley with its ethereal glow. Two doors at the base opened up and revealed a blinding white chamber within the statue itself. The four guards moved forward with a wave from Captain Hayator. They pushed the Queen's coffin inside of the chamber until it masked the light utterly.

On its own, the chamber's door closed and the electricity along the statue subsided, leaving only the little light of the sun to cover the five men. They knelt down in reverence for their fallen Queen. Captain Hayator muttered to himself, "I'm sorry that I have failed you again my Queen. First your husband, then your daughter and now you, all fallen on my watch. I swear, no matter the cost, no matter the time, I shall avenge you. On my own blood I swear."

He stood up, his men followed suit and the sun disappeared, leaving them covered in darkness.

In the heart of Mathea, the Sophos Capital, spun into the Great Mavros Forest, laid the Apelesia Amphitheater, home to the Sophos Senate. Fashioned into the surrounding hillside, the amphitheater seemed almost natural in its formation. It was truly fused with the very landscape itself, created structures blending seamlessly with environment. Four gigantic metal orbs dotted the corners of an invisible square. Their archaic black metal was worn from years of use and exposure. They had no external features outside of a simple antenna that rose from their crown.

The orbs, when activated, could shield the council from all manner of invasion from the elements. On a pleasant day, such as this one, the Apelesia was able to enjoy the benefits of their home world while still conducting their business.

The Apelesia consisted primarily of members from each ruling house. A caste based society, the Sophos elite were those that made the majority of their races decisions, though they afforded an elected minority as well.

Today they were gathered to discuss who would rule their people. The tragic loss of their Queen had struck more than just an emotional blow to their people; the political ramifications were proving to be fatal.

In the wake of her loss, numerous houses had laid their claim for the throne. Some had created an elaborate connection to the King's bloodline, while others focused on a level of financial gain they could afford, yet none focused on the trait most needed at such a time, leadership. All at once they spoke, talking over each other in a frantic dash to be heard.

BANG! BANG! BANG! The loud thumps echoed up through the amphitheater from its base. The trees that rose up in between the senators seats shook from the force. Down on the stage below stood Minas, the leader of the Sophos church. His staff, having caused the senators to halt their voices, stood firmly planted in the ground at his side. His eyes hung low as the weight of the collective gaze of so many rested squarely on him. In the silence, he found his strength, even after so many times speaking in front of such large masses of people, Minas still found dread in the entire process.

"My fellow people, today we mourn the loss of Queen Helaya. Her passing has robbed us all of that which we need most at this dark time compassion, principle, regality and more important than all those, her leadership. I have received word and I am certain all of you have as well, that the Great Council at Ter'Ar'Tor has been attacked and consequently disbanded. War now bites on our heels, as the Belgae threat is no longer mere rumor or speculation, but rather a real and personal threat. They have struck at us far deeper than any other race can make a claim to, stealing our beloved Queen with their most recent attack."

He breathed a deep sigh, "Yet I know that there is a greater end in sight, if only we can find the means to reach it. I know that if we are faithful and stick the tenants that have formed the foundation of our people, that our faith will see our people through this darkness."

"But who will lead us?" shouted a senator from the crowd.

"We have no heir," yelled another.

This caused the senate to roar once more with discussion. An overweight member of House Gondrola stood up and bellowed, "It should be a member of House Gondrola. We are the last clan with blood ties to Menalae's own, as you can plainly see in these documents." He pulled a long silver cylinder from his breast and it snapped a thin translucent form out of its side.

The members of House Ephora stood up in vehement disagreement. Paroth Ephotrata, head of House Ephora yelled, "Your claim to his bloodline is far too stretched to have any relevance. Menalae has no heir and his line has no immediate connection, thus no family may make a justifiable blood claim to the throne."

The Apelesia erupted with discussion, threatening to pore over to physical confrontations. A lighthouse amongst the storm, Minas simply raised his hands in the air at his side. "Enough," he roared.

When the room was silent he continued, "He speaks the truth. Menalae has no immediate successor, a fact the church has spent numerous hours confirming. Tradition holds that the Apelesia must choose who now sits on the throne."

Almost in unison, the Apelesia broke out with claims for nomination. Minas's eyes scanned the ruckus and a deep sadness welled up inside of him. His eyes swelled with a wetness that he forbade to show. His people, so disciplined, so ordered, were now succumbing to the lustful temptation of power. Disdain filled him and he struck his staff down once more. The bang silenced the crowd.

"Have we strayed so far as to come to this? In the face of such tragedy is there no one here who can see to our people's needs before they see to their own? Is there none here who have not become inebriated with the taste for power? Our people need a leader. They need guidance now more than any time in our past. I implore you my Apelesia, is there none here that retain the desire to see our people returned to glory?"

A single voice came from the back of the Apelesia, "There is one."

Senator Odesea Ephimira walked down toward the Patriarch and the rest of the Apelesia stared in awe. Odesea was beyond respected amongst even this elite congregation of the Sophos people; he was one of their most decorated warriors. Unusually tall for a Sophos, Odesea carried a sense of strength in his stride. His confidence could be felt as he walked by.

Odesea was nearly bald, what little black hair that remained around the base of his head was pulled back into a multiple clasped ponytail. His face was extremely boney, more so than any of the other Sophos around him. Usually a rim of hard boney exoskeleton protruded along the brow and cheekbones of a mature Sophos, but in Odesea's case, the growth nearly engulfed the whole of his face. He wore facial hair, also a contradiction to the norms of Sophos society, but the two strands of grayed black hair that stretched from the outer edge of his lips to his chest had become his own commentary on the rigid society he grew up in. Tightly fitted black robes, trimmed in gold, hung on his body in such a way that it nearly seemed as though they were a suit instead. The Patriarch smiled at his approach.

"Odesea Ephimira, yes, if ever there was one amongst us worthy it would be you," said Minas as he bowed to the man.

Odesea chuckled to himself as he now reached the stage and stood directly in front of the Patriarch. "No old friend, I do not come to nominate myself for such an honor, though I am humbled by even the thought of it. I have no aspirations for the throne and I have had beyond my fill for the wonders of politics. My time has come and passed. Now it is simply the shores that I owe allegiance."

Puzzled Minas replied, "Then who is there here amongst the Apelesia that you feel shall answer my call? Who is worthy?"

Odesea grabbed the Patriarch by the shoulder and waved toward the congregation of Houses above them. "No, not amongst the Apelesia," he said and a few snickers followed.

"Then who?" Minas asked.

Odesea took a step back and paused. He stared directly at the Patriarch and smiled. "I would think you would know old friend. There is only one amongst us who is fit to answer this call. Our people need a steady hand to bring them through the darkness that approaches. They need an example to look up to, to pattern their own behavior after. I know of only one such person, one person who possesses a natural ability to lead. You."

At first only whisper spread through the senators, then an uproar of approval, most applauded and some screamed their endorsement. The Patriarch raised his hands to quiet them once more.

"No, no, no, I have no desire to rule our people, I only seek a solution that is best for them," Minas said.

"Which is why you must accept this path."

"I cannot."

"You have no choice. Above all else you respect and honor the traditions of our people, and we have few which are more sacred than this. Your fate I'm afraid is in the hands of the Apelesia," said Odesea.

The Patriarch paused and then nodded in consent. Odesea turned to the Apelesia and said, "A vote then my senators."

Nearly unanimously, they voted in favor of the Patriarch. He stared in awe as they all rose and applauded him. The tears in his eyes finally gave way, accompanied by a bright smile.

Inside the Main Hold of the Slai'Nor, Colin, dressed in his Reaper squadron jumpsuit paced. His eyes darted to the different artifacts that now rested along the walls. Mementos of adventures that spanned the chasm of time, from epic battles to simple tokens of friendship, they all were items that Colin had never even imagined existed. He pressed in close to look at one particular piece, a sword. By all appearances, the ship's hull seemed like a simple metal, but as his hand made contact with it, the feel was anything but lifeless steel. Somehow, the metal under Colin's hand was warm, as if alive. He pulled himself away, startled by the strange sensation.

O'Tel's voice boomed behind him, "The Slai'Nor is unlike any other starship you've ever encountered."

"I've noticed," Colin replied.

"Come Colin, sit with me," O'Tel said. He waved his hand and two globules rose up from the floor. They morphed into steel chairs. "What ails you young Kinison?" O'Tel asked.

O'Tel waved his hand again and another globule rose up, this time forming a black glass table and on top of the table two white cups, simple cylinders with no design or features. O'Tel raised a hand and a decanter containing a dark green liquid flew across the room into his grasp.

"Never have I seen such sorrow as that which hides behind your eyes now," O'Tel said as he filled their cups.

Colin looked down at the liquid, it seemed the same consistency of tea, yet it moved about in his cup of its own volition. The green was so dark that it reflected the image of his face back up at him. He sipped the drink, taking the path of caution for this one time in his life.

The drink was tepid at best, yet as it passed down his throat, great warmth spread out across his body. Its taste was sharp, sweet but not overly fruity. The drink seemed to enliven his mind as well. It was as if someone had just hit him with a shot of adrenaline.

Colin placed the cup back down on the table. He kept his gaze upon the walls surrounding him. "Why me? Why am I so important to you in this?" he asked.

O'Tel hung his head at the question. He breathed a deep sigh, exhaling the weight off his shoulders into the air about him. "You have a destiny Coin. It was always thought best to shroud that fact from you, but such deception, even as well intentioned as it was, has proved to be our most fatal mistake."

Colin stood up. "What?" he exclaimed!

O'Tel pointed to Colin's chest. "You still have the mark, do you not?"

Colin's hand covered his heart out of mere mention of the mark that rested upon his breast. "That's not proof of anything; it's just a birth mark."

O'Tel shook his head, took a sip from his cup and then stood up. "Doubt me child, but do not blind yourself to the truth."

He grabbed Colin by the collar and pushed him to the wall. They stopped next to the sword that Colin had been drawn to earlier. The Jahn'Do'Tor hung on the wall, sheathed in its scabbard and not any more recognizable than any other plain sword. In a single motion, O'Tel pulled the sword free and swung it directly in front of Colin's heart. Colin tried to pull free, but O'Tel's grip was to sturdy. "Look, look upon the sword's blade Colin."

Colin looked down and saw that the blade was visibly glowing, something that a piece of cold steel should not be doing. O'Tel pressed the blade in Colin's chest, not with enough force to pierce, but enough that Colin could feel the subtle bite of its edge.

His chest exploded in a burning sensation, as though hot water had suddenly been injected into his heart. Colin screamed and crumbled to the floor. O'Tel swung the blade away, sending it back to rest in its scabbard once again.

The burning began to subside and slowly Colin was able to breathe normally once more. He spoke between gasps, "What was that?"

"That was truth. The mark on your chest is far from anything ordinary," O'Tel responded.

The old king walked back to his seat. He took a sip from the cup, as Colin could do no more than simply stare in wonder. Colin rubbed his chest, hoping to erase the memory of the pain and wipe away the sense of responsibility that was no creeping into his soul. He shook his head and said, "It can't be me, I'm not special and I've never done anything but fail. How am I supposed to confront Xyrus? I can't do the things he can, the things you can."

"You think control of the uR is unique?" O'Tel asked.

"I've only heard of such powers existing in your race, at least until. . ."

O'Tel interrupted before Colin fully had to revisit the memory. "Perception blinds you to the truth of such things. We Ter'Ok'Zhu are born with a greater connection to the uR and thus are ability to wield its wonders seems inimitable, but the uR itself is not something that is unique to our race. Have you never had an unexplainable push of intuition? Has your desire for something never been so great, that your will alone has seemed to bring it to you?"

Colin paused; he had no argument, "Well of course."

"Then you too have walked the same path as I, simply with your eyes closed instead," O'Tel replied.

Colin said, "You speak of it as though it were as simple a breathing."

O'Tel laughed at the statement, for its truth was bold. "Conceded young Kinison, yet it is as simple as that. The uR is a part of everything. It holds no explanation, control of it cannot be found in some simple form of understanding, nor can any instrument measure it. It is life, an energy that exists in us and around us. We are all bound to it as much as it is bound to us. It is in that that everything, every piece of life is connected.

Now some, such as the girl we must save, are born with a natural ability to connect with the uR, beyond even the level that those of my race have. To those few Mavens, the things that you see as wonders are no more fanciful than how you view your own ability to walk and talk. It is simply an extension of themselves, a natural part of their being. Yet even those not touched this way are connected to the uR, as it connects us all. It is through looking within that you find the path to such control."

"So how did Xyrus come to possess this power?" Colin asked.

"I fear his new found ability may be from a dark source, rather than any natural cause and that prospect chills me to the core."

"But how?" Colin asked.

O'Tel breathed deep, "A question I myself have been disputing that since his attack at the council. I have denied the truth for fear of the consequences of accepting it."

O'Tel waved a hand over the glass table at his side. A holograph of Xyrus attack on his home planet appeared inches above it. O'Tel froze the display on an image of Xyrus holding the Jahan; it was glowing in his hand. He spoke to Colin, "Do you see the sword that he wields?"

Colin looked closer and noticed that the sword was visibly glowing, far brighter than any weapon Colin had seen before, save one. "It radiates like that one, but how?" No energy blade can emit power like that. It defies logic."

O'Tel shook his head, "No. It defies logic as you've come to know it. That blade is as old as time itself, the twin of the one that now hangs on the wall before us, that Xyrus wields the Jahan, the dark blade of the Malef can mean that he is their herald; their sword bearer."

Even more confused Colin continued to stare at Xyrus as he said, "Who are the Malef?"

"A race consumed with destruction, as old as my own. We thought them gone, banished from the known universe, bound by an ancient pact sealed by those very swords. It seems as though they have found a way to sever that pact and Xyrus seems their agent in doing so."

"Banished? Pact? How do I fit into this Master O'Tel? What are we doing? What is Xyrus's ploy?" Colin asked.

O'Tel rose up and walked over to Colin. He placed a hand on his shoulder and spoke, "The Malef King, upon his defeat in the battle that bound his people from this space, spoke of a dark prophecy. He spoke of a child, one that would be born baring the mark of his people, and this child would break the pact, which was sworn on the swords, allowing his people to return and rule over all.

This chosen child would not only bear the mark, but be born of mixed and royal blood.

For ages we Ter'Ok'Zhu have watched for such a child, for the few that knew of the prophecy feared it. Ours is a dying race Colin. Our time in this realm is spent. More and more of my people have crossed on to the next existence, freeing themselves from the cycle of life, but the cost of our own enlightenment is the uncertainty of the legacy we leave behind. The coming of this child was inevitable however; what few refused to look at was the greater consequence of such a child's fate. You see there are some things in this existence, which defy our ability to change; events that are so tied to our existence that no matter what choices we make we must meet them.

Fools would see this child dead, rather than accept such a truth and thus we have watched, waited for this chosen child to be born. We have found two children born in this generation, one is the princess that Xyrus has now kidnapped; the other Colin is you."

Colin shook his head and walked away frantic. "That's impossible. It can't be me. My father was a senator, not of royal blood. Humans don't even have royalty anymore."

O'Tel did not move, "What of your mother Colin? Did Arthur not speak of her to you?"

Tears in his eyes, Colin refused to give a vocal response. The memory of his mother cut too deep for him to pierce into too deeply.

"I know why it brings you pain Colin, but..."

Before O'Tel could finish Colin slammed a fist into the wall. The ship squealed in response. "Don't patronize me; you can't know that kind of pain," Colin shot back.

Colin walked over to the side of the bay, stood next to the window and stared out into the depths of space trying to escape the conversation. He fought hard to expel the memories, to withhold the tears. Even the briefest mention of her had been like a spark to the gasoline that was his pain. Colin had so long avoided his past and especially now he did not want to face it.

O'Tel could feel Colin's pain pulse through the uR, so deep seeded that it was nearly overpowering. He wanted to let the boy escape, to avoid prodding such an agonizing memory; but Colin's pain showed a lack of understanding concerning his true heritage.

Finally, O'Tel offered, "Your mother was royalty Colin, a fact that was no doubt hidden from you."

"I told you there isn't any royalty on earth anymore."

"Did you know her Colin?"

At last, the dam burst and the tears escaped his prison, his voice cracked as he spoke. "She died after I was born. I only knew her for the briefest moment of my life, memories that I'll never be able to enjoy. So no, I never truly knew her."

O'Tel said, almost in a whisper, "She was not human Colin. Your mother was Fa'Sham's sister, a princess of the Bellat people. Your birth was hidden from them, for such a thing would carry a great dishonor amongst their people, regardless of their birthright."

Colin's mouth hung agape. He could only mutter one word in response, "Why?"

"Her love for your father was instantaneous, but utterly forbidden amongst her people. They risked a great deal for each other, but love will do such things to people."

The realization of what O'Tel was saying began to sink in and the weight of his fate began to settle in on Colin. He looked back to space, "Then I'm doomed, we're all doomed. More sorrow, more dead and it's all going to be because of me."

O'Tel reached his side. "No. There is no certainty that you are the child that the Malef King spoke of, only that you fit the prophecy itself."

O'Tel waved a hand and a hologram of Zhu materialized before them. "She's beautiful," Colin said.

"She too has the mark and could be the child of the prophecy."

"But you said that there is no escaping this prophecy, so what are we doing then?" Colin asked.

"I fear the Dark Lord plans to use her to fulfill the prophecy," O'Tel said.

"You think he will turn her to his cause?"

"No."

"Then what?" Colin asked.

O'Tel stared at the image of the girl in front of him, the child that he had raised and come to know as his own. He stared at her and a feeling of dread took over his face. He replied, "I fear he plans to kill her."

CHAPTER TWENTY

In the horizon, the sun slowly rose over the crest of Mount Arras. Through the swollen black clouds that hung high in the sky, its ray filtered across the countryside in a haze of crimson. A great wind tore across the landscape, causing the stalks of red grass to dance about as if they wished to be free of the soil below.

Planted in the middle of the field was a giant white Ziggurat, home to the Temple of A'Zag. The temple, a pentagon shaped building lay on top of two square sections. Pillars and statues carved from black stone, that spoke of violent wars and their triumphant heroes lined the middle section whereas the lower section was simply plain and functional. A staircase sprung up from the ground and reached all the way up to the base of the temple.

The temple's exterior was solid stone. It bore no markings, not any detail that would lend to its identification. At first glance, it seemed as though the temple was dropped from the heavens and that, the earth had spewed forth the sections below to catch it. On the eastern side of the temple, at the base of the pentagon was a simple arched opening that allowed the sun to rain its warmth on the inner chamber.

Inside the temple it was dark as night. The sun had begun to rise on the horizon, but its position had not gotten high enough for the room to bask in its glow. The only light in the room was from the red glowing timbers that rested in five black steel bowls. These bowls were placed in direct relation to each corner of the building. Their fire had since burned down.

Behind each bowl of fire, resting beside the wall were five white pillars. Like five outstretched fingers, these pillars were obviously not part of the temple, but rather clearly, the temple had been build around them instead. The pillars were not smooth, nor did they rise in a perfect line. Time had taken its toll on the white rock, carving countless deep wrinkles into the rock.

Black metal bands wrapped around each digit of the pillar, ominous rings that belched power into the air. Dark red runes lined each ring in a language unfamiliar to any of the Belgae.

In the center of the room, carved into the stone floor was a giant ring. Large Belgae runes that bore the words, *Strength*, *Power*, *Victory* and *Death* were inscribed in gold. In the center of this ring, which was bordered by the bowls of fire, was an X shaped altar.

Stains of blood decorated its base, speaking silently of its malevolent purpose.

The archway at the base of the room was by far the most intricate piece of decoration within the room. Along the extended frame, a serpent's body was relieved into the stone, appearing as though the architect was more of an alchemist and had turned the beast's flesh into stone. Even more elaborate then that was the keystone. A'Zag's face screamed out in anger and hate. Sharpened teeth, deep cheek bones and a heavy brow were the most prominent features, but even the smallest hair seemed alive, even though the stone was frozen in time.

The sun rose and broke over Mount Arras in the distance and its light suddenly flooded the room. In the back, two steel doors slowly opened. From their base entered Xyrus, followed by a high priest and two of his disciples.

The high priest wore a crimson robe that covered his body from his neck to his toes, save for his left arm, which was fully exposed. Golden ropes were wrapped ceremoniously around his elbow, shoulders, rib cage and waist. On his head, a large skull of a Dzarth obscured the majority of his face. Small horns dotted its crown and the top of its skull rose up to a crest. Huge eye sockets dominated the front of it, with two nostrils below them. On each side of the skull were two oversized tusks.

His bare arm was covered in tattooed runes. He wore a golden bracer on his forearm and a black leather glove. He carried a long golden staff.

His disciples were much less clothed. Their physiques chiseled and perfect were a reflection on their dedication to their faith. The only clothing they wore was a black hood, enough material to cover their more private areas and half sleeves that began at their elbow then billowed out past their hands to a gaping opening. Along their body, bits of bones were attached as if by some permanent adhesive rather than chained together. On their waist they wore a leather belt with an oversized buckle that bore the image of A'Zag.

The two disciples held in their grasp an unconscious Zhu. Her outfit was wet and stained with dirt. Her hair was matted to her head, which fell down slumped and lifeless. Zhu's feet dragged along the floor as the two men took her further into the room. Xyrus rose a hand up and stopped the other all followed suit.

Xyrus spoke, "I never fully tasted the power that lies in this temple such as I do now Malak."

The high priest dipped his head in respect. "A'Zag, it is said, raised the five pillars himself. I am sure it is his mark on this sacred site that you now feel Lord Xyrus."

Without looking back, Xyrus replied, "She must be prepared, the filth of the Ter'Ok'Zhu washed from her body."

Malak, the high priest nodded and then clapped his hands. His two disciples dragged her to the back of the room. There they held her in under an ornate arch. Crafted from random bits of skeletal remains, the top of the structure had two large holes on either side and a channel that spanned from each edge to the center.

Malak walked to the wall next to the arch. A large chain and pulley system rested, though its purpose was difficult to discern. Along the floor next to the chain was a lever, a simple steel rod that extended up to Malak's chest. He reached out, pulled back on it and the enormous chain creaked to life. Above the chamber, the sounds of an ancient mechanical system crept to life. Metal that had seen rare use, screamed out as it turned and the vibrations of its movement shook the whole room. The chain, with links nearly as thick as half a man, began moving up into the ceiling counter clockwise.

On the ceiling above the arch, two circular hatches slowly lurched open. Behind was not light, but rather the murky darkness of the crimson liquid that poured forth, as mere drips at first and then a solid stream. It filled the holes on both sides of the top of the arch.

Soon the channels spewed forth a solid black liquid stream toward the center of the arch. Not only did this process change the color of the once crimson liquid, but also its consistency, turning it far more thick, much like tar.

Beneath the center of the arch, still limp, was Zhu. Each disciple firmly held onto one of her arms. The liquid, having reached the center of the arch, flowed down in a solid stream, oozing over her forehead, staining her once white clothes.

The contact woke Zhu back to life. Her mind was disoriented; she remembered a battle, her Master Paow, such pain and then that horribly evil face of the man responsible for it all. His laugh echoed in her ears, vividly real. She blinked her eyes, trying to focus them and gain a bearing on her surroundings. Shock and hatred overcame her as her vision cleared and before her she saw that the laugh was not emanating from her memory but rather its source was real and directly in front of her; the very man that had kidnapped her and killed Master Paow.

"NO!" she screamed out, releasing her pain into the word.

Xyrus stalked over to her, his confidence concentrated into the smile on his lips. "Still such fight, it's no wonder why they want you dead."

Zhu struggled against her captors as he snaked his way even closer. She loathed everything about him and wanted nothing more than to strike out and find a piece of revenge for the loss of her master. She was still too weak, a problem she knew that time would eventually remedy.

Xyrus stopped mere inches in front of her face. He raised his hand up to her cheek and ran the back of his fingers along her jaw. "So much like your mother." Xyrus grabbed her by the throat and looked over to Malak, "Increase the stream to full."

Malak nodded and walked over to the arch. He grabbed a bone jutting along its side, pulled it out fully and then began turning it clockwise. In response, the black stream of ooze increased its flow exponentially.

It poured down over Zhu's body, saturating her. Xyrus released his grip and walked toward the altar, her screams echoed out behind him.

Pain, searing pain tore across her body. The breath in her lungs was pulled away, as if by millions of microscopic invisible hands. Zhu looked up and saw his back to her. The liquid burned like fire against her flesh, but this was her chance. A surge of anger took over her body, she felt it try to overcome her training, begging her to feed into such a primal emotion, its power threatening to consume her. The image of Master Paow came to her mind and she calmed herself. She washed away the feeling, focused her mind and searched for some sense of peace amongst the chaos about her.

Strength was needed and deep within her core, she found a small reserve. Zhu stopped fighting and flailing against her captors. She pulled her body towards the ground into a ball. As the two disciples pulled against her, trying to raise her back up, she exploded out with them. Not only physically, but a surge of unseen force from the uR, drawn from that deep reserve, rode behind her movement.

The disciples flew up off her, unable to maintain their grip against such a force. They smashed into either side of the arch; their bodies giving where as the structure did not.

The loud thud of the two of them hitting the floor did not give Xyrus any pause. He continued to the altar. With a wave of his hand, the archway in front of him began to creek and shudder. From within its core a large worn steel door, exceedingly decorated, began to extend down toward the floor, closing the room.

Zhu stood up and stepped out of the ooze after him. The flash of gold headed for her face caused her to stop. She raised both arms to her face to block the blow. The horned head of the staff made contact with her forearms, sending her back a step. Malak spun in front of her, blocking her path to Xyrus.

He used the momentum of his spin to thrash the staff at her again. This time she was ready for him. A swift kick both caught the staff and pinned it to the floor below. A solid push down with her foot, reinforced with the uR and the staff snapped under the force. Malak pulled the broken half of his staff away and thrust it toward her. Zhu simply grabbed the end and pulled hard. The high priest flung forward, flailing off balance. Zhu struck him in the chest as he reached her and sent the high priest flying across the room.

His body landed beside Xyrus's feet. The Dark Lord did not even offer so much as a glance down at him. "You know the price for failure Malak," Xyrus said.

Purple electricity rose up along Xyrus's forearm and he whipped it down at the high priest. Malak's scream was as loud as it was short lived. Then in a breath, the high priest was cold and still.

Zhu charged at Xyrus, the broken piece of Malak's staff at her side. She lunged forward and stabbed at the Dark Lord. He spun about and raised a hand to intercept her blow. The steel of the staff melted into liquid as it met his flesh. As she came near, he snatched her by the wrist and pulled her close. "You fight a battle you cannot win child."

She tried to strike him with her free hand, but no blow could reach its mark. Eventually Xyrus caught that hand as well and spun her around so that her back was pressed up against him and her arms were crossed over her chest. "Let me free coward," she yelled.

"Do you not feel its bite?" he countered.

Zhu bent down and sprung into the air, kicking her legs back into his chest. The momentum from the blow sent her flying forward out of his grasp. She rolled back up to her feet and readied herself for another assault. Then the pain took hold of her, striking deep into her chest at her heart. Zhu collapsed to a knee and screamed a muffled yelp of pain.

"I see the poison has finally taken its course with you."

Zhu felt the vileness of it beginning to surge throughout her veins. It attacked her body like acid burning her from the inside out.

Xyrus laughed as she writhed about. "The blood of the Dzarth now has made its way into your system. To most this pain you now feel would signal the inevitable sign of your impending death, though you are not like most are you? You too have a mastery over the uR and it is that skill that saves your life here in this moment."

Once more Zhu searched down inside of herself for the strength that she had called upon earlier, her own personal connection to the uR itself. She allowed the bits of life that were pure in the room to flow through her and give her strength. It brought her life, where now only the threat of death existed.

Crouched in meditation she did not hear or see Xyrus approach her. He grabbed her by the throat and hoisted her into the air. "Do not shift your focus child, the poison is strong and will require every bit of your concentration if you are to survive it."

Zhu struggled against his grip as he moved her over to the altar. "You can try to strike me down and you may indeed succeed, but I assure you that the cost will be your own life as well."

As Zhu attempted to focus on her attack, she felt the truth of his words. The sting of the Dzarth's blood bit ten times harder and so she relented and refocused her mind on sustaining her own life.

Xyrus slammed her down upon the altar and with a wave of his hand black steel bands clamped down her arms. Tiny needles inside the bands pierced her flesh and she screamed out in pain. "The binds shall feed your body with the poison to ensure that your mind stays focused on that task, rather than some foolish attempt at escape."

Xyrus ran a finger down her cheek. She recoiled away at the touch. "Your suffering will be at an end soon enough my sweet child, soon enough indeed!"

Colin awoke from his dream, slightly confused, the firm grip of O'Tel's hand clasped onto his shoulder. He began to fight then calmed down and asked, "What's wrong? Are we there?"

Colin shook his head as he rose out of bed, still in his jump suit for that very reason. O'Tel stepped back and replied, "No, but the Slai'Nor tells me that we must drop into real space earlier than I had planned. It would appear that Xyrus anticipated a direct assault."

"How could he?" Colin asked.

"He is a great general Colin, though his goals may be corrupt; do not allow that to cloud your perception of his skill in the game of war."

O'Tel stepped closer to Colin and placed a hand on his chest, it glowed a bright white as it made contact. The energy carried into O'Tel's eyes and he spoke, "We are soon to come to a difficult crossroad Colin, where the darkness shall threaten to consume us from all ends. When all seems lost, let this light your way."

With that said, the energy channeled off into Colin and then disappeared. O'Tel released him and looked away, as if listening to an unreal voice in the room. After a beat, he looked back to Colin and said, "We near the drop to real space, we must move to the cockpit."

AS they walked out of his room, Colin asked, "How do you know that?"

O'Tel looked at him, "The Slai'Nor told me."

Colin shook his head, "Amazing."

They entered the cockpit of the Slai'Nor; control panels lit the interior in a soft glow. O'Tel took his seat in the center and a second one formed up behind him for Colin. O'Tel reached out to the panel in front of him, his hands flowing across them like a bird over water. His presses of each button were so subtle that they could barely be seen by the naked eye. The large panel at the front of the cockpit sprung to life, dissolving into a landscape of the space before them.

The Slai'Nor did not travel through space like most ships. Being born from the masterful hands of O'Tel himself, the technology onboard the ship was unique unto itself. Outside of the ship, the familiar stream of a wormhole, much like that seen during passage through the jump gates, streamed along past the ship. This stream however was not the familiar blue as that of the jump gates, but rather a cacophony of color that seemed to move independently of the ships direction.

"What is that?" Colin asked.

"The uR Colin, at least in part. We pass through it, moving within the streams of energy that connect the universe, a feat you'll not find in any other ship. It is what allows us to make this trip with such speed."

O'Tel pressed a group of buttons and two faces cut into the display, Fa'Sham and Lieutenant James Johnson. "Prepare yourselves; we drop to real space shortly. I fear our arrival is expected as well."

Fa'Sham roared his approval, "By Wo'Tinath's will, I have no taste for sneaking about. We shall be ready to face our glory and allow death to judge the honorable."

"We shall follow your lead Master O'Tel," Johnson said.

"May the uR be our guide," O'Tel said to both of them. He pulled a lever back and reality began to blur. Space and time slowed and bent. A pinprick of real space tore into the sea of color and came screaming toward them.

In space, orbiting around Belga was four massive security stations. Each sat cross sectioned on either side of the planet, allowing them the ability to cover the entirety of its surface.

The stations themselves were cylindrical at their center. Two interconnected cones that flowed together spun in opposite directions. Time had taken its toll on the stations, leaving countless spots of scars and burns. Blackened windows allowed its occupants a view to the outside but prevented anyone from seeing within. Hundreds of small lights decorated the bulk of the cylinders.

On the top was the command tower. A saucer that peaked off the main section, the command center's movement was independent of the rest of the station itself. Large triple enforced eight-foot thick panels of glass ran along its center. Inside was a hive of movement.

From the center of the station extended four arms set out in a cross that connected to a ring, which also rotated. The center ring had two giant bay doors that housed an armada of Belgae Nergal star fighters.

The Nergal fighters were extremely sleek and petite in their design; primarily functioning as fodder to hold over the battle, while their larger warships inflicted the main casualties. The Nergal fighters were highly agile, but packed only a small amount of firepower.

The cockpit was oval shaped, with a glass hatch on top. A long neck connected it to a wide body, which in turn housed scythe shaped wings. Two gun ports rested within concaved ports below the cockpit.

At both the top and base of the station were thick antennas that extended obnoxiously far out into space. A beam of energy shot out to the other stations, as well as two satellites that hovered above the planets poles, interconnecting them and then creating a sphere of energy that protected the planet. Though not as impervious as the shield on Ter'Ar'Tor, this sphere of energy prevented any physical mass from reaching Belga.

Inside Security Station One's command center sat Commander Gal'Mator. Dressed in yellow and black armor, he sat in the center of the room, a literal overlord watching over those in his command.

Suddenly an alarm went off and the room's lights switched nearly off, red lights replaced the normal white glow that filled the room. Commander Gal'Mator shouted, "On screen now! Fetch me an answer for these alarms you foul dogs or heads will roll!"

On the main screen in the front of the room, a giant radar appeared, displaying the space around Belga. In the distance far away from Belga, a small blip flashed to life.

"Spatial anomaly in beta sector," an officer from the lower portion of the command deck said.

"Launch all fighters. It is as Lord Xyrus has predicted. Ready the station for battle."

In the hanger bay of the Security Station, Belgae pilots rushed to empty chairs, sectioned in large open pods. As they sat down, two assistants rushed up to their side, locking them into their chair. A large black metal circlet lowered onto their brow. Connected to it were a mass of tubes, wires and a single large ribbed grey tube in the rear.

As the circlet found its place snug on the pilots head, a solid glass plate hissed as it extended down past his chin.

When the pilot was secured, the entire chair shot down through the floor to the hanger bay below. In the bay, the pilots were careened through a series of metallic racks until they found themselves above an empty Nergal fighter. A crane then took hold of their chair, like some giant metallic beak enveloping them whole, and lowered them into the front of their vessel. As the chair secured itself, the pilot grabbed a hold of the control stick between his legs, a long vertical pole that stretched from his sternum down to the floorboard. His other hand gripped the throttle, which rested along the left of the cabin. The hatch closed as the engine of the Nergal fighter roared to life, a blast of white-red energy spat forth from behind the craft and then it rose into the air. Ship after ship followed this procedure, running smoothly as though they were all on a giant unseen factory line. In the distance, the giant bay doors opened to the black of space and vomited out the fighters within.

In the black of space, hundreds of miles away from Belga and the Security Stations, a pool of energy tore into the fabric of space. Through it exited the Slai'Nor, followed by the Harin'Horn and the eighteen Hammer Class Fighters of Reaper Squadron.

They flew together without any specific formation, though all clearly headed for the same destination; Belga.

In the approaching distance the armada of Nergal fighters progressively grew in size and speed. It would be only a matter of moments and the two sides would converge.

The Security Stations burst forth with movement as plain exteriors shifted aside allowing massive gun turrets and torpedo stacks to emerge. Without hesitation the Stations opened fire on the incoming threats. Giant beams of energy screamed across the dead of space.

The stations were twice the size of most battleships and thus the armament was made to match that mass. In the case that such large targets were to assault the planet, they would prove a most formidable match, however, against this small attack force their weaponry was as effective as swinging a sledge hammer to kill a fly.

The Slai'Nor pushed forward, taking a noticeable position as the leader of the force. The Reapers formed up in a line two by nine deep and the Harin'Horn took the rear. The Belgae fighters were a breath away from entering firing range, but their impatience overrode their prudence. Lasers poured forth at random, lighting up the void of space, but equally missing their targets in whole.

The Slai'Nor and its group pushed forward, anxiously waiting for their own weapons to come into range. As they did, they opened fire in return. The Slai'Nor's forward batteries erupted in a stream of fire, nearly as thick as the core of the ship itself. The blast tore through the oncoming enemy fighters, those not consumed by the beam exploded along its shaft.

Each side screamed past each other, dotted with explosions from shots that connected on either side. Neither group deviated from their course and the Slai'Nor answered those who dared to attempt to challenge its dominance.

As O'Tel and the others neared Security Station One, the mass of the Belgae fighters doubled back and poured back down upon them.

Inside the Slai'Nor, O'Tel pulled the image of Lieutenant Johnson to the front of his display. "Lieutenant Johnson, engage the second station, but be cautious of the main canons. I fear a direct shot to any of your fighters may prove fatal."

"Understood Master O'Tel, Reaper Two out," Johnson replied.

Another wave of his hand and Fa'Sham now filled the screen. "Provide them with cover Fa'Sham. The Slai'Nor is more than capable of defending itself for this."

"Of course M'Lord," Fa'Sham replied.

The screen snapped back to a dual display of the space in front of the ship, as well as a three dimensional layout of the battle field. O'Tel pressed the control sticks forward and the ship accelerated forcefully in response. His left hand tilted slightly and the Slai'Nor banked off from the formation toward Security Station One. Six of the Reapers broke off in the opposite direction toward the next closet Security Station.

The other twelve Reapers veered up and flipped around in an elegant one hundred eighty degree turn that sent them back toward the oncoming mass of Belgae Nergal fighters. Laser fire poured forth from both sides, most connecting with the Nergal fighters.

The Reapers skill was by far superior to that of their opponents and they danced in and out of the oncoming laser fire. The Nergal Fighters were primarily used as fodder in the overall agenda in the Belgae offensive, as was apparent by their blatant disregard for their own safety and their deficient fighting skills. Their losses were an acceptable statistic of this battle.

The Reapers formed into four groups of three. They engaged the Belgae force, taking out as many fighters as would cross their path. The field of battle became a fast dance of laser fire, explosions, debris and chaos.

Inside of the Slai'Nor, O'Tel focused on the main screen. Every subtle movement of his hands on the control sticks adjusted the Slai'Nor's path. He wove the mighty ship between both the oncoming foray from the Security Station and the multitude of laser fire from the few fighters that trailed behind them.

O'Tel said something in a language that Colin did not remotely recognize. As if in response to the Ter'Ok'Zhu king, a console rose up to his side. On it was a Holo display of the fighters behind them. Directly in front of that were two controls, shaped like gloves with a comfortable sized opening for one's hand to be inserted.

O'Tel looked back to Colin, "Rear weapons. The controls are self intuitive and will react to your movements. Simply squeeze your hand to fire, do you understand?"

"No, but I'll manage," Colin responded.

Colin turned to the new console and inserted a hand into each control. As his flesh made contact with the steel a liquid seemed to seize up around him. He jumped back at the sensation.

"Do not fear it Colin, she simply conforms to you, though I know the sensation may seem odd at first," O'Tel said before Colin could ask him a question.

"Oh is that all that was," Colin said, the sarcasm thick off his tongue.

He stared down at the Holo display, thin crosshairs now appeared amongst the ships that followed them. Colin sat down and took hold of the controls once more. As he moved his hands the crosshairs moved in response. As one locked onto one of the Nergal fighters, Colin squeezed his grip tight. A bright blue laser bolt fired out and tore through his target. The fighter exploded in a burst of flame. The attack sent the other ships into a frenzy of movement, now aware of the danger that lay before them.

The Slai'Nor was now upon the security station. One of the shots from the station's canons grazed the Slai'Nor's hull, leaving a deep black singe. Next to the massive station the Slai'Nor seemed no more than a gnat flying along its hull.

The main guns lit up space as best as they could. The Slai'Nor passed by the station's outer ring. The number of Nergal fighters that pursued the ship doubled, filing their ranks from the station itself as the extra launched out after Ter'Ok'Zhu ship.

O'Tel weaved the ship down along the center core of the station, preventing the main guns on the outer ring from firing anymore. Now all he had to concern himself with was avoiding the incoming fire of the Nergal fighters that so viciously pursued them. Then bits of light shot up from the station. A small group of light canons along the core section emerged from the station.

Colin's learning curve was extremely quick and the bolts fired from the Slai'Nor almost all found their mark on the enemy ships. Though just as quickly as one fighter would be destroyed, two more would appear to take its place.

Finally they reached the bottom of the station. The giant antennae which fired off a huge stream of energy as bright as a sun toward the other two stations, passed below the Slai'Nor as it shot back into space away from the station.

The main guns instantly opened fire on the ship, one bolt made direct contact on the ships belly, causing a large explosion that rocked the ship.

The metal of the antennae was different from that of the station itself. A black metal that was it not for the sheen of light reflecting on its surface, would have blended seamlessly into the space around it.

O'Tel banked the Slai'Nor around, bringing it into a straight descent at the base of the antennae itself. The Nergal fighters screamed past them, unable to match the vicious maneuver.

Inside the ship, O'Tel fired the main guns of the Slai'Nor and the giant beam poured forth, this time its target was the Security Station's main antennae. A large explosion billowed up toward the Slai'Nor as the beam made contact with the black steel, but still the Slai'Nor pushed forward, its main cannon still firing.

In the distance, the other members of Reaper Squadron cheered at the sight of the massive explosion.

On board the Harin'Horn, Fa'Sham raised a hand to silence his own cheering crew, "The shield still stands, hold your cheer till it falls."

He saw O'Tel's face on his display, along with that of Lieutenant Johnson's. O'Tel spoke, "Lieutenant Johnson, abort your attack. They've forged the antennae out of Trillium, your weapons will have no effect on it."

Fa'Sham hung his head, "Then we are lost?"

O'Tel looked up to him, "No, Fa'Sham, hope has not yet escaped our grasp."

On the Slai'Nor O'Tel looked over to Colin, then back to the display. "Brace yourself," he said.

"How?"

"Not you Colin, the ship."

"Colin's eyes went wide, "What?"

The Slai'Nor bent its course down slightly, yet still towards the base of the Security Station. The main guns continued to fire, tearing into the hull of the station, rather than the antennae. A second explosion belched up and engulfed the Slai'Nor.

The ship crashed into the hull of the station as flames erupted up around it. The Slai'Nor bore its way through layers of metal, its own hull burning bright as the main cannon melted away as much of the station as was possible.

O'Tel was utterly focused on his current dissection of the station, Colin simply fired all of the Slai'Nor's rear weapons, inflicting as much collateral damage as was possible. He looked over at the ancient king, "My father never told the Ter'Ok'Zhu were crazy."

"When convention does not offer us a viable solution, then sometimes we must find an create our own answer, regardless of how far removed from sanity it may seem. We must find an alternative avenue for success."

"If that's the Ter'Ok'Zhu version of improvisation okay, but this is one hell of an alternative avenue. Where are we headed?"

"Our goal is the station's central power core," O'Tel said.

"How are we suppose to find that?" Colin asked.

"With faith."

Laser fire struck the ship, shaking its interior. Colin looked up and saw four Nergal fighters on the Holo. He fired back at them, though with the constant shifting in their own trajectory it was greatly more difficult to get a clean shot.

Colin focused hard and time seemed to slow down slightly. He could feel and almost see where the Nergal fighters would be rather than where they were. He knew that he needed to finish them off prior to entering the core and his hands squeezed, then time snapped back to its normal pace.

The Nergal fighters exploded as the shots tore into them. The last fighter passed through another as it exploded, but then it crashed into the hull and tore apart into pieces.

The Slai'Nor burst through a layer of the station and shot into the central power chamber. A huge open space that housed a single generator which powered the entire station. The generator was made up of four posts that converged together halfway down their length at the center of the room. In their center was a great ball of fire, like a very small sun. Below that was a large hexagon, with claws at each point that shot out beams of energy into the sphere.

"A fusion reactor, unthinkable that a race so bent on conquest could master such a beneficial technology. A shame it is wasted on such warmongering."

The Slai'Nor fired its main gun at one of the claws around the sphere. The blast tore through it sending shards of metal and fire into the air. The sphere began to fluctuate, growing and then shrinking in no calculated manner. Its surface began to bubble with energy, spirals of flame blasted out around it. Then, in the blink of an eye the sphere imploded down upon itself and was gone. The posts went dead, black and lifeless. The Slai'Nor simply hovered in midair watching.

O'Tel stood up and looked to Colin, "Brace yourself Colin."
"For what? Why aren't we going?"
"There is no time to escape this."
O'Tel clasped his hands together. He focused his mind, drew in the uR from the world around him. In the distance he could sense the surge of power about to burst forth, time was short. In between his palms he felt the warmth of the orb of energy as it was forged along his flesh. His hands began to glow a bright gold. The hue intensified until it took on a supernatural appearance that consumed his body.

The reactor blew as a surge of unseen force erupted outwards, tearing apart the posts and sending a giant shockwave out toward the exterior of the station. Directly in its path sat the Slai'Nor.

O'Tel thrust his arms out, no longer able to wait and the orb which was in between his palms expanded exponentially fast.

The orb consumed the Slai'Nor, covering it in a golden sphere near seconds before the shock wave hit.

O'Tel remained still, his eyes closed as he stood in meditation. He spoke, "Colin, take the controls. We must leave. NOW!"

"I don't know how. . ." Colin began to say.

"Now is not the time for doubt or argument, only action."

Colin moved into O'Tel's chair and took the helm. He mimicked the motions he had so recently seen O'Tel making earlier.

Shockingly the ship moved, not nearly as fluid as before, but still it responded to his hands. The Slai'Nor veered back down toward the opening at which it had entered the chamber. O'Tel's voiced was sharp, "No. Head to the walls, it will be swifter."

Colin nodded and moved the controls. The ship obeyed and they banked back to the nearest wall. The shockwave had severely compromised the station's integrity. O'Tel said, "Fire the main cannon Colin. The generator is about to explode."

Colin squeezed both hands and the main cannon fired out toward the station's wall, tearing through it and exposing the black exterior of space. The Slai'Nor sped forward as the reactor went nova behind it.

A giant fireball tore through the Security Station sending metal and death exploding outward. Through that explosion spat out the Slai'Nor, still protected by the golden orb O'Tel had created.

The rest of the Reapers and those onboard the Harin'Horn erupted in cheer as the smoldering remnants of the Security Station sunk down into the atmosphere of Belga. Gravity and the friction of reentry tore it apart.

With the station destroyed, the energy beam and shield around the planet was fractured and gone. The battle in space however did not rest. Nergal fighters continued their assault on the rest of Reaper Squadron and the Harin'Horn.

The golden orb surrounding the Slai'Nor dimmed and the ship screamed through space, back towards the battle. Onboard the Harin'Horn, Fa'Sham sat in his chair, his fellow warriors cheered. Again, he waved them silent. "Ready the ship for descent. The time for honor and death is at hand."

Together the Harin'Horn and the Slai'Nor dove down toward Belga's surface. Reaper Squadron continued to dart about space, engaging the Nergal fighters in a fierce battle. "Safe journey my friends," Johnson said to both ships.

"Pray we are successful and shall be rejoining you soon enough," O'Tel responded.

"If we die, make sure they sing fanciful tales of this day Johnson." Fa'Sham offered.

Both ships tore through the planet's atmosphere, friction lit their hulls on fire as they descended to the surface. As they reached the lower atmosphere, the ships flew across the landscape, coming to rest along a mountain range.

The hatches to the Slai'Nor and the Harin'Horn opened simultaneously. O'Tel and the others dispensed forth and gathered in between the two ships. As everyone made their way out, O'Tel stepped forth and pointed into the distance. A large Ziggurat sat along the horizon.

"The Temple of A'Zag, a most corrupt place," O'Tel said.

Fa'Sham stepped forward, his eyes pressed into a pair of binoculars. He lowered them from his eyes and asked, "Are you certain he holds the princess inside of it?"

O'Tel stared out across the plains before the, his vision clearly seeing that which no other there could, streams of uR, overall much darker than those elsewhere, flowed along the planet's surface. His eyes took in the flow, thousands of years of staring into the streams had taught him how to read its subtleties. His vision shifted to the Ziggurat itself. At its peak, a small bit of brightness shone through, vibrant blue sparks of life amongst the sea of darkness. They fought for freedom, but were drowned down by the mass of darkness around them. His gaze locked onto the Ziggurat as he spoke, "As much as I wish to be wrong, I am certain that the Dark Lord keeps her there. Worse yet I fear her life wanes and our time grows shorter with each passing breath. Let us hope that he does not know the true nature of that structure."

Colin stepped up to their side and Fa'Sham passed the binoculars to him. In the distance, Colin saw how dire a situation they had gotten themselves into. An army sat guard at the base of the Ziggurat and not simply men, but large war machines as well amongst them. This was not a group that was called together in response to the attack above the planet, but rather a force that had been ready and prepared for this exact situation.

Alone the Ziggurat itself, countless numbers of Shahd patrolled the walls. Large cannons were interspersed at different sections.

He spoke, "We're out numbered nearly fifty to one, they have heavy artillery at every strategic point and there is no chance for use of the element of surprise."

O'Tel and Fa'Sham looked at Colin as he lowered the binoculars and continued, "When do we start?"

Fa'Sham let out a hearty laugh and slapped him on the back, a loving blow that still sent Colin stumbling forward. "Such pride in this one Master O'Tel, so much like his father at that age."

"Overconfidence is the fold the fool wears as he walks along the cliffs edge Fa'Sham."

"Then what do we do?" Colin asked.

O'Tel said, "We offer Xyrus a prize that he cannot resist, so that his eyes are forced to focus on what we wish him to, rather than what he needs to."

Colin chided, "That bait would be what?"

O'Tel's eyes locked onto the army at the base of the Ziggurat. "My young Kinison, I shall strike the chord that lures the beast from his cave, while the rest of you rescue the princess."

Anger rose from the pit of Colin's stomach. How many would he have to lose before the world felt his debt was paid? "That's suicide; even your powers have limits."

O'Tel smiled and placed a hand on Colin's shoulder. Though he did not want it to, the move had an unnatural calming effect on Colin. O'Tel spoke, "My days draw to a close Colin and beyond that, Zhu's life carries a far greater significance in their future than my own."

"If you go to face that army, you'll die. I saw it in a dream on the Slai'Nor," Colin said.

"Perhaps death does indeed wait for me. Such is the risk required if her life is to be spared. I would gladly sacrifice my life for her."

"Then what of us?" Fa'Sham asked.

"When they have shifted their attention to me, you must make your way to the base of the temple. I fear anything more direct will only serve to alert them to the true nature of my own attack. The princess will be held in the highest chamber. Hurry now, time is against us."

Tar'Sham stepped up to them, "What of the ships? Who shall stay to guard them?"

"We cannot afford any men to do so my son," Fa'Sham answered.

"Allow me," O'Tel said. He closed his eyes and reached out a hand. The ground below the ships began to tremble. Then with a simple motion of his hand, the earth followed suit, as if he were simply playing with nothing more than dirt. A giant ring of dirt and rock rose up around the ships and engulfed them. Within the time it took, to make their getaway the dome of earth had consumed both ships.

A clench of his fist and the dirt solidified into a firm dome. Tar'Sham said, "I see then, you have solved that crisis Master O'Tel."

"Now hurry, I know not how long my distraction will hold their attention," O'Tel responded.

The others grabbed their gear and hurried off down the side of the mountain. Colin was the last to move, his feet refusing to cooperate. He looked back on O'Tel; though their time together was so short, he still felt a deep connection to him. He dismissed it to the shared qualities O'Tel and his father had and a simple sense of nostalgia for the man he had lost. That thought of his father fueled him. He turned back to the group of Bellat warriors and hurried to catch up with them.

O'Tel stopped at the crest of the mountain and stared at the hundreds of soldiers that covered the plain below. He thought of the countless battles he had endured the numerous opponents who had challenged him and how none prior could equal the importance of this single one now.

O'Tel closed his eyes and opened himself up to the world around him. O'Tel's true vision superseded a simple biological processing of optical impulses. His deep connection to the uR allowed him a sight within his consciousness. In this sight, he could see, feel and interact with the uR on an almost primal stage. He allowed that stream of power to surge into him, gathering up the natural uR that emanated from the planet itself. As it filtered through his body, penetrating his every cell a faint glow began to emit from his flesh.

As O'Tel opened his eyes, they burst with power, their natural blue beaming as if they were mere panes of glass holding back a raging river.

O'Tel reached up to the sky with both hands. Electricity shot out, arcing into the heavens above and generating a series of deep dark grey clouds that obscured any natural light.

He lowered his hands and the earth below him rose up like a giant board. O'Tel leaned forward and the piece of earth shot down the mountain, carrying him down toward the soldiers below. A massive sheet of dust rose up and trailed after him, marking his path.

CHAPTER TWENTY ONE

Captain Koral sat perched on the first level of the might Ziggurat that housed the temple of A'Zag. Fat, scarred and broken down from countless battles, Koral now simply moved the pieces on the board, a facility he readily accepted. His time entrenched amongst laser fire and other countless forms of assault had honed his perceptions to a point where he could quickly identify anything even slightly abnormal in his surroundings.

This present disturbance however, even his youngest child would have been able to notice. It also did not take a great deal of deduction to figure out that the man in the distance who shot electricity from his hands was none other than the Ter'Ok'Zhu King that Lord Xyrus had forewarned them about.

He yelled out to his company below, "He comes. Light up the cannons. Fire without mind or mercy and that goes for all of you filth. Pray he does not make it down that hill alive."

In response the four square bases below him in front of the Ziggurat whirred to life. Roughly three hundred feet across at their base, these giant cannons were primarily used against incoming spacecraft.

A huge saucer shaped command center elevated into the air on a large column. The saucer was roughly two-thirds the width of the massive base that housed it. Two discs on either side of the saucer extended out and from those two fifty foot cannons came. The sheer size of the parts moving created a tremor along the ground.

All four towers became erect in unison, swinging their cannons to bear aim on the man quickly approaching along the mountainside in the distance. One after another, they opened fire, enormous bolts of red energy tearing into the air and screaming out as they charged toward O'Tel.

In the distance, as the clouds above began to provide a shroud of darkness, O'Tel continued his descent down the hill.

Even as far as he was, he could feel the towers as they moved. He felt the first shot through the uR, sensed its trajectory. O'Tel did not alter his descent; rather he simply pressed forward, his natural instincts screaming at him to stop. His mind was sharp and he knew the bounds of his ability.

As the first bolt neared, he focused his mind on it. They would meet in but a beat more of time, yet that single beat was an infinite gap of time in relation to the time that O'Tel was able to perceive. His mind so in tune with the uR, that his every move was more automatic in process, as he had total control over his surroundings.

He grabbed a hold of the earth before him and pulled a large sheet up as a wall between himself and the incoming blast.

It exploded into a cloud of dust. The move was one that required a surgeon like precision, one second off in either direction would have resulted in death. However, the reward was a fine cloud of cover that would allow him to gather himself for a few more seconds before he made his final assault on the hundreds that sat waiting below.

The bass of the impacts from the cascade of fire told O'Tel that his identity was no secret to the Belgae soldiers. As he exited the dust cloud, he saw that not only the cannons were laying down fire at him, but a barrage of laser fire also shot forth from the soldiers as well.

Six groups of them formed in five by five battalions, stretched back three deep on the battlefield below. In front of the back third was a line of eighteen light tanks, the Galguran. The Galguran were as beautiful to behold, as they were deadly effective. A sleek body that hovered above the ground held two guns along each extended arm. In the middle of the that base was a small chamber for the pilot, slightly raised above him was a circular pod, that rotated and housed the tanks gunner. A large single cannon sat on one side of the pod, a smaller blaster on its other.

The smaller fire provided a nuisance which O'Tel either avoided or deflected with the uR, however, the blasts from the four main canons are what drew his utmost attention. Their strikes caused a mass of destruction about the hillside and O'Tel could only imagine his fate were he to have to encounter such a meeting.

His mind dashed for a solution when one of the shots hit all to close. The sheer amount of bedlam was beginning to cloud the uR and hinder his ability to react. Another blast tore into the ground directly in front of him. The explosion sent a sizeable boulder into the air. Something in O'Tel's mind clicked. Within seconds his consciousness focused on the hillside, searching desperately until he found it. His mind pulled hard and it tore through the dirt and rubble until it burst forth into the air before him.

The boulder was massive, easily fifty feet in diameter and like a pet; it followed its master, hovering in the air alongside of him. O'Tel's hand reached out and felt the boulder's smooth surface. Energy flowed out from his body and covered the entirety of the stone's surface. O'Tel reached back and then hurled it forward.

The boulder streaked across the plain, careened over the mass of soldiers and drew not only their fire, but that of the towers as well. O'Tel focused on keeping the stone on its path, protected by the shield he had placed around it.

BOOM! It smashed into the tower at the edge of the Ziggurat. The impact sent an eruption of flame and smoke into the air around it. The flame consumed the side of the Ziggurat in a grey shroud.

O'Tel landed at the base of the hill and smiled. Koral screamed, "KILL HIM!" and his forces roared forth their approval.

Colin, Fa'Sham and the rest of the Bellat warriors sat at the edge of the hillside. They stared at the side of the Ziggurat. The cannon that had risen at its base was massive and it poured forth fire at O'Tel in the distance. Colin pounded the rock in frustration. "We should be helping him, not ever he can hold out against those kind of odds."

Fa'Sham laid a hand on Colin's shoulder; his mighty grip calmed the young man's nerves. He spoke, "I bare no doubt in my mind that Master O'Tel has seen circumstances that dwarf the duress of even this situation Colin and more so than that it is his part to play in this. Remember, her rescue is the only end that qualifies this mission as a success."

Tar'Sham leaned in, "How are we even to approach without gaining notice?"

Fa'Sham looked back, "That my son is a question that even I have no answer for. Colin, how say you?"

Colin lifted his binoculars up and scanned the base of the Ziggurat. Belgae patrols guarded every portion of the wall. They were well trained as well, ignoring the chaos that was taking place in the field before them.

"I don't see any choice but a direct assault."

BOOM! The boulder smashed into the gun tower. Smoke and fire consumed the side of the Ziggurat where its fresh remains now laid. The Belgae soldiers, even with their extensive training, drew their attention away from their posts to the annihilation.

Fa'Sham smacked Colin on the back, "You see the old man has things well in hand. Now come, let us go to our glory!"

They charged out into the open, a hushed mass, fearless of the consequences. One of the Belgae guards saw the bit of movement and turned. Before he could vocalize a warning to his fellow guards, a bolt from Tar'Sham's blaster slammed into his chest. He flew back into the wall and his body fell limp.

That was enough of an alert in and of itself. The other Belgae turned their attention from the explosion to the intruders. They opened fire, which was gladly returned by the Bellat warriors. The whole of the provided cover as Fa'Sham, Colin and Tar'Sham hurried to the exterior wall.

Colin asked, "How thick do you think the wall is?"

Tar'Sham answered, "At least ten feet. Two detonators should be enough."

Colin nodded and he removed a small pack from his back. He withdrew two small circular discs, three inches wide and barely a half inch thick. Without a word, Fa'Sham took reached a mighty hand into the pack and pulled out two more of the discs. Tar'Sham looked at him, thoroughly irritated. "Father!" he said.

"Are you trying to take down the entire building?" Colin asked.

Fa'Sham laughed, "I hardly think such a structure would be so vulnerable. More importantly though is that this effort has but one chance for success, best to over compensate."

Colin shook his head, but relented and placed the two discs he had removed alongside of those that Fa'Sham had taken. Fa'Sham's large finger pressed each of them, a red light flashed to signal they were active. "I suggest we run now," Fa'Sham said.

The three followed his advice and rushed back to their cover, laser fire trailing after them. When they reached the cover of the rocks, Fa'Sham smiled over at Colin and Tar'Sham. "Would it really be such a loss if it did fall?"

"FA'SHAM!" Colin yelled, but before he could say anything more the bombs exploded.

A plume of fire and smoke barreled out into the air and then dissolved. Behind it, a large hole now gave entrance into the Ziggurat.

"Ha, you see more is always better," Fa'Sham exclaimed as they hurried their way into the new opening. The incoming fire had also lessened. A secondary benefit from the extra detonators.

Lasers fired past O'Tel like horizontal drops of rain, yet none could find their mark as he slowly danced through their mist. The first four battalions charged in behind the fire. Those on the outside of the front line rushed in around O'Tel. The rest of the Belgae simply help their position, firing their blasters in vain.

The ground rumbled as the tanks that rested in the middle of the troops came to life. Turning to the side, they rushed out to the side as well, bristling past the edge of the troops. Their cannons volleyed shots that tore into the ground beside O'Tel, sending charred remnants of the earth up around him.

O'Tel's mind quickly assessed the situation. It was getting direr with each passing second. He barely had enough focus to deflect the laser bolts that he could not evade. Even as strong and skilled as her was, to press on into this sea of death was to guarantee his own fate as such. He stopped and with a motion of his hand erected a towering wall of rock. This platform of earth absorbed the oncoming fire. It was twice his height and three times as wide, allowing him just enough cover. O'Tel press a palm to it and the wall lurched forward, moving in tandem with his pace.

Within a few steps, the mass of Belgae soldiers flooded past him. Without the distraction of the laser fire, their attacks were little more than an inconvenience. O'Tel was able to dodge with such fluidity that it at times appeared as if he were simply a walking ghost, moving through the soldiers rather around them. Occasionally he would strike back, launching whichever poor soul that received the blow flying through the air into the massive horde that continued to assault O'Tel.

As the Belgae numbers mounted, O'Tel used the uR to bolster his attacks. Unseen hands pushed the masses back against the oncoming flow. All the while O'Tel slowly pressed forward toward the Ziggurat.

BOOM! The massive laser strike tore into his earthen shield, disintegrating a large portion of it. O'Tel knew the source of the blast was the light tanks steadily approaching him. Their main cannons glowed red as it charged for another strike.

Their volley shot through the sky of the battlefield in a magnificent procession. The sea of red lasers flew straight at the old Ter'Ok'Zhu king. He had seconds to react. O'Tel mind moved to instinct and he pulled the uR in around him in a bright gold orb in between his palms. As he extended his hands, the orb expanded.

Age had finally begun to catch up with O'Tel and the orb did not nearly expand at a fast enough pace.

One of the beams struck him in the shoulder tearing through his flesh. His nerves threatened his concentration for a second, but he silenced them and fully focused on the orb that surrounded him. The rest of the blasts exploded around him, absorbed by it rather than him. The residual from the explosion consumed everything within a fifty-foot radius. *Such disregard for their own,* he thought.

O'Tel crossed his hands and then shot them out. The orb burst apart into a ring of force that tore through those that remained on the battlefield near O'Tel.

In the distance, the tanks gathered themselves and pressed forward. Their main cannons smoked and once again began to glow as they readied for yet another barrage. O'Tel had had enough. He reached out with both arms, allowing the uR to take a tangible form and shoot out in two individual streams of energy. They consumed the Belgae tanks in a sea of gold. Then with a clasp of his hands, all of them were crushed together into two separate balls of metal and energy. O'Tel could sense the blasts from the tower cannons before they even left their barrels. Both came crashing down beside him, leaving wide craters in the earth, but both missing direct contact with O'Tel. Molten earth flew into the air about him, some burning his clothes as they made contact.

O'Tel spun his body back toward the toward the tower cannons and flung his arms over his head. The spheres of metal and energy that were connected to him by the uR flew past him, like a slingshot through the Belgae soldiers on a path to the towers.

The barracks inside the temple filled with smoke from the explosion. Bunks lay burnt and scattered about the room, the only casualties of the forced entrance. Fa'Sham was the first to enter, followed by Colin, Tar'Sham and the rest of the Bellat warriors.

"Father, your shield," Tar'Sham said.

Fa'Sham scoffed at the request. "Leave your worries for more important matters my son. I have no need for such silly trinkets. Glory is not won on the back of caution."

BAMF! Colin raised the energy shield on his forearm to deflect the shot from hitting the Bellat king. He looked up at the mighty man.

Fa'Sham shook his head and laughed. "You see, I have the young Kinison as my protector."

BAMF! BAMF! BAMF! Colin raised his arm to deflect another series of shots.

"Enough of this foolishness," Fa'Sham roared, reaching to his back and withdrawing a large war hammer.

It was colossal, even by Bellat standards. The hammer's head was roughly two feet wide and both a foot tall and thick. The hammer bore a great amount of detail etched along its surface, but also an equal amount of wear. Only for Fa'Sham's massive frame was he able to hide such a weapon. He reared back and threw the hammer with vicious force. The soldier at the doorway caught the blow with his face. It shattered the Belgae's helm and tore into his skull sending him crashing to the floor beneath its weight.

Fa'Sham charged forth and picked up his hammer as he passed it. He looked back to the others, pausing for a brief second. "Pray he did not set off an alarm prior to his entrance."

"I think our doorway was alarm enough," Colin replied.

Fa'Sham laughed, "Then let us hope that O'Tel is able to draw as many eyes as possible."

They nodded and pressed into the hallway.

The hallway itself was long and narrow. It bore no visible marking and as such offered them little direction. "How are we to find a single girl in such a place?" Fa'Sham asked.

Something pulled at Colin's mind, as if some unseen hand was tugging on a rope around his neck. The feeling drew him north. Almost as an afterthought he spoke, "This way."

The clamoring of feet at the south end of the hallway broke him from his trance. The Bellat party hurried down the hallway as the Belgae soldiers entered it. The two sides exchanged fire as they moved east.

Fa'Sham and the rest turned down the north end of the hallway. Belgae lasers snapped into the wall behind them. Colin took the lead yelling, "Come on hurry!"

Colin's eyes focused on a double door along the hall. It was silver and the metal was no longer glossy from prolonged use. Colin pointed to it down the hall. "In there."

The doors opened and a group of Belgae soldiers exited into the hallway. They were prepared, weapons drawn and movements calculated.

Fa'Sham rushed in at the sight of them, unsheathing his sword and letting out a primal scream. Both his weapons in hand, the taste for battle on his lips and his enemy at hand had sent the Bellat king into a near rage. The Belgae could taste his rage and so they charged forward as well. The rest of the Bellat followed their king in suit.

Blades clashed in a burst of chaos. Fa'Sham tore through those unfortunate few who crossed his path, dismissing them equally with his sword and hammer in a dance of death. Tar'Sham fared nearly as well, though lacking the experience of his father; his path was not as swift or effortless. Colin pressed past them all, dealing out death only as a last resort on his path to the silver double doors.

As the flow of Belgae soldiers subsided, those that were pursuing them entered the fight. Luckily, Colin reached the door, but he had no way of opening it. "Move aside," bellowed Fa'Sham at full pace.

With one large swing of his hammer, he hit the center of the doors. The head crushed through the gap enough to pry a small opening.

"Hurry now before the chance is lost," Fa'Sham said, straining to hold the hammer in place.

Tar'Sham and Colin each grabbed a side of the door and pulled. Their muscles strained and flexed as they fought against the force of the mechanisms holding the door closed. They creaked and groaned a horrific death gurgle before finally yielding to the two young men.

Fa'Sham turned his hammer and used it to brace the door open. The remaining Bellat hurried past him into the room and as the last rushed up, he pulled his hammer free. The doors closed swiftly behind his as he just barely made it into the room himself.

"Seal it!" Fa'Sham ordered.

Instantly the Bellat warriors rushed up to the doors and with their blasters began welding the door shut.

Fa'Sham walked over to Colin and Tar'Sham then spoke, "So where have you led us Colin? By what name shall we call this tomb?"

Colin looked around the room, the numerous computers and displays spelled out to him the purpose of the room in an instant. "This is some sort of maintenance room, a central hub that monitors and maintains the entire facility."

"No wonder they had so many soldiers protecting it," Tar'Sham said.

Fa'Sham looked back at his men, "What are our losses?"

"Three have fallen my lord," one of them responded.

He turned back to Colin, "So what now?"

Colin moved over to one of the terminals, his fingers attacked the keyboard, pressing buttons at a furious pace. The display above his showed the entire temple in a three dimensional picture. Then the three levels of the temple split and rotated so that a bird's eye view of them could be seen. On the lowest section one of the rooms near the center blinked red. "Here we are," Colin remarked.

"But where is she?" Tar'Sham asked.

BAM! BAM! BAM! The vibration of the laser fire outside the door was becoming increasingly more audible. "I fear that the doors life near an end," Tar'Sham said.

Colin nearly screamed as he found her location. He popped up and pointed to the top level on the screen, the temple. "She's there," he said, "but getting there is going to be a problem."

Fa'Sham point on the screen and asked, "Why? Is this not a stairwell? Can we not just take it?"

Colin shook his head, staring at the display. Scores of green lights flooded the screen and a majority sat along the stairwell. "No, it's too well guarded and we can't afford to lose any time or the princess may be lost."

"Then what do you propose?"

Colin tapped another of the rooms on the display; it was slightly below their position. He spoke up, "This room is unguarded and has a direct line up to the Temple. It's our best bet. Only. . . "

"Only what?" Tar'Sham demanded.

"They have it marked as the 'Blood Room'."

BOOM! BOOM! Two colossal explosions rocked the entire building and power in the room shut off leaving the group in total darkness.

The two main cannons erupted in a ball of fire as the spheres made contact. The blast left little but a blackened frame, like some mechanical exoskeleton or carcass of a steel bug.

Three of the main cannons were now laid to waste, but the fourth did not hesitate in its next move. It fired at O'Tel, huge beams of energy tearing through the air in an instant.

It was all he could do to brace himself for the blast. O'Tel raised his hands above his face, his arms straight and rigid, the uR coursed through his veins as the beams made contact.

He bent as much of the blasts as his ability would allow him, arcing the blast around his body. The flesh on the palms of his hands began to blister and burn under the force. His robe smoked and singed from the heat of the beam. Finally it passed and he was able to relax, his eyes focused from the cannon in the distance to the growing number of soldiers now taking up position around him from every direction. He breathed a deep breath, drawing in what little fresh air still existed amongst the smoke and carnage.

A large black circle of scorched earth sat at his feet, not to mention the death and butchery of the entire battlefield. The uR pulled at him and he sensed that the main cannon was charging for another blast. The roar of the Belgae soldiers were upon his ears as he refocused his sight on the main cannon. If they fired, they would guarantee a large number of casualties amongst their count, a fact that he had already borne witness to in this current battle.

His own reserve was near empty and the land had little left to offer him to supplement that need. His odds against so many soldiers were not great, but to face another strike from the cannon would certainly result in death.

O'Tel closed his eyes; shut himself off from the world around him, drawing his body in close. He searched inside himself, searched for any bit of strength that would lend itself to him. He could sense the proximity of the Belgae soldiers, sense the time and opportunity slipping from his grasp, he could sense the cannon ready to fire on him and he could sense his own propinquity to death. Then in the darkness, deep within his heart he found strength, strength from the memory of the love he felt for Zhu. That love had strength and he allowed it to fill him up, to pour through his being until it rushed to the edge of his flesh.

O'Tel shot his hands out at the canon, a blast of blue energy streamed out from his burnt hands. It charged across the battlefield.

The cannon lit up with energy, the air crackling with electricity from its force. It fired its main guns, but the blasts were too late as the blast from O'Tel struck the cannon just as it was discharging. The barrels shattered and the main cannon exploded, sending shrapnel through the air and leaving a plume of smoke behind.

The explosion did not halt the Belgae soldiers. They behaved as though it was no more than a figment of O'Tel's imagination. Within seconds they were on him, this time they did not attempt to attack him, but rather they simply aimed to tackle and smother him instead.

O'Tel attempted to fight back but eventually the sheer number of Belgae's attacking him became too much to overcome. One by one, they grabbed him, piling on top, until he was crushed under the weight of their mass and lost.

The lights slowly flickered back to a half-life, casting the command room in an eerie yellow glow. The laser fire outside of the main door ceased.

"It seems our pursuers are either distracted or dead," Fa'Sham offered.

"Does it really matter which," Colin offered.

"Your words of this being a tomb may still prove true father," Tar'Sham said.

Fa'Sham scoffed, "I have seen far more dire situations than this. We need to get to this 'Blood Room' while they're occupied with whatever it is that O'Tel is doing right now," Colin said.

Tar'Sham said, "Agreed, but we've no way out of the room."

Fa'Sham patted his son on the shoulder lovingly. "You must learn to think out of the normal realm of things son. Sometimes solutions to the most complex problem can be found in the simplest choice."

Confused, Tar'Sham looked to Colin for some hope of insight. A shrug of his shoulders was his only answer to the unspoken question. Fa'Sham walked by his son and grabbed a blaster from two of the Bellat warriors. He walked to the wall opposite of the main doors and placed both weapons on one of the computer terminals, fidgeting with them as he laid them down. Both weapons began to beep as Fa'Sham returned to his son and drew out his war hammer. He looked over at Tar'Sham and said, "You see son, when a problem offers you no solution and it has you boxed in, such as our present situation, sometimes the only answer is to simply blow up those walls around you."

Colin understood in enough time to shout his protest, but not to actively stop Fa'Sham. The Bellat king kissed the top of his hammer, smiled wickedly and then threw it at the two beeping blasters.

The company of men, save for Fa'Sham himself, ducked and turned away from the impact. Fa'Sham's accuracy was perfect and his hammer struck the weapons head on, causing them to explode in a very violent manner.

However, Colin's protest stemmed not from the anticipation of the blasters, but rather of the terminal, on which they rested. Though not functioning, they still remained connected to an emergency power source and the blasters explosion ignited that source, causing a significantly larger explosion than Fa'Sham had intended.

The force of the blast tore a vast hole in the wall, but also sent pieces of equipment all over the room. Fa'Sham also took a brunt of the blast, sending him back on his rear.

Colin stood up and dusted himself off. The emergency lights flickered on and off, threatening to fail at any moment's notice.

"You could have killed us all Fa'Sham. People think I'm reckless," Colin said.

Tar'Sham picked up his father who was covered in soot and laughing fiendishly. Fa'Sham composed himself enough to respond, "We still live and now we have an exit, a success by all measures, though perhaps a muddled one at that, but success none the less."

Colin raised his blaster and waved toward the Bellat warriors as he rushed to the exit, "Come on, we've no time to lose."

They poured into the hallway behind Colin, blaster ready. Within moments, they had cause to use them as Belgae soldiers charged in firing. They exchanged fire; Colin pressed forward picking off enemies with his every shot. At the end of the hallway, he reached a doorway, laid a hand on it and said, "This is it."

Fa'Sham and Tar'Sham arrived at his side, along with the other Bellat. More and more Belgae soldiers began to make their way into the fracas. Soon laser fire began to illuminate the corridor more so than even the lights. Colin smashed the end of his blaster on the control panel for the door. It fell free, connected scarcely by its wires like a mechanical umbilical cord.

Colin tore out wires and tapped frantically at the pad, looking up at Fa'Sham only to say, "Don't try to force the door. We can't risk damaging whatever might be in there. Just give me a few more seconds, I've almost got."

The pad beeped and the door slid open. Inside the room was a rancid odor, which flooded into the hallway. The Bellat warriors were barely able to maintain their composure. Fa'Sham gagged out, "By the gods, more than death rides on that tang. What have you brought upon us Colin?"

The floor of the chamber was a pool of black liquid, but that was only half the source of the tainted smell of death that corrupted the air. Hung from the ceiling, bound by a mass of barbed chains, were a mass of Dzraths. They dangled above the pool half-alive, blood oozed from their bodies into the pool below. Those with enough strength moaned out, a woefully deep ache of a call.

In the middle of the room was a single platform. On that platform stood a giant machine, which seemed to not only draw in the blood from the pool around it, but also to somehow process and pump it up to the levels above. Next to that machine was a giant chain, which served to power the machine. It ran up to the ceiling as well.

Colin looked over to the two Bellat nobles, the only family that he had left. He knew what needed to be done and before his mouth could convey those thoughts, his eye did. Fa'Sham grabbed him in a great hug and then pulled Colin to arms length. "You face this path alone now Colin. All our hope lies in you."

Blasts from the Belgae soldiers tore into the wall behind them, but they paid it no notice. Tar'Sham placed a hand on Colin's shoulder. "Safe journey Colin," he said.

"Thank you Tar'Sham," Colin replied, nodding his head in respect of the gesture.

Fa'Sham grabbed his sword by the blade and handed it to Colin. As Colin grabbed the handle, Fa'Sham squeezed the blade causing Colin pause. "Make sure the bards sing our praises for the generations to come and Colin," he let go of the blade, "make certain they embellish us properly. Now GO!"

Fa'Sham laughed as the door closed behind Colin. He reached into his armor and pulled out two of the explosive discs. Tapping both on Fa'Sham looked at his son and smiled.

Colin stood in the chamber, the door slammed shut behind him. The stench was even more overwhelming now that he was locked in the room. The Dzraths bellowed out, begging for death. Colin searched the room for some way to access the center platform for a control panel or anything of use. He looked back to the door and saw the control panel along its side. It sparked with electricity, compliments of his earlier handy work outside of the room to gain access.

Colin wished he had more time, time to devise a plan, any plan that excluded the ultimate reality of the situation, which was swimming through that putrid pool of black to reach his goal. Time was the one thing he did not have and thus he did not have any other option as well.

BOOM! A large explosion from outside of the room drew Colin's attention. He glanced back for fear of its cause. Colin's practical mind took control, even as his hand involuntarily reached for the door, and forced himself to draw back to his task. He gathered his bearings, placed the sword in his belt at his side and leapt as far as his legs would propel him.

The center was roughly fifteen feet away, just far enough that no man could reach it by natural means, yet still Colin tried, as his desire to stay out of the pool of black was so great. Colin flew over the pool, barely avoiding the hanging Dzraths, but he was only able to cover slightly over ten feet.

Colin's body splashed down into the black pool. It enveloped him in a breath, sucking him into its depths. His skin burned as the liquid made contact. Colin kicked hard and shot up to the surface, flinging himself out of the pool. He reached out for the island and caught it in his grasp. Colin pulled himself up onto its base. He looked over at the massive chain churning and powering the pump.

The links of the chain were nearly as thick as one of his legs and they moved at a pace that tempted Colin to grab onto it. Colin's stomach bit hard, buckling him to his knees. His trip through the black ooze obviously did not agree with his body and it was clearly relating that fact to him. Had he anything in his stomach it would have been brought to display, instead he was treated to the sharp pain of his body contracting instead.

As the discomfort passed, Colin focused his attention back to the chain. His eyes followed its path, his mind processed its speed and gauged its most favorable time to strike. He dove out; leaping into the air and his whole self caught the chain. In an instant, he was propelled upward toward the ceiling.

The hole, which the chains passed, was not large by any means, but as he held the chain tightly to his body, he was barely able to fit. The chamber above was pitch black, only the sounds of the chain moving let him knew he was still in motion. He reached the top of the room and passed into the next chamber.

Light hit his eyes and as soon as he was able, he let go of the chain and landed on the floor of the temple. Instantly he recognized the room from his dream, yet now faced with it in reality the temple seemed even more menacing, in its center stood the altar and in its grasp was the Princess Zhu.

Colin's heart dropped as he saw her face. She was vibrant and full of life in his dream, but now she lay on the altar, a mere shell. It seemed as though the slightest wrong breath might end her. Colin ran to her side and leaned over her face, placing one hand under her chin. The beat of her heart was faint, but it still pounded enough to be felt by his fingers. "Princess Zhu, are you able to move? I'm here to rescue you."

Laughter filled the room, its source stood in the shadowed corner of the room. Colin stood up and pulled the sword from his side. Out from the darkness stepped Xyrus, clapping slowly. "What heroism boy. Have you come simply to save the girl or do you plan to avenge your dead father as well?"

Colin screamed at the mention and charged the Dark Lord, his emotions taking full control of his actions. He swung the sword with all of his hate, praying for a single blow to land so that he could exude it from his system. Xyrus barely moved, simply raising an arm an instant before and of Colin's strikes could find their mark, the Na'Dral on his forearms deflecting the blows. Unusually Xyrus moved in a completely defensive mode, as he stepped out of the way of one of Colin's blows, the young human fell to the floor.

Thousands of sharp needles suddenly pierced his stomach and his flesh. He cried out in pain as he stood up, it was etched in both his posture and face. The Dark Lord simply laughed as he stepped away from Colin. "Stupid boy," he quipped, "Did you think yourself immune to the poison of the Dzrath's blood or were simply so ignorant as to not know that it was dangerous."

The pain overcame Colin again and he dropped his sword as he buckled over. Xyrus approached and grabbed him by the throat. "I should squeeze the life from your lungs this instant, but first I want for you to see something," Xyrus said.

He waved at the huge steel door on the other side of the room and walked over to it, Colin dragging behind. Xyrus stopped as they reached the opening, grabbed Colin by the top of the head and forced him to look. The sight horrified Colin and caused him an even greater pain than that of the poison. "NOOOO!" Colin managed to squeeze out in a broken voice.

Tears flowed from his eyes as in the distance he saw the battlefield in front of the temple. On that field in the center of a circle of cheering Belgae Soldiers, amongst the devastation laid a single body, a body that even from such great distance was clear to Colin whose identity it belonged; O'Tel.

Xyrus flung Colin back toward the center of the room. He slid to a stop slightly in front of the altar, which held Zhu. Broken in every way Colin screamed in pain.

"Now you know the utter failure of your feeble little mission, now your soul may break and now most of all young Kinison, as the poison seeps into your system and death beckons , I shall deliver you into her cold icy grip as salvation," Xyrus spew.

The Dark Lord pulled the Jahan from its sheath, the uR danced along its blade as he stalked his way over to Colin.

Colin felt his life slipping away, felt his system beginning to fail. Pain was slowly numbing his body in a slow death. He curled up like a child in pain; his world began to fade, as did his vision. Colin's chest was heavy, as if someone had laid a large weight vest on top of his shoulders. He felt the burn of acid rise in his throat and could taste it on his tongue.

In what remaining bits of consciousness he had left, he was able to see Xyrus arrive above him, the Jahan raised and ready to strike. Xyrus began to swing his blade down, but Colin blacked out before the blow reached him, his body had reached its end.

Then something inside Colin began to grow. It was foreign and it started from his core, a warmth that consumed his being. It grew exponentially in both size and speed until this energy seeped into his skin. His flesh radiated a warm white light that continued to expand into the air surrounding him. It gave Xyrus pause, so pure and powerful that he stopped his attack and back away shielding his eyes.

Colin looked up and opened his eyes, the energy shot forth from them as well, like two giant floodlights, and it filled the room with an ethereal light. He screamed out from the sheer force of the raw energy now consuming his body. His arms stretched out, reaching for some way to siphon away the force within him. As he rose to his feet, the energy began to subside until only the natural light illuminated the temple.

Colin's eyes were the only part of his body that retained the energy. As it became a soft glow above his iris, the color of the energy shifted from white to a subtle blue. Colin's vision began to change and the room came to life, a sea of flowing color poured forth, overwhelming him. He lifted his hand to try to shield his eyes from the brilliance that the world had now become, but it did yield in its force.

"Cheap parlor tricks may delay your demise, but they cannot save you from it," Xyrus said.

The Dark Lord moved in a quickened pace, the Malef sword in tow. Approaching Colin, he whipped the blade forward and over his head.

Through the madness, Colin saw movement and behind that, he heard Xyrus's words. Something inside him screamed of the danger before it was upon him. Suddenly Xyrus snapped away from the rest of the energy, becoming as clear as he was mere seconds before. Colin saw the blade move, knew he was its target, but his own sword was out of reach. Still his hand reached out for the blade, more out of instinct than some processed thought.

As Xyrus's blade neared Colin's neck, he braced himself for the blow, but just then, the weight of Fa'Sham's sword found its way into his grip. Colin almost hesitated, unsure if the sensation was real or not, but he brought the sword up to parry the blow.

The deflection sent Xyrus, a few steps back. Anger mixed in with disillusionment in a wretched boiling stew that spilt out of his face. "What madness is this? How is it possible?"

He struck again at Colin, this time each blow was blocked. He shot his off hand into Colin's chest, the uR amplifying the blow and sending him sliding backwards.

Colin reached a hand back and stopped himself, yet without touching anything to do so. The sensation was odd, yet natural. It seemed as though in some way his hand extended beyond its own fleshy limitations and braced against the floor. He gave a press and slid back, sword striking as he approached Xyrus.

"Your Ter'Ok'Zhu trickery shall not fool me boy," Xyrus said as he thrust a beam of energy at Colin.

It caught him in the shoulder and sent him flying in a spin back onto the floor. Colin pressed himself up, blocked Xyrus's blow and then delivered a punch that sent the Dark Lord back nearly five feet. The blow was one that his body did not possibly have the strength to deliver without some exterior assistance. The uR was flowing through Colin without his full knowledge and thus it was reacting in an almost primal way. Energy began to amass in his fists, growing into orbs of light that encompassed his fists.

Xyrus reached out towards the massive chain that churned by the arch and ripped it asunder. He flung the mass of linked steel toward Colin, whose focus was so intense on the Dark Lord that he did not see it coming.

They struck into his side, taking his wind from his lungs and tossed him to the floor. His sword flew from his grasp across the floor as well. Quickly Xyrus weaved the chains around Colin's body, ensnaring him. Colin fought to get free, but Xyrus reinforced the steel with his own strength, using the uR to press it further into Colin's flesh.

"You failed Kinison," Xyrus gloated as he moved closer, "Just as your father did before you."

Xyrus squeezed his fist closed and with every bit that his fist tightened so did the chains. Their grip pressed hard into Colin's body crushing the air from his lungs. He could feel the bones of his rib cage ready to give into the pressure. Xyrus stepped even closer to gloat, "You simpleton, what chance did you think you stood against me? Why sacrifice yourself? Why walk into the beast's den with so much to lose? WHY?!?"

He squeezed again and Colin screamed out. Colin looked up as the grip around his chest relinquished. "HOPE!"

The word angered Xyrus and as he began to roar out his frustration, the blade of Fa'Sham's sword pierced his side. Xyrus stopped and turned. Standing before him was Zhu; sickness still covered her face like a sheet of white silk.

"Such heart," he spit out smiling.

Xyrus withdrew the blade from his back, his lip and eyes twitching were the only reveal of the pain it caused him. He tossed it aside and said, "It pains me that you must still die. How much of your strength did you sap to deliver that blow and yet like your savior you still fail?"

Xyrus raised the Jahan as the pain overcame Zhu and she collapsed to her knees. Colin looked up to her face, their eyes connected. Something inside him erupted and he forced his will over the chains that had enveloped him. Colin screamed out, "NOOOOO," and thrust out. The chains exploded from his body, flew across the room and drew Xyrus's attention back to Colin.

"If you'd prefer to taste he kiss of the Jahan first boy I will oblige you."

Colin forced himself to his feet and reached out for his sword as Xyrus moved toward him. It flew across the room back to Colin's hand. He and Xyrus exchanged blows, but as they did the Jahan began to glow. It exuded uR, its blade spat out purple energy that was visible to even the naked eye, but to Colin's new vision it became an increasing beacon of light, a tiny sun that was growing in strength with each passing moment. Colin tried to shield his eyes as he fought, a fact that Xyrus clearly noticed.

"You see, the blade senses your weakness boy and exploits it. It is no mere piece of molded steel such as that which you hold."

Xyrus increased the fervor with which he struck at Colin until the shattered Fa'Sham's blade and sent Colin falling to the floor, Zhu also collapsed. Once more Colin and her eyes connected. It was as though he could feel her pain, hear her thoughts. She was clear as if separated from the rest of the world.

The tip of the Jahan stretched up toward the ceiling ready to be plunged into Colin's chest. Xyrus spoke, "Now young Kinison, YOU DIE!"

As he brought the blade down a burst of gold energy tore into his back sending him flying across the room into the far wall. Standing at the opening of the temple, tattered and torn was O'Tel.

Colin looked up and though he could not define what stood before him through the sheen of color he could feel the warmth that radiated off the man and instantly knew it was O'Tel. Colin dared say his name, "O'Tel?"

O'Tel leapt into the Temple, landing on its floor with barely an audible sound, as if he had landed on a cushion rather than the stone floor. He rushed over to check on Zhu, laying a hand on her cheek. It began to glow, a soft warmth like that of a candle. It quickly left his own flesh and drank into hers. O'Tel rose up and hurried over to Colin.

"How? I saw you on the battlefield, there were so many and you looked dead," Colin began.

"You saw what was needed to be seen, but that is neither here nor there. The shock of my attack will surely be wearing off Xyrus any moment we have but seconds. You must take the princess out of here; the cold grip of death grows stronger with every second she spends in this forsaken place. Take her back to the Slai'Nor, the ship will care for her."

"But," Colin tried to interrupt.

O'Tel waved away his comment and continued, "There is no time for argument, take and go, NOW!"

O'Tel reached out and put both hands on Colin's head. Again, his hands glowed a soft golden hue then faded into Colin's. He said, "Hopefully that shall help you with the vision, give you a sense of control for it."

The sea of color began to fade back into the world from whence it came, nearly all of it sucked down into an invisible drain. Colin shook his head and reoriented himself. He hurried over to Zhu and picked her up into his arms, holding her body close enough to his own that her scent overpowered his nose. It overwhelmed him, she was so fragile and yet he could sense the strength that radiated from her heart. He nearly found himself lost staring at her, so slender and pale.

"COLIN!" O'Tel snapped, bringing him back to the situation at hand. O'Tel waved a hand and the floor rose up into a makeshift ramp leading up to the main opening. Colin rushed up it as fast as he could.

Two blasts of red energy spat into the wall above them. As Colin looked back to find their source, a third blast came streaking at him. Just as quickly, a bright gold shield of energy appeared and deflected the bolt harmlessly away, mere inches from his face.

In front of O'Tel, Fa'Sham's broken sword hovered. The blade turned red hot, pieced itself together and then cooled as if it were being assembled in some imperceptible forge. O'Tel grabbed it from the air and said, "They are no longer your concern Xyrus."

Xyrus stood up, the Jahan glowing in his hand. He was covered in soot and blood, but still he carried himself with a sense of arrogance. Xyrus replied, "Then what is old man?"

O'Tel paused and allowed his free hand to gather golden energy about it, then said, "I am!"

CHAPTER TWENTY TWO

Colin exited the temple, Zhu still unconscious in his arms. Before them at the edge of the short ledge was a drop down to the next level of the Ziggurat. Colin knew that he could make the jump down on his own, but he was unsure of what the result would be with Zhu in his carriage. Still, he had no choice, the bass reverberating from behind as the giant steel doors slammed shut assured him of that. Colin braced himself for the descent when a familiar sound caught his ear.

"Colin! You're alive!" Tar'Sham screamed from below.

Colin stopped and looked down at his old friend. Tar'Sham held Fa'Sham at his side. The Bellat king was badly injured and his left side from the waist down was soaked in a deep crimson. At a count, only three of the Bellat warriors remained beside them. "As are you," Colin yelled back.

"Barely. Is that her?"

Colin replied nodding, "Yes. She's badly hurt. We need to get her to the Slai'Nor. How bad is your father?"

Tar'Sham looked over to his father's wound which was still wet and bleeding, "He lives, but only because he is stubborn and refuses to yield even to death."

"Is there another way down?" Colin asked.

"None but this staircase. Send the girl, my men will catch her."

"I don't know if she can survive the drop."

"She will not survive at all if you don't Colin. Time runs thin for all of us."

Colin nodded and the Bellat warriors gathered below him. Colin dropped to his knees and held Zhu out over the ledge. He closed his eyes and dropped her. Her body sank through the air, nearly lifeless into the waiting arms of the Bellat warriors. She gasped as they caught her, then she fell back flaccid.

Seeing she was all right, Colin leapt down. His feet smashed through the rock as he landed, splashing bits of rubble into the air. It took him a second to recover, blood rushed to his knees and ankles, but they were still functional, all the reassurance he needed. Colin hasted over to Zhu, "Lay her down," he ordered the Bellat warriors.

Colin leaned in by her face to listen to her breathing, soft and slow, but still there. He rose up and said, "Watch over her," then rushed over to Fa'Sham.

The wound on his side was large, a gash from his hip to his armpit. It had been bandaged enough to slow the bleeding, but no enough to stop it and Fa'Sham was barely a shell of his usual boisterous self as a result. "What happened?" he asked Tar'Sham.

"The Foolish old man is always questing for glory. He got that lovely mark saving us from an ambush below."

"It looks serious."

"I still live cubs," Fa'Sham barely could grit the words through the pain, squeezing his eyes to look up at Colin.

Tar'Sham shook his head, "Just barely father," he looked over to Colin, "it is serious enough to slow his tongue but not silence it."

Colin looked around, the steps which seemed to be the only direct way down were now impassable, collateral damage from both O'Tel's and the Bellat assault on the fortress. At the ground level, Belgae troops began to fill the battlefield once more. Laser fire from their ranks shot up at Colin and the others. They backed away from the edge and huddled together.

Colin looked over to Tar'Sham, "No reasonable way out that I can see any ideas?"

"I am at a lost my friend," he replied.

Fa'Sham coughed up some blood and smiled through his pain. His words slid past his throat like a snake moving through a much too small pipe. "We fight. . .and we die. . .with honor."

Fa'Sham coughed harder and the bite of his dressing cut into him. Tar'Sham looked up to Colin, "What of Master O'Tel?"

"He's inside the temple with Xyrus right now, he saved us."

"Then I assume he can offer us no assistance," Tar'Sham concluded.

"Does your ship have a remote system?"

Tar'Sham nodded, "Yes, but the transponder was destroyed in our last skirmish." He looked down at his father's side.

"DAMN!" Colin exclaimed.

Zhu whispered, "Call for her."

Both of their attention snapped to the sound of her voice, so quiet they barely could hear her over the chaos of the battle about them. Colin leaned in and asked, "What? What was that?"

Zhu opened her eyes and looked into his. "Do you not feel her? Look into your heart; seek her within yourself. She is listening for you. She can hear you. Call to her, quickly before the chance is gone."

Tar'Sham stared quite confused at Colin. "Her? Who does the princess speak of? Is there someone else on this mission that we are not aware of?"

Colin shook his head and stepped away. "No," he said as blasts from the Belgae lasers screamed overhead.

He paused, closed his eyes and focused himself inward. It was as if he had opened a door to another world, his sight from inside his own mind into the world around him. The life of the world flowed around him, as if each creature, each being reverberated with his or her own unique song of color. Then in the distance, as if calling to him in a language of light that only his heart could understand, was a most innocent voice, feminine as Zhu had said, but utterly alien in nature.

Colin focused harder on it and it seemed as though he was pulled in closer to the source of the voice. His consciousness flew through the world until it stopped in front of the source. He was shocked at how simple the answer was, so maddened that he had forgot in such a short period. In front of him, singing was the Slai'Nor. "Help. Hurry," was all Colin could manage to say before his consciousness was torn back to his body.

Colin yelled out and fell to his knees. Tar'Sham's hand was instantly on his shoulder. "Are you alright Colin?"

"Yes," he smiled as he spoke. Tears dripped from his eyes. "She's coming."

O'Tel thrust his free hand out towards Xyrus and a beam of energy shot forth. Xyrus charged forward, he raised the Jahan up, allowing the Dark Blade to deflect the beam away. As he neared O'Tel, the Dark Lord leapt into the air and raised his blade high above his head.

O'Tel stood poised as a statue, only his eyes moved as they followed Xyrus's flight and more importantly the flight of the Jahan. AS the Dark Blade came screaming down at him, nearing his flesh, so close that he could feel its cold evil breath; he stepped to the side and used his own sword to guide the Jahan deep into the floor.

Enraged Xyrus screamed and ripped the blade from the floor's grasp, tearing a large section of it into the air with it. He reached out and grabbed each stone with the uR, then hurled them at O'Tel.

The Ter'Ok'Zhu master simply swayed as each came near him, using his sword to deflect those he could not simply avoid.

Xyrus charged again, this time firing a blast of energy from the blade as he moved. O'Tel waved a hand and a golden shield of energy appeared to absorb the blast. Within seconds, Xyrus was there, the Jahan slicing and disintegrating the protective barrier. His blade tore wildly at O'Tel, great heaving blows that were more about domination then precision.

O'Tel moved as a true master, shifting his body and blade in the subtlest movements, but enough that Xyrus could never draw a blow even close to hitting him.

Frustration mounted in the Dark Lord as the realization of how futile his skill in swordplay was when compared to the ancient master in front of him. Xyrus slammed the Jahan down on the floor like a hammer and a wave of energy exploded around O'Tel in a giant cocoon. Xyrus reached up to the ceiling and pulled down. A giant chunk tore out from the rest and came crashing down on top of O'Tel, smothering the orb of energy around him.

Not satisfied, Xyrus slammed the Jahan into the floor and then with both hands blasted a mammoth beam of energy into the rubble. The stone burned under the heat. Xyrus stopped, smiled and pulled the sword from the floor. He strutted over to the burning pile of rock; parts had blackened while others still shone a hot molten orange. Steam and smoke rose into the air as Xyrus strolled by. He stopped at the center and chided, "Perhaps you are not as strong as my masters had feared old man."

Just then, as if in response to his comment, the pile of rock exploded, sending Xyrus flying across the room, at its center stood O'Tel, sword at the ready. "It will not be so simple a task as that to kill me Xyrus," he said.

Xyrus picked himself up and reached out for the Jahan, it flew into his grip. "Then I shall try harder this time."

The Belgae soldiers now littered the battlefield below and worse they had begun their ascent up the broken stairway. A group carried a large platform to bridge the gap to the upper level.

The Bellat warriors vainly took shots at the oncoming threat, taking out the occasional target, but unable to sustain an offensive over the barrage that assailed them. Mere moments and the Belgae would be upon them, hope would serve them no purpose if that happened.

"Fall back," screamed Colin and the Bellat warriors complied. "Protect the princess at all costs."

Together they formed a wall to protect both Fa'Sham and Zhu. Their rifles ready, they stared at the edge of the ground they stood on.

BOOM! The loud crash of metal on rock echoed up to their ears as the Belgae Bridge slammed up against the side of the Ziggurat. As the first Belgae hand reached up to make its way onto the second level, something glinted in the distance, a small fast moving reflection of light.

The Bellat warriors opened fire on the Belgae as they leapt over the platform. Numerous Belgae were hit and tumbled off the side of the Ziggurat, but their numbers were simply too much for Colin and the others to overcome. Soon the second level of the Ziggurat was filled with enemy soldiers. Colin knew they could not fight any longer and with all of the enemy weapons aimed on them, Colin lowered his own defeated. "Lay down your weapons," Colin ordered.

The Belgae moved forward as the Bellat followed Colin's lead, but then a gigantic roar screamed forth overhead and the Belgae turned and opened fire. Their target was no longer Colin and the Bellat, but rather the Slai'Nor.

The mighty ship maneuvered itself in between the two parties and flared its engines to press the Belgae soldiers back. The forward hatch lowered in front of Colin and the others. Tar'Sham's open jaw was enough of an opening to cause Colin to offer up, "You see old friend, she came."

"But how did you call her?"

"That is a story for another time. I suggest we move while we have the chance."

Together they all hurried inside of the ship. With the last of them inside, the Slai'Nor closed its hatch and turned upward, blasting off toward space.

Inside the ship, Colin pointed the Bellat warriors to the sick bay. "Take King Fa'Sham and the Princess there, the ship will tend to their wounds."

They did as instructed. Colin grabbed Tar'Sham by the shoulder, halting him from following. "I need you with me in the cockpit," he said.

Tar'Sham nodded and followed Colin.

Inside the cockpit, Colin stopped and reached out with his mind as he had seen O'Tel do. *Chairs*, he thought. The same siren voice seemed to answer and as the chairs rose up he knew that the ship had understood. The controls rose up to his hands as he sat down.

"Sit Tar'Sham, I need your skill on the weapons if we're going to survive this," Colin said.

Tar'Sham sat down, his face a direct conduit for his confusion. "But I have no idea how to operate such machinery."

"It's intuitive like the Tyr fighter. The ship will adapt to you, but the system operates off of your movements and reactions."

Two control sticks rose up to greet Tar'Sham and on the HUD five enemy targets now trailed in after the Slai'Nor. Laser fire exploded around them.

"I don't think we can outrun them, so we'll just have to out gun 'em."

Colin banked the Slai'Nor hard back over itself, propelling the ship back toward the planet's surface. The five Nergal fighters came screaming up at him. He squeezed his right hand and the forward batteries fired a splatter of laser fire back. One of the Nergal fighters took a direct hit and burst into flame. The other four tore past, spun around and chased after the Slai'Nor.

Tar'Sham saw all four in the HUD. As he moved his hands, the crosshairs from the Slai'Nor's rear batteries danced along the screen synchronously.

"Grip your hand to fire," Colin told him.

Tar'Sham did so and a mass of laser fire tore into the space behind them. The Nergal fighters easily avoided the random shots, returning fire in kind.

"Your other hand fires the secondary weapon."

Colin weaved the ship through the sky avoiding as much enemy fire as he could. Tar'Sham maneuvered his hands until one of the crosshairs locked onto an enemy fighter and went red. He clenched his left hand tight and the ship fired a plasma torpedo.

This time the shot hit home and the Nergal fighter erupted in a ball of fire. Colin pulled up hard and pushed the ship to full throttle, still the remaining Nergal fighters trailed behind. All three Nergal fighters fired their missiles. They screamed through the sky, leaving a trail of smoke behind as they raced toward the Slai'Nor.

"Take care of those missiles Tar'Sham."

"I'm trying," Tar'Sham replied.

Tar'Sham gripped his right hand and fired his guns at the incoming missiles. A stream of laser fire tried to catch the missiles. He hit one and then another, but the third made its way past his assault and slammed into the bottom of the Slai'Nor, erupting in a black plume of fire.

The ship rocked from the impact and it screamed out in pain. Information scrolled up on Colin's screen detailing the damage from the impact. "That hit took out the rear shields. Those aren't standard Belgae missiles," Colin yelled.

He dropped the throttle to zero and flipped the ship around in a one hundred and eighty degree turn. The Belgae pilots were ready for the maneuver and followed suit, their ships turning as they just passed by the Slai'Nor. Colin, however, pulled open the Slai'Nor's flaps and the mighty ship snapped back down toward the planet in reverse, as if someone had connected it to a large anchor. He closed them shut and engaged the thrusters, placing himself directly behind his targets. "Everything we have Tar'Sham! NOW!"

The massive Bellat squeezes both hands as he turned them, flipping the rear guns toward the front of the ship. The sky lit up as Colin followed suit. Both Nergal fighters exploded before them and the Slai'Nor flew through the debris. On board Colin and Tar'Sham screamed out a cheer in victory.

Colin tapped some buttons and the ship resumed its course away from the planet. "Not the prettiest victory, but I'll take it."

O'Tel pulled his sword back behind his back, resting it along his spine. His eyes tightened, focusing hard on the Dark Lord. He spoke, "Yield Xyrus. End this futility and abandon your path. Do you not see the tides? Can you not foresee the end to this game you think you are playing?"

Xyrus slammed the Jahan into the floor, its power seeped forth, a dark fountain of vile energy that sloshed about his feet. He pointed and shot his words at the Ter'Ok'Zhu king, "It is you old man who cannot see this game's end. You think I am simply a novice to your world, that I am so your lesser. I AM THE SWORD BEARER!"

The pool of energy began to creep up Xyrus's legs as his fury mounted. O'Tel shot back, "No. I know the strength that that title encompasses."

Xyrus paused, "What?"

O'Tel offered a small laugh, "You are so focused on the now, that you forsake the then and yet to be. Did you truly think that I would not recognize the sword you wield? Rather, do you simply not understand its true legacy? Did your masters hide such a fact from you, in this Sword Bearer?"

Xyrus's frustration erupted into rage, exiting him in a scream. He thought, *How could he know so much about my masters? How could they have hidden this from him? What else did the old man know?*

The sea of energy that had been amassing at Xyrus's feet was now overflowing, feeding off the Dark Lord's rage. "NO!" he screamed as his arms shot forth at O'Tel.

The energy poured up along his body and funneled its way out from his arms at O'Tel in two giant purple streams of energy.

O'Tel raised his hands up, deflecting the streams around him, as though he was encased in an invisible bubble. The energy poured into the room around him, destroying it in the process. He felt the weight of the floor begin to shift and crack. The entire structure of the temple was giving way. The ancient pillars hummed to life amongst the destruction, as if Xyrus's anger had somehow ignited something hidden away in the old stone. O'Tel looked up to the hole in the ceiling and leapt. The uR reinforced his legs, sending him soaring up into the night air.

Even through his fugue of rage, Xyrus saw O'Tel's escape. His eyes locked onto the movement like a hawk. He ceased his attack, which now had torn through most of the far wall, grabbed the Jahan and leapt up after his prey.

The air licked at his cheeks as he rose up to the top of the Ziggurat. His boots crushed into the stone as he landed. A beam of golden energy greeted him and he deflected it with the Jahan. Xyrus lunged toward its source, O'Tel, the dark blade still deflecting more of the same attacks as he moved.

As he reached O'Tel, their blades clashed. Again, they entered into a dance of attacks and parries, however this time Xyrus's attacks were increasingly more violent. What he lacked in skill, he attempted to compensate with brute force. His blows though blocked, pressed O'Tel back toward the edge of the roof. Laser fire erupted as he neared its edge.

He pressed each of his hands out in opposite directions using the uR to send an invisible wave towards both Xyrus and the incoming fire. An explosion in the upper atmosphere drew O'Tel's eyes away from his current predicament. He used the uR to enhance his vision and saw the Slai'Nor in battle.

Xyrus laughed. "You see the end to this game now, Death."

O'Tel refocused on the Dark Lord, "At that you are terribly correct Xyrus, though blind to the truth in its nature."

O'Tel went on the offensive, attacking Xyrus for the first time. His blade, though insignificant compared to that of the Jahan, was more than its equal in the hands of O'Tel. Xyrus did his best to deflect the incoming blows, but bit by bit, they began to find their mark, cutting fine lines along his body and arms.

Another large explosion in the sky drew Xyrus's attention for but a split second, but it was enough of a distraction to cost him a vicious scar across his cheek. Xyrus recoiled and grabbed at the wound. O'Tel looked up and said, "You have failed Xyrus, the princess is safe and her blood shall not be spilt on this day. The Slai'Nor and its crew have nearly escaped your clutch. Your lack of focus and lust has been your undoing."

A most foul laugh began to pour slowly from the bowels of Xyrus's stomach. Such a sickening joy wrapped in hate and delivered by the sharp tone carried forth in his laugh. He touched the cut on his face, tasted the blood on his fingers and continued to laugh even harder. "Failure? Failure! Oh yes indeed old man. A deep failure, but not my own. Not mine indeed."

Suddenly O'Tel felt a surge of dark energy grow beneath his feet. He could see the uR gathering below him and through the hole, he could see one of the pillars glowing with an increasing furiousness. Xyrus tapped a pad on the top of his hand and raised it to his mouth. "Engage the secondary shield."

In orbit above the planet, near where the security station had been, the Fahn'rir uncloaked. More than half the size of the other security station, the Fahn'rir was enormous by any comparison. Two beams of energy fired out towards the remaining security stations and within an instant, the planetary shield was reactivated.

Alarms screamed as red lights flashed in the cockpit of the Slai'Nor. Tar'Sham turned to Colin, "I swear I've touched nothing."

Colin shook his head frantically tapping buttons in an almost random pattern. The forward display sprang to life, showing the space before them. "It can't be," Colin stammered.

He pulled the controls back as a hue of energy filled the space in front of them. The Slai'Nor responded to him and banked back toward the planet, just barely avoiding the shield itself.

"What is happening?" Tar'Sham asked.

"They've reengaged the shield."

O'Tel stared up at the sky as the shield formed. His eyes went wide from shock and then narrowed in realization. He looked over at Xyrus, who now carried a very smug look upon his own face.

"You see you old fool, you see now what was truly hidden from you; YOUR FAILURE! My masters foresaw all of this, your entire attack, your every move," Xyrus said as he drew the Jahan ready to strike. "You thought yourself so wise, thought you knew of this sword, knew that she must die at this moment, but your own arrogance has now blinded you to the means of which that blow shall be delivered. Only now, as everything has already been played out, when all of the pieces are finally in place do you see your grandest mistake and realize your failure."

O'Tel looked at the pillars below, energy surged between them, bolts of electricity danced along their bodies. Xyrus nodded as his gaze returned to him.

"Yes," he said, "though you knew this sword, you could not know this temple. Stamped onto our world and lost to nearly all of history, save for a privileged few. This place is one of my lord's darkest secrets and now the Jahan and my hatred for you have fully unlocked its power. So this final blow still flows from my hand and I shall claim the glory from it."

O'Tel's eyes glistened with realization as he took in the entire scene. "She was right. I was a fool to think I could change this." He stepped to the edge of the hole, looked down at the pillars below and fell to his knees.

Xyrus's eyes glowed with hate at the sight. He stepped behind O'Tel and raised the Jahan. His body filled with an uncontrollable bloodlust and his eyes went black with rage. "You have failed. Soon they will be dead and the pact will be broken. My lords will be free again to reign and none of your own race shall be here to stop them. Your death, however, shall be my glory alone."

A voice in Xyrus's head screamed, *NOOOOO!!!* He would not hear it this time; O'Tel's death was his reward. To kill the Ter'Ok'Zhu king would stain his name with glory for ages to come.

He thrust the Jahan deep into O'Tel's back and it screamed along with the old king.

CHAPTER TWENTY THREE

Golden energy consumed the Dark Blade and rose up its handle to Xyrus himself. The pain of it caused him to recoil back and the sword came with him as he moved.

The wound in O'Tel's chest and back poured blood and golden uR together. He looked up to the heavens as the life drained out of him and scratched out a single word, "Zhu!"

On board the Slai'Nor Zhu sprang up from her cot. She screamed out in shock as a series of robots attempted to calm her.

O'Tel spoke again, "I will always be with you my child and I will always love you."

"FATHER! NO!!!" She screamed as she reached a hand out for him. The Bellat warriors rushed into the room and assisted the robots in restraining her.

O'Tel fell forward into the temple. The pillars erupted with a beam of black energy, consuming his body and headed straight for the Slai'Nor.

In the cockpit, Colin's eyes went wide with terror. "Oh my god it's all been a setup, this whole time. Look at the temple, LOOK!"

Tar'Sham looked at the screen in front of Colin and saw the forth-coming blast. "Can we evade it?"

"No, it's too big."

"Then we're doomed."

The beam tore up into the sky, a vile black geyser of energy; it rushed up toward the Slai'Nor, death on its heels.

Then, at its base, the stream changed to a brilliant gold. Faster than the beam itself, the surge of golden energy raced up the black stream, consuming it as it rose. It met the peak just as the stream devoured the Slai'Nor and then smashed into the planetary shield.

Colin and Tar'Sham braced for the impact, but as the stream consumed the ship, there was only a sense of peace and serenity that overcame them. It seemed as though the great Ter'Ok'Zhu king stood at their side, his large hand resting on their shoulder. Then just as quickly as the feeling arrived, it disappeared.

The stream tore through the shield and crashed into the Fahn'rir, before dissipating. Along the hull of the Fahn'rir, a pulse of energy coursed, leaving a lifeless wake that of disabled system behind.

On board the Slai'Nor, the ship began to warble at Colin frantically. "I understand, I get it," he responded.
"Get what?" Tar'Sham asked.
"The shield is down. I don't know how he did it, but O'Tel just saved us all."
"By the Gods, is there nothing the Ter'Ok'Zhu cannot do?"
Colin pushed the ship back around toward space. It shot out of the planets grip with an even great speed than before. Colin tapped some pads and the remaining Reaper Squadron appeared on the screen.
"What the hell was that?" Johnson asked.
"No time for explanations. We have to go now!" Colin responded.
"Understood, we'll be on your wing when you exit orbit."

As the Slai'Nor reached the black of space, the Reapers promptly fell in line behind. Together they sped out past the falling Capital ship.

"Do you know what you're doing Colin?" Tar'Sham asked.
Colin moved his hands around the control pad, in what seemed like familiar moments. "I think so. I don't know how, but it all feels right. What choice do we have?"
"Point taken."
"Engaging the jump drive, brace yourself."

From the Slai'Nor's nose a bright beam of light shot out into space and from that, a large tear in space burst open into a bright circle of energy. The Slai'Nor and Reapers flew straight into it, disappearing as the portal did behind them.

On the planet the temple was deathly quiet and devoid of movement. Then, Xyrus rose to his feet, the Jahan still in his hand. The pillars below him were now broken and crumbling. "NO!" he screamed in frustration.

Xyrus walked to the edge of the roof and leapt off. He flew through the air and slammed into the earth below. A shock wave flew outward, billowing dust into the air and sending the nearest soldiers into the air.

Xyrus rose up and whipped the sword from shoulder to shoulder. Purple energy lashed out and consumed his fallen men. In an instant, they were gone, washed away by the wave of energy. The other soldiers backed away, save for one man. He stepped forth and kneeled before Xyrus. "Your order m'Lord?"

Xyrus looked to the sky, "What of the Fahn'rir?"

"Disabled m'Lord. The blast has rendered the ship inert for the time being."

Xyrus reached down, physically grabbed him by the throat and raised him to eye level. "Fix my ship. Gather the armada. We storm Ter'Ar'Tor and leave none alive who stand against us!"

"Yes m'Lord," the man gasped out.

Xyrus tossed him to the ground and stormed back into the temple.

The black of space suddenly burst open, as if a blade had sliced through the nothingness. It expanded into a giant glowing circle and as it reached its apex, the Slai'Nor and Reaper Squadron came tearing through. Bits of electricity crackled along their hull as the ships entered real space.

Alarms flashed and rand as Colin frantically attempted to correct the problem. "What's wrong? Were we hit?" Tar'Sham asked.

Colin smashed a fist on the control pad in frustration. The ship screamed at him in response. "Sorry," he said.

Colin's hands scrambled around the cockpit searching for something that he did not know where to find. "I don't know what's wrong. I think something happened during the jump."

"Can we land?"

Colin focused on the controls again, the irritation washing away and emotion from his face, "It'll be bumpy."

The Slai'Nor banked down toward Ter'Ar'Tor, engines sputtering and the ship itself shaking violently. As it entered the atmosphere, the hull lit up and smoke began to billow out from the stress.

When the ship got close enough to the planet, it turned away from the city center out toward the sea. The Reaper fighters followed closely behind.

Colin tapped a button and Johnson popped up on the screen. "Johnson, take the Reapers to the space port. I'm going to land the Slai'Nor by the shore. I'm afraid she won't survive putting down anywhere else."

"Aye sir."

Colin tapped another button and the display returned to normal. The ship continued to buckle as Colin eased it toward the water. "Hold on."

The Slai'Nor slammed into the water, a giant wave washed up over it. The ship pushed toward the shore as it decelerated, coming to a halt as it reached the shoreline. The lower ramp lowered down onto the shore.

The doors to the council chamber opened. Silence filled the room; such an unusual condition that it created the illusion that time had suddenly stood still. The only remnant of life was the destruction from Xyrus's earlier attack. Tar'Sham, Zhu and Colin walked in. Zhu held onto Tar'Sham's arm, still weak from her earlier ordeal.

As they reached the center of the room, Colin waved a hand, snapping the Holovid to life. He looked over to Tar'Sham. "Fa'Sham should be here for this. We could use his experience."

Tar'Sham laughed, "My father has rarely been one for any strategy that did not simply involve a direct assault. No, action is his trade; strategy is something he would easily defer to you."

Colin smiled and nodded. His eyes focused on the star map that rose up around him. Then something caused him concern. Each Jump Gate on the star map was a deep shade of grey. "That's odd."

He reached out with a hand and touched one of the gates. It enlarged and a great deal of data poured into the air around it. Colin touched it and it shrunk back down. He checked another and then another, all gave the same result.

"What happened to all the gates?" Tar'Sham asked.

"They've shut down. None of them seems to be damaged, but they're all dead. It doesn't make any sense," Colin said.

Tar'Sham walked around leaving Zhu to sit. "Perhaps being that they are of Ter'Ok'Zhu design, the loss of this planet's generator has somehow affected them as well."

"At least that bides us some time to come up with a plan. It'll take Xyrus nearly double the time to get here without the gates."

"No," Zhu whispered.

They both looked at her. "What did you say?" Colin asked.

Zhu looked back, their eyes met and she paused for a second. Since his transformation at the temple, Colin's eyes were now a permanent hue of blow, so bright that nearly glowed against his skin. Something about them brought her such a sense of warmth. "What do you mean, No?" Colin asked.

The question snapped her out of her gaze. "He is adept with the uR and thus he has no need for something so mechanical to travel."

Tar'Sham growled in anger. "It is as if we have pulled ourselves from drowning, only to find that we rest on the cliff. Is there no fortune that will smile upon us other than bad?

"We have our lives, is there no better fortune than that?" she said.

Her voice was so soft, so pure and so regal that its sound eased Tar'Sham's mood. The power of her message was a reminder of those who had sacrificed their own lives up to this point and as true a reminder of their luck as anything.

Colin waved at the Belgae home world and the Holovid focused on it. "How long do you think until his Capital Ship is ready for battle?"

"There is no way of knowing the extent of the damage, but I would venture ten hours at the most," Tar'Sham answered.

"If he indeed uses the uR to transport his fleet, he will be severely weakened upon his arrival. We shall at least have that to our advantage," Zhu said.

"What advantage does that present us? Even weakened we are outnumbered more than one hundred to one," Tar'Sham said, "We should abandon this place, regroup and strike when we are better equipped."

"NO!" Colin stepped up to Tar'Sham. "We cannot abandon this planet; it has far too much value to simply be sacrificed so we can escape."

"There is no chance for survival in this fight Colin. Anyone that would offer assistance is too far away to arrive in time. You must face the reality of this," the Bellat replied.

"We have to at least try."

Tar'Sham turned and walked away, "This is madness."

"You always were afraid to risk anything, always so ready to take the cowardly path rather than risk the chance of failure," Colin spat back.

Tar'Sham roared, turned and charged at Colin. He grabbed him by the collars and pulled him next to his face. "There are none left to impress with your foolhardy ventures. How many need to for your glory?"

"Get your filthy paw off me!"

Tar'Sham pushed him back, "YIELD!"

"NO!" Colin answered. He grabbed the Bellat's wrist and twisted his own body under and around him. The momentum swung Tar'Sham's larger frame up into the air and then sent him crashing down to the floor.

"STOP!" yelled Zhu. With the uR, she pressed them both apart and held them at bay. "Your arguing serves only the Dark Lord's purpose. Look at yourselves."

Colin waved a hand and broke her hold on him. He walked to the hole in the wall on the far side of the room, stopped and turned back to look at them. "I am staying and I am fighting to defend this planet, even if the cost is my own life."

With that, he turned back and left the room. Zhu began to go after him, but Tar'Sham's large hand on her shoulder stopped her. "No, he needs to be alone right now."

Xyrus sat upon his chair, which more resembled an ancient throne torn from some gothic castle, then a piece of the warship it resided in. His anger poured into the air, palpable. The bridge of the Fahn'rir was sizeable, giant panels offered a direct view of space and a high vaulted ceiling provided the ambiance of power needed for such an environment. The crew moved about at a rapid pace, both out of duty and fear of reaping Xyrus's wrath.

"Repair status," Xyrus demanded.

The ship's computer responded as a Holo of the ship rose in front of him. "Eighty five percent complete."

He slammed his fist down onto the armrest of his chair. "Do I need to find a more proficient way to motivate you knaves?"

Xyrus waved a hand at the Holo and it disappeared. A middle aged Belgae general stepped up to take its place. He was met by a dismissing wave from the Dark Lord, but the general would not budge. "Lord Xyrus the armada is assembled and ready for your orders."

"Excellent General, once the Fahn'rir is fully operational we shall begin our siege of Ter'Ar'Tor."

The general paused, his eyes darted about the bridge and then he spoke, "M'Lord, do you think it wise to commit so much of our fleet to this task? Intelligence has said that the planet is a virtual wasteland and. . ."

Before he could finish his sentence, Xyrus was upon him. He grabbed the general by the throat and hoisted him up into the air. Xyrus's rage at being question filled his strength so much that he did not even need the assistance of the uR. The general grabbed at Xyrus's arm and tried desperately to free himself from the crushing grip.

"Do I think it wise General? DO I?!? Who are you to question my orders? What glory have you tasted on your lips? How much blood have you spilled in the name of our people? How many Belgae have you seen die before your eyes for the honor of our people? I do not THINK this move is wise, I KNOW it to be. I have crossed the stars, fought in battles that the bards sing about and you have the audacity to question my will?"

Xyrus squeezed his hand closed, the general's body kicked and flailed as the life was crushed out of him; and then just as swiftly he stopped. His body fell limp and the Dark Lord tossed him across the length of the bridge.

The crew went silent, their tasks stopped as they stared waiting for their leaders next move. His eyes scanned theirs, he drank up their fear, as a shark would blood. "Are there any other objections?"

They knew better than to do anything that would further draw his wrath. After a pause, he spoke again, "Then we move. To Ter'Ar'Tor!"

Another wave of his hand activated the Fahn'rir's communication system. It broadcast his image to each ship in orbit.

"Tonight my brothers we take our rightful place in this world. Tonight we strike Ter'Ar'Tor, the famed home of the former Galactic Council and much as it has crumbled in the face of my vehemence, so shall the planet fall under the weight of our assault. The time for preparation has passed and now is the time for action. Today I shall show you such wonder, such glory, that our peoples name shall stain the lips of all who live and breathe."

Xyrus shut off the communicator and stepped to the front of the bridge, so that he could see out into the depths of space. He closed his eyes and stretched out his hand to either side. Slowly he lowered his head, a silent muttering on his lips.

In his mind's eye space unfurled out before him. His perspective began to pull away from his own body out into space itself. The universe than began to change, erupting into a sea of color as the uR came into his vision as well. He opened his eyes, which now were consumed in the purple energy and his vision returned to normal.

He looked up and the uR exploded around his body in a giant hue of purple and black energy. The crew jumped back from shock, the sight was so foreign, as if a fable had somehow come to life before them. Were it not for Xyrus's composure, some may have thought their leader was covered in some sort of flame.

His chest flexed out and his arms shot back as the energy poured forth from his body into the space in front of the ship. It exploded like a geyser, brilliant, intense and streamed into a giant cylinder of energy until it stopped and poured into a giant pool of energy several thousands of feet in front the Fahn'rir.

After several seconds, the stream stopped and Xyrus fell to one knee. Steam rose up from his body. He took a second to compose himself then stood and turned to his crew. Xyrus was visibly drained; all the color was gone from his face, though he still strove to maintain a level of dominance. "Take the ship into the anomaly," he staggered as he spoke, turned and stalked over to his chair, nearly collapsing as he reached it.

Soon, he thought as his chest heaved, *soon I shall have what is deserved!*

Colin sat on the edge of the broken bridge. His mind trailed off to the past, to when O'Tel had asked him for help. His heart sank at the thought of his fallen teacher. How many had perished, how many had sacrificed their own lives for him? Yet here he stood, on the brink of failure and he felt the encumbrance of life bear down on him.

Colin grabbed a rock and tossed it into the ravine. He took another and rubbed it in his hand. He could feel its life, the subtle energy that rested not only within the stone, but around it as well. He threw it at the generator to its certain doom, but then it stopped in the air and hovered, silently mocking him.

Colin did not need to turn to know that Zhu now stood behind him. No other on the planet could do such a feat. He simply sat, silent and stoic. His eyes focused on the rock that floated in front of him.

"Has the rock bothered you in some way?" she asked as she sat beside him.

"No."

"Then why do you treat it as such?"

"It's just a rock Zhu."

"Is it?" Zhu raised her hand and the stone floated to her grasp. She rubbed her fingers gently along its surface. "Can you imagine all the years this simple rock has seen? How many lifetimes have come and gone and yet it this rock remains. What are we but a flicker of light in its lifespan?"

He looked over to her. "You act as though it's alive, as thought it has thoughts and feelings. It's a rock."

She reached up and touched his cheek with the outside of her hand, gently caressing his flesh. He did not jump, but the contact caught him off guard. Her flesh was warm against his own and her touch both calmed and excited him. He looked into her eyes as she spoke, "I know you have the sight. That you know of the uR and now wield it as your ally."

"Yes, but. . ."

She pressed a finger to his lips. "The uR exists in everything, every facet of life, no matter how small. Every choice we make affects that pool of life, altering it and leaving its mark on the world around us. Some things in life are so important that they leave their mark on time itself. Look at the rock again Colin, but this time open your mind and see more than just the stone in my hand."

Colin looked into her eyes, so thirsting, so caring, and then he looked at the stone in her hand. He focused on it and as his mind did, it seemed as though his vision was zooming in on the stone itself until he was lost within it.

Suddenly Colin was surrounded by darkness, but then that was replaced with the landscape of the broken bridge. Before him stood O'Tel and by the Ter'Ok'Zhu king was himself. The scene played out briefly before him until it faded away and was replaced by O'Tel running to save the shield generator. That too dispersed and was replaced by another moment in time, and so on and so forth in more and more rapid succession until it stopped on a scene from a time long lost to the stars.

Great black ships covered the sky line and along the planet's surface were thousands of Ter'Ok'Zhu ready for war. They were strikingly different in everything about themselves in comparison to O'Tel. The ships in the sky struck fear into Colin. His mind recognized them instantly as the same ships that had destroyed the Ares. Behind him lay an endless field of grass, but no shield generator.

One of the black ships in the sky fired its main gun. The beam cut into the surface of the planet behind Colin. The earth melted under its force and then began to fracture into a giant crevice. Suddenly the Ter'Ok'Zhu around him began to speak in their native tongue.

Then just as quickly, the very planet itself began to shift. Large cannons erupted from below the planet's surface. Within minutes, the once peaceful landscape was transformed into a full-scale war machine.

The cannons fired, launching a sea of laser fire into the sky and tearing through the enemy warships.

Colin snapped back to the bridge and Zhu, breathing in sharply as he did. "What did you see?" she asked.

He looked deeply into her eyes and that spark shone in his own as he said, "Our salvation."

CHAPTER TWENTY FOUR

Nearly broken and seated stooped over in his chair, Lord Xyrus no longer had a visible air of terror about him. Transporting so many warships, not to mention the behemoth that he now rode aboard, had clearly sapped him of his spirit. At a glance, his body seemed close to death.

Suddenly, the shimmering sea of energy flowing outside of the ship snapped back to the darkness of real space. The ships tore into the bleak emptiness orbiting Ter'Ar'Tor. The planet though defenseless and abandoned still inspired awe amongst the crew of the Fahn'rir. They stared in amazement at the giant orb that rested outside of the main view port.

"Analysis," Xyrus snapped weakly through coughing breaths.

A Holo of the planet popped up in front of him. Lines scanned over the orb, small cross hairs locking on to key points and producing data in the air surrounding it.

A crewmember spoke up, "The planet appears practically abandoned sir. Limited signs of life. Main shield is confirmed down. Shall we begin our ground assault sir?"

Xyrus reached a finger out and pointed to a small area on the upper half of the planet. One of the small crosshairs had begun moving more slowly along the planet's surface. "What is that?" Xyrus demanded.

The crewmembers moved at their stations with an increased intensity, "Scanning, we should have the target identified in ten seconds sir."

The image magnified, showing a group of small blurs. Xyrus waved away the rest of the planet before him and pulled the blurred image to the forefront. The image froze and the computer began to scan its blurred contents. From the shapes, it pulled skeletal images of a series of Bellat and Terran ships. The last one was unable to be identified, but Xyrus knew its origin already.

The Holo resumed its motion and the image became nearly crystal clear. Another crewmember spoke up, "Sir we have confirmation of targets. It appears to be a small squadron of mixed Bellat and Terran fighters along with a group of four Bellat Warships. Your orders sir?"

Xyrus paused and coughed heavily. Some of his strength was beginning to return to him. "Is this the best they can do? Is this how little they respect my might?" he asked himself.

Xyrus tried to stand, but his legs would not cooperate with him. They would not straighten as he leaned forward, instead choosing to shake. He relented as the image on the Holo revealed the Slai'Nor and the rest of the Alliance Ships. Xyrus slammed a fist on his armrest. "KILL THEM," he screamed with what little strength he could muster, "KILL THEM ALL!"

On board the Slai'Nor, Colin and Zhu sat beside each other, the black of space rushed toward them on the view screen. A small haze filled the bottom of the screen as the ship pressed up through the atmosphere. In the distance, the Belgae armada tore into space. The view screen lit up with alerts identifying the threat in the distance. Colin hammered some buttons and said, "I know, I know, obviously the whole point of being out here is to intercept them."

Zhu touched his shoulder, trying to calm him down. "She only means to inform us."

"Of information we already know."

The ship squealed angrily at him in response.

"That's not what I meant," Colin said.

A foreign symbol flashed at the bottom corner of the screen. "Incoming transmission," Zhu said.

Colin tapped a solid blue flashing button. "Finally. Tar'Sham?"

The Bellat prince appeared on screen, taking a primary position on the display. Behind him was a mass of mechanisms that seemed both ancient and alien in their design. It very much seemed as though he were trapped in the inner workings of some giant clock.

Tar'Sham replied, "Colin, are you positive that this system is still in working order? Half seems rusted over and the other portion seems ready to collapse in upon me."

"No, that entire system was built by the Ter'Ok'Zhu, don't be fooled by the ascetics, I'm certain it'll run."

Tar'Sham looked around befuddled, "Assuming that it does indeed still function, how can you be sure that I can operate it?"

"I can't," Colin admitted, "but the specs of the system seem simple enough. Just think of it as a giant game of Darbash, multiple levels functioning on different planes but all working as a single unit."

Tar'Sham shook his head. "Only you would bet our fate on blind faith. Pray it is that simple."

The Slai'Nor erupted in a much more anxious tone. More alerts filled the view screen, pushing Tar'Sham's image to the bottom corner. Colin scanned the alerts, "I told you. . ."

"Incoming fire," Zhu snapped.

"Damn it," Colin yelled as he hit a dark red button above the flashing blue one. "We're coming in hot boys, take your girls to the ball because this is going to be a tricky dance."

"Walk with honor brother."

"In life or death," Colin replied. He banked the Slai'Nor hard to the side.

The Slai'Nor and the rest of the squadron broke off from their formation as they exited the atmosphere. A hailstorm of thick red lasers greeted them. The smaller fighters were easily able to weave their way back and forth between them. The larger Bellat warships were not as lucky.

Made for combat, not maneuverability, the warships absorbed most of the incoming fire. Their heavy armor plating was able to take the beating as they fired back, sending their own flurry of green laser fire back.

Seated in the center of the command center of the Planetary Defense System was its most uncomfortable operator, Tar'Sham. The Bellat people in general were not admirers of technology, yet here he sat, utterly encapsulated by thousands of mechanisms.

The sea of metal looked beyond worn, a result of centuries of stagnation. Levers, buttons and other odd controlling devices surrounded Tar'Sham like hundreds of tiny invaders frozen in their attack. Were it not for Zhu's translation of the equipment, scraps of parchment adhered to the devices; he would have no bearing on where to start.

Tar'Sham turned a lever, which was marked power, a half turn to the left, then pressed it into the console. Streams of light flooded the control panel. Eventually it streamed its way across the entire room. The blue glow of light from the freshly activated system also carried with it a hum of life. In front of Tar'Sham, a small Holo of the planet materialized. A prerecorded voice began to speak in the Ter'Ok'Zhu language and consequently whatever bit of knowledge it was trying to impart on him was lost.

Below the Holo were four switches. Zhu had marked them, *Northern, Southern, Western and Eastern hemisphere.* Under the switches were dials. Presently they were turned all the way up. Tar'Sham pulled the switches down. The nameplates lit up and then the sections on the Holo of the planet did as well.

Along the planet's surface, amongst the fields, the buildings and deep in the sea, a deep rumbling began to shake the surface. Certain areas lit up with blue energy, lines outlined giant squares. Then down their center, another stream of energy lit up.

The surface of the squares shook violently, sending clouds of dust into the air. Then the earth split open from their center, pulling apart.

Tar'Sham stared at everything around him, his eyes glazed over in amazement. Hundreds of different mechanisms were springing to life, moving slowly at first, but then picking up speed. Centuries of rust began to shed itself from the metal beneath. As the pieces picked up their pace, they began to shine with a new glow.

As the machinery sped along, more screens began to materialize before Tar'Sham. They reacted to his touch, zooming in and out, as he moved his hands along their ghostly surface. On one screen to his right, he saw the ships in space as though they were physically there before him.

Their forces were viciously outnumbered and if Tar'Sham could not figure out how to make the system work soon, they would all be dead. His hands darted along the board trying desperately to find some button or lever that would control the weapons.

By chance, his hand glanced over the Holo of the planet and a slew of targeting sensors lit up along the display of the space battle. Tar'Sham stopped and his attention locked onto the screen. His eyes shifted from it to the Holo of the planet. The upper half of it glowed red. Tar'Sham touched it again and the targeting display disappeared.

Again, he reached up and touched the Holo, once more the planet lit up, and the targeting sensors appeared. He pulled a hand away from the planet, the Holo enlarged, displaying different gun turrets, and torpedo ports scattered along the planet's surface. With his other hand, he touched one of the Belgae ships in the space display. The targeting sensors darted across the screen and one after another followed his touch. As he pressed his finger on them, each individual sensor stuck in place glowing a brighter red. Then he looked at the turrets and ports, as individual sensors locked onto the Belgae ship, corresponding turrets and ports turned red as well.

Tar'Sham's mind raced, his own mechanisms spinning furiously. His hand dared to move to a large turret near the center of the planet. As his finger touched the ghostly red hologram, its color changed to a bright green and the Turret fired.

On board the Fahn'rir, the Dark Lord watched the display of the battle unfold before him. A steady stream of laser fire poured forth from his armada towards the Terran and Bellat fighters. They were small enough on the whole to make their execution a difficult task to accomplish, but time was now the Dark Lord's ally and soon enough he would see the end of those foolish enough to stand against him.

Then one of his crew spoke up. "Lord Xyrus, there appears to be an unexplainable amount of movement along the planet's surface. Also a large surge of energy is stemming from near the planets core."

"On display," Xyrus said waving the battle scene to the side. Ter'Ar'Tor rose up to take its place before him. He stared at the planet, examined the bits of movement along its surface. His mind puzzled as to what its cause could be. "Thermal signatures."

The display changed, shifting from a physical view of the planet to a more colorful version. Seas of reds and blues melted in and out of each other along the planet's surface. As they grew larger and larger, their color melted in a pool around them.

Realization snapped into Xyrus's mind. As unfathomable as it seemed, he knew what was about to happen. "Raise our shields. NOW!"

Crewmembers hustled to heed his order and within seconds, a faint glow snapped around the Fahn'rir, then just as quickly it disappeared.

BOOM! One of the midsized Belgae warships took a direct hit to its port side. Before it could raise its own shields another two beams of green energy came shooting up from the planet's surface. They tore through the ships metal leaving gaping holes in their wake. Then a screaming green ball of energy came screaming up from the planet's surface. It collided into the ships belly. The Belgae ship exploded into a giant ball of flame.

The other ships near the rear of the line followed the Fahn'rir's example and put up their shields as well.

Tar'Sham furiously darted his hands back and forth amongst the enemy ships and the gun on the planet. He had discovered that each weapon had a significant refractory period and as such, he needed to balance how they were used.

Streaks of red streamed down toward the planet in response to his attack. This barrage was welcome, as it meant not only was his assault garnering success, but also that his comrades were now able to proceed with less interference.

As the enemy fire met its target, the entire command center shook under the weight of the impact. Two turrets exploded from the barrage. Tar'Sham focused a number of the guns at the Fahn'rir. Together he fired them and a nearly united stream of green raced up from the planet's surface.

The explosion as they hit the Fahn'rir consumed nearly half of the ship. Tar'Sham spun in his chair and began punching numerous buttons on a new control panel. In the display, the Fahn'rir appeared and was thoroughly scanned. Data streamed forth revealing that even as massive as the strike had seemed, it only had minimal effects against the Fahn'rir's shields, which were promptly recharging themselves with every passing second.

Tar'Sham spun again and tapped yet another portion of the control panel. This time Colin appeared before him. "I'm afraid his ship is too well protected. Even the planets weapons in have had little to no effect on the Fahn'rir's defenses."

Colin's attention was focused past Tar'Sham, as he was more focused on navigating the incoming fire than making eye contact. "Just focus on taking out as many of those secondary ships as you can. We'll take care of the Fahn'rir."

The Slai'Nor pressed on through the battlefield, streaking past the giant Belgae warships towards it target in the rear of the fracas.

On either side of the front of the Fahn'rir, giant bay doors opened and like a swarm of locusts, hundreds of Nergal fighters poured out into the battle.

The green of the planetary lasers ripped through their numbers as they passed through the protective field of the Fahn'rir. The Nergal fighters scattered and opened fire, adding even more chaos to the sea of death that now filled the void of space around Ter'Ar'Tor.

The Slai'Nor would not be deterred, nor would any other of the group that followed behind it. Both sets of fighters neared each other, closer and closer in a dangerous game of mortality, neither side willing to yield.

They shot past each other, metal passing by metal by mere feet. It was a beautiful dance, which showed how skilled both sets of pilots were. Both sides opened fire as they passed by each other. The Slai'Nor's shields glowed as they absorbed the incoming hail of fire from the Belgae fighters, returning in kind and sending streaks of color that stained the sky in explosions. The sheer mass of steel that stood between them and the Fahn'rir was seemingly impassible, yet still they pressed forward.

The Slai'Nor drew closer to Xyrus's ship and had nearly passed through the entire swarm of Nergal fighters, when the Belgae changed their tactics. Instead of continuing a direct assault on the Slai'Nor, the remaining wave of fighters stopped and formed a blockade between the Ter'Ok'Zhu ship and its goal. Those Belgae that had passed, circled back, half to reinforce the blockade and the others to attack the Terran and Bellat fighters.

Zhu fired the secondary guns as quickly as they would allow, yet for every enemy fighter she destroyed, it seemed that two more would take its place. "There are simply too many fighters to allow for a clear path."

"We don't have any other choice. Our shields are getting too low to break off now. We only have one shot at this," Colin replied.

The ship spoke up, catching both of their attentions. Colin banked it to the side, "Why didn't you just mention that in the first place?"

The ship chirped back, obviously annoyed with the brashness of its new pilot. "Here it is," Zhu said.

Along the consol was a single switch with what appeared to be a black flower and a skull of some form. She flipped it up and pressed the flashing red button underneath. The Slai'Nor began to shake forcefully.

The top and bottom of both of the Slai'Nor's wings detached slightly and then swung up towards the rear. Filling up their underbelly were foot long cylinders that each housed a missile.

On the screen before Zhu, targeting crosshairs began to lock on to every enemy ship that lay before them. The last crosshair found its target, a solid beep sounded, and then the thunderous bass as the cluster of missiles launched together.

In the forward display, hundreds of jet streams dotted the space before them. The missiles sped off at the stagnant fighters at such a speed that it allowed the Belgae pilots no time to react to the assault.

The onslaught exploded into the barricade and the blast lit up space into a giant plume of white fire. The Slai'Nor tore through it and spat out the other side. The Fahn'rir now stood directly in front of it. Energy snapped and hissed at the Ter'Ok'Zhu ship passed through the Belgae shield.

Colin opened fire with the main gun, cutting a large line of destruction through it outer hull. Bolts of laser fire shot up in return for the Fahn'rir's surface.

Soon, other members of Reaper Squadron joined in behind the Slai'Nor, adding to its assault. Moments later the sea of remaining Nergal fighters gave chase.

Colin looked on his display screen at Lieutenant Johnson. "Keep those Nergal fighters off my back Johnson."

"We're on it."

Colin looked over to Zhu as the image of Johnson faded away. "Are you sure you want to do this?"

She looked at him, saw his face and saw such compassion behind his eyes, such concern. Colin was striking and confident, but in this moment, there was something utterly vulnerable about him. Her heart drew into a knot and she paused. The feeling was so foreign and new and yet so right; yet it frightened her to her core. She could not place where its origin came from, anxiety about knowing what her task was in this plan, or was it simply from seeing Colin care for her, for her safety. O'Tel had never prepared her for such questions, or for such feelings.

The reality of the situation took hold of her as a laser bolt struck the ship. She focused her mind and relaxed, taking a sharp concerted breath. "Yes this is the only way to protect the planet, and ultimate the galaxy. I believe in you Colin."

Colin paused, the words distracting him from the situation at hand. "He did not know how to respond to the statement. They had known each other for such a brief amount of time, yet when he looked at her, it seemed as though they had always known each other, as if they were connected on some unexplainable level that transcended time. He wanted to reach out to her, but his focus needed to remain on the Slai'Nor's controls. "Be safe then," was all he could manage.

They exchanged a glance and she got up and left the cockpit. Colin watched as she walked away, but the ship's squealing brought his attention back to the view screen. He weaved the Slai'Nor down closer to the hull of the Fahn'rir.

The Slai'Nor weaved its way through the oncoming fire until it was mere feet from the Fahn'rir's hull. At such close range the exterior gun could no longer target the Ter'Ok'Zhu ship, but that did not mean that they were safe. Laser fire still shot past them, fired from the growing number of Nergal fighters that now chased behind them.

The Reapers and the Slai'Nor shifted back and forth, dodging portions of the Fahn'rir that cropped out from the hull, as well as the laser fire from the enemy ships behind them. A shot ripped into the Slai'Nor and lit its hull up with a small explosion.

Colin scrambled about at the main consol; the ship cried out in pain and then screamed at him in anger as he flicked a series of buttons with his free hand. Lieutenant Johnson popped up on the view screen. "Johnson, my shields are too weak to take any more abuse. Break off and see if some of those bastards will go with you."

Johnson smiled, "Just like Omega Nine eh Cap? If they won't follow, we'll give 'em a good reason to." He tapped a pad off to his side and his attention turned to something off his screen. "Reapers, Delta Gamma Ninety Five, follow my lead boys. Hope you all ate light for lunch." He returned his attention to Colin. "Good luck to you both Cap."

"Walk with honor Johnson," Colin replied and then Johnson disappeared from his display.

Behind the Slai'Nor, the Reaper's engines turned a bright blue as the reversed their thrust. Giant flaps opened from the top of their ships, causing the force from the change of inertia to flip the fighters in a one hundred and eighty degree turn.

The pilots dropped the flaps, hit their afterburners and opened their guns full bore. The Belgae could not react fast enough and the first wave of Nergal fighters quickly met their death.

The Reapers burst through the sea of fire and headed up away from the Fahn'rir. Half the Nergal fighters broke formation and gave chase, not allowing them to outflank the rest of their numbers.

The brief pause allowed Colin the time he needed to adjust the consol to not only allow him control of the ship's navigation, but also limited control of the weapons systems. The view screen split to show both the front and rear views of the Slai'Nor.

Colin opened fire and took out a couple of the Nergal fighters following him. Though not as accurate as when done separately, he still showed considerable proficiency in his use of the weapons system. Along the side of his display was a three dimensional skeletal display of the Fahn'rir along with a general display of the ships flying along its surface. A single red target flashed on one particular part of the Fahn'rir directly ahead of the path of the Slai'Nor.

Colin punched up Zhu onto his display. She was heavily strapped into a chair, awaiting some sort of impact. "We're almost there Zhu. It might get a bit bumpy at the end, but theoretically this should work."

She smiled and nodded trying not to show her concern, "I understand the risk Colin and I am ready to take it. You have a saying I believe, walk with honor."

Colin nodded, "In life and death." He looked up and saw that the red target was nearly upon them. "Here we go."

The Slai'Nor pitched up away from the Fahn'rir. The Nergal fighters followed suit, forming into a funnel as they chased after their prey. The nose of the Slai'Nor glowed as its main cannon charged.

Suddenly the mighty ship arched back down towards the Fahn'rir and fired its main gun. The glow from the beam tore through the sea of red laser fire, then through the stream of Nergal fighters and finally into the hull of the Fahn'rir itself.

The remaining Belgae were lost as the Slai'Nor tore through their ranks, penetrating into the cloud of fire and debris from its attack. As the ship pierced through the Belgae ranks, it emerged just above the Fahn'rir's hull, pulling up to skim across it. The Slai'Nor fired a projectile into the hole it had created from the blast of its main cannon and then sped off into space.

The shimmering black metal of the underside of the pod was now scratched and scorched from its impact into the hull of the Fahn'rir. Bits of shredded metal, melted and charred, rested around its edges, the wake from the pod's collision. The lower half of the pod's casing popped open, letting out an exhale of steam as it separated itself from the rest of the pod.

A group of Belgae soldiers charged into the hallway and stopped as they made visual contact with the pod. Their leader stepped forward and threw an inspecting glance at the situation.

A bright white light began to pour forth from the edges of the open section of the pod. The leader of the soldiers spat out as he pointed toward it, "FIRE!"

The rest of the group opened fire, sending bolts of red energy flying across the hallway into the hull of the pod. It shuddered briefly and then exploded outward, flying through the air towards the soldiers. Behind the piece of the pod, a sea of white energy erupted that filled the entire room.

The metal of the pod crashed into the soldiers and carried them back into the opposing doorway, crushing under its weight.

The light in the hallway faded and both the soldiers and the bottom half of the pod fell to the floor. Standing at the now exposed interior of the pod was Zhu. A slight glow of energy still enveloped her body, encasing her in a glow.

Her hair pulled back and braided, she wore a white and gold tunic with skintight sleeves that opened to a more billowy portion from her elbow down. It was cut at her hips so a flap of cloth extended past her pelvis, black tights and white knee-high boots covered the rest of her legs. She carried no weapon, as she was enough of one on her own.

Zhu stepped forth from the pod and looked at the scene before her. She placed a finger to a small device that rested in her ear and applied pressure. "I'm in," she said.

"That was the easy part," Colin's voice echoed in her ear. "You know the rest, good luck."

"Hopefully luck will be something I shan't need."

Zhu clasped her hands together and pulled them apart, forming a sword out of the uR. The blade was sleek and more ornate than usual. It hummed with energy as she spun it behind her arm. With her free hand, she gathered in the uR, forming a growing ball of energy that enveloped it. She charged forward and thrust it toward the door. A stream of energy poured forth and struck the steel.

In the cargo bay, a group of Belgae soldiers charged toward a closed door. Behind that group, hundreds more began to filter their way into the room.

BOOM! The door exploded out into the cargo bay, carrying hot shrapnel along in its trail. A large fireball followed closely behind. The destruction took out nearly all of the Belgae that so foolishly had been charging forward.

White energy crackled along the new opening in the wall and through the chaos stepped Zhu. Immediately laser fire tore through the air to meet her. Zhu's skill with the uR was matched only by her skill with the blade. The sword moved as though it was simply an extension of her body, as forced as taking a breath. It rose up and around to deflect any shot that might hit her otherwise.

As she walked into the bay, the Belgae soldiers rushed toward her. Zhu's eyes darted along the outline of the room, the streams of uR danced with each new movement of the enemy soldiers.

Suddenly something clicked in her mind and time seemed to slow down. O'Tel had always talked about reading the uR, about it being an extension of life, time and space. He had told her how everything was interconnected and that those who knew how to look could see the subtlest swings in its flow, such that even an action as simple as a butterfly flapping its wings could be observed across galaxies.

Zhu danced through the ranks of soldiers who fruitlessly continued their charge to her. Her every subtle move was beautiful, a choreographed dance amongst the chaotic storm that flowed against her. Zhu weaved in between blows, dodged out of the of laser blasts and struck only when threatened. Thrusts of her palm into the Belgae soldiers were amplified by the uR so that each one sent hordes of them flying aside.

The battle was taking its toll on the cargo bay itself, as missed shots had blackened the walls and destroyed several pieces of equipment. In one move, Zhu sheathed her sword, spun around and reached out to two giant columns on the other end of the bay.

She could feel the steel on her hands even though her flesh touched only the air. Zhu pulled back and the columns tore out from their bases. They screamed a horrible high-pitched whine as they fell down crushing the Belgae beneath them. The columns landed on either side of Zhu, sending a cloud of dust and metal into the air.

The moment was all that Zhu needed. She crouched down and her body became consumed by white energy. She used the uR to spring herself up like a missile. The floor exploded with shock wave from the force as she flew up to the ceiling. Zhu made impact with it and the metal melted into liquid as she easily passed through it.

CHAPTER TWENTY FIVE

The engines on the Slai'Nor burned bright as a supernova. The mighty Ter'Ok'Zhu ship pitched up away from the Fahn'rir, splatters of energy spat out at the base of its engines as it fought hard to gain enough momentum to pull away from the hull of Xyrus's Capital Ship. As the Slai'Nor pushed back into the black of space the Fahn'rir opened fire. Giant red streams of death flew past the ship coming dreadfully close. Colin maneuvered the ship in a twisted dance around them as he pushed into space.

The battlefield in front of them was no more inviting than that which they had just left. Hordes of Nergal fighters dashed about and Colin fired the ships weapons forging a path to escape through.

Colin tapped his control pad and Johnson appeared on the screen. "We need to create some sort of distraction."

Johnson looked up at Colin. On his HUD a radar display of the battlefield showed thousands of tiny blips between the massive Belgae warships. "Why? You feeling dangerous Cap?" Johnson asked with a wry smile.

Colin could not help but smile back and nod. "Bout time we got to have some fun."

"You've got the lead Cap'y, we'll be hard on your six."

"Keep it tight boys, things are gonna get a lot dirtier before they get clean. I think I'm gonna ask one of the big girls to dance."

Colin tapped another series of buttons and Tar'Sham appeared. He spoke before Colin could get the chance, "I heard your conversation Colin. It is fool hearty, unconsciously dangerous and complete idiocy to even attempt what you are thinking."

Colin simply stared at the display, unsure how to respond to the scolding. Then, Tar'Sham smiled. "Father would be proud. I am clear with what my role to play is. Honor in life brother!"

Colin nodded, "and in death." As Tar'Sham disappeared from the display Colin sighed, "Let's do this."

The web of fighters between the Slai'Nor and its target was inconceivably dense. The chaos of their movement overpowering, a dance of metal and energy that nearly sucked in Colin's vision. A giant bolt of green from the planet tore through their ranks and snapped Colin out of his trance.

The Alliance ships' guns opened up as they neared the fighters, returning fire against the sea of red. The Slai'Nor's front shields deflected what shots the ship could not avoid.

It was a precise dance that the Reapers had to perform. The Ter'Ok'Zhu's technology was vastly superior to that of its enemies on this field of battle and thus it provided cover to the squad, a virtual flying shield. The slightest mismanuver would render that cover meaningless. Suddenly a large green bolt flashed past the ship's hull.

Colin pulled hard on the control stick, banking the Slai'Nor away from the deadly blast. Two of the reaper fighters unable to match the move fell to the enemy fire.

Even as advanced a craft as the Slai'Nor was, Colin knew that under the never-ending barrage, eventually the ship would give. The Belgae fighters were more numerous then he had gauged and the Slai'Nor was too damaged to try the same tactic that had gained him access to the Fahn'rir.

The ship buckled and shook as the onslaught of fire pierced its way through the ships shields and lit up the hull. Colin's hands tore around the control panel, desperately routing auxiliary power to the shields.

"What's the play Cap'y? Seems like no matter how many Nergs we take out there's double between us and that warship."

Colin looked at the radar; the Nergals they had passed were turning back to engage them. Another reaper disappeared from the display. He breathed heavy and said, "Take the reapers and break off, get out of this mess. I've got a plan. Be ready to make your run, but not until I give you the call."

"Aye, aye Cap'y."

The reapers streamed away from the battle, back toward the openness of space. A fraction of the Nergals broke off with them, but the majority focused their attention on the Slai'Nor.

Colin tapped a series of commands into the panel of the Slai'Nor. "I need you to take the wheel. Just follow along this course."

The ship chirped back at him questioningly.

"Trust me," Colin said as he pushed the thrust all the way forward and stood up from his seat. The Slai'Nor's engines roared to life and the ship shot out at a furious speed.

As the Slai'Nor neared the warship, it suddenly turned away sharply. The ship curved up and away, circling in a large spiral in front of its target.

On board the Slai'Nor Colin closed his eyes and lowered his head. He did not know if what he was planning would work. It seemed so fanciful, yet he trusted Zhu and some unknown part of his soul calmed his nerves and whispered for him to have faith. For a brief second he thought he could hear O'Tel's voice. He brought his hands together to form a triangle at his chest and energy radiated from the empty space between them. At first, a tiny ball of green fire grew and consumed his flesh. It climbed up his arm, consumed his chest and then finally his entire body.

Colin looked up and his eyes snapped open. Energy spilt out from them like sparks from a forge. He turned, faced away from the screen and spread his arms wide. A beam of green shot forth from his torso, seamlessly traveling through the hull of the Slai'Nor.

From the aft of the ship the brilliant beam of green shot out, blending in with the thrusters and then extending past them. It consumed the Nergal fighters behind the ship, freezing them and dragging them along.

Every fighter that made contact with the beam or the growing mass dragging behind the Slai'Nor was sucked in and captured. The weight of so many fighters pulled on Colin's body, dragging him across the floor of the cockpit. "Now!"

The Slai'Nor stopped its spiral and angled back towards the Belgae Warship. It opened fire on the Nergal fighters as they once again formed a wall to impede them. Explosions lit up space and the Slai'Nor continued its charge. Laser fire absorbed into its front shields and then as they failed into its hull. It shook from the blasts, but did not waver from its course.

Sweat poured off Colin's body as his muscles flexed to their maximum from the strain of his task. The ship screamed as it shook from the barrage of laser fire. "Faith old girl, you must have faith," Colin struggled between labored breaths.

Colin dared a glance back at the display, "Now Johnson."

The Slai'Nor smashed through the blockade, tearing through the Nergal fighters as if they were made of paper. The remnants of their destruction slipped into the mass of ships trailing behind the Slai'Nor. They exploded as the debris tore through their hulls and send a series of shock waves rippling through the ball of energy. The Slai'Nor, charred, damaged and smoking from its assault, pulled up just in time to avoid colliding with the Belgae warship.

Inside the cockpit, Colin screamed out as the exertion of what he was doing finally caught up to him. His body slid across the room and he released the beam just before he hit the far wall. His connection broken, Colin allowed the strain to sink its teeth into his body and he collapsed down to his knees.

Behind the Slai'Nor, as the beam diffused, all of the carnage contained within smashed into the hull of the warship like a giant molten asteroid. A plume of death rose up behind the Slai'Nor as it shot away to safety. The remaining reaper fighters tore through the plume and dropped rows of their own bombs into the opened section of the warship's hull. They pierced deep within the core of the warship, doubling the damage they unleashed.

Two of the planetary lasers tore through the warship's belly, striking the death knell. The warship exploded in a giant ring of fire, sending a shockwave out into space. Colin stood up turned and nearly stumbled back to his chair. "You see, I told you; you have to faith in me if this relationship is going to work."

Suddenly something deep inside of Colin took over and his body was flooded with the uR as primal instinct took over his action. On the screen in front of him, a second Belgae warship was rapidly approaching on a collision course with the Slai'Nor. Colin screamed out, "NOOOOOO!!!!!"

Alarms screamed out across the bridge of the Fahn'rir, lights flashed, massive amounts of data spilled onto the Holo and the crew moved at a hastened pace. Xyrus sat apart from the madness as motionless as a statue.

An image of the intruder popped up onto the Holo, he grabbed at it, pulled her image to the forefront and brushed the rest of the information away. Her image froze as his eyes glowed with intrigue and glee. Fate had bestowed a gift on him as his lost prize had returned to him and this time he would see the princess dead.

Suddenly he felt a tug at the back of his mind, so bitingly familiar and yet so horribly foreign, as if some tiny insect was burrowing into his spine. Xyrus refused to hear their call. His skill with the uR was increasing and he knew that Zhu was headed directly for the bridge. He would not have his glory taken away again, not even by their command.

Xyrus forced the thoughts aside, blocking out the voice of his master. Suddenly, what seemed like a ball of acid burst inside of his head. Xyrus yelled out and grabbed at the sides of his skull. "ENOUGH!"

Xyrus pointed to a door on the bridge and commanded, "Leave me!"

The majority of the crew knew to obey. They stood and hurried off the deck. One of the officers walked up and knelt before the Dark Lord. "Lord Xyrus, the battle still need our atten..."

Before he could finish speaking, Xyrus's hand gripped around his throat and lifted the officer into the air. The Dark Lord's anger had become tangible as deep purple tendrils licked their way from Xyrus's hand to the officer's face. "I am aware of the girl's chances of reaching her goal and I am even more painfully aware of the inadequacies of our fleet. You, Captain, have underestimated two most crucial things in this moment," the officer's flesh burned beneath his grip.

Xyrus thrust him down to the floor, slightly buckling it under the force. He stood domineeringly over the man. "You underestimate the girl's ability, for she wields a power your simple mind could never comprehend."

He raised a hand in the air next to his own face, staring at it as his hand erupted in a purple flame of energy. "Power I myself had once dismissed as myth and magic."

Xyrus clenched his fist and the flame's intensity increased. He shifted his gaze back to the officer. "Yet it is real and there lies your second failure. For you underestimate me. So allow me to better illustrate that point."

As Xyrus thrust his hand the uR shot out from it, consuming and burning the officer. The blaze intensified until it was blinding and then in an instant it disappeared leaving only a scorched stain where the officer had been. Xyrus turned to the other remaining crewmembers, "Leave me," both his hand erupted with the uR, "NOW!"

Terrified the remaining crewmembers rushed off the bridge. Xyrus waved a hand and two giant blast doors sealed off the room behind them. The lights flickered and faded, though the reason was not mechanical in nature. Out of the shadows walked an all too familiar figure, the Malef King. This time he was more than just a shadowy figure, this time he appeared all too real. He stood a good foot taller than Xyrus and his build was obviously muscular. The King was large and lean, he seemed sculpted from stone for he bore no visible flaws in his physique. The Malef King was covered in a smooth black armor that bonded to him like a second skin.

The King's armor not only protected him, but also served to intimidate those that stood before him. The shoulder and arm pieces were embellished with spikes and blades. The tips of each finger were even pointed to give the appearance of claws. At the center of the King's chest, he bore the symbol of not only his people, but of his royal lineage as well. His helm was demonic, as if fear itself had been forged into some twisted tangible idea that now rested upon the King's head. Shades of black and gray created gothic, beastly angles and the eyes were shaped to express a constant glare. The jaw piece was separated and allowed the king to open and close it as he spoke. Along his mouth sharp metal teeth sat between two yellow fangs. Gold horns crested the back of the helm, matched by a faceplate along his brow. Together they served as his crown. The red of the King's eyes glowed even brighter beneath the sea of gold. As the Malef King stood there, evil forged into one single living being. Contempt overwhelmed Xyrus's emotions.

The bass of his voice shook the room, the power behind it became almost tangible as he spoke. "Lord Xyrus. Come, kneel and show your Master respect."

Xyrus did as was commanded of him. Again the King spoke, "I sense your blood lust for the girl, but you are our herald and it is not the time nor the place for her blood to be spilt. It does not serve our purpose, you threaten to undo all the plans we have laid for you."

Xyrus looked up and the uR raged forth around his body as his anger took form. He felt the strength of the sword flow into him and so he dared to speak, "You would deny me this glory?"

The Malef King slammed a foot down and a wave of black energy washed through the room and over Xyrus. The Dark Lord suppressed the pain as best as he could, unwilling to yield his point. "Your glory is insignificant. You have been given a task to complete for MY PEOPLE and you will OBEY MY COMMAND!"

The Malef King raised a hand and a black tendril of uR snapped out, wrapping itself around Xyrus like a coil. It stopped just below his chin, pulsed and smoke rose off his skin. "Do not think yourself greater than your destiny Xyrus! You were picked to play a role. You are ours to command and you will obey me boy or YOU WILL DIE!"

The tendril pulsed and Xyrus screamed as every fiber in his body cried out in pain. He knew the Malef King was strong, had tasted the bite of his anger once before, but his own strength had grown since that time. Xyrus had never lived his life a slave to anyone's will. His hatred for such a misuse of power burned bright within his black heart. He was no one's pawn. Bile rose up from his stomach and his flesh glowed purple as the uR consumed him. Xyrus lowered his head and screamed through gritted teeth, "NO!"

Xyrus focused on his hatred, allowed it to consume his soul and fuel his strength. He could feel the Jahan's thirst for his defiance, its need for chaos. The Jahan fed him strength to fight back. Xyrus flung a hand up at the tendril and a blade of energy cut through it. The Malef King stared in utter shock. The portion wrapped about Xyrus's body disappeared and he rose to his feet.

"I shall not be your lap dog any longer. I am the Sword Bearer and so I shall write the course of destiny myself!" Xyrus said.

"Fool. You allow pride to cloud your judgment. I should crush this ship and end your life where you stand."

Black uR spread out from the Malef King like a deathly fog threatening to consume the whole of the bridge. Xyrus simply laughed at the display. "But you cannot, for you need me."

"NO!" the Malef King corrected him. He shot a blast of energy at Xyrus with both his hands. The beams struck the Dark Lord in the chest and grabbed hold of him. The Malef King pulled his arms back and the beams retracted, pulling Xyrus in with them. The Malef King increased their intensity as he drew near and Xyrus dropped to his knees. He could feel the life being sucked out of his body. Still defiant, he refused to scream through the pain. The Malef King snapped, "You will obey me! CONCEDE TO MY AUTHORITY!"

Xyrus refused; death was a preferable option to conceit. Xyrus knew he did not need to serve anyone any longer. He had tasted too much power to yield to anyone. Then it came to him, a slight whisper at first, barely audible in his mind.

It grew louder!

The Jahan, called to Xyrus and with his last bit of strength he reached back and grabbed hold of the hilt of the ancient sword. As he pulled it free, a warmth flooded over his body. For a second he mistook the feeling for the sweet release of death, but as it intensified, he knew it was the sword feeding him power. With its strength Xyrus rose up and yelled, "NO!"

He swung the blade at the Malef King, it cut across the front of his helm. The King recoiled back, bewildered that he had been struck. He reached to his face as his body dissolved.

The room instantly snapped back to life; Xyrus its only occupant. He stood with the Jahan in hand and spoke, "I alone shall shape my destiny. I bow to no King."

BAM! The blast doors exploded into the room and behind them stood Zhu, proud and waiting to attack.

Free me

FREE ME

CHAPTER TWENTY SIX

Wisps of smoke filled the edge of the room, rising up from the charred opening where the blast doors had been. Xyrus smirked, his newfound confidence clearly on display.

"Come child," he said placing the Jahan back in its sheath, "face your death."

Zhu charged forward, her sword hidden behind the back of her arm. She reached out with her free hand and a blast of uR shot at Xyrus.

Xyrus crossed his arms in front of his face and the beam splashed out around him, deflected by an invisible bubble.

Zhu pressed forward and as she drew close, Xyrus thrust his arms apart. A wave of force flowed through the room, pushing Zhu's beam back towards her. Zhu stopped, thrust both of her hands out. As they collided their impact rocked the bridge and buckled its steel.

As Zhu neared Xyrus, she could feel the hatred pour out from his body. Their eyes locked and for a second she felt the breath of hesitation within her mind the weight of Xyrus's own bloodlust. Something had changed in the Dark Lord; he seemed unhinged, darker and far more sadistic than the last time she was before him.

Zhu swung her blade at his head, but the dark steel around his wrists snapped up and absorbed the blow. She did not stop to take even a single breath. Her blade freed, Zhu spun her body, adjusting her grip and struck yet again. Once more Xyrus blocked the blow. No matter how Zhu attempted to strike him, Xyrus was there to deflect the blow. The Na'Dral, once a death sentence, now served him as valuable tools.

"Good child, you fight with such passion, such emotion, such a hatred to strike me down," he spat at her between blows, "yet like your masters, you are WEAK!"

Xyrus deflected a blow and kicked Zhu square in the chest. She flew across the room and crashed into a computer terminal. It crackled as she pulled herself free of its debris and backed up to her feet Xyrus skulked towards her, taking in the moment.

Her feet braced against the fractured metal, she pressed off it and leapt. The consol buckled as Zhu flew through the air at Xyrus. Her foot slammed into his jaw sending him spinning around. Just before Zhu's body cleared past his, Xyrus reached out and took hold of her. He used his own momentum to swing the young princess into the crew area below.

Like a wrecking ball, she once again tore through the steel of the deck as her body made impact. Pain shot through her body and she threatened to slip in unconsciousness as Zhu lay in a pile of mangled steel and wires. Xyrus stood over her, disgust filled his eyes as he stared down at her broken body. Zhu fought her eyes open and pulled herself to her feet. He spoke as the uR flowed through his hands, "Your masters were blind to the true nature of the uR. Power lies not in control, but in the sheer force of our own emotion; it feeds our strongest desires."

He fired a stream of uR at her. Zhu pulled herself free from the metal and leapt back up to his level. "It is you who are weak."

Xyrus shot another blast of purple energy at her, but this time Zhu anticipated it. She moved her body, as if walking through a well-choreographed routine and as the beam of energy reached her, she manipulated it around her own body, then redirected it across the bridge. "Your indulgence of your own ego leaves you vulnerable."

As Xyrus's frustration grew the uR wrapped around his hands grew with it, bubbling over and dripping off his flesh onto the floor. "That indulgence saw to the death of both your masters child and I assure you it shall see to yours as well."

Xyrus screamed as he blasted beams of energy at her. They were far too strong for Zhu to deflect, so instead she used her agility to weave her way through the hail of the oncoming fire. She neared close enough to engage him hand to hand again.

This time as Zhu struck Xyrus grabbed her sword with his bare hand. Blood trickled down his flesh as he squeezed his hand tighter. His other hand snapped up around her throat. "Your skills are nearly unmatched in all those I have faced in this life."

He clenched his fist and the blade shattered under its strength. He pulled Zhu in mere inches from his face, "Though they still are not a match for my own."

Xyrus tossed her across the room into the remaining blast doors. Her body indented into their steel frame upon impact. She looked up and fell forward onto the floor. He gathered up the uR in his right hand as, his eyes locked onto her body. Zhu stood up, slowly and with visible pain, but still she rose. Her resilience frustrated him and fueled his anger even further. He yelled, "Now you DIE!"

Xyrus slammed his fist onto the floor and a wave of purple energy shot forth towards Zhu. She looked up and saw the oncoming attack; instinct took control. In a motion, she spun around and a cocoon of white energy took form around her. The cocoon spun about, burned a hole through the floor and sank through it to the deck below. The purple wave rushed over her just as she disappeared, instead slamming into the blast doors and turning them into liquid. Xyrus screamed out, "NO!" He shot beams of uR at his feet, melting the deck and sending himself down after her.

Xyrus slammed into the floor of the lower deck. He stood up and stepped out of the small crater that his impact had left. The uR spoke to him before his physical senses could; danger. Xyrus reached up and caught the Nergal fighter in the air just before it crashed into him. He held it in his grip as though it weighed nothing.

The fighter bay was an environment that favored Zhu's abilities. Numerous items scattered about to provided her both weapons and cover. Xyrus tore the empty fighter in half and tossed the remnants aside. He walked forward and two more fighters flew at him. Xyrus waved a hand, dismissing the attack with a razor like sheet of purple uR. It cut through both of the fighters, splitting them in two. He stopped, looked around and then paused to open his senses to the uR itself.

The floor beneath the Dark Lord quaked as he focused on finding the young princess. "I can taste your fear and hear your thoughts princess. Why play this foolish game? The moment you use your power I shall have you."

The steel rose up at Xyrus's feet and seized hold of his legs. Though the move came at the cost of her location, Zhu now had an advantage and as Xyrus went to strike, she was upon him. Zhu had reformed her sword and furiously struck at the Dark Lord. "You may take my life this day, but it will not be without the cost of your own," she spat between strikes.

With one thrust her blade found its way to Xyrus's shoulder, cutting deep into his flesh. The physical pain hurt him considerably less than the blow to his pride. He thrust his palm into her chest shooting Zhu crashing back through a group of fighters.

Xyrus reached over to his wound, felt its warmth on his fingers and brought a bit of crimson to his face. He bellowed out his disdain, "For that your death shall stain time with the suffering it shall entail."

His hands became engulfed in radiating purple energy, which grew exponentially fast. Bolts of white lightning snapped out from them as their power surged. Xyrus laughed, a hideous sound of sadism sprinkled ever so finely with a dash of hatred and topped with a bit of insanity.

Zhu looked up as she recovered from his attack. She saw him rise up into the air; the orbs surrounding his hands had grown to half the length of his body. Xyrus's arms stretched out and he arched his back awkwardly over, all the while continuing to laugh his sickening cackle.

Zhu could sense the potency of the force he was gathering. She knew that there was only seconds before he struck. She sat down on the deck, legs crossed and hands at her waist. Zhu slipped into a deep meditative trance and the uR took form around her.

She focused her mind inward and searched for her center, her own personal connection to life. It was a skill she loathed practicing so often in her past, yet now it became vital to her survival. Zhu found that place of tranquility and for a second she saw O'Tel's face, felt the warmth of his embrace wash over her.

White streams mixed with blue as they wrapped themselves around her body and just as quickly numerous Nergal fighters flew into a giant orb of crushed steel around her.

Xyrus looked forward; his laughter stopped and was promptly replaced by the deep guttural scream of a single word, "DIE!"

He thrust his hands forward and all the energy that had been accumulating in the orbs burst forth in a wall of energy that was nearly triple Xyrus's own size. It tore through the room decomposing everything in its path. As it hit the ball of metal that surrounded Zhu, Xyrus pressed himself forward. The ball slowly melted away and flew back to the far wall. Metal poured to the ground as the blast continued to burn through her shield. Soon all that remained was the white and gold orb that protected Zhu.

Seeing it only intensified Xyrus's attack until the very wall that Zhu's orb was pressed against fractured. Then the orb cracked and exploded outward, sending the Dark Lord back across the room. Zhu looked up, broken out of her trance. She saw the destruction Xyrus had laid on the room and then saw the new opening in the wall behind her. Zhu snapped up to her feet and out of it.

The moment Zhu entered the new room; she knew she did not want to be there. She looked down at her wrist; a small bracelet flashed a single red light. Zhu seemed frustrated at the sight of it. The room was filled with life, both from the hum of the reactor core in its center and from that of the workers, who now ran to grab weapons.

Structurally the room was intimidating. Giant pillars stretched all throughout, siphoning power from the core and distributing it throughout the ship. They glowed brightly and pulsed in a random sequence based on the ships needs. The core itself was shaped like a giant red diamond. It burned brilliantly, like a giant piece of coal, spewing out streams of thick yellow plasma along its exterior. On the top and bottom were two golden rings that encircled the core. They spun and floated up and down its surface, connected together and to the hull by beams of energy.

Laser fire peppered Zhu's entrance as she moved behind one of the giant pillars. Her attention could not suffer such a distraction and so she reached out with the uR and crushed their guns.

A larger explosion above her proved that even that brief distraction could have cost her her life as Xyrus had entered the room. His mind reached out to the pillar, crushed its base, ripped it from the hull and sent it collapsing down at Zhu.

She ran towards another pillar for cover, deflecting the laser fire from the workers and dodging the uR blasts from Xyrus. He shifted his attention to the workers. "Fools, you shall not steal this prize from me."

Xyrus tore the pillar near Zhu and sent it crashing on top of them. Their screams muffled instantly under the crunching metal as it smashed into the floor.

Zhu looked down at her wrist and this time the bracelet flashed green. A smile came to her lips, she crouched down and her body became consumed by energy. Zhu launched herself up through the ceiling. "Coward," Xyrus yelled.

He too leapt up toward the ceiling. The two collided as they reached the metal roof, their impact sending them tearing through the decks of the Fahn'rir. Finally they stopped and burst back up onto the bridge.

Xyrus rose up, as did Zhu. She formed a new blade in her hand as blood dripped down from her lips, now stained bright red.

Sweat and dirt covered her body and she wheezed as one hand clutched broken ribs.

"Enough," Xyrus called out as she charged. He pulled the Jahan from its sheath; black energy licked his flesh as the sword was allowed its freedom. With his other hand Xyrus reached out, black strands of liquid webbing shot forth and grabbed hold of Zhu's body. Purple energy danced along them, forcing her to her knees in dreadful pain.

"You see now! You HAVE lost!" he spat. Xyrus stepped in closer to her, the pulses of energy increasing with each step, drawing louder more agonizing screams from Zhu. "You were a fool to face me alone. Now you taste the power of the Jahan. Now you hear the call of Death beckon to you. All your efforts for victory have crashed down in failure at your feet. Where are you left now child?"

He released his dark grasp on her and laid the tip of the Jahan under her chin. "At the end of my blade."

She raised her sword to strike the Jahan away, but it shattered as it made contact with the dark blade. The move puzzled Xyrus. "You still fight, even now, when all is lost, WHY?!?"

She smiled up at him. "Because it is you who stand defeated. Your blind rage has seen my task completed. If my own life should be sacrificed to see an end to such an evil as you, then I die with honor, willingly embracing death. Look around Xyrus and see all that you have wrought."

Xyrus scanned the destruction about the bridge. Alarms blared and what screens that did still work displayed the level of destruction he had unwittingly waged on his ship. Zhu stood up, shaking, a light from out in space behind her glared through the bridge's main panel. Realization struck Xyrus as he drew the Jahan back to finish her. The Slai'Nor fired and its main gun tore into the bridge, consuming everything in its wake.

When the main gun stopped, the bridge was left blackened, charred and open. Immediately the vacuum of space pulled at all that was not attached. Zhu and Xyrus were sucked out into the darkness, their bodies blackened and burned from the blast. As Zhu passed by the Slai'Nor, unconscious, an invisible hand took hold of her and pulled her inside its bay doors.

Xyrus awoke as he passed into the cold black embrace of the galaxy. He still held the Jahan in his hand and so he thrust the sword toward the Fahn'rir. It propelled him down until it implanted into the ship's hull. Black uR slipped out of the sword over his flesh, masking him from the ill effects of space and anchoring him to the ship as well.

He walked along the hull and watched as the Slai'Nor sped away back into the heart of the battle. From behind him a large explosion tore through the bridge of the Fahn'rir. Xyrus knew the reactor would be the next to go and with that, the rest of the ship was doomed.

Xyrus stopped at a panel and reached down, tapping a small number pad on the hull. A hatch popped open and the Dark Lord entered it. As the hatch closed, it became clear that Xyrus had entered an escape ship, the Niit'Horg. A ring of energy glowed around its edges as the ship detached from the Fahn'rir and flew out into space. The Giant capital ship burst forth with a series of explosions and then went nova, taking the nearest warships out with it as well.

Xyrus tapped a small pad in his ship. On his screen he saw his capital ship explode and slammed a fist into the main consol. His ship's engines glowed bright and then jumped through space. What warships that remained turned away from the battle and followed suit.

On board of the Slai'Nor, Colin rushed through the hallways until he reached the cargo bay. Resting on the floor was Zhu. He charged over to her side, held her and placed a hand behind her head.

Zhu awoke and coughed in pain. Her vibrant skin now seemed deathly pale, as if the life was slowly leaking out from some unknown hole. She looked up at him staring into his eyes lost in their familiarity. She whispered, "Did we succeed? Is the planet safe?"

"Yes Zhu. Xyrus is defeated and his fleet is retreating."

She reached a hand up to his cheek. "Then my sacrifice was worth it. Thank you for saving me."

Zhu's eyes fluttered and her head dropped to the side. With his sight altered, Colin could see the life fading out of her body. His heart ached at the thought of losing her. He pressed her body close to his own as tears threatened to consume his vision. Then something in his mind clicked, he was losing her and that was unacceptable, not now and definitely not like this. "NO! I won't lose you. I can't lose you too!"

His body suddenly erupted with power. The uR consumed his flesh. Starting at his chest green light poured out of his body, his skin transforming into pure energy. Slowly it stretched out until he was no longer recognizable. Zhu lay still in his arms, the life all but slipped from her heart. He bent down and pressed his lips to hers. As they embraced the energy along his skin flowed directly into Zhu. It flowed into her veins glowing under her skin.

Suddenly she flung her body back and gasped. The green energy consumed her, leaving Colin and then in one sudden instant it was gone; absorbed into her. As she looked up and opened her eyes, she could see not only into Colin's eyes, but into his soul. The knowing reflection in his own eyes told that Colin was sharing in that bond, knowing every moment of each other's lives; souls interconnected. Then the world came back to prominence and they were in the bay together. She reached up and placed a hand gently on his cheek. "Thank you Colin," she purred weakly.

Words were lost in his mind, not that any would properly suit that moment. Instead he allowed his eyes to speak for him. He had lost so much recently, lost so many people that were close to him. Life as Colin knew would never be the same, but no matter what the future held, he knew that he would always find peace in this moment of time and so he relished in it.

EPILOGUE

In the Great Hall, Colin, Zhu, Tar'Sham and Fa'Sham stood together. Kale gingerly walked in and stopped before them, proud and humbled. Colin stepped forward and nodded, a token of respect for the Baan's service. Colin spoke, "Thank you for today Kale."

Kale laughed, "Death on ground, death in sky. Xyrus not known for mercy."

Colin nodded knowingly and replied, "I fear this battle is only the beginning. War stands before us all. You'd be a welcome ally."

Kale slapped Colin on the shoulder. "My blade, your blade. Others?" Kale shrugged, an utterly awkward movement for his giant frame. "I not sure. War not taste so good to all. They fight, I bring. This I promise."

"We are in your debt Kale," Zhu stepped next to Colin and placed a hand on the mighty Baan's shoulder.

The giant Baan stomped his way, heavy footed out of the hall. Colin turned to the three people before him, people who had been through so much with him, who he now looked to for guidance, council and support. Fa'Sham was still injured, but enough of his strength had returned that he was able to stand without assistance. The red-tinged bandaging and labored breathes kept his usual boastfulness in check. He placed a had on Tar'Sham's and Zhu's shoulders, taking a deep breath and then speaking through gritted teeth, "Dark days loom before us now. I have seen such times in the past, before the last Great War. I fear it has been too long a memory for most to know the sorrow that comes. Xyrus has gone mad with this newfound power. He seeks to scorch the fabric of space and build his throne on its embers."

Tar'Sham asked, "What word from Earth Colin?"

Colin lowered his head, bearing a shame not of his own. "Vulcanon would see the whole of the U.T.A. Set on his campaign of glory. I know not everyone will listen, but after this attack fear will blind the masses to his true intensions."

"To what end?" asked Tar'Sham.

"He'll send the Alliance into Civil War," Colin answered.

Zhu sighed, "A war on two fronts." Zhu closed her eyes in mourning. "So many innocent lives shall suffer in the wake of this."

"But even more shall fall if someone does not stand up against this madness," Fa'Sham added.

"Dark days," Colin said, "we'll be the beacon in the dark then."

"Aye," Fa'Sham roared and then clutched his ribs.

"Father!" Tar'Sham called concerned.

Fa'Sham waved him off, "I'm fine son. Let today be the first glint of light against that darkness. Tomorrow shall be a time for war, but for today, Celebration!"

"Agreed old man," Colin said, winking at Zhu.

Fa'Sham embraced her in giant arm, leading her out of the hall. With a sly smile he said, "Come princess and let me introduce you to the wonders at the bottom of a glass of Krell!"

"Father!" Tar'Sham roared in objection, following after them. Colin stared at them and a smile came to his lips.

GLOSSARY

Ka'Dre'Kall - (Kah-drey-call) The Cliff of Kings on Ter'Nag'La, sacred spot where the first King of the Ter'Ok'Zhu was chosen.

Ter'Nag'La - (Tear-nahg-la) Homeworld of the Ter'Ok'Zhu.

Ter'Ok'Zhu - (Tear-ock-zhoo) An ancient race, adept with the uR.

uR - (Oo-er) The unseen energy the binds the universe together.

Ar'Tor - (Ar-tore) First King of the Ter'Ok'Zhu people.

Mor'Dair - (More-dare) Leader of the Southern Tribe of the ancient Ter'Ok'Zhu.

Scrib - (Scrib) A poisonous hard shelled bug native to Ter'Nag'La.

Fahl'ak - (Fall-K) a uR sensitive animal native to Ter'Nag'La. Combination of a lizard and bird.

In'an - (Een-non) The greatest of the Fahl'aks.

O'Tel - (O-tell) Last King of the Ter'Ok'Zhu.

Slai'Nor - (Slay-nore) Living ship that was shaped by O'Tel.

Tair Dal - (Tear-doll) Capital city of Ter'Nag'La

Paow - (Pow) Ancient Ter'Ok'Zhu Master, trainer of the Ter'Ok'Zhu Mavens.

Xyrus - (Z-eye-russ) Dark Lord of the Belgae.

Na'Dral - (Nah-drawl) Ancient bracer/cuffs, the ultimate punishment in the Belgae culture.

Belgae - (Bell-guy) Warrior race whose primary goal is conquest.

A'Zag - (Ah-zog) Dark God of the Belgae.

Jahan - (Jah-hahn) a cave with no exit on Mount Akasha, also the ancient Malef sword.

Dershaz - (Dur-shah-zz) The leaders of the Shahd.

Zheresy - (Z-air-see) The leader of the Dershaz who recruited Xyrus.

Shadaz - (Shah-da-z) The day when all ten year old Belgae children are gathered to fight for their place in society.

Shahd - (Shod) The Belgae military and citizen class.

Orphiannon - (Or-fee-an-none) The Queen of the Belgae people.

Yashin vines - (Yah-sheen) Peaceful flowered vines found in the Great Hall.

Sophos - (So-fo-s) An isolated race that bases its societies' values on an equal balance of science and religion.

Bellat - (Bell-lat) A feline-like warrior race that adheres to a strict honor code.

Voro - (Vore-oh) An opulent race driven by greed.

Navia - (Nah-eve-ah) A sloth-like race that makes up for their lack of intelligence with brute strength.

Ter'Ar'Tor - (Tear-are-tore) The home to the Galactic Council, a former planet of the Ter'Ok'Zhu.

Mita Delosham - (Me-tah Dell-lo-sham) - a Voro Senator who is as obese as he is greedy.

Dahaumn Tar'Sham - (Dah-how-m Tar-shah-m) - The heir and lone child of Fa'Sham.

Fa'Sham - (Fah-shah-m) - King of the Bellat.

Yaggrahal - (Yog-rah-hull) - The Bellat version of heaven reserved for those who die an honorable death.

Tokar sector - (Tow-car) - A sector in Bellat territory.

Kodos sector - (Ko-doe-ss) - A sector in the utmost edge of Terran territory.

Odesea Ephimira - (O-dess-ah Eh-fem-rah) - A respected senator of the Sophos people.

Krell - (Kr-eh-el) - An ale native to Bella Prime.

Zha'Toh - (Shah-toe) - Student in the Ter'Ok'Zhu language.

Zhi'Fah - (She-fah) - Teacher in the Ter'Ok'Zhu language.

Jahn'Do'Tor - (Jon-doe-tore) - An ancient mystical sword that predates the Ter'Ok'Zhu people.

Crocena - (Crock-key-nah) - A violent wild animal found on Belga.

Mardral - (Mar-drall) - Xyrus's personal Crocena that he found outside of the Jshan.

Herak - (Hair-ack) - A super dense white stone native to Belga.

Malef - (Mall-liff) - An ancient race and enemy to the Ter'Ok'Zhu.

Grimwurm - (Grim-worm) - Advisor to the Belgae queen.

Simura - (Sim-mer-ah) - A general in the Belgae military.

Lordakai - (Lor-dah-k-eye) - Second in command to Xyrus.

Nahk'Bet Pe Wahjet - (Nah-k pay wah-jet) - The Temple of the Prophet.

GahngNr - (Gong-ner) - Spearlike weapons.

Kah'gashi - (Kah-gah-she) - An ancient whip/staff of the Belgae nobility.

Andromedean - (An-drab-mo-deen) - An alien race.

Alecean Coast - (Ah-lee-see-in) - a se on Ter'Ar'Tor.

Desh'Kai - (Deh-sh-k-eye) - A bladed lance wielded by the Senate Guards.

Darbash - (Dar-bash) - A Bellat game of skill similar to chess.

Darka - (Dar-Kah) - Shouted for a good move in Darbash.

Mount Arras - (Ah-rass) - Mountain on Belga that contains the Jahan.

Queen Helaya - (Hell-lay-ya) - Queen of the Sophos.

Menalae - (Men-ah-lay) - Fallen king of the Sophos and husband to Helaya.

Vysan - (V-eye-son) - Home world of the Sophos.

Imana - (Ee-mah-nah) - Religious caste of the Sophos people.

Jonella - (Jah-nell-ah) - Handmaiden of Queen Helaya.

Ichar - (Ee-car) - A Sophos snack, vegetable flavored.

Ambrita - (Am-br-ih-tah) - A Sophos drink.

Niit'Horg - (Nit-hor-g) - Xyrus's personal ship.

Alea - (Ah-lee-ah) - A Sophos child.

Helos - (Hee-low-ss) - Sophos peasant or farmer.

Isris - (Ih-ss-riss) - Queen Helaya's personal ship.

Horg - (Hor-g) - A native beast of Vysan.

Ta'Lor - (Tay-lore) - A Sophos child.

Jabril - (Jah-br-ill) - A Sophos child.

Noth - (Nah-th) - Ancient spider-like assassin robots.

Sefas - (See-fah-ss) - A Sophos soldier.

For'Dowas - (For D-wah-ss) - Belgae afterlife for those killed in battle.

Captain Hayator - (Hay-yah-tore) - Head of the Sophos Royal Guard.

Ha'Trag - (Hah-track) - The Ter'Ok'Zhu word for charge.

Toros Dampel - (Tore-oh-ss Dam-pell) - A Senator.

Bellat Senator Mor'Dral - (More-dray-l) - A Bellat Senator.

Harin'Horn - (Hare-in-horn) - The personal transport of King Fa'Sham.

Captain Safir - (Sah-fear) - The head of King Fa'Sham's personal security.

Mathea - (Mah-thee-ah) - The Capital city of Vysan.

Great Mavros Forest - (Mav-roh-ss) - The largest forest on Vysan.

Apelesia Amphitheater - (Apple-lay-shah) - The meeting area of the Sophos Senate.

House Gondrola - (Gone-droh-lah) - A great House of the Sophos people.

House Ephora - (Ee-for-ah) - A great House of the Sophos people.

Paroth Ephotrata - (Pah-row-th Ef-oh-trah-tah) - Head of the House Ephora.

Dzarth - (Zar-th) - An animal native to Belga, whose blood is extremely poisonous.

Malak - (Mal-ack) - The High Priest of the Belgae people.
Wo'Tinath - (Woh-tih-nath) - A god of the Bellat people.
Belga - (Bell-gah) - Home world of the Belgae people.
Nergal - (Nur-gah-l) - The main class of Belgae star fighter.
Commander Gal'Mator - (Gall-mah-tore) - Commander of one of the Belgae Security Stations.
Captain Koral - (Core-all) - Old war master of the Belgae military.
Galguran - (Gah-l-ger-ron) - Light tanks of the Belgae military.
Fahn'rir - (Fah-n-rer) - Xyrus's Capital Ship and flagship of the Belgae armada.